# Hell hath no Fury

Ashuan Lust 1

Janna Ruth

First published in New Zealand in 2024

Copyright © 2024 by Janna Ruth

www.janna-ruth.com


This is a work of fiction. Names, characters, businesses, places, events, locales, and incidents are either the products of the author's imagination or used in a fictitious manner. Any resemblance to actual persons, living or dead, is purely coincidental.

All rights reserved.

No part of this book may be reproduced in any form or by any means without written permission from the publisher or author. Except for the use of brief quotations in a book review.


ISBN-13: 978-1-73861608-4

also available as ebook: 978-1-73861607-7

ASHUAN LUST BOOK 1

# HELL HATH NO FURY

## JANNA RUTH

*For Fabian & Benji*

*.*

*Who each typed up a paragraph in this book and deserve to
be mentioned. Love you guys!*

*.*

*You too, Kai (sorry you missed the typing session)*

# A note about sensitive topics

There is a lot of magic and fantastical creatures in this book, but the teenagers at the heart of the story are just that: teenagers. And as such, they deal with a number of very real issues in addition to their magical ones.

If you don't like spoilers and you're cool with everything, skip this note and start the book. If you want to be prepared, read on. I'm writing this because reading should be fun, not a nasty surprise.

While this series started out as a YA fantasy, all the main characters are now eighteen or older, and over the legal drinking age in Germany. As this trilogy is about the Archdemon of Lust, there will be various sexual encounters, though no actual sex on the page.

This series deals heavily with demons, hell, and the seven deadly sins. Demons have no morals to speak of, and can be found engaging in incestuous relationships, most of it merely suggested. If any of this makes you uncomfortable, this isn't the book for you.

As fun as it sounds, hunting monsters and using magic is dangerous. In this series, people will get hurt and some will die. This includes characters you've come to know well. Their deaths will not be meaningless, although it may feel that way to the surviving characters. I'm a big fan of consequences, which means you'll see depictions of grief in various stages.

In this book in particular, you will encounter a demon attack that reads very much like a school shooting, complete with lockdowns, fear, and police intervention. I understand that such themes can be upsetting.

You can skip this storyline altogether by not reading **Part 3: Hunter & Prey.**

The last part deals with an infectious disease and the consequences of its spread. Any similarities to Covid are purely coincidental (it's modelled on the plague from the Middle Ages). However, there are quarantine measures and perhaps gruelling depictions of boils and blood.

Finally, there is mention of burnout and financial stress, as well as family strife.

The characters live in a dangerous world, but it's also a beautiful one. For every dark spot there is light and humour. And, of course, magic. Lots and lots of magic.

Enjoy it!

Love, Janna

# Here's what you missed... on Ashuan Greed

Our story begins with 17-year-old Lucille de Cerque leaving boarding school to attend public school in her charming little hometown of Greenvalley. The small town in the Harz Mountains is famous for its rich history of witchcraft, a history that Lucille loathes until she discovers she's a witch. Together with her new friends—Samantha, a fellow witch with a penchant for potions; Fabian, a reluctant water elementalist; Rachel, a shy dreamwalker, and her twin brother Nico, an apparent healer; Jan, a good-for-nothing troublemaker obsessed with magic; and mysterious, handsome Matt, who carries a sword—Lucille sets out to hunt the various monsters that haunt the town.

The group faces vampires, demons, ghouls, and more as they stumble through their awakening powers and the daily struggles of teenage life. Lucille has a crush on Matt, but he's the epitome of emotionally unavailable and quickly breaks her heart. Meanwhile, Samantha and Fabian, best friends since childhood, have a history that prevents Rachel, who's always been in love with Fabian, from making a move.

But there's more to their meeting than chance when Samantha and Lucille discover an ancient prophecy. Six ancient heroes will be reborn at the same time, in the same place, to fight an age-old battle until they all die or their enemy fails twice. The Emblems of Power, powerful magical artefacts, have begun to appear in Greenvalley, including the amulet Lucille inherited from her witch grandmother and the legendary sword Matt carries. Soon after, Fabian comes into possession of a magical feather that allows him to draw anything to life and control the wind.

But before the seven teenagers can get too excited, tragedy strikes. Nico is bitten by a werewolf, and in this world, there's no cure. His only options are death—something Matt is willing to bring—or a life in some kind of werewolf end-of-life care. Samantha refuses to give up and works on a potion to remove the curse. She manages to turn Nico back into a human, but he bleeds to death from the bite, which unravels in the process. It's a terrible wake-up call for the six remaining friends that monster hunting is not without risk.

In the aftermath, Rachel finds comfort in Fabian's arms and the two begin a tender relationship. Meanwhile, Matt is the only one who can get through to Samantha, who blames herself for Nico's death. Something sparks between them, but neither Samantha nor Matt really know how to deal with it.

However, Nico's death wasn't an accident. It turns out that he and Jan have angered a powerful demon in town. The demon has set his sights on the Spring of Magic, the source of all magic in Greenvalley. When the remaining six confront him, they quickly learn that they're no match, and barely escape with their lives.

Jan remains on the demon's death list and becomes involved in a magical drug scheme that slowly kills his old junkie friends and threatens his own life. With the help of Meg, Samantha's annoying little sister who starts dating Jan, and the fourth Emblem of Power, a bracelet with a single thread of golden magic, the friends manage to turn Jan away from his self-destructive path and foil the demon's plans once again.

Over the course of several adventures, Matt and Samantha have grown closer, but Matt is hiding a dark secret. Just as he's about to confide in her, his old friend Chay, who sees the future of everyone he touches, shows up to warn him. Matt, who has never experienced such feelings before, remains stubborn. Samantha, on the other hand, doesn't really believe in his intentions, as he's always sleeping around. Then she meets singer Daniel at a Christmas function and falls head over heels for him.

Meanwhile, Chay reveals to the group that the prophecy is indeed about the six of them. Together, they will have to fight the Greedy One, a description that perfectly fits the demon they've already faced on several occasions. The fifth Emblem of Power has also appeared. The Dreamweb of Old Orenja falls to Rachel, who has developed a connection with a mysterious figure in her dreams who bears her brother's face.

Things heat up at New Year's when another demon goes on the rampage in town, Matt celebrates his 18th birthday, and his unsavoury relatives start to turn up. Unable to hide his intense jealousy of Daniel, Matt begins to suffer from blackouts. When the six decide to hunt the demon down before he kills more people, Lucille finds out that Matt is the one they're looking for.

Chay confirms that Matt is half-demon and that he's going through his Blood Night, a demonic coming-of-age ritual that sends them into a killing frenzy. Unfortunately, his human feelings get caught up in the process, and he murders Daniel in front of Samantha. While the friends manage to stop him and drive out his demon relatives, Samantha vows never to forgive him.

In the aftermath, Matt takes a break from Greenvalley, while Samantha mourns Daniel and discovers her own magic. She's able to weave the rivulets of magic into spells and is slowly getting better at it. When Matt returns, she knows how to protect herself. Meanwhile, Lucille struggles to keep the group together. Fabian has taken Samantha's side without question and Rachel follows his lead. Even Jan doesn't know how to handle Matt's revelation. But Lucille believes her friend is trying his best and is willing to learn after a lifetime in Hell. In the end, the prophecy forces them back together, but the animosity between Matt and Samantha remains.

Matt's biggest problem is his denial. He claims his actions during the Blood Night were beyond his control and refuses to take responsibility for Daniel's death, causing Samantha further pain. But no matter how hard he tries, he can't seem to let go of her.

Samantha's chance for revenge comes when three vengeance goddesses latch onto her, Lucille, and Rachel. For Lucille, it's a rivalry between her and school queen bee Cheryl that gets uglier and uglier, while Rachel has doubts about Fabian as their relationship gets stuck. Both Cheryl and Fabian have a series of accidents before the vengeance goddesses' grip is broken, but none as bad as Matt, who seems doomed to an early death if Samantha can't forgive him. Samantha struggles with the implications, but ultimately puts her own life at risk. She can't forgive Matt, but she doesn't want him dead either, giving up her desire for revenge. For Fabian and Rachel, it's the end of the road, and the two part amicably.

The last Emblem of Power, Flowers from Freya's Garden, turns up in Samantha's hands, just in time for the Greed Demon to strike again. It turns out that he's not just any demon, but the Archdemon of Greed, one of the seven most powerful demons in Hell, and Matt's uncle, Malcolm. In his efforts to gain control of the Spring of Magic, he begins to drag Greenvalley into Hell and kidnaps Samantha's grandmother for her witch blood.

The six gather their emblems and set out to face him. But for all their powers and cooperation, they're still no match for an archdemon. Their only chance is thwarted by Matt, who suddenly finds himself unable to slay his relative and abandons his friends instead. The remaining five refuse to give up and give it one more shot. By sheer luck, Rachel's dreamweb returns one of Malcolm's earlier attacks and strikes the demon down. Greenvalley is saved and the prophecy seems to be fulfilled.

Despite their survival, the friends are angry with Matt. Only Samantha shows an ounce of understanding, believing that his decision has shown his human side. Just when she's ready to move on with Cian, a school friend, Matt shows up at her door and gives her the apology she's been craving.

When Matt returns home, Chay is waiting for him with terrible news. Malcolm wasn't the Greedy One the prophecy spoke of. Their true destiny still awaits them.

**For the summer adventure, A Summer of Love & Death, and a bonus Matt scene, join my newsletter at www.janna-ruth.com/newsletter.**

Over the summer, Fabian and Lucille started dating. How will their relationship fare in the new school year when new monsters appear? And how will Matt and Samantha's relationship develop now that he's finally taken responsibility for his cruel actions? Turn the page and dive into a brand new season: Ashuan Lust.

# Part 1

## Beaks & Feathers

# Samantha

Green hills rose outside the train's window, replacing the endless fields from before. The familiar sight eased the pain in Samantha's chest a little. She was seated on her father's side next to the window, with her sister and mother opposite them. None of them looked at each other. Meg was busy on her phone, her father was reading a car magazine, and her mother was asleep, or at least pretended to be. Samantha had her headphones in and looked at the scenery, glad for the momentary silence.

Her family was returning from a three-week trip to Canada. What should have been a nice relaxing holiday had been the stuff of nightmares. The landscape had been mesmerising, the history interesting, and she'd even found some magic in unexpected places. But all of that had been spoiled by her parents' constant bickering.

Money had been tight before they left. At the beginning of summer, the Archdemon of Greed had tried to suck her hometown into Hell. Samantha and her friends had managed to stop Malcolm, but not before some parts of Greenvalley had slipped into another dimension, including half her father's workshop. The garage had lost most of their precious tools and a customer's car. To make matters worse, they couldn't even explain what had happened, since most of the people in Greenvalley had forgotten something had ever been wrong with their town.

From money woes, her parents had continued old quarrels, such as her father always spending too much time at the workshop, or her mother not having a stable income due to her misplaced acting aspirations. And from there, all the little issues they'd collected over twenty years of marriage were thrown into each other's face.

Now, the torture was finally coming to an end. They'd return home, her father would hide himself in work, bringing some much-needed distance between them, and Samantha would be able to escape the tense atmosphere, if needed. The familiar sight of the mountains promised respite, but it also carried dread. While her friends awaited, so did the monsters. And so did Matt.

Before she'd gone on holiday, Matt had apologised for the terrible crimes he'd committed more than half a year ago. It hadn't made much of a difference—he was still her boyfriend's murderer—except for healing the pain he'd inflicted on her again and again by not acknowledging his fault in the matter. On an intellectual level, Samantha understood where he was coming from. He was a half-demon who'd grown up among the demons in Hell, after all, and the night he killed Daniel he hadn't fully been himself, but that did little to ease the horror-images of Daniel's blood in the snow. And even after three weeks of holiday, Samantha still didn't know how she was going to respond. Was she going to forgive him? Forget what had happened? Or would she hold onto her grudge, because letting go of it would mean letting go of Daniel as well?

"Meg, wake your mother. We're almost there," her father said suddenly.

Meg stared at him, annoyed, and probably wondering why she had to be the one to do it when he could've done it just as well. But their father was already up and grabbing their luggage from the overhead storage. With an eye-roll in Samantha's direction, Meg gently nudged their mother with her elbow. "Mum, we're—"

"I'm already awake. Thanks."

So, she really had been pretending then. Samantha sighed and turned her gaze back towards the scenery. The sights were even more familiar now. Looking ahead, she saw the familiar shape of the Witches' Hump in the distance. Once the train ran around it, they'd be home, and hopefully could all go back to normal.

The train whistled and the Greenvalley train station came into sight. Despite her worries, Samantha's heart suddenly soared. This was home, where her friends, her beloved grandmother, and all the beautiful magic of the mountains were waiting for her. She forgot about Matt and even pushed aside Daniel. This was where she belonged, where her destiny was awaiting her.

With an intense screeching sound, the train came to a stop. Samantha was the last of her family to get up and grabbed her suitcase to exit onto the platform. The Greenvalley train station was small, so it didn't take her long to register that not a single one of her friends had come to welcome her back. Only Meg's best friend, Anne, was there, gleefully throwing herself at Samantha's little sister.

"You're back!" Anne cried. "I missed you so much. Jan couldn't come, unfortunately." Her older brother was a friend of Samantha's, but more importantly, he was Meg's boyfriend. "He's working until ten tonight. I can't tell you how weird it is that he's constantly working nowadays."

It had most definitely been a surprise. Faced with having to repeat the year if he stayed, Jan had decided to quit school, and surprisingly managed to get hired at the local youth hostel. So far, he seemed to be doing a passable job.

Meg's eyes sparkled. She had immediately latched onto Anne, locking arms with her. "You've got to tell me everything!" With a quick glance at her parents, Meg announced, "I'm sleeping at Anne's tonight."

"Is that so?" Their father sounded disgruntled. "What about your luggage? Is that going to go home alone?"

Their mother clicked her tongue. "Gosh, Ben, let her go. She's been with us for three weeks." She turned to Meg. "You go, darling. We'll take care of the luggage."

"As if you ever helped," their father shot back.

Meg rolled her eyes again, whispering to Anne, "Let's go before they get really into it."

Samantha watched them flee the scene with a pang of jealousy. What she wouldn't do to escape with her best friend just like that. But Fabian was disappointingly absent from the train station, and so she followed her parents to the parking lot that had been home to their trusty old car for the last few weeks.

"What's that even supposed to mean?" her mother was arguing before they'd even reached the vehicle. "I never help? Is that another way of saying my job's not good enough for you?"

"Just forget it."

"Can I remind you that *I'm* not the one who's in financial trouble right now?"

Her father harrumphed. "Oh yeah? I want to see you take care of this family with nothing but your meagre acting payments."

"It's not the only thing I do," her mother said, climbed into the car, and slammed the door shut behind her.

Cautiously, Samantha checked with her father. His jaw was working overtime, but for once, he kept to dark looks and dumping the luggage into the back. Samantha helped him as much as he let her and cast one last glance around.

The train had already left the station and those who had arrived were all leaving via bus or car. No one else had shown up. Within minutes, the whole place was deserted, save for a black crow on top of the station clock. Its beady eyes seemed to return Samantha's gaze, causing her to shudder. It felt like an omen, and in Greenvalley, that never meant anything good.

Her father's silence only lasted until they'd left the parking lot. Now, he and her mother were back at bickering. Even with Samantha's headphones turned as high as she could bear, she couldn't completely tune them out. Instead, she grabbed her phone and texted Fabian. Perhaps she could stay at his place tonight.

*Samantha: Anyone home?*

Apparently, he saw the message, but Samantha waited in vain for the three dots to appear that would indicate he was typing. Just as she was about to give up, her phone rang.

Relieved, she took the call. "Fabian."

"I'm so, so sorry. I forgot the time!" Fabian sounded so dismayed, Samantha forgave him immediately.

With just a bit of a tease, she answered, "You *and* Lucille—"

"How did you find out?"

"Find out what?" Uneasiness swelled in her stomach.

A short hesitation on the other line, then a sigh. "Well... Lucille and I... we're dating."

That was the last thing Samantha had expected to hear, though it explained how both of them had missed meeting her at the train station. "You and Lucille?" It was probably unkind of her to think so, but he didn't seem like the kind of guy Lucille would be into. Her fellow witch usually had a crush on hot and popular guys, and while Samantha loved Fabian dearly as a friend, he was neither. "Umm, no, I didn't know."

The next voice she heard was Lucille's. "Hello, Samantha. We're extremely sorry to have missed your train and also for learning about us this way. We were actually planning something else."

"No, it's fine. I'm happy for you." What else was there to say? She liked Fabian and she liked Lucille. They were an unlikely pairing, but if they were happy, so was she.

"Ha, see!" Fabian said triumphantly, obviously proving a point to Lucille. It made Samantha breathe a bit easier learning that her best friend hadn't planned to keep it a secret. It hadn't really seemed like him.

Samantha forced herself into a happy mood. "I can't wait to hear the story." She truly couldn't.

"Do you want us to come over, or is that too much?" Fabian asked. "You must be exhausted."

If only exhaustion was the cause of her parents' constant fighting. "No, don't. You two enjoy your evening. I'll call you tomorrow when I've had a chance to sleep."

As expected, Fabian didn't suspect anything. "Okay. Sleep well. And welcome back."

"Sorry again," Lucille said before Fabian ended the call.

The car turned into the parking bay at home. Samantha got out as soon as they stopped and went to the back to grab her bag. Her mother went straight inside and started to air out the house. Once again, her father was left with the luggage and positively seething.

Samantha decided not to get involved and carried her bag upstairs to her bedroom. She'd barely made it to the second floor when her mother started shouting.

"You can't be serious!"

"What now?" her father grumbled.

"You didn't take out the rubbish!"

"Is that all? Don't you have anything else to worry about?"

"You never do what I say! I told you to take out the rubbish before we left, and now it's grown legs."

"Fantastic. It can take itself out then."

Her mother groaned. "This isn't funny. Can't you smell it?"

"I don't smell anything."

If Samantha concentrated very hard, she could smell a whiff of what her mother was talking about. It must have been absolutely horrid in the kitchen.

"That doesn't surprise me at all," her mother said. "The way you always stink when you come home from work."

"What did you say?" A dangerous undercurrent had entered her father's voice.

Samantha had heard enough. She dropped her suitcase and backpack onto the floor and ran down the stairs again, then past her parents into the kitchen. The stench was truly overwhelming, while the bin was disgusting to look at. Fungi in five different colours were blooming on top of what might have been potato peels long ago. Samantha held her breath as she grabbed the handle and yanked the bin out of its hold.

Her mouth set, she carried it past her parents who were still fighting, and stormed out of the house, slamming the door behind her. Blissful silence awaited her outside.

It was slowly growing dark. Samantha made her way to the big bins and poured the disgusting kitchen rubbish into the brown-coloured one. A flutter of wings was all the warning she got before a bird tried to land on her head, its claws raking through her hair.

Startled, Samantha screamed and let go of the bin. She threw up her arms as the wings beat around her ears. Something sharp hit her wrist and a claw scratched her elbow. Samantha tried to hit the bird, when it suddenly rose again. Then she heard fast approaching steps.

"Sam!" His voice out of breath, Cian arrived at her side. "I heard you scream. Is everything okay?"

Samantha stared at him. He was the other reason she'd been kind of dreading returning to Greenvalley. Before she'd left—in fact, before Matt had apologised—she'd told Cian all about magic. And kissed him.

None of that mattered right now, though. "I think so. Did you see the bird?"

Cian glanced up and quickly found the black bird sitting on the roof of her house. It looked like an exact copy of the one that had stared at Samantha at the train station. Finding its intelligent gaze again made Samantha shudder.

It seemed to have the same effect on Cian, who slowly bent down and closed his fingers around a stone. Samantha put a hand on his arm. "Don't. It's already aggressive enough."

Cian let go of the stone but kept glaring at the bird for good measure. At last, he turned away and turned his gaze on Samantha. "You're hurt."

Following his eyeline, Samantha felt around her head. At the back of it, her fingertips came away wet. In the meantime, Cian had produced a tissue for her. She took it, well aware of the feel of his skin when their fingers touched, and pressed it to the back of her head.

"That's a strange bird."

She agreed silently. "It probably wanted our weeks-old rubbish." Disgusted, she stared at a banana peel covered in thick white fur. With pointed fingers, she picked it up from the end and threw it into the bin.

Cian grimaced in response. "Yum."

"I know." She snorted softly. "What brings you here?"

A charming grin appeared on Cian's lips. "You told me not to come to the train station. This isn't the train station." He took a step closer. "I missed you."

Samantha blushed. "You can't say things like that."

"Can I not?" Cian asked amused. He bopped her nose with his finger. "It's true, though."

She stared into his eyes until she noticed she was doing so, quickly blinked and changed the topic. "Well, I missed peace and quiet the last three weeks. My parents are tearing each other apart. Meg fled the second she could." It wasn't her smoothest transition.

Unsurprisingly, Cian seemed a little taken aback. "Wow, that sounds horrible. You mentioned them fighting, but..." Nervously, he rubbed his ear. "If you need... My house is only a couple streets away. You're welcome to come by whenever you need to."

Samantha sighed as he successfully brought the conversation back around. "Cian. You..."

Cian raised his hands in defence. "I know, I know. It's all a bit fast for you." He looked absolutely smitten with her.

Samantha should've felt the same, or at least something. Instead, she only felt bad about not reciprocating the feelings the way she should.

He sighed. "Why does it have to be so complicated?"

"Because, apparently, I am complicated. If you want simple—"

"I only want you."

Samantha blushed. She liked Cian a lot, but her heart felt as if it was wrapped in cotton wool and foam, numb to the world.

"Alright, here's an idea," Cian said, trying his best to sound upbeat. "We still have a full weekend before school starts again. Your vacation was the opposite of relaxing, so let's do something fun tomorrow." When Samantha looked at him doubtfully, he grinned. "And I'll try my best not to kiss you, promise."

She couldn't help but laugh. "What do you have in mind?"

"I'll tell you tomorrow." He took two steps back, still grinning from ear to ear.

Samantha had to chuckle. "Alright. But it's not a date."

"Call it whatever you want."

"Thanks for coming by." He'd successfully managed to lift her mood.

Cian smiled. "Anytime. I'm just a text away."

He turned around at last and walked down the street. Samantha picked up the bin and faced the house. Her good mood was wiped away when she noticed how the bird was still watching her.

She kept her eyes on him as she made her way to the overflowing post box. Most of it was for her parents, but a thick and heavy envelope was addressed to her. When she saw who the sender was, the puny rest of her good mood evaporated. "Daniel."

The sudden beating of wings made her forget all about it. She threw the bin at the bird and rushed to the door. Within seconds, she'd let herself in and closed the door behind her. A moment later, something heavy crashed into the door, making Samantha jump.

"There you are," her mother said, apparently alone in the living room. "Thanks for taking out the rubbish. Is everything okay?"

Samantha listened for the bird outside but couldn't hear a thing. "Yes. I'm good. I think." She deposited the mail on the cupboard close to the door and cradled the heavy letter to her chest. "Goodnight."

"Goodnight, darling."

As soon as Samantha made it to her room, she dropped the letter on the desk as if it was poison. A rustling in the leaves of the nearby tree made her jump. Without looking outside, she drew the curtains shut, her heart racing unnaturally.

Matt, Daniel, and now an evil bird. When was she supposed to find time to worry about Cian?

# Lucille

Her guilty conscience was eating Lucille alive. She sat on the sofa, absently touching her slightly swollen lips and tried not to jump into action as she usually did. Everything inside of her wanted to call Samantha and apologise again for not welcoming her at the train station.

Fabian and she'd planned to, of course, but while they'd been waiting to leave, they'd passed the time the only way they currently knew how: by making out heavily at her place. The plan had been to tell Samantha together, how they'd been the only ones left in Greenvalley for the summer, and how helping a vampire couple reconnect had made them fall for each other. It wasn't anything serious. Just a flirtation Lucille was enjoying tremendously. Surely, their friends would be cool with it once they'd let them know gently. Naturally, though, Fabian had to put his foot in his mouth, and now Lucille was analysing how Samantha had taken the news.

The words had been positive, but there had been some tension in her voice. Lucille didn't think Samantha would mind the two of them going out. She had been over Fabian for more than a year, and had fully supported his ill-fated relationship with Rachel, but in some ways Lucille still felt like the newbie of their friend group. And since none of the others had been around during the holidays, she also felt like she'd somehow stolen Fabian while no one was looking.

It wasn't like she'd planned the whole thing. If anything, she was probably the most surprised. Fabian wasn't exactly her type and he'd been nothing but a dorky friend before. And then summer had come, and she'd been alone with him, and somewhere along helping the vampires, Lucille had fallen for Fabian's softer, romantic side. He hadn't seemed like much of a dork when he'd been willing to risk his life for love.

Lucille called it the *Fabian Paradox*. There was no doubt about it that he was one giant coward, often whining about the various monsters prowling Greenvalley or how his own powerful water magic freaked him out. But as soon as one of his friends—or some innocent—was in danger, he threw all caution to the wind and fought tooth and nail for them, even if it meant going up against crazy archdemons or ruthless vampires.

She touched her lips again, wishing he would hurry up—how long could a man take in the bathroom?—when someone else suddenly appeared in her bedroom.

Lucille jumped, before she recognised him, her heart racing. "Matt?"

The handsome blonde raised a hand in greeting. "Hey, there."

"Have you forgotten how to open doors?" Lucille asked, slowly recovering from the surprise of having a demon space-jump into her room. Well, a half-demon.

Matt rubbed his neck. "Sorry. I'll have to get used to it again."

Lucille chuckled. Then she got up and gave him a big hug. "It's nice to see you again. How was it back home?" She hadn't seen him since summer had started.

Matt was about to say something when Fabian returned.

"I was thinking a surprise party would—" Fabian stopped cold in his tracks, instantly glaring at Matt. "What's he doing here?"

Frowning, Matt answered, "*I* could ask the same about you."

Lucille was aware of the tension in the air. Their battle against the Archdemon of Greed, who also happened to be Matt's uncle, had opened a rift between the half-demon and the rest of their group. Instead of dealing Malcolm the final blow, Matt had abandoned them, practically consigning them to a brutal death. That they'd been able to turn it around in the end was enough for Lucille, but not for Fabian.

It was the last topic Lucille wanted to start with, so she smiled and said instead, "Uhm, Fabian and I have been dating for the last week and a half."

Matt stared at her, bewildered, as if he, too, couldn't fathom what she saw in someone like Fabian. The latter, however, closed the gap between them and put his arm around Lucille's waist. She couldn't deny the little spike of exhilaration inside her when he pulled her close to him while glaring at Matt.

"I see." Matt frowned, then shook his head as if to free himself from the strange images inside his head. "Well, then... I'm back."

"A shame," Fabian said coldly.

It was a side of him Lucille didn't particularly like. Fabian was fiercely loyal to his friends, to the point of deliberately shunning some of his others. At least, she hoped, Fabian still saw Matt as a friend of sorts. "Give him a chance, please."

"Why should I? He didn't give us a chance either."

Matt set his jaw, stubbornness creeping in. "If you want me to leave, just say so."

"I don't have the power to tell you what to do or not," Fabian replied in a similar tone. "But I'd like to spend some time alone with my girlfriend. If you don't mind." It wasn't a question.

"Yeah, yeah." Matt rolled his eyes, then searched Lucille's gaze. "The surprise party is for...?"

"Samantha," Lucille confirmed, well aware of how much her friend meant to Matt, even though he shouldn't even be capable of caring so much. "She arrived today, and well, we thought about surprising her tomorrow."

"Don't you dare think of turning up," Fabian snarled, destroying all of Lucille's vague hopes to use the tentative party as a bridge for Matt as well. "The party is for Sam, so you've got no business being there."

Matt's face tensed, but he didn't hit back this time.

Nevertheless, Lucille tried to soften the blow. "It's probably not a good idea. I would be all for it, otherwise, but we want to lift Samantha's spirits, and if you come, it'll be a bit complicated." Now that she thought about it, Fabian was right. Samantha wasn't going to appreciate having to deal with Matt.

"I got it the first time," Matt snapped. "You don't want me here or there. Well, have fun with... whatever." He vanished without giving them the chance to reply.

Lucille sighed and extracted herself from Fabian's embrace. "You didn't have to go so hard on him."

"After what he did to us? He left us to die, Lucille, and then he vanished for six weeks. Did he think he could just waltz in here and all would be forgotten?"

Knowing Matt that was a very likely thought process. He'd done the same after his involuntary killing spree on New Year's, not understanding how they wouldn't be over it after a few short weeks.

"But we're a team." They were more than that; destined heroes of an ancient prophecy. And even though that prophecy had been fulfilled, their fates remained intertwined.

Fabian snorted, obviously thinking differently. "Are we? Does he know what being a team even means?" He sighed, the fight leaving him. "Let's talk about the party instead. Please." He opened his arms.

Lucille smiled, returning to his embrace. When he kissed her gently, she melted into him. "What were you thinking of?"

# Matt

Matt returned home after the failed reconnection. Frustrated, he kicked his bed, stubbing his toe in the process. The pain throbbed for a hot minute before it was gone. Finding no relief, he dropped onto the side of his bed and buried his face in his hands.

He'd made a royal mess out of everything last spring. Even before then, in winter, when he'd destroyed all that was good for him. And now he was going to mess it up again. Matt clenched his fists so hard his nails drew blood. No, he was not going to bring his demon mess to his human friends this time. They didn't want to be around him? Fine with Matt. That would keep them much safer.

A soft knock sounded at the door. His father, the only one he'd told. "Yes."

René opened the door, but the first to come in was Matt's puppy Crumbs. Not that he looked much like a puppy anymore. The golden Labrador was excited to see Matt, as if he hadn't only left home ten minutes ago. Six weeks of absence did that, probably.

"Hey, cutie. Did you miss me?" He rubbed Crumbs' big furry head.

"How was your visit?" René asked.

"Good. They want nothing to do with me."

René sighed. "Matt."

"What? That's a good thing."

"No, it's not. You need your friends." As usual, his father was adamant that he had human needs.

Matt shook his head. "No, it's better this way. This has nothing to do with them. There's no need to involve them."

"You sure?" René didn't seem to believe a word he said, but fortunately, he gave in quickly. "Alright. I suppose, as long as you show no interest, you're relatively safe here, and you're not interested, right?"

With blazing eyes, Matt shook his head. "Of course I'm not." That was the whole reason he'd come back to Greenvalley. Well, part of the reason. "I don't know about safety. Caspar and Balthasar weren't exactly overjoyed when Melaney nominated me."

"I saw that," René said in a tense voice.

When Matt had returned home, he'd been pretty beaten up. He'd been barely able to drag himself under the shower to wash off the blood, most of it his own. By the time the shower was done, he'd healed, but his soul had remained torn. What his mother wanted from him was unthinkable to him. Not so to his brothers.

He held René's gaze. "You don't need to worry. I can take care of myself."

"I'd worry less if you'd told your friends."

Matt clenched his teeth. "Not going to happen."

René sighed. "Well, then. Let me know if you need anything."

Matt waited until he was gone before burying his face in Crumbs' golden fur. "I can't do this to them," he whispered. "They already hate me enough as it is."

His night had been restless, so Matt decided to walk Crumbs early, while the town was still asleep. The fresh air brought him a little relief, but his heart wasn't in it. Bored, he scrolled through his friends' social media posts. Lucille and Fabian had made their relationship official last night, and he couldn't help but assume it was to spite him. As if he cared. Jan was posting weird stuff about his new job at the local youth hostel, his crystal collection, or random shit as usual, while Rachel's feed was as good as empty. She'd never been one to post a lot about her private life. She didn't really talk about it either.

Predictably, Matt got stuck on Samantha's feed. For the last three weeks she'd been posting pictures from her trip; beautiful scenery with barely a description beyond the location of the pretty sights. There wasn't a single picture of herself among the vacation shots. Matt wondered if that had been a conscious choice to avoid her school bullies or whether there was more to it.

As he kept scrolling, he came across a picture of Robert in a bright yellow chicken costume. "Ridiculous."

"Oh, absolutely."

Matt jumped when the dark timbre of his oldest brother reached his ear. Crumbs barked excitedly and sniffed Balthasar's feet. Before something could happen to the dog, Matt jerked his lead, bringing him back to heel. "What do you want?"

Balthasar was like a hidden grenade. He smiled, but under that smile was layer upon layer of threat. "My dear, so rude. I had some time off the Small Council and thought to myself, let's visit the little one. You know, just checking how much you've grown since last time."

Almost a thousand years lay between them. A thousand years of experience in the harsh battle for survival in Hell. Matt knew he wouldn't have the slightest of chances if Balthasar wanted to go head-to-head with him. "It wasn't my idea."

"And yet, here we are."

Matt groaned, not knowing how to extract himself from the danger his older brother clearly posed. This wasn't like Caspar, who you had to strike back as hard as you could to make him back off. "Listen. I don't want anything to do with this. You two can battle it out amongst yourselves for all I care, or even better, just leave it as it is. Why aren't you taking care of Caspar? He almost went for it right there and then."

Balthasar dismissed him with a scoff. "I know Caspar. He's a lot of bark and bite, without much brain to back it up. Once in a while, he goes crazy, and in that case, you need to lay low for a bit, but truth be told, he's not much more dangerous than your sorry excuse for a hellhound." He nodded at Crumbs.

"The General of Terrors isn't dangerous?" Matt asked doubtfully. His experience was a decidedly different story. Caspar had been beating his hide ever since he'd been old enough to cross his path.

"Like I said, he doesn't have the necessary mental faculties to make things happen, otherwise you wouldn't be here. Which brings us to you. I admit I haven't really paid you much attention in the short span of your existence."

"No hard feelings."

Balthasar seemed amused. "However, I noticed how much stock Chay is putting in you, and that's enough to pique my curiosity. Why is he wasting his precious time with you?"

Matt shrugged, uncomfortably. "Because he likes me?" He knew Chay was a far better man than he could ever dream of becoming.

A short laugh erupted from Balthasar's lips. "I thought it was sentimentality at first. Some silly half-human sympathy, but I'm beginning to think there's more to it. That I should pay you a little more attention."

One murderous brother was more than enough, in Matt's opinion. He'd fared just fine without the older one's attention. "No need, really."

"Nice try, pup. But you've got Melaney and Chay to thank for this. If they weren't so obsessed with you," Balthasar ran his gaze up and down Matt's body, "and I really don't know for what reason, I'd leave you alone to live whatever sorry existence you're carving out for yourself."

He waited for a moment, as if to expect Matt to jump at the insult like Caspar would've. At last, he nodded. "Very well, keep your little secrets. I have other ways of finding out." The smile Balthasar gave Matt made him think of Malcolm. It was full of sadistic promise. "It seems like Chay's interest extends to your friends."

Sudden panic shot through Matt. "What did you do?"

The smile deepened. "So, it's true. You care for these little humans." While Matt's pulse was racing, Balthasar leaned forward to whisper in his ear, "There's something you should know about me: I hate getting my hands dirty. That said, you should check with your friend, you know the one. The little girl you practically devoured with your eyes on your Blood Night. The one you killed for."

Samantha.

Matt felt as if his heart was being squeezed by a steel press. His breaths came harder and shorter. Black spots danced in front of his eyes. "What did you—?"

But when looked up, Balthasar was gone.

# Samantha

The bird was still there in the morning. Apparently, it had moved into the tree outside her window while Samantha had been away. It was the only natural explanation that made sense. Unfortunately, there were a bunch of supernatural explanations that made a lot more sense, each of them more distressing than the last.

Samantha pulled the curtains closed again when her gaze caught on the letter Daniel's parents had sent her. She hadn't yet managed to open it, scared of what it might hold for her. What could they possibly want more than half a year after they'd buried him?

Unable to come to an any conclusion that made her want to open it, Samantha stuffed it into her purse. She went downstairs in search for breakfast. Since they hadn't gone shopping last night, she was mentally prepared to do a bakery run, but when she reached the bottom of the stairs, her father almost bowled her over.

"Just leave me alone," he shouted over his shoulder, then slipped on his shoes.

"Papa?" Samantha asked but failed to receive an answer.

Instead, her mother hollered, "Yeah, go, hide in your workshop, as you always do."

The door slammed shut before the sentence was finished. With a sigh, Samantha checked the living room. "What happened this time?"

"Nothing. Nothing ever happens in this household." Her mother glared at the closed door for good measure. Then she loosened her stance and sat down. "It's just your father sticking his head in the sand instead of facing the consequences. As if that ever helped anyone."

Samantha's heart missed a beat. "What consequences?"

"Well, closing the garage and finding a secure job before that damned thing ruins us all."

"Oh." That was a lot better than the consequences Samantha had initially thought of. Though not by much. "We're going to be okay, won't we?" For as long as she could remember, her and Fabian's fathers had run their workshop. She'd learnt to walk in the office and helped out with accounting for extra cash in more recent years. She was no expert, but the finances had always looked okay to her. "I mean, surely, Jo's settled things with the insurance by now, and—"

"You think so?" her mother asked, her voice full of doubt. "If he has, he hasn't exactly told us. And I think we need more than just a settlement with the insurance company to get the workshop back on track. No, it's a dead horse. We managed to pull it out of the muck a couple of times, but I'm tired of putting my career on hold, just so those boys can live their dream."

Samantha hadn't been aware that her mother had done so in the past. Juliane had always dreamed of becoming a movie actress but had never really made it beyond a bunch of ads and small background roles in TV. If the workshop was merely a dream, her mother's acting career was nothing but an illusion. Samantha doubted things would've been different if she hadn't worked part-time for the council as well.

Her mother got up, rubbing her eyes. "I'll give my agent a call, see if they have something for me." She forced a smile. "We'll find a solution. I just have to make your father see sense for once." And with that said, she left Samantha alone.

*It's going to be alright,* Samantha told herself. It had to be. Maybe if she picked up a part-time job, they could get over this hurdle together.

As expected, the kitchen was empty. She found some old cornflakes turned chewy in the cupboard and forced a few spoons down without milk. Then she went back upstairs to get her phone and text a quick message to the group chat and see if anyone wanted to meet up.

After a minute of waiting, the replies came back as if they'd coordinated it.

*Jan: Got work, sorry.*

*Lucille: We're on a date.*

*Fabian: What she said.*

*Rachel: I'm boarding a plane in two hours. I'll be home tomorrow.*

Matt was the only one who didn't reply, but then she noticed that he'd left the group. Or had been made to leave.

A tear fell onto the screen, startling Samantha. It shouldn't affect her this much, and yet it did. Her nerves were taut, and she was in desperate need of a pick me up.

Just then, her phone vibrated and a call was incoming. Cian. With a shaky finger she accepted it. His cheerful voice filled her ears. "Good morning. Did you sleep well?"

"It was alright."

"Ready for some fun?"

"Definitely." Samantha shocked herself by how readily she accepted his offer.

Cian laughed. "Awesome. I'll pick you up in twenty minutes, then."

She needed to go out of the house, and since her friends were all wrapped up in their own business, Cian would have to do. In fact, she was sure he'd do splendidly.

Cian's idea of fun was taking her to the local adrenaline park. High up in the trees, several courses consisting of swinging blocks, knotted ropes, and flying foxes had been laid out. They'd taken his car and stopped at a bakery on the way, but Samantha regretted eating something as her stomach did a weird little flip.

Amused, Cian followed her line of sight. "Don't say you've been monster hunting all year long, but you're afraid of heights."

"I just respect wonky obstacles at a ten-metre height, that's all." She wasn't usually squeamish about heights, but despite the safety measures, this didn't look safe at all.

"We'll start small. I've only done the ten-metre parkour once, and yeah, I get what you mean about respect."

He patted her shoulder and turned towards the lockers, where they stored their belongings. As he did so, he accidentally knocked her purse with his elbow. It fell from her hands to the ground, the letter spilling out.

"So sorry." Cian was quick to pick it back up. "Did you want to send this? I can stop at the post office on our way back."

Samantha snatched the letter from his hand and pushed it back into her purse before stowing it in the locker. "No, that one's for me." Only then did she remember she'd told Cian all about what happened to Daniel. "It's from Daniel's parents."

He immediately grasped the gravitas of the situation. "Oh. What do they want from you?"

"I don't know," Samantha admitted. "I haven't managed to bring myself to open it yet."

"I see."

She appreciated him leaving it at that. Determined, she made sure her stuff was secured and handed him the key. "You promised to distract me."

Cian offered her his hand. "Then let's make sure I keep my promise."

Together, they went back around to the front to get their gear fitted and listen to a short introduction. Then Cian picked a course he deemed fun and challenging, but not too scary, and they climbed up the ladder.

Going up was surprisingly easy. Samantha only had to concentrate on the next rung of the ladder and managing her security line until they reached a little platform three or four metres in height. From here on, they had to climb around the tree towards the first obstacle; a horizontal ladder made up of short logs that swung more sideways than back and forth when they set a foot on it.

Cian went first, crossing the obstacle with admirable dexterity. He made it look easy, but Samantha quickly found out it was anything but. She held onto her safety rope for dear life as she balanced on the logs, taking a whole minute to get across, while Cian encouraged her with a big smile on his face.

Together, they made it through two more obstacles before Samantha decided she couldn't do this anymore. The next obstacle was a narrow beam with nothing but the safety line to hold onto. Even Cian went slow on that one, though he sped up towards the end of it.

Samantha made the mistake of looking down, and her head instantly started swimming. She pressed herself against the tree trunk behind her and breathed through her nose, while staring up into the foliage. Somewhere above her, the leaves rustled, as if a bird had taken flight.

"You can come," Cian called.

"No, I can't," Samantha replied shakily.

He chuckled and stretched out his hand, as if that was going to help when she had to cross a distance of ten metres before getting into his reach. "Just one foot in front of the other. You've got this!"

At least one of them believed in her ability to do this. Since the only alternative was to admit defeat and get one of the employees to bring her down, blocking the entire course for the duration, Samantha finally decided to give it a try. She put one foot on the beam, then the second. When the wood beneath her feet started swaying, she quickly stepped back.

"The rope keeps you safe. You can even hold onto it," Cian suggested, referring to the safety line above her head.

Unfortunately, it was just out of her reach. Instead of stretching up, Samantha tried to lower herself onto her knees, finding the thought of being on all fours comforting. This time, the rope around her belt pulled taut, only allowing a small amount of vertical movement. At least, that proved it was doing its job. If she fell, it would only be half a foot.

She held onto the rope in front of her chest and gave it another try. Unable to face the swinging beam, she kept her eyes locked on Cian, while using her feet to feel her way across. By the time she reached the middle, each step on the swaying beam made her legs tremble.

"I can't."

"Just keep going. You're almost here."

Samantha took a shuddering breath, willing her feet to move. Just then, leaves rustled and wings beat. A bird screeched, and something flew into her left cheek.

Screaming, she swung to the right and lost her balance. She came to a sudden halt and her shin hit the beam, while the bird's talons missed her by a hair's breadth.

It rose, banked, and came for her again, its dark eyes glistening in the morning sun. Samantha pulled her shoulders up and lowered her chin, causing the bird to scrape across her helmet. Still, it caught bits of her hair, and Samantha cried out.

Suddenly, Cian was there. He grabbed her by the elbow and helped her back on the beam. "Come on. Quick!"

Her fear of heights was forgotten as Samantha scrambled after Cian. He pulled her with one hand, while trying to fight off the bird with the other. Just as they reached the opposite platform, the bird dove under Cian's arm, its beak hitting Samantha just above the brow.

Cian reached into the bird's feathers, grabbing hold of something, and smashed it against the tree trunk. The bird crashed onto the platform, no longer moving.

Samantha wiped blood from her forehead, breathing heavily. "Is it dead?" Her heart was nearly jumping out of her chest, pain throbbing in her brow.

"Looks like it." Cian caught his breath, his hand shaking. "Are you okay?" He turned to her and gently rubbed his thumb over her wound. "Did you hide bird food in your hair or else why are they so crazy for you?"

"I wish I knew!" Samantha exclaimed, trying her best not to start crying. "How many more obstacles till we're back down?"

Cian glanced over his shoulder. "Hard to tell. I'd say we're close to halfway—"

"It's moving!" Samantha screeched.

At their feet, the bird was bulging and twitching. Cian raised his boot, ready to stomp the creature, when the bird suddenly exploded into a mound of feathers. Three birds rose in its stead.

Samantha felt the blood drain her face. "Oh my god."

"What the hell?" Cian asked, pushing backwards against the tree.

Samantha shoved him. "Go. Go. We need to get out of here."

There was no more natural explanation for the birds that flocked to her. They were hunting her, and with killing them turning out to be a disastrous option, Samantha had no idea how she'd ever escape them.

# Fabian

Fabian had barely let Jan into his room when Samantha's text had arrived. After a short discussion with Lucille and Jan, they'd decided to all feign being busy. He felt a bit sorry about blowing Samantha off, but he knew the surprise they were planning would make up for it. In the meantime, he got busy drawing streamers with Shitaten's feather for Jan to hang around the room according to Lucille's expert advice.

"A bit higher, Jan," she called out, an ice block in her hand. "Otherwise it'll look all crooked and weird."

"Really sorry, but I can't grow on command," Jan replied grumpily. "How about you help?"

Lucille innocently sucked on her ice-block, causing the heat to rise in Fabian's face. "Hazard management is hard work, you know?"

Jan snorted. "Be careful. You don't want to split a nail or something."

"Stop fussing, work!" Fabian called over, feeling a bit defensive over his new girlfriend. He was also afraid the surprise wouldn't be good enough. "Should I call Samantha?" he asked after finishing another beautiful streamer.

Lucille raised her finger in warning. "Don't you dare. You can't have a surprise party when the surprise is ruined."

"I wasn't going to tell her about the party," Fabian protested. "Just talk a bit, so she doesn't think we all suddenly stopped caring about her."

Lucille rolled her eyes. "Samantha will be fine. And you can last a few more hours without your best friend."

It occurred to Fabian that Lucille might be a bit anxious about co-existing as his girlfriend with Samantha back in the mix. It had been the downfall of his last serious relationship. But if he'd learned one thing from it, it was that Samantha was part of the package deal. Abandoning his best friend was out of the question, but he'd make sure Lucille knew she was his number one priority.

He kissed her on the head before stealing a piece of her ice block. Sweet coldness spread in his mouth while she mock-gasped at him. "Naughty."

"You're one to talk," he whispered cheekily. As if she hadn't made a big show of sucking on it whenever he glanced at her.

Lucille gave him a devilish grin. "It tastes better from my lips."

Fabian wasted no time in testing her claim and found she'd spoken true.

Behind him Jan groaned loudly. "Not this again. I thought you guys wanted to make this the biggest party ever. If you're not helping, I'm going to get Meg and start making out, too. I'm not going to do this alone."

Lucille broke off the kiss, her cheeks flushed. "I wouldn't expect you to do anything alone."

"Wouldn't expect me to or wouldn't trust me to?" Jan asked with a grin, causing Lucille to throw a package of balloons at him.

Fabian chuckled as he returned to the drawing board. So far, the new school year was lengths better than the last. And the best thing was, school hadn't even started yet.

An hour later, Fabian made his way over to Samantha's house to pick her up for her surprise. He'd volunteered not only because he'd be the most inconspicuous, but also because he was hoping to have a few moments alone with her to ask about her trip and explain how he'd suddenly found himself Lucille's boyfriend. After yesterday's failure to pick her up from the train station, he owed her as much.

He reached the Kollmer house and rang the doorbell. A few seconds later, her mother Juliane opened the door. "Hello. Is Sam home?"

"Hello, Fabian." Her face was a bit tense as she recognised him. "I'm afraid she isn't. She left this morning."

That came as a surprise. They'd all turned down her request to meet up. "Did she tell you where she went?" Perhaps Samantha had gone to visit her grandmother in the forest. That actually made a lot of sense. They hadn't seen each other for three weeks, either.

"You know, the times she used to tell me what's going on are long past. She probably got that from her father. But hey, why don't you call her and ask?"

A little taken aback, Fabian blinked. Juliane usually didn't leave him standing outside the door, even if Samantha wasn't there. "Sure. I'll do that." He buried his hands in his pockets and took a step back. "Welcome back."

Juliane gave him a weak smile before closing the door. Still confused, Fabian turned around and pulled out his phone. Just as he was about to call Samantha, he saw Matt coming down the street.

"He can't be serious," Fabian muttered. Pulling his hands out of his pockets, he crossed his arms and glared at his former friend. "What do you want?"

Matt balked at Fabian's aggressive greeting, but managed to keep his own voice calm. "I'm here for Sam."

Fabian snorted in disbelief. "She's not here, and even if she were, you'd be the last person she'd want to see."

"Did she say that?" Matt asked with a frown. He had the audacity to feign surprise, as if Samantha had any reason to forget what he'd done to her.

"She doesn't have to. I know how much she hates you. I thought you'd got that by now." Foolishly, they'd all given him a second chance only to be disappointed again in the worst possible moment.

Matt took a deep breath. "Things change."

"Things do. Demons, however..." Fabian left the sentence unfinished on purpose.

It finally did the trick and broke Matt's composure. "As if you have any idea what it means to have demon blood," he hissed.

"What's there to understand?" Fabian shot back. "You kill as you like, abandon anyone who's stupid enough to trust you, and still expect the world to fall at your feet."

"Hey," Matt snapped, "Just because you're finally getting screwed doesn't mean you get to have an attitude now. One of that sort is enough."

"Are you referring to yourself?" Fabian couldn't think of anyone with a higher opinion of himself and blindness to his own faults than Matt.

In response, Matt clenched his fists, reminding Fabian how dangerous the half-demon truly was. "Listen, Sam is in danger and I—"

Fabian immediately switched into alert mode. "What? What did you do this time? Are you—?"

"Stop wasting our time!" Matt barked. "She's in grave danger and I need to find her. So, where the hell is she?"

"I have no idea," Fabian admitted. "Not home, but I was going to call her." He finally did and anxiously waited for a reply. After a few rings, the phone went to voicemail. "She might be with Elda," he said, calling Samantha's grandmother instead.

While Elda answered the phone relatively quickly, she didn't know where Samantha was either.

"Matt says she's in danger," Fabian explained, glaring at Matt for good measure. "We need to find her."

"I can ask the pendulum," Elda suggested. "Just stay on the line."

The phone went silent, leaving Fabian to wonder what asking the pendulum meant. Another thought pushed the question aside. "What kind of danger are we talking exactly?"

Matt was pacing next to him, impatiently waiting for a trace of Samantha. "I have no idea, but whatever my brother came up with can't be good."

As soon as he heard the word "brother", Fabian narrowed his eyes. "I thought we were finally through with your blasted family." Matt only winced, making Fabian groan. "Which brother? The mad one who hates your guts?"

"No, the oldest one. Balthasar."

"The one who kissed Lucille?" It probably wasn't the most logical association, but the image came to Fabian unbidden.

Matt stopped in his tracks. "He did?"

It had happened at Matt's birthday party, when the birthday boy had been busy with a little celebratory killing spree. "Doesn't matter. Why's he after Samantha?"

"I have no idea," Matt said, after the slightest bit of hesitation.

Fabian was about to question him further, but he suddenly heard Elda's heavy breathing again. "She's at the adrenaline park in Harzgerode."

"What?" Fabian stared at the phone. The location was a total surprise. It sounded so mundane, and yet so out of character. "That can't be right. Why would she go there on her own? How would she even get there? You must be wrong."

"The pendulum has never lied to me," Elda said sternly. "Samantha is at the adrenaline park in Harzgerode. Now, will you check on her, or—?"

"I will. Thanks." Fabian ended the call and stared at Matt, hoping he had a better explanation, but the other guy only shrugged.

"Perhaps Balthasar kidnapped her and brought her there. What's an adrenaline park?"

Fabian had no patience for explaining that particular Harz attraction to Matt. "We need to get there as quick as possible. Do you have a car—?"

Matt grabbed his arm, and suddenly, the world turned black. Coldness spread through Fabian's body and he felt like passing through wet slime. Just as he was about to throw up, they reappeared twenty kilometres further east from the boundaries of the next big city.

"Harzgerode," Fabian said, feeling a bit weak in his knees.

Next to him, Matt's jaw was set. "Well, where's that stupid park?"

This time, Fabian was prepared to give him proper directions.

# Samantha

The height and flimsy obstacles no longer mattered to Samantha as she raced through the course with Cian. He took care of switching over their snap hooks, while she concentrated on upholding the quick shield she'd woven around herself. The birds seemingly ignored the taller boy and solely went for her, their talons extended, beaks ready to do as much damage as possible. Every time they came down on her shield, the magic gave a bit more.

She climbed along a spiderweb of thick ropes, barely registering the strain on her muscles, when the first bird broke through. Hair was ripped out of her scalp, but Samantha kept climbing. The only thing that could save her was to get out of the park and into a building, something where the birds wouldn't—or couldn't—follow.

"We're almost there," Cian called.

The magic barely held on. It prevented deeper cuts but the birds still got to her, scratching her arms and tearing her hair. It was hard to balance and keep renewing the weaves. When she tried to hook her line onto the last obstacle—a long flying fox—the birds descended on her fingers, wings beating into her face.

"Let me do that. They don't care for me." Cian stepped in and did the hooks for her. "There you go. Don't wait until I'm through."

And with that, he jumped off the platform to soar through the forest. Samantha waited merely a heartbeat before she followed, ignoring all standard instructions. As she took on speed, she crashed into one of the birds, leaving it to drop dead on the ground. The other two quickly began to fall behind.

Cian reached the opposite platform, gripping the auxiliary rope to pull himself up and turn around to catch her, just as Samantha slammed into him. They stumbled under the impact, but Cian managed to hold on to the rope, while Samantha found her own balance.

They barely managed to loop their hooks around the guiding rope when the birds—now five—came down on Samantha.

She'd never been more thankful for a helmet as when the wings smacked into her face. With her head pulled tight between her shoulders, she rushed down the ladder, missing a step in the process. With a cry, she dropped down onto the grass, rolling her ankle.

Unable to get back on her feet, Samantha crossed her arms over her face when a shadow blocked her. Blinking, she saw Cian crouching over her, defending her with his body. The birds tried to get around him, not interested in going for him, though his position meant he couldn't quite escape the sharp claws.

"Take off the belt and run! I'll take care of the rest," he promised, his eyes wide with terror.

"Are you sure?" Despite her question, she began to shimmy out of the safety gear, dropping it to her ankles.

Cian nodded tightly. "Perhaps you can hide in the toilets until I get the car key."

Samantha pushed the belt off her feet and sprang out of Cian's trap. Immediately, the birds followed, their shrieks ringing in her ears. She'd made it almost back to the huts when Matt and Fabian appeared out of thin air. Fabian was stumbling, but Matt set his jaw and raised his hand.

Terrified, Samantha shouted, "Matt! Don't!"

Too late. His black energy tore through three birds at once.

"Sam!" Fabian had noticed her now too.

"If you kill them, they spawn more!" Samantha whimpered, ducking behind Fabian.

Matt's eyes widened. "What?"

In front of them, nine new birds joined the other two. A cloud of black came towards them.

"How are we supposed to stop them if we can't kill them?" Matt asked.

"Perhaps—" Fabian started, then quickly got moving when the flock of birds aimed at him. He formed a delta with his fingers and water shot out.

A few birds were forced to bank, but there were too many of them to keep them in check. Samantha cowered on the ground, trying to make herself as small as possible. "They won't stop coming for me."

"I'll meet you at home in your room," Matt called out, making no sense at all. Then he grabbed Samantha and the world went black.

They reappeared in front of Fabian's bedroom. Samantha fell forward, landing on all fours and retching from the disorienting experience and the heightened adrenaline rushing through her blood.

"You're bleeding."

Matt. Matt had come to save her. He—... Samantha shuddered again, trying her best to keep in the meagre breakfast she'd had before.

"I'll go get Fabian." He vanished moments before Lucille and Jan rushed out of the room, alerted by the ruckus outside.

"Sam!" Lucille cried, falling to her knees in front of her and pulling her into an embrace.

Samantha clutched her shoulders with desperation. "Lucille." She was still breathing hard and reeling from the panic. "What...?" She wanted to ask what Lucille was doing at Fabian's but then remembered that they were a couple.

"Are you okay?" Lucille caressed her cheek, making Samantha wince as she caught a scratch. "Obviously not. Jan?" Jan just stared at them. "Your healing powers."

"Oh. Yes. Sure. Come on in." He gesticulated to the colourfully decorated room.

It wasn't until Samantha was sat on Fabian's bed with his cat Merle in her arms that she noticed how weird it was that Jan and Lucille had been alone in Fabian's room. But then Matt and Fabian appeared, both looking unharmed.

While Jan healed her scratches and beak wounds, Samantha sipped at some juice and explained what was happening. "It was only one bird yesterday. I didn't think much of it, but then it attacked me just as I was most vulnerable. I managed to kill it"—it had been Cian, truly, but Samantha was going to keep that secret—"but that didn't stop it. Instead, three new birds rose from it. That happens every time you kill them, so now, there's a whole flock of them."

"But what do they want from you?" Fabian asked. "The moment you vanished, they stopped attacking and flew off."

Samantha had no idea and shrugged helplessly. "Beats me."

"I suppose it's my fault." Matt had kept his distance from the others, standing near the window. When he spoke, everyone's heads whipped around to him. He grimaced as if in pain. "Balthasar... My half-brother hinted at having put a mark on you. To test you or something."

Instantly, Jan and Fabian started shouting at Matt. "What the hell is wrong with your family?" Jan cried, while Fabian snarled. "Haven't you done enough harm to her? Did you have to send your brothers after her now?"

Jan picked up Fabian's thread, "Yes, first your uncle, now your brothers."

"You should've just stayed in Hell and left us alone."

"What do you mean—?" Lucille tried to get a word in but failed miserably when Jan shouted over her.

"Yeah, why did you even come back? You've already proven you'll always side with your psycho family."

"And most importantly," Fabian interjected, "leave Sammy out of this. She's been through enough, thanks to you."

Lucille groaned. "Boys!"

"Go to hell, Matt!" Jan snarled.

"Stop that!" Samantha shouted. She'd let go of Merle and put herself in between Matt and the other two. Unsurprisingly, Fabian stared at her in confusion. "Why don't you let him explain before you tear him to pieces?" It wasn't that she wanted to defend Matt, she told herself. She just needed answers.

Behind her, Matt sounded surprised when he whispered, "Thanks."

Without really looking over her shoulder, she nodded at him. "No worries."

Lucille used the stunned silence to ask, "What exactly did Balthasar say?"

Matt sighed. He stepped away from the window and sat down on Fabian's desk chair. "He mentioned finding out why Chay has such a huge interest in me. Apparently, friendship doesn't cut it."

"He's got a point," Jan muttered.

"If you say so," Matt said, sounding slightly tired. "However, he noticed that Chay's also interested in you. I assume that he doesn't know about the prophecy. It's not like he'd care. So, I'd guess he just wants to see how dangerous you could be if he decided to attack me."

"Attack you?" Samantha asked.

Matt evaded her gaze and shrugged. "Just demon family issues. You know the kind."

"Oh yes!" Jan sneered at him. "We know. Well, you can tell him, he's got nothing to worry about. I won't be standing in the way if he wants to kill you or beat you to a pulp for fun."

"Good to know." Matt sounded pressed, and Samantha couldn't fault him. What Jan suggested sounded almost as bad as what a demon would do.

"No, I mean it." Jan doubled down. "You left us to die!"

"I'm sorry."

It shocked Samantha how easily those elusive words slipped from Matt's lips. It had taken him more than half a year to apologise to her, but it seemed as if he might have learnt a thing or two from that.

Fabian heaved a big sigh. "We don't want you to die," he declared, ignoring how Jan huffed. "We just don't want anyone else to die in the crossfire. Especially not one of us."

Matt's face hardened. He nodded and rose from the chair. "I'll take care of it. It's my psycho family, as you said so aptly, so it's my problem to deal with. This time I won't shirk my responsibility." His eyes found Samantha.

Like her, he seemed to remember the moment he took responsibility for his actions after the battle against Malcolm. After all those months of protesting and denial, he seemed to have changed for real.

Matt swallowed, and Samantha blinked, quickly looking away before anyone noticed. Instead, her gaze caught on the colourful decorations. Before, adrenaline had made her blind to it, but now she recognised streamers and balloons. She turned to Fabian. "Were you planning a party?"

Startled, Fabian's eyes widened. "Uh... yes. Surprise!" he said, with little impact.

Instantly, Lucille was at her side. "We wanted to surprise you to make up for yesterday's failure. Welcome home."

Warmth spread inside of Samantha. It looked like they hadn't blown her off, just tried to protect their secret. "That's so nice of you..."

The room darkened all of a sudden. Something tapped against the window, as if a surprise hail storm had started in the middle of summer. Everyone stared at the window behind Samantha. The warm feeling was replaced by cold dread as she turned.

All twelve birds—or more—were hammering their beaks against the glass.

# Matt

The birds had followed them here. Without fail, they'd flown all the way from Harzgerode towards Greenvalley, and from there to the one house that Samantha was in. Cold spread in his chest and he swallowed as he realised what monsters Balthasar had trained on Samantha.

"Kerxes," he breathed. "Those are kerxes." When none of his friends replied, he explained, "They're practically airborne bloodhounds. They don't let go of their prey until they hunt it down."

"And how do you kill them?" Jan asked.

"You can't!" Samantha cried, her voice full of terror.

That's right. She'd been running from them all morning long and had already realised how futile her flight was. "You don't kill them. That only increases their number."

"Like the Hydra of Lerna?" Lucille asked.

Since Matt had no idea what kind of monster that was, he simply shrugged. Samantha, however, knew. "Yes. Pretty much. And they want me."

"There must be something we can do," Fabian exclaimed.

They were all keeping a healthy distance from the window, stunned by the surreal display of nature. Or rather, demon nature.

"I've got an idea," Lucille proclaimed, and Matt desperately hoped it would be one of her better ones. "I'll turn Samantha into someone else."

Matt bristled, only inches away from ripping her head off.

"With an illusion," Lucille added, and quickly went to work.

He let out a soft sigh of relief. An illusion might actually do and leave no nasty aftereffects on Samantha, as so many other ill-found spells of Lucille had.

Half a minute later, he was staring at Meg, Samantha's little sister.

"Creepy," Jan said, and Matt silently agreed.

The younger Kollmer sister was Jan's girlfriend and entirely unappealing to Matt, but she also looked quite different with her blond hair and blue eyes, and vastly different fashion style. Only the way she crinkled her nose in dismay was entirely Samantha.

"It's not working," she cried.

There hadn't even been a pause in the birds' onslaught of the window. Matt sighed. "They knew where to go from twenty kilometres away. They're probably too intelligent."

Dismayed, Lucille let go of the illusion. "What else can we do?"

"We have time to think," Fabian said. "Right now, we're inside and they're—"

A teeth-shattering chink tore through his words, and a crack appeared in the window, running from the sill to the top of the frame. Five seconds later, the glass shattered, and the black flock dove in. One of the birds cut its own head off on the jagged edges of the remaining shards and burst into three new birds.

Jan, who'd been closest to the window, smashed his arms about without any sense or reason, while Lucille dove under the bed with a shriek. Fabian's cat Merle had the right idea and bolted from the room. Samantha followed her, Fabian not a step behind.

"To the basement," Fabian called. "It only has tiny windows."

The two of them were running for the stairs, but the birds were faster. Matt could already see how they'd tear Samantha apart with their vicious claws and sharp beaks. A moment later, he was between her and the talons, pressing her against the wall as he shielded her with his own body.

Claws raked through his hair and over his arms. A particularly sharp beak hammered into the back of his head, nearly splitting his skull. A bird landed on his shoulder, its talons biting into his skin despite the shirt he wore, as it tried to peck at Samantha through the gap. Blood was seeping from several wounds.

A stream of water nearly took his head off. Fabian was trying to flush the birds away. But he couldn't use too much power or the annoyingly fragile birds would multiply again.

Squeezed between Matt and the wall, Samantha was breathing hard. She bit her lip and repeatedly closed her eyes, clearly fighting the sudden despair that had come over all of them. If he didn't make a move soon, Balthasar would succeed.

"I'll bring you to the end of the world," he hissed through gritted teeth. "Or into another world. That'll give us time." The birds would follow them, even then, but it would take them considerably longer to catch up, and by then, they'd move again, always keeping ahead of them, until Samantha found a permanent solution. She always did.

Even now, despite her panic, he could see the wheels of her brain turning. "My room will do."

Matt shook his head, wincing when a bird bit his ear, while another rammed its beak into his exposed cheek. Big mistake. "That's too close." The birds would be at her house within minutes.

But Samantha had made up her mind. "I've got an idea."

And when Samantha had an idea, Matt trusted her.

The sudden silence in Samantha's room was deafening. They hadn't been followed through the abstract space Matt had jumped across, and he almost moaned with relief when he realised no birds were assaulting him. It gave his body the chance to heal the dozens of little wounds.

He let go of Samantha, knowing how much she hated being close to him, and took a couple of steps back. She didn't even bother looking at him before dashing to her nightstand and grabbing her Emblem of Power; the Flowers from Freya's Garden.

Meanwhile, Matt's cellphone rang. Lucille was calling him. "Yes?"

"Where are you?" Lucille asked, sounding a little out of breath.

"We're at Samantha's. She said she has an idea." It was all Matt knew.

Samantha grabbed the phone from his fingers and pressed the loudspeaker. "Did the birds leave?" she asked.

"Yes. As soon as the two of you were gone, they turned around and left. They're probably on their way to you."

Just as Matt had predicted, the dark cloud was already visible from the window. "They'll be here within a minute or two." Whatever idea Samantha had needed to be executed fast.

"Listen," Samantha said to Lucille, not hurried in the slightest. "I've got a plan. No idea if it'll work, but let's give it a try. Do you know where Bear Gorge is?"

Matt had no idea, and neither had Lucille. "Not really..." Lucille paused, obviously listening to someone on the other side. "Fabian knows it."

Samantha wasted no time to launch into her plan, sounding almost confident. "You'll need about forty minutes to get there. Matt and I will meet you there. Tell Fabian to bring his feather. And if you've got any wind spells, review those."

"What are you planning?" Lucille asked.

"Tell you later. We've got to go." Samantha ended the call and pressed the phone back into Matt's hand as she glanced at the window. The flock of Kerxes was already darkening the sky.

Matt knew what was going to come next. "Where to?"

"Have you ever been to Canada?"

If Samantha's room had been quiet, Canada—or rather this particular part of Canada—was the exact opposite. They were seated on a stony ledge close to one of the biggest waterfalls Matt had ever seen. The water thundered from the top into the lake beneath, the spray obscuring them from the many tourists on the other side. It was both beautiful and awe-striking.

According to his watch, they had about half an hour left until they'd have to return to Greenvalley. Half an hour with just the two on them on a tiny ledge next to one of the natural wonders of Ashuan. Matt was painfully aware of the tension between them.

He'd apologised to Samantha after their fight against Malcolm, but that didn't mean Samantha had forgiven him. She'd barely said a word after he'd spilled his confusing heart out to her, leaving him strangely nervous in her presence.

Samantha seemed a lot more relaxed, as if the sight of the massive waterfall filled her with peace. Perhaps it wasn't just water that tore down the ledge but magic as well. Without looking at him, she said, "You're probably waiting for an answer."

Had she been thinking what he'd been thinking? "Possibly?" Matt replied cautiously.

She nodded to herself, her lips thinning. It didn't bode well for Matt, but he finally accepted what would be the most likely outcome. Samantha didn't owe him anything. Not in the slightest. Instead, he'd owed her an apology, and now that he'd given it to her, she'd probably want her distance.

"I thought about it for a long time," she admitted. "Way too long. I... I can't forget Daniel."

Matt sighed. If only she'd never met the charming singer. No, if only he'd never picked him during his Blood Night.

"I still dream of that night," Samantha continued. Matt lowered his face in shame. He too still dreamed of what he'd done, though his nightmares all revolved around Samantha telling him how much she hated him.

"It's horrible. I no longer see his face very clearly. It's pretty stupid. I know what he looks like, but then again, I don't." Samantha's shoulders lowered, as if pressed down by the weight of the waterfall next to them. At last, she looked up at him. "Your face is always clear."

Matt had no idea what to make of that. He held his breath, waiting for her to continue.

She locked eyes with him, but seemed to look right through him. "The spray of blood on your forehead, the wild look in your eyes, that cruel smile on your lips."

He grimaced, his stomach churning painfully. As much as he'd fought responsibility initially, he'd now do anything to take it back.

"That's what I see when I think of Daniel, or when I think of... your demon form." Samantha licked her lips. "And that doesn't really make it easy to forgive you."

"I get it," Matt said softly. If he were human, he wouldn't forgive himself either.

Samantha snorted. "But my mind tells me that it wasn't truly you." She took a deep, shuddering breath, that weight bearing down on her again. "You weren't in control of yourself. Not by much, at least. You *did* pick Daniel—but you said it yourself, if it weren't for the Blood Night, you wouldn't have killed him. Hated him, ostracised him, but not murdered him the way you did. At least that's what I choose to believe." Her voice faltered ever so slightly. "And I do believe that you feel sorry in your weird unhuman-like ways."

Surprised by the gentle tease, Matt had to chuckle. Though the words were harsh, and the truth in them even harsher, there seemed to be a flicker of hope.

"I can't promise you that I'll ever forget your face that night," Samantha said with a pained voice, "or that we'll ever have what we did before I met Daniel, but right now, I've got enough to worry about. My parents are fighting day in, day out, and I no longer have the energy to hold a grudge against you. It doesn't change what happened."

It wasn't nearly as much as Matt had hoped for after pouring his heart out to her on her doorstep. There would be no forgiveness, nor any hope of anything more than a good-willed tolerance. At least, not yet.

"It's more than I deserve," he said and meant it. One apology, no matter how extensive, didn't reverse the pain he'd caused her. It definitely didn't guarantee him anything beyond a tentative rekindling of their friendship. But it would be enough. It had to be.

Samantha clicked her tongue and rolled her eyes at him. "Oh, stop it. This eating-humble-pie business doesn't suit you."

He had to laugh. Maybe friendship wasn't as far out of reach as he'd thought after her speech. She even smiled softly as she said it, and Matt's stupid half-human heart soared with hope.

"Then let's leave it at thanks for giving me another chance?" he asked when the laughter had fled again.

With a deep breath, Samantha's shoulders relaxed. "I suppose so."

She returned her gaze to the natural wonder. For a moment longer, Matt studied her profile; her intelligent green eyes, the slight upward tilt of the tip of her nose, and the bow-shaped lips he wanted to kiss so much. But instead of scooting over or putting his hand on hers and searching for a semblance of intimacy, Matt followed her gaze, at peace with their current truce.

# Lucille

After Samantha had ended the phone call and Lucille had relayed the plan to the boys, Fabian immediately started packing a backpack. He seemed to know exactly what he was going to take, as if they'd been planning to go on a multi-day hike for weeks. Meanwhile, Lucille was scanning the extensive list of spells she'd made in her phone's notes app for any wind-related spells.

As usual, Jan didn't do anything useful, but took full advantage of the snacks they'd prepared for the party. "Got to hand it to you, Lu," he said with his mouth full. "You know how to throw a welcome party. I bet Samantha already feels right back at home, running for her life."

Lucille couldn't help chuckle, while Fabian groaned. "Who would've thought Matt's family would mess it all up again?"

Jan raised his eyebrows. "Honest answer?"

"Guys, please." Lucille pushed herself up from the chair and put the phone away. "I know what Matt did was wrong but he apologised."

"Yeah, that makes it all okay," Jan said, with a heavy dose of sarcasm.

Anger distorted Fabian's face. He growled, "We could've died."

Lucille's mind flashed back to that day in July when their world had turned upside down. Greenvalley had been slowly sinking into Hell, and they'd had to fight the Archdemon of Greed with their Emblems of Power to save it. Samantha had nearly bled out, and they'd all received a horrible beating, but then Matt had had the chance to end it... and he'd run away, instead, leaving the archdemon to his severely incapacitated friends. If it hadn't been for Rachel's dreamweb suddenly throwing back his own attack at him, they would've all died that day.

But Matt hadn't done it out of maliciousness or cowardice. He had grabbed the bloodstone that had been sucking Greenvalley into Hell in the hopes of destroying it. He just couldn't bring himself to murder his own uncle, even if said uncle was a raging psychopath. As Samantha had said back then—and she hated him—it was a testament to his growing humanity, not the betrayal the boys saw it as.

Since Lucille had always been a lot more open-minded in regards to demons, she decided to throw her lot in with Matt. Even if that meant going up against her boyfriend. "But we didn't die," she said. "There have been so many times we've been in mortal danger. All of us made mistakes that put the others at risk, me most of all." Her confidence grew. "Look, we can't spend months trying to make Samantha see we're a team despite everything that happened, and then turn our backs on him for a relatively minor thing."

"Minor my ass," Jan grumbled.

"I'm just saying. If Samantha can handle working with Matt, we can too."

Fabian shouldered his backpack. His anger had turned into disgruntlement. "Yeah, what was that about? Why did she take his side all of a sudden?"

"I blame jet lag." Jan grabbed some more food for the way. "Meg is a bit testy, as well."

Slowly, they made their way down the stairs. "Didn't you say Matt went to her before he left for the summer?" Lucille asked Fabian. "Perhaps they finally cleared the air."

"Don't you think she would've told me then?" Fabian grimaced. "All she said was that she had to think about a couple of things."

Lucille opened the door. "Well, perhaps she's done thinking now."

As Samantha had said, it took them about forty minutes to hike out to Bear Gorge. Lucille had never been to this part of the woods. The gorge was next to the Witch's Hump, cutting through the eastern section of the mountain. The hiking trail wound its way close to the cliff-sides. At a few points, it was so narrow, only one person could pass through.

Now in summer, the trees high above them filtered the sunlight, painting the gorge in a mottled, dusk-light darkness. Jan put his hands together around his mouth and called out, "Helloooooo!" He grinned when a faint echo sounded back.

"Is this it?" Lucille asked. The shoes she'd worn at Fabian's hadn't really been made for hiking, and her feet hurt after skirting past all the stones and roots on the way here. Despite that, she managed to appreciate the sight. "Why is it called Bear Gorge?"

Fabian leaned back, his shoulder grazing hers as he pointed upwards. "Do you see that rock face near the top? From the right angle, it looks like a bear."

Lucille squinted her eyes. It took her a moment to find the mentioned rock face, but then she found it. It would've never occurred to her on her own, but since she knew what she was looking for, she was able to see the bear in it. "That's quite imaginative."

"It's the Harz for you." Fabian smiled. He really loved living here.

The smile didn't hold for long. As they turned a corner, Matt and Samantha appeared in front of them.

"He's still alive," Jan muttered, sounding surprised and a little impressed.

"Do you have the feather?" Samantha asked, wasting no breath on a greeting or an explanation. "We should have a bit of time to prepare. Forty minutes to be exact. Assuming the birds are turning around this very moment."

Lucille wondered where Samantha and Matt had spent the better part of the last hour that the birds were that far away, but she kept her mouth shut.

Meanwhile, Fabian pulled the feather from his backpack. "I did. What do you need it for? Do you want me to draw some birdcages?"

Samantha shook her head. "Almost, but first I need wind magic. Lucille, did you find some spells?"

"I did. Two, in fact. I'm just not sure about the effect they have." Last year, she would've just gone with any spell. It had led to accidentally sending her stepmother away, turning Jan into stone, and nearly burning down her house. Now she knew she had to be careful around unknown spells. "One of them is more storm-like. The other might not be more than a breeze."

Samantha pondered the information for a moment. "If you do a storm, they could get hurt. That makes matters worse, since they're just so damn fragile, but the breeze could work."

She went into the middle of the gorge and took out her flowers from her purse. "I want to try putting a sleeping spell on them, but for that I need wind, otherwise, the pollen will just fall to the ground or might hit us instead. Anyway, I chose the gorge, because this way, they won't be able to come at us from all directions. I need you two—" she pointed at Lucille and Fabian "—to take position on either side of me. Lucille, you'll use the breeze spell. Fabian, you use your feather to create a similar wind. I'll take care of the pollen. Any questions?"

"Yeah, what are Matt and I suppose to do?" Jan asked.

"You can watch for the birds and warn us when they come. Don't worry—if this works, I'll need you both afterwards."

Matt nodded sharply and walked to the end of the gorge. Jan shrugged as he was left with no choice but to go back the way they'd come. Soon, it was only the three of them.

"How was it with Matt?" Fabian asked softly, making sure his voice wouldn't carry.

Samantha sighed. "Okay."

"Okay?"

Lucille was bursting with curiosity, but she knew that Fabian had a far better chance at getting information out of Samantha.

"He apologised at the end of last term," Samantha said, sounding a bit tired. "It was... nice, I suppose. A bit surprising. He gave me a lot to think about."

The news sent Lucille buzzing, and she exchanged a look with Fabian over Samantha's head. What she'd yearned for had finally happened. Hopefully that meant they could all move on from it soon and go back to being the awesome monster-hunting team they'd been before. Not that the monsters had stopped knocking after they all fell apart.

"And?" Fabian gently prompted Samantha.

Samantha took a deep breath, her eyes fixed on her flowers, which she'd turned a soft pink shade. "I decided to let it go. Or at least, try."

Lucille very nearly squealed. She managed to hold the sounds in by the width of a hair, her face hurting from the exercise. She had to say something, though. "Thank you."

"Don't thank me yet," Samantha said with a snort. Nervously she looked up at the sky. There was nothing to see or hear. "Hey, Fabian?"

"Yeah?"

"How are Joachim and Caroline?"

Fabian sighed. "Alright, I suppose. A bit stressed because of the workshop. Mum's been helping out a lot, closing the Magic Circle more often than she opens it, and I've been doing my bit, but school's starting next week, so that counts me out. Did yours manage to relax a bit in Canada?"

Samantha did an impressive snort. "Nobody relaxed in Canada. I can tell you that much." She sighed. "No, they've been fighting about money the whole time. I don't think it helped that there were the natural expenses. If the flights and accommodation hadn't already been paid, we probably would've cancelled it. That might have been better."

While the two discussed their family's financial woes, Lucille kept an eye out for the birds. Her family had more than enough money. It had never been a cause for strife or stress. If anything, they had too much. Perhaps, she could get her father to invest in the workshop, though that wasn't really his line of work. Maybe if she played the guilt angle right.

Suddenly, Matt appeared at their side. "They're coming."

At first, Lucille thought it was the wind that was rustling the leaves above, but then she heard the unmistakable flapping of a multitude of wings.

"Ready?" Samantha asked, grim-faced. She had shaken some pollen into her hand.

Lucille and Fabian took their respective sides. Once more, Lucille went through the spell in her head. It wasn't a hard one. Then the birds descended on them, just as Jan came running.

"Now!" Samantha called.

"Venti Volti!" Lucille called, while Fabian waved his feather in a desperate manner.

Two vortexes of wind blew outwards towards the birds, carrying Samantha's pollen. They glowed pink as they spread and clouded around the few birds that hadn't tried to avoid the wind. Three birds fell asleep and dropped to the ground. The moment their fragile bodies slammed into the earth, they erupted into a multitude of not-that-sleepy birds.

"I'll catch them," Matt announced and jumped into the air to catch the errant birds as they trundled down dozily.

Unfortunately, the birds were now trying different angles of attack. Samantha had to avoid the ones directly above them so the sleeping pollen wouldn't fall on her, forcing Lucille to cast a different spell. "Scutum Protecto!"

The shield covered all three of them just in time for the first birds to rake their claws across it. Lucille winced when she saw them attack the shield with their beaks. "It's not going to hold," she said worriedly. The continuous attacks decimated the magic rapidly.

"Let's just keep going as fast as we can."

Fabian produced another gust, forcing the birds back in the air, and Samantha threw more pollen in the air. Four more birds dropped, but as Matt tried to catch them, he accidentally stepped on a bird on the ground, startling himself when three birds erupted from under his foot. Instantly, Jan ducked in and started collecting the sleeping birds in a pile closer to the entrance of the gorge.

"More," Samantha said, exhaustedly.

Fabian whipped his feather into a frenzy, when suddenly, a bird broke through the shield and tore into his shoulder on its way to Samantha. With a cry, Fabian turned and the wind flurry hit Matt in the face. A mere second later, Matt sank to the ground and fell asleep.

"Shit!" Fabian cried, cradling his shoulder as three birds that also been hit fell to the ground next to Matt and multiplied. So far, they'd created more birds than they'd managed to put to sleep.

"Lucille!" Samantha had her arms in the air, trying to protect herself as the whole cloud descended.

"Venti Volti!"

The ensuing gust nearly ripped the flowers out of Samantha's hands. Instead, pollen flew into the air along with the birds and managed to put eight of them to sleep, two of which died on impact.

Lucille very nearly burst into tears. They were fighting with all they had, and they'd still made barely any progress. By the time they got the birds down to a manageable number, they'd all be too tired.

Samantha clutched her flowers close to her chest, breathing heavily. "Alright. Plan." She pointed at Fabian. "Water." Then Lucille. "Wind." At last, she pointed at herself. "Featherfall weave. Here." She pushed the flowers into Lucille's hand and closed her eyes to weave.

Momentarily overwhelmed, Lucille stared at Fabian.

"Let's do it. Quick!" he said, pointing at the sky.

"Sure." Lucille shook the flowers until it poured pollen. "Venti Volti."

The pollen was swept into the air, where Fabian's stream of water catapulted them even higher. The wind spread both water and pollen until it rained upwards for a few precious seconds. Then the birds started dropping. And with them the sleep-laced water.

"Scutum protecto!" Lucille cried, before covering her mouth and nose with her hands, hoping it would be enough to escape her own spell.

A second later, birds and water came down on them. Through splayed fingers, Lucille watched them rain down on an invisible barrier and gently lower themselves on the ground. Soon, they stood in a sea of black feathers, and silence ensued.

"Was that all of them?" Fabian whispered, as if afraid he'd wake them.

"Looks like it." Despite her words, Lucille checked the gorge. Nothing moved.

Samantha leaned against the rock face, sweat covering her scratched face. "Don't step on any, Jan."

Lucille had all but forgotten about Jan, but he was still there, swiftly but carefully collecting the sleeping bodies of the birds. "I'm being super careful." On his way to the pile, he nudged Matt's fallen body with his foot. "Hey, this isn't time for a granny nap."

"Oh, I hope he keeps sleeping a while longer," Samantha said.

Jan grunted appreciatively. "Mean. I like it."

Samantha scrunched up her nose in frustration. "No. Because if he wakes, the birds will wake too."

"Right," Fabian exclaimed. "What do we do with them now? Killing them in their sleep won't work."

Lucille shuddered at the idea of more birds erupting from the sleeping. "Please tell me you have a plan for that." She handed the flowers back to Samantha.

Samantha smiled weakly. "I do. Fabian. Please draw us some spades."

Hiking, fighting, and shovelling. It was too much for Lucille. With a self-pitying moan, she sank to the ground in defeat.

# Samantha

It took Samantha, Jan, and Fabian nearly an hour to dig up a hole large enough to hold all twenty-eight birds. When they couldn't reach any deeper, Jan jumped in and continued until it went up to his chest. In the meantime, Samantha and Fabian collected enough rocks to cover the surface.

Gently, Fabian and Samantha handed the birds to Jan, who laid them at the bottom of the hole before climbing out and reaching in from the top. "Stones now."

Samantha left it to Fabian to heave the rocks as gently onto the birds as he could, while she started to fill the soil back in, hoping to get enough of it into the empty spaces between the birds that they'd be unable to move. When they were done, they covered the area with more rocks, like a fancy burial ground.

"You think that's enough?" Fabian asked. "Won't they suffocate and multiply?"

If they did, Samantha was fresh out of ideas. "Well, I'm hoping that confining them like we did will keep them from doing so. There's simply no space for them to multiply." To be absolutely safe, she wove a confining web of magic that she generously spread across the area.

When she was done, the sound of clapping echoed through the gorge.

"Not bad," a vaguely familiar voice called. "I'm impressed."

All four of them whirled around to see Matt's brother Balthasar leisurely strolling towards them. Jan instantly took up a fighting stance, while Fabian held out his feather. Lucille heaved herself up from the floor where she'd been sitting with Matt, her lips moving.

Balthasar gave them an appreciative nod. "Not bad. I would've thought you'd lose an eye at least."

"You ba—"

Samantha quickly shot her arm out to keep Jan from going up against the demon. Balthasar might not look like much of a fighter—instead, he had the suave politician look down to a T—but by now she knew looks were deceiving. Meanwhile, her gut was telling her that they were screwed if they made a wrong move now.

"What do you want from us... me?" Samantha asked. In the end, the birds had been solely trained on her.

Balthasar smiled. "To find out what you're worth. Both in your own right, and to my dear brother."

Behind them, Matt was groaning softly, slowly waking up.

"It's fascinating, really." Balthasar tipped his chin. "I'm looking forward to continuing this soon. Meanwhile, tell the little one that I'll be keeping him alive for a little longer." And with that, he simply vanished.

"Damn it!" Jan stomped his foot in anger, but his lip was quivering. "I've had enough of this demon psycho shit."

Fabian moaned softly. "It's going to be Malcolm all over again, isn't it?"

"But I thought the prophecy was done," Lucille protested. "We defeated the Greedy One. We—"

"It has nothing to do with the prophecy," a tired voice interrupted them. Matt pulled himself up from the ground, rubbing his eyes. "Are the birds gone?"

"Yeah, you missed all the action," Jan announced gleefully. "As you see, we do splendidly without you." Samantha tensed, but then Jan grinned. "You can be useful, though. Occasionally."

Matt snorted. "Glad to hear."

Fabian wasn't quite as welcoming. "Your brother says hi. Why does he want to kill you, and by extension us?"

"Balthasar was here?" Matt asked, sounding uncharacteristically worried. "Did he—?" Frantically, he looked around until he met Samantha's gaze. With a sigh, he relaxed again, then pulled himself up to his feet. "It's complicated. Some family drama. The usual stuff. I'll take care of it, I promise. You don't need to worry about it."

Samantha raised an eyebrow. She was tempted to point out how worrying the birds had been and that Balthasar had promised them a next time, but there was something strange in Matt's behaviour. It wasn't his usual avoidance or misjudgement. No, it felt much more like a deliberate choice. And in that case, she needed more information before she blew his cover. Most importantly, *why* he preferred to choose to go up against his family on his own.

"Oh well," Lucille said. "There's not much we can do about it today. Shall we have our welcome party, instead?"

"The decorations have probably vanished by now," Fabian said, as he watched the spade disappear from his hand.

"To be honest, I've had more than enough excitement for one day." Samantha checked her watch, shocked it was only early afternoon when the day had already felt like half a week. "How about we do drinks tomorrow night. Something easy, straightforward." Without nasty surprises. "Rachel will be home by then, too."

Lucille's eyes lit up. "Cocktails? Should we do Maverick, eight o'clock?"

"Works for me," Jan announced. "I'm off this weekend."

They all agreed to the plan and slowly started to make their way back home. Somehow, Samantha found herself walking next to Matt.

She wasn't quite sure whether it was coincidence or whether her subconsciousness had put her here, but after watching him study the forest floor in silence for a few minutes, she made herself ask, "This thing with your family. Is it something serious?" For all she knew, demons randomly tried to kill each other for fun.

Matt looked up, only now realising she was there, as if he'd been expecting to walk alone. He quickly shook his head. "Don't worry about it."

It only made her worry more. "You sure?"

"Absolutely." He flashed her a quick smile. "My family, my issues."

She sighed heavily. The temptation to leave it at that was huge, but Samantha couldn't do it. Not after she'd promised. "Prophecy or no prophecy, we're a team, Matt."

"Yeah, about that prophecy..."

It hadn't truly shocked Samantha to learn that Malcolm hadn't been the Greedy One the prophecy had proclaimed. As frightening as the battle had been, the prophecy was about the end of all worlds. And Greenvalley sinking into Hell was hardly a world-shaking event, no matter, how much they loved their hometown.

Fabian had been straight into denial, while Jan had threatened to quit, but by the end of it they'd all agreed that they'd wait and see. After all, they didn't need a prophecy to keep the town, and maybe more, safe. And as Samantha had said, they were a team. A huge dysfunctional team, but a team, nevertheless. They'd face whatever fate was going to throw at them.

And in all honesty, the prospect scared Samantha a lot less than what was currently happening at home. She was in Meg's room, leaning against the door, and listening to their parents having a go at each other yet again.

"We need to do something," she said at last.

Meg was sitting on her bed and looked at her with a mixture of hope and helplessness. "What's there to do? They already ruined our vacation."

"I know. We never should've gone with the workshop in trouble, as it is."

Meg bit her lip. "Do you think it's bad? I mean the whole workshop thing? Are we in trouble?"

Samantha shrugged, fending off the same wave of despair that was rolling over Meg's features. "I don't know. They've always pulled through before. I honestly believe the workshop is a safer bet than Mum's acting aspirations."

"I don't know. With the right projects, there might be way more money."

"I know it sounds terrible, but she's too old. She'll never get cast beyond a supporting role at this point. It'd be better if she let that dream die." Samantha hated how horrible it felt speaking those words. "I mean, I don't know."

Meg nodded slightly, still chewing on her lip. "You know, I don't care for the money, not really. I just wish they wouldn't tear each other apart because of it all the time. I'd even give up my allowance, if that helps."

"I suppose we could do that." Grateful, Samantha grasped at the thin line of hope. "I'm going to get a part-time job. A proper one." So far, the only money she'd made had been directly from her father's or Caro's pocket, the very same pockets she hoped to fill now.

"Sam?" her mother called loudly from below, causing Samantha to flinch. "Can you come here, please."

For a moment, Samantha froze, expecting to be called down as a judge for an argument, but then she realised it had been quiet for at least a minute. "Wish me luck."

Meg put her earphones in. "Good luck."

With a rapidly thumping heart, Samantha went downstairs and sighed in relief when she saw Cian standing there, holding up her purse with an awkward smile. Next to him, her mother glared at her. "You've got a visitor."

Samantha tried not to take it personally. Her mother was probably still riled up from her fight. She nodded upstairs, indicating Cian to come up. Fortunately, he got the hint and didn't hesitate to follow her to her room.

Carefully, Samantha closed the door behind her, then she let out a sigh of relief. When she turned around, Cian held out her purse to her. "I would've called, but your smartphone is still in here."

"Thanks!" Samantha took the purse and dug through it to find her phone. "I was looking for this."

"Were you able to get things sorted with those crazy birds?"

"Yes, I think so." She suddenly felt terrible. For the past few hours, she hadn't wasted a single thought for Cian. To be fair, she'd also been fighting for her life. "Look, I'm sorry that our date was cut short and... well, it was also pretty dangerous."

The words made Cian grin. "Hey, we managed a new record on route four. No one's ever done it that fast."

Samantha had to chuckle, suddenly feeling the tension slip from her shoulders. "And I wasn't even afraid. Well, not afraid of the heights."

"There you go. Mission accomplished." Cian's grin widened. "And you just called it a date. My day is made."

That sobered Samantha up a little. She obviously enjoyed being around Cian. He was a great guy and all, who made her laugh. Right now, he was the only one who'd managed to bring a bit of sunshine into her life, and she was wary of ruining that.

Fortunately, Cian didn't push. Instead, his face became a lot more serious. "You've still got Daniel's letter in there."

Samantha swallowed. The letter had been another thing she'd managed to forget for a few hours.

"I know I'm not Fabian or Rachel, but if you want to, I'll be there for you while you read it."

She winced at the suggestion, then sighed. "I suppose, I *should* read it."

The purse in her hands suddenly seemed to weigh more than the rocks they'd shifted earlier. If she didn't take care of this, it would continue to weigh her down for the rest of her life.

Taking a deep breath, Samantha walked to her bed and sat down, putting the purse on her lap. Then she looked up at Cian and patted the space next to her. He came readily, sitting neither too close nor too far.

Samantha took the letter out and placed it on her knees. "I hope I don't have to give yet another statement."

"It's way too thick for that," Cian said softly. "Besides, it hasn't been issued by the police or a court."

He was right, of course. Samantha took another deep breath before she gingerly opened the envelope. A handful of pictures and a letter fell into her lap. The very first photo took her breath away. It was a selfie of her and Daniel pulling faces during one of their earlier song practices.

Tears filled her eyes, and her throat tightened suddenly. Cian scooted a little closer and carefully put an arm around her shoulders. "Read the letter first."

Samantha followed his advice and unfolded the letter. Daniel's mother had handwritten it, detailing how the police had shelved the investigation. It was officially a cold case now. Samantha felt a pang of guilt since it had been her testimony that hadn't been nearly as comprehensive as it could've been. She sincerely hoped she'd made the right decision but doubted it.

As a result of the withdrawal of active officers, Daniel's phone had been released. Or rather his SIM card, since the phone itself had been completely smashed. "They thought I'd like the photos he took."

Her own phone had only a dozen photos or so. Daniel had taken much more. A whole pile of them.

Cian leaned in, smiling softly. "So, this was Daniel?"

Samantha appreciated his gentle show of interest. She relaxed into him and nodded, slowly going through the photos one by one with him. "This was our first meeting. And here we visited the Christmas market and shared a hot cocoa." Seeing Daniel again brought tears, but she also found herself smiling at his goofy grimaces and the loving memories that came to her when she looked at the pictures.

They'd had less than a month together, and only a week as a couple. His face might have been fading in her dreams, but the memories would live on. No matter what happened with Cian or what her tentative rekindling of her friendship with Matt would bring, she would always keep a part of Daniel in her heart.

Twenty-four hours later, Samantha joined Fabian, Lucille, Jan, Meg, and Matt at the club for a round of cocktails and pool. She still had to get used to Fabian and Lucille being a couple, but Fabian and she had spent the entire morning catching up. He had finally told her the story of how their summer romance had come to be, and Samantha had decided she would've much preferred helping a day-walking vampire girl be reunited with her long-lost love, than listen to her parents fighting every day.

She and the new couple formed one team, while Jan and Meg had adopted Matt for the other. Just now, Matt was aiming with his cue. He looked good as he did so, but the result was shocking.

Jan groaned. "Can I have Sam? She hits something at least."

Meg put her elbow into his side. "Hello?"

"This is my first time," Matt complained.

Immediately, Jan started grinning. "To think I'd ever hear you say that."

While Samantha and Lucille rolled their eyes, Matt scrunched up his nose, only succeeding in making Jan laugh before he gave Meg a kiss to smooth the wave over. Samantha came forward and took careful aim, sinking first the red three and then the yellow one into the pockets, before her turn ended.

Expectantly, she glanced at Fabian and Lucille, but the two were too busy making out to have seen her feat. Meanwhile, Matt was the one who looked impressed. Jan only groaned and snatched the cue from her.

He pointed at Matt before bending over the table. "Watch this."

Suddenly, Samantha saw a familiar face searching the crowd. "Rachel!" She raised her arm to wave.

Rachel's eyes widened with delight. Moments later, she was doing the rounds, hugging everyone. "Hey, everyone."

"Welcome home!" Lucille cried, for once letting go of Fabian. "Go get yourself a drink. The first round's on me."

"And then you're joining our team," Jan declared. "You can replace this loser here."

"Please," Meg added.

Matt grinned widely, not taking the slightest offence at Jan's comment. "Hey, Rachel."

"Hey." Rachel ordered a drink, while Fabian took his turn, spurred on by an air kiss from Lucille.

"How was LA?" Samantha asked her.

"As always. Full of people, big, and colourful. But it was nice. Dad was able to take two weeks off and we went up to San Francisco and Yosemite."

"Your turn, Rachel!" Jan called.

It came to no surprise to Samantha that Rachel was a fairly decent pool player, with her affinity for maths. She actually managed to balance the teams out, since Lucille was nearly as useless as Matt when it came to playing pool. Or perhaps she only pretended to be clueless, so Fabian would help her out, practically draping his body across her.

"When I saw that group text, I thought they were joking," Rachel admitted to Samantha.

Samantha laughed. "Trust me, I haven't got used to it yet, but Fabian seems to be on Cloud Nine. He told me all about it."

"Count yourself lucky," Jan chimed in. "You haven't had to experience these two as a double much, yet. Imagine how I feel."

At that moment, Lucille managed to sink a ball. Excitedly, she bopped up and down, then leaned into Fabian and kissed him passionately.

Rachel shuddered, whereas Samantha felt a little pang. It reminded of her and Daniel's first and last week together. To distract herself, she pulled out her phone. For the last eight months, a picture of Daniel had adorned it. Now, the Niagara Falls greeted her, along with a text from Cian.

*Cian: How are you feeling today?*

She quickly texted him back before watching Matt fail at the pool table again.

Fabian and Lucille were retaking their places at the table and apparently only now realised how their showy display of newfound happiness must seem to his most recent ex-girlfriend. Nervously, Fabian glanced at his hand clasping Lucille's. "Hey, Rachel, we need to…"

Rachel huffed and waved them off, looking as if the very thought of sitting through a painful explanation and declaration of their love scared her. "I already know."

"I hope it's okay," Lucille added, equally shy all of a sudden.

"Yes, it's all good." Rachel nodded eagerly. "Please, it never truly worked between the two of us. You two look very happy."

"Way too happy," Jan crowed. "You need to get a room!"

Playfully, Fabian tried to kick Jan, who danced away, laughing hysterically. Samantha couldn't help but laugh along, ruining her shot as she did so.

Rachel's drink was delivered and the seven of them paused the game for a second to toast each other.

"To a new year of school," Lucille called.

Jan shook his head, pretending to be disgusted. "Not for me, I'm part of the working class now."

"You were always—" Lucille started, but Fabian shut her up with another kiss.

Swiftly, Rachel took over the toast. "To a new year of kicking monsters' butts."

"Hear, hear!" Jan crowed, as they clinked their glasses. He leaned over to Meg and kissed her gently.

Meanwhile, Samantha and Matt locked gazes. He mouthed something that looked suspiciously like, "To second chances," and she found herself nodding generously. If anyone deserved a second chance after the year they'd had so far, it was her.

It was time to turn things around.

# Part 2
## Myths & Stones

# Lucille

Lucille was dreaming of colourful birds filling the skies as she floated on a bed of pink pollen, when she was gently woken from her dreams. Yawning, she opened her eyes and found her butler, Albert, hovering by her bedside. Instantly, Lucille was wide-awake. Had she overslept? No, it was Saturday. Her heart started racing. Had something happened to her father?

She nearly fell out of her bed in her hurry to get up and onto her feet. "What happened?"

Albert smiled gently at her and raised his hands. "Nothing. Your parents asked me to wake you for breakfast. They have important news to share with you."

News? Lucille pushed an errant lock behind her ear. "I hope it's nothing bad?" Her mind galloped ahead, considering terminal illnesses and sudden divorces. Or what if they had to move? In that case, Lucille would have to find a way to stay in Greenvalley, no matter what.

"I don't think so. I'll let them know you'll be down in a couple of minutes." Without further information, Albert left the room and closed the door behind him.

Lucille took a deep breath to calm her racing heartbeat before she quickly picked a casual outfit and tamed her hair into a ponytail. Normally, she wouldn't be caught dead in one, but there was no time for proper hair and make-up. With the bare minimum applied to her face, Lucille made her way over to the salon Linda preferred the family to take breakfast in.

As she entered the room, Lucille caught her father checking his watch. It told her how important this meeting was. "You called?"

"A while ago," her father mumbled.

Linda slapped his hand playfully. "Oh, don't be like that. She was still asleep." She flashed a Lucille a bright smile. "Come, sit. Your father and I have to tell you something."

Nervously, Lucille took place on the edge of her usual seat. She folded her hands on her lap and regarded her parents expectantly. "Is everything all right?"

"Better than alright." Linda giggled, frequently checking with Bastien to see if he shared her excitement.

Not even close. "Stop making such a big thing out of this. I'm expected on a call in a few minutes."

Linda pouted, but then the excitement got the better of her and she grinned wildly again. With a barely contained giggle that worried Lucille, she said coyly, "Well, my dear. You've grown to be a fine young lady."

That didn't bode well in Lucille's experience. Poised to the maximum, she waited for the other shoe to drop.

"Your father and I always wanted to have a child."

"A child?" Lucille asked, dumbfounded. Was Linda really going to tell her that she wanted a child the moment Lucille had ceased to be one? What did she expect? For Lucille to turn herself back into one?

Linda's enthusiasm was only slightly curbed. "At the beginning, it was out of the question, of course. Naturally, I had my career to think of, but after a while, I started to want for a child of my own. We never told you, because it just wasn't happening."

The admission caught Lucille out of the blue. She blinked, trying her hardest to process the news with a neutral face. A child of their own. Her father had a child of his own.

"*What* didn't happen?" Lucille forced herself to ask. She looked at her father, hoping to see some sympathy there, but her father's face was blank. He neither shared Linda's enthusiasm nor seemed to feel any empathy for Lucille.

Slightly embarrassed, Linda stared at her fingers. "It turned out, I couldn't have children." She struggled with her composure for a second, then found her happiness again. "So, a few years ago, we decided to adopt."

She beamed at Lucille, clearly expecting her to jubilate at the news. All Lucille felt was dread. This whole speech about wanting a child, of going to all sorts of lengths, while she'd been locked away at boarding school, never to be seen, completely stunned her. What were her parents thinking? What was her father thinking?

Apparently not much, as he decided he'd endured the grand reveal for long enough. "You're going to be a big sister to a little boy." He shook his head in mild annoyance. "I don't know what takes so long to say that."

Next to him, Linda visibly deflated. "Bastien, I…"

"He'll be here soon. I'm sure you have a lot to prepare. I'll leave you to it." And on that dismissive note, he got up and walked out of the room.

Linda took a deep breath through her nose before the plaster-smile was back on her face. "Would you like to see—"

But Lucille didn't want to see anything. She jumped out of her chair and ran after her father, catching him just in front of his office. "Dad!"

Bastien stopped at the door and turned to her with a frown. "What is it, Lucille?"

"This child… You want another child?"

"Your mother has wanted a child for a while."

"She's not my mother!" Lucille thought Linda and she had reached a new understanding, but apparently she'd been mistaken. Linda had never seen her as her child. Not then and not now. "Why didn't you get her a dog instead?"

Bastien heaved a sigh, as if all of this was incredibly inconvenient to him. "Lucille, I'm about to receive an important call."

"More important than this new son of yours?" Lucille shot back. Her voice was quivering and she took a step back. "Or me?"

Her father paused in thought. "Lucille." Inside his office, the phone started ringing. "We'll talk about this later."

The door shut behind him before Lucille found her breath again. Blankly, she stared at the marbled door behind which her father took the call that was so much more important to him than his own daughter and soon-to-arrive son.

"Lucille." Linda entered the hallway behind her. The big smile had been wiped from her face, her eyes full of empathy now. "Would you like to have breakfast with me? I'd like to tell you more about Pascal."

"Don't bother!" Lucille turned on her heel and strode past Linda. "I'll be spending the rest of the weekend with my boyfriend."

Linda and her father could be glad if it was only for the weekend.

Even though Lucille turned up at the Bendtfeld house with barely any warning, she was invited to join them for lunch. The four of them settled around the slightly wobbly dining table tucked away in a corner of the living room. Several bowls of simple food were freely shared around. No one, not even Fabian, had brought their phone or the paper to the table. Every Bendtfeld clearly treasured this time as a family.

Fabian's parents were some of the kindest, most welcoming people Lucille knew. And despite their busy jobs—they were both running businesses, after all—they always made time for each other.

"How's school?" Joachim asked. "Now that you're the top dogs."

Fabian winced. "Uh, Dad. That's embarrassing."

Lucille laughed at his overdone outrage. "It sure is nice, though also a bit scary."

"Scary?" Caroline asked, while handing her a bowl of peas.

The food at the Bendtfelds wasn't the exquisite cuisine Lucille was accustomed to at home, but it had been made with love.

"Well, it's a constant reminder that this is our last year at school and exams are approaching. Before we know it, they'll want us to apply to universities and decide what to do for the rest of our lives." At the moment, Lucille had no idea what to do. She was interested in a variety of subjects. History was one of her favourites. But she also liked languages and could see herself doing something with that. Or maybe cultural studies. Or philosophy.

"Oh, yeah, there's that," Joachim said and the wrinkles of laughter around his eyes deepened. "It's physics for you, Fabian, right? If you pass your exams." Even that little sting came across as much more of a tease than true criticism.

Fabian, however, pulled a face. "Actually, I'm leaning much more towards biology at the moment."

His father frowned. "Is that because of Herbert? Because if you need me to talk to him again..."

"Oh, please no!" Fabian's eyes widened with horror. "Last time you did, I had to hand in my experiment reports for six weeks straight."

Caroline frowned at that. "Fabian, you know that's not right. You need to let the school know. If you need me to—"

"I'm good, Mum. Really."

"This is important."

"And I'll take care of it," Fabian said quickly. "I promise. Just please, no more interventions. He already hates me enough as it is."

Lucille had often downplayed Fabian's woes regarding his Physics teacher. She simply couldn't fathom how any teacher would lead a personal vendetta against his student like that. Surely, Fabian was just exaggerating. The fact that both his parents seemed to worry, though, gave her pause.

"Why does he hate you so much?" she asked.

On the opposite side, Joachim coughed, nearly choking on a piece of meat. Fabian threw him a pointed look before answering flatly, "Because Dad and Ben bullied him in high school."

"We did no such thing," Joachim swiftly explained. "Played a couple of tricks on him, perhaps, but all in good fun."

Caroline's eyebrows shot up. "Don't believe a word he says. The two of them were awful." She reached over the table to cover Fabian's hand with hers. "Still, that doesn't give him a pass for treating you like this. Your dad was a kid then, Mr Herbert is not one now. And you're hardly responsible for your father's actions."

Lucille wholeheartedly agreed. "You should definitely report him, and probably sue him." That was the de Cerque way. A lawsuit, any time, but no time for comfort.

"Nah. I'll just keep my head low," Fabian said with a shudder. "It's only one more year. Herbert can't fail me on the big exam. Even if he wants to, the external examiner will make sure he follows the rules. As long as I pass that on the first try, I'll be fine."

"But if you need us to talk to him..." Caroline started.

"I'm not a baby, Mum," Fabian protested before rolling his eyes at Lucille, making it clear he didn't want her to think he needed his mum to fight his battles.

If Lucille knew one thing about Fabian, it was that he was perfectly capable of fighting his own battles. He'd whine and moan, but he'd always pull through. "You're going to show him," she said, and kissed him on the cheek.

Caroline withdrew her hand, looking almost relieved. "I'm so grateful Fabian's got you."

"Oh, absolutely," his father chimed in. "He's not paying you, is he?"

"As if I could afford her!"

Lucille noticed how Caroline flinched at the mention of money and quickly decided to change the topic. Unfortunately, there was only one thing she could think of. "Oh, there's something I need to tell you. I'm going to be a big sister."

Fabian's hand froze midair, and a bunch of peas rolled off his fork. "Come again?"

"That's wonderful news," Caroline said. "Congratulations."

"Yeah, about that." Lucille grimaced, wishing she could take it back, but now that she'd announced it, she had to follow through with the rest of the details. "My parents are adopting. According to the papers"—Linda had sent some through despite Lucille's blatant disinterest—"it's a hyper-intelligent ten-year-old boy. Only the best for the de Cerques."

"Are you okay, darling?" Caroline asked.

The sudden show of parental empathy made Lucille choke up. How was it that her boyfriend's mum cared so much more than her own parents? "Not really," she admitted in a thin voice.

Immediately, Fabian let his fork fall and scooted his chair closer to wrap her in his arms. "Why didn't you say something earlier?"

"Because it feels stupid," Lucille admitted, while tears sprung to her eyes. "Just because my parents adopt a child doesn't mean they don't love me, right? Right?" Her voice hitched around the last word. It absolutely felt as if her parents didn't love her. "They never wanted to be my parents." The words were suddenly spilling out of her mouth and she had no idea how to turn them off again. "So, what makes this child better? Why does *he* get to be their child?"

"Oh, sweetie." Caroline came around the table, put her arms around Lucille's head, and pulled her into a motherly hug. "I'm sure that's not the case. Your parents love you very much. This has nothing to do with you or their feelings for you. It doesn't change anything."

Although Lucille knew for a fact that Caroline was wrong, she greatly appreciated the support. It was everything she'd wanted to hear from her own father's lips.

She took a few shaky breaths and extracted herself from Caroline's embrace again. As she wiped her eyes with a tissue, she even managed a wan smile. Just like Linda. The thought made her shudder, resetting the calming process by a few breaths.

"Thanks. I know. Intellectually, I know. And the boy isn't at fault. I'm happy he's getting adopted. He probably thought he'd be too old by now." With another shuddering breath, she came to a decision. "I want to be a good big sister to him. Kind. Attentive. Because if anyone knows what my family is severely lacking, it's me."

Unless those things wouldn't be lacking for Pascal. Unless he was the little prince that Linda doted on and her father was proud of.

"Look, if you need anything, we're happy to help," Caroline promised.

Lucille felt a strong desire to hug her again. Rachel had it absolutely right: Caroline was the best mum in the world, and Fabian was the envy of all unloved children.

"It's okay. I'm going to be fine. Apparently, I'm going to meet him next Wednesday. There's going to be a big welcome dinner." Even her father wasn't going to miss that one.

"Hey, if it helps, I can come," Fabian suggested, causing Caroline to nod proudly.

Surprised, Lucille stared at him. "You want to come? For dinner?" The idea had trouble registering in her brain. Fabian and fancy de Cerque dinners just didn't mesh in her head.

"Yes. If things go south, you won't be alone. I could be your buffer. Someone in your corner."

"Do you have a suit?" Lucille blurted without thinking.

Fabian stared at her, a vertical crease forming on his forehead. "A suit?"

"For the dinner." At last, her brain was catching up. "Sorry, I'm probably overthinking this. You want to meet my parents?" Suddenly, Pascal seemed to be the least of her worries.

Still confused, Fabian checked with Joachim and Caroline. "You've met mine. Several times."

"Yeah, but yours…" Lucille caught herself. "Uhm, I'm not sure that's a good idea." It pained her to see the hurt in Fabian's eyes.

"Oh, don't worry, I'm sure we can find a suit for Fabian. He can wear one of Joachim's," Caroline suggested.

Joachim snorted, spraying a bit of water on his plate. He set down the glass he'd been drinking from. "One of mine? You mean the only one I own?"

The bridge between their parents had never been wider. Lucille was almost embarrassed by her family's fortune. The Bendtfelds deserved it so much more than her parents did.

"We'll make it work," Caroline promised. Meanwhile Fabian looked like a deer in headlights, as if he'd only just realised what he'd signed up for so willingly. Again, Caroline put her hand on Lucille's. "The important thing is that you're not completely alone at that dinner. And as I said, if you need anything else, just ask."

Lucille sighed. As worried as she was about her parents' reaction towards Fabian, she'd feel so much better with him there. "Okay." Belatedly, she added, "Thanks."

# Samantha

With a desperate gasp, Samantha threw back the blanket, and sucked in the fresh, cool air that filled the room via the half-open window. It was dark outside. The only light in the room came from the TV, which was showing the crumpled body of a forgotten game avatar.

Next to her, Cian dropped himself into the pillows, breathing nearly as heavily as she was. "You know, you're really welcome to come by more often."

Samantha managed a short laugh, before she gasped for air again. "Funny."

"I'm a little afraid to ask, but... what brought you here?"

Slowly, Samantha's breathing calmed. She turned onto her stomach and watched Cian. His blond hair was sweat-plastered to his neck. "Honestly? Stress relief."

It was a testament to Cian's character that all he did was laugh. "Did you just use me?" he asked between giggles.

Samantha grinned at first, but then her guilty conscience washed over her, and she felt horrible. What was she doing, taking advantage of Cian's obvious affection for her? Since when was sex her go-to stress relief? "I'm so sorry," she said, absolutely mortified. "I have no idea what came over me."

Cian turned on his side and kissed her shoulder, his lips cool against her heated skin. "Don't be sorry. You made me a very happy man." When she winced, worry entered his eyes. "What's the matter?"

"I don't know." She suddenly felt as if she was drowning. "I didn't plan this. It's just... you helped me so much with the whole Daniel thing last week. And I... I came here to talk."

"And then your clothes fell off," Cian said with a nearly straight face. "Happens all the time."

"Stop it!" But it was too late. Samantha was already giggling. "I took advantage of you." After all, she knew exactly how he felt for her.

Cian nodded sagely. "Yes, terrible. I don't know how I'll cope." He was obviously still enjoying the post-coital bliss.

And so was she. She just knew it shouldn't have happened. "Cian. I like you a lot. But..."

"The sex was bad?"

"The sex was great."

He smiled smugly, which did something funny in her stomach or perhaps even lower. With a lot of effort, Samantha forced herself to continue her train of thought. "I don't think I can reciprocate your feelings the way you want me to."

This time, Cian wasn't smiling. For a flash of a moment, she saw him tense. "Then what was this?"

"I don't know," Samantha replied honestly. "Sex?"

The tension fell away and he laughed again, falling back on his back and running his hands through his sweaty hair. "You're killing me, Sam."

"I'm sorry," she said for the second time. "I like you. As a friend. And I don't mean that in a bad way. I greatly enjoyed myself just now." Even with a guilty conscience, she couldn't deny that the sex had given her exactly what she'd needed at the moment.

Cian crossed his arms under his head and grinned at her. "I repeat. You're welcome to relieve your stress anytime."

"Even if I might never truly love you?" She didn't want to rule it out completely. Obviously, she was still hung up on Daniel, but Daniel was dead, and she needed to move on. Why not with a nice, charming guy like Cian?

He shrugged. "You can't force feelings. But look, I enjoy being friends with you. And if we're going to be friends with benefits now, I'm not going to complain." He chuckled lowly.

Carefully, Samantha studied his face. There was no hint of the hurt earlier. Cian seemed to mean every word. "Are you sure?"

He unwrapped his arms again and slung one of them around her, his hand grasping her butt cheek and pulling her closer to him. "You like me and you want me. What else could I possibly need from you?"

Instead of pondering that question, she lowered her mouth to his lips. As long as they were honest about their feelings, maybe this really was okay. His kisses were definitely more than okay. As was everything else.

Samantha had thought school would be awkward after her weekend adventure, but Cian had greeted her as usual in Chemistry and they'd spent a fun period continuing their experiments from last week. There had been a few hungry looks and conspiratorial smiles, but that only added to the excitement.

Now, during the break, they'd returned to their respective friend groups. Cian seemingly ignored her presence as he chatted to Alan and Björn in the atrium. But from time to time, he glanced over his shoulder and immediately found her, as if an invisible line connected them.

It made it extremely hard to focus on Lucille's report of her disastrous weekend. The blonde girl was sitting on the bench next to her, her voice growing tighter and tighter as she told them. Meanwhile, Fabian, who sat on her other side, had his arm slung around Lucille's shoulder.

"I mean, of course they wouldn't adopt a baby. That's way too much work, plus it might turn out ordinary." Lucille performed a shocked gasp. "No, he's ten and a little genius. And he'll arrive in two days. Can you imagine? A child will join our household and they only tell me a few days beforehand." She laughed mirthlessly. "They probably forgot I was part of the family. I mean they obviously forgot they already had a child when those parenting urges overcame them"

Samantha rubbed her hand in commiseration. "You know Linda. She's always a bit awkward with these things." In her opinion, Lucille's parents had no business having one child, much less two. Add to that they were adopting a ten-year-old with emotional needs that neither parent seemed to be even close to capable to fulfil.

"I know. I mean, I honestly don't blame her. I get it. She got thrown into this family and had a lot of maturing to do, plus her career was kicking off. I get that it took her ten years to develop a maternal instinct, but my dad!" Lucille sounded so hurt when she said that. "My dad doesn't even have time to inform me. To be honest, I got the impression he's only going along with what Linda wants. Or rather, he's supporting her wish so she'll stop bothering him as much."

"I already feel sorry for this child," Fabian admitted.

"Me too," Rachel said. "If anyone knows what it's like to grow up in a house where your presence is considered nothing but a nuisance, it's me."

Samantha was of the same opinion. It didn't seem right to force an innocent child into the dynamics at the de Cerque villa. But money always talked, and at least in that regard the kid would have nothing to want for. "At least he's got you."

Lucille heaved a gargantuan sigh. "Yeah, but I didn't want him. Look, I'm not saying that to be mean, but he's being dumped on me quite literally out of the blue, and while I feel incredibly sorry for him, I don't think it's exactly fair on me."

"Oh, it's not," Samantha hastened to say. "It's very much not. You've got enough to worry about with school..."

"Monsters..." Fabian threw in casually.

"That prophecy," Rachel added.

Lucille's face looked like she was about to explode. "Yes! I don't have time to take on responsibility for a child. And let's face it, it won't be my dad who'll step up."

"But Linda might," Samantha interjected gently. "Give her a chance."

"Speaking of monsters and that prophecy," Matt started. He hadn't really added anything to the conversation, which was probably a good thing, considering how screwed up his family dynamics were. "How are you going to hide your magic from him?"

Instantly, Lucille groaned. "Oh, gosh. I hadn't even thought of that yet. What if he walks into my room and finds all those spellbooks?"

"He'll probably get lost long before that," Fabian quipped.

Against her will, Lucille had to giggle. "There's that." Then she glanced at Samantha. "How do you keep your magic hidden from Meg?"

"I don't," Samantha said, then thought better. "Well, it has become increasingly harder this year. I honestly think she knows." Jan had hinted at that. "But she's got no interest in it, probably finds it embarrassing."

"Yeah, so embarrassing how we keep saving this town," Fabian joked.

Samantha chuckled. "Pretty much. Look, I honestly don't think you need to worry about it. You never had a problem with keeping your activities secret from your parents, even when you made Linda disappear or we had a full-blown witch fight in your hall. Unless you tell him, Pascal won't know any better."

Slightly calmed, Lucille nodded. "Thanks guys. That's really helped. I'll try and give Pascal a chance. He's probably a good kid who deserves the world. Just not from me." She clapped her thighs and got up. "Time to get back to class."

Somehow, Samantha managed to time her exit from the atrium perfectly with Cian. As she walked through the door, he ran his hand across her backside "accidentally", his head turned to the other side. Samantha felt the heat rise in her stomach. She couldn't help but secretly smile to herself.

# Matt

Tuesday came with lots of rain and cold wind. As usual, Matt took Crumbs on his walk right after school. While he couldn't wait to get back inside where it was dry and warm, the puppy seemed to find great joy in rolling around puddles, before shaking out his fur and spraying Matt from head to toe.

"One more time and I'll drag you home, whether you want to or not," he warned the dog, despite knowing he'd stay as long as Crumbs was having fun.

They were almost alone in the park, which meant Matt noticed *her* as soon as she came into view. A woman with green-coloured hair was swiftly walking towards him. While the hair should've been the most obvious thing, it was her eyes that drew him in. Even from this distance, they seemed completely mesmerising.

Matt frowned, but he couldn't take his eyes off the woman. She wasn't particularly pretty, and yet there was something in her golden gaze that completely disabled him. Even as she stopped right in front of him, then slowly made her way around him, regarding him in excruciating detail, Matt couldn't move as much as a finger.

Only, when she returned to face him and nodded with great satisfaction, he managed to draw a breath. He hadn't even noticed he'd been holding it in.

"Can I help you?" he asked, mortified at his body's inexplicable reaction to this stranger.

"You really are as good-looking as she described you."

Matt's frown deepened. This was getting weirder and weirder. "Who described me?" He could think of way too many people who might use that descriptor, and none that mattered.

"Your mother."

Any kind of spell the woman held on him was instantly broken. "Crumbs, we're going." He pulled on the leash and started walking, the dog loyally following along and quickly running ahead.

Naturally, the woman followed him. "She sent me."

"Nice." Of course, Melaney would send someone for him. He counted himself lucky she hadn't come herself.

"I'm supposed to lead you to her."

And there it was. Matt winced, trying his hardest to avoid thinking of the reasons for it. Even for a half-demon like him, they were simply too upsetting. "I'm not interested."

The strange golden-eyed woman didn't leave him alone. "I know you haven't seen her in a while."

"And I don't want to see her for an even longer while." Not until his mother's momentary insanity had passed.

"Melchior..."

Without a glance at his surroundings, Matt jumped through space to catch up with Crumbs, grabbed him by the fur, and did another jump, leaving the stranger behind. Hopefully, she wouldn't find him again.

His reprieve held for about an hour. By then Matt had completely forgotten about the weird encounter. He was lying on his bed, reading a passage in his Geography text book, when the doorbell rang. Without thinking, he'd crossed the small apartment with Crumbs at his toes, and opened the door to find the woman standing in front of it.

She smiled from ear to ear. "Found you."

Matt nearly slammed the door in her face. "Who the hell are you?"

Apparently, his question must've indicated an invitation, because the woman entered the flat and took an interested glance at the sparse design. "Humans." With another eerie smile, she turned to Matt, who somehow hadn't found it in him to prevent her from trespassing.

"I'm Euryale, sister of Medusa and Stheno. I'm a gorgon. That means—"

"I know what that means," Matt barked, annoyed at himself for not realising it first. The sudden lapses of mobility had nothing to do with fascination or awe, and all with the woman being a petrifying monster. Literally.

Euryale clapped her hands in delight. "Fantastic. I've heard the Latin classes in these parts of Ashuan are excellent. I personally prefer the Greek version, but tempora mutantur et nos mutamur in illis et manus manum lavat hoc signo vinces."

Once again, Matt stared at her dumbfounded. "I've never had a Latin lesson in my life." Nor did he understand why Latin lessons should help with what to do when dealing with an obnoxious gorgon.

The woman seemed entirely clueless to her effect on him. She kept smiling and wandered into the flat, curiously investigating the most mundane things. Meanwhile, Crumbs wasn't quite sure what to make of the strange visitor, fluctuating between wanting to greet her happily and whining in confusion.

Matt decided the fastest way to get rid of her was to find out what she wanted. "How do you know my mother?" The gorgons were creatures from Ashuan, and while they were known to demonkind, they weren't exactly known for being great lovers.

"Oh, she helped me with a little problem a few centuries back. I owe her." She turned to Matt, fixing him in place yet again. "She wants you to accompany me back to her."

"As I said, I've no interest in that. So, you can go back to her, tell her you tried, and leave me alone."

All Euryale said to that was a little "huh", then she glanced over her shoulder, and suddenly, a ripple ran through her stringy hair. Before Matt had blinked twice, the long green strands had transformed into little snakes, some of which were hissing at him. But Euryale's gaze didn't hit him.

Crumbs barked once, then he was quiet. His beautiful golden fur coat became stiff and grey as he turned into stone.

Matt saw red. He strode towards her, black magic crackling in his hand. "Turn him back, instantly!"

"Don't worry, boy, your dog will be alright." Nothing had changed in her cheery voice or her disturbing smile, but the snakes on her head had calmed, regaining their hair-like disguise. "He won't remember a thing. I just want to talk to you in peace."

"I won't answer a single question while my dog is a statue. Turn him back or I'll turn you into a corpse." He didn't care whether the gorgon had the power to petrify him. He'd kill her before she could move a snake.

This time, Euryale sighed theatrically and waved her hand about. Crumbs turned golden and fluffy again. With a high-pitched whine, he ran into Matt's room, to hide under the bed, most likely.

"Oh well, you seem to have your mother's temperament. Have you actually met her before?"

Matt was still seething with anger. "Of course I've met my mother," he spat. Melaney better had a good explanation for this Greek tragedy.

"I see." Euryale sounded surprised. "Well, look, a long time ago, I had trouble controlling my... gaze. Anyone I looked at turned to stone. Try keeping a relationship alive that way." She sighed. "Your mother helped me turn things around, so now I'm going to help her."

"Is this sob story going anywhere?"

"I'm here to tell you the truth."

Hopefully, it wasn't another truth about a gorgon life's woes. "The truth about what?" Matt asked impatiently.

"About yourself. Where you come from. Torn from your family, raised in strange lands." Euryale seemed to be near tears, while Matt wondered whether he'd been caught in some surreal nightmare. "I know. You probably think you're human like everyone around you, but your true powers were hidden from you."

Matt was speechless. The situation was getting weirder and weirder with every word.

Euryale put her hands onto his shoulder, looking deep into his eyes. "Matt, you're a half-demon."

The reason Matt couldn't move had nothing to do with Euryale's petrifying glance and all with this supposed revelation.

"I'm sure this is a shock for you."

"Not really."

Her face lit up. "You must've felt it then." When Matt only frowned in response, she continued with her bubbly chatter. "You know, demons aren't all that different from humans, but they have some special abilities humans don't. Did you ever ask yourself why your injuries heal so much faster than those of your fellow humans?"

Matt finally managed to snap out of his stupor. "I know what demons are."

"Amazing. That makes my task so much easier." Euryale offered her arm. "Shall we, then?"

"I'm not coming with you. If my mother wants to talk to me, she'll have to come here." Away from Caspar and Balthasar, he might be able to make her see sense.

Euryale's eyes widened dramatically. "You can't speak like that about your mother. A woman like her doesn't come to you. You come to her."

"Well, I won't. If she doesn't have time to deal with me, that's her problem." Though, it wasn't *time* that was the issue here.

Offended on his mother's behalf, Euryale clicked her tongue. "Your mother is very busy. She has an important task to fulfil."

"Yes, hopping from one bed to the next." Not that Matt blamed her. It was what it was. Melaney was the Archdemon of Lust, after all, and he was hardly one to judge.

"No, no, no, it is much more than that." As disappointment hit her, Euryale shook her head. "She satisfies needs."

Matt took a step away from her, unable to keep up this pretence of a conversation. "I don't want to talk about my mother's sex life."

"Very well. I just don't want you to have a false impression of her. She's a wonderful woman, and you mean the world to her."

He whirled back around. "Oh, do I now? Is that why she set my brothers on me? Because I'm important to her?"

Euryale sighed deeply. "I see we have a lot of work to do before I can take you home to her."

Matt heavily massaged the bridge of his nose. "I. Don't. Want. To go. Home!" With great effort, he took a deep breath and smoothed his voice. "Look, it's late and my father will be home in a bit."

"He might make a good statue."

Stunned, Matt stared at her. "You're not going to do that."

Euryale smiled sweetly. "I gave your mother a promise and I intend to keep it. Now, are you ready to learn what it means to be a demon?"

The threat was still curdling Matt's blood. There was no way he was going to endanger René. "Fine. Let's talk."

All those hours in drama class last year paid off when Matt managed to hold off Euryale by feigning that he was too overwhelmed by her sudden revelation. By the end of the conversation he'd been ready to stuff his ears with hot coals, but he'd managed to arrange some reprieve. Euryale had left him alone, though not without a promise to return soon, and there had been no further petrifications. That said, he needed a plan fast.

And the only person he knew who would come up with a perfect plan without too much fuss was Samantha. Thus, Matt was delighted when he found her alone in the cafeteria during his free time. Well, alone apart from Robert and that stupid Elite Idiot who'd dared to declare his intentions of going after her. Now, he dared even more, sitting so close to Samantha, their legs were practically glued together.

Matt felt an uncomfortable heat rise in his chest. Before he knew it, he'd strode over and towered over Cian, growling, "Scoot off."

"Oh, hey, Matt," Robert greeted him, completely disregarding the tone in his voice. "Do you want to sit here?" He pointed at the chair next to him.

"No."

Meanwhile, Cian and Samantha exchanged a glance. Then Cian wisely made the decision to grab his bag and get out of his chair. "Come on, Robert. I'll teach you enthalpy somewhere else."

"Great idea," Matt snapped, immediately grabbing the chair the other boy had vacated. He watched them take a seat in the furthest corner before sitting down, only to find Samantha glaring at him. "What?"

"What was that?"

Taken aback, Matt made sure *his* legs weren't glued to Samantha. "What was what?"

"Chasing Cian off?" For some reason, she sounded really angry.

Matt dismissed it, having far more important things to deal with. "Nah, he deserved it. Now—"

But Samantha wouldn't let it die. "And why is that? Please enlighten me. Why does Cian deserve you being rude to him."

"He's an Elite Idiot?" Didn't that explain everything?

Samantha huffed, then started to pack up her books. "The only one acting like an idiot is you."

Confused, Matt stared at her. "I thought we were good." They'd made up, so why was she once more acting like he was the worst?

Samantha had been in the process of standing up, but now she sat down again. "Are we? I thought you meant it when you said you didn't want to hurt me anymore."

"How did I just hurt you?"

She groaned and got up for real this time. "I should've known it was nothing but pretty words."

"I don't understand." He grabbed her wrist, forcing her to stay and explain herself.

Samantha gave his fingers a withering stare. "Of course you don't. Now let go of me."

He ignored her. "What did I do wrong? I only came here to talk to you."

"And to do so you acted like a complete ass to Cian—"

"Who's an Elite Idiot." Matt still didn't get it.

"Who's my *friend,*" Samantha stressed.

Matt leaned back, letting go of her arm at last. "You and Cian are friends?" It shouldn't have surprised him. After all, the other boy was obsessed with Samantha and had recently hung out with her at any given opportunity. He'd even gotten himself dragged into fighting Malcolm's creation because he didn't know what was good for him.

"We are, so I would appreciate it if you'd stop acting like an ass around him. I don't need your protection." And with that, she strode away and rejoined the other two boys.

Though Matt supposed she only meant that she didn't need protection from Cian—of course, she didn't—the comment still stung. It was only made worse by watching her slide right back into a seat next to Cian's without even glancing at Matt in the process.

After their heart-to-heart in Canada, Matt had thought they were finally on the mend. They'd worked together so well while fending off Balthasar's birds, he'd let himself believe he was finally on the right path to regaining her trust. But apparently, he was far from it. Samantha only tolerated him. She didn't actually care for him.

Still stunned, Matt watched her interact with Cian and Robert. When he'd met her last week, even he'd been able to see how down she was. She even told him that she was too exhausted to keep up her vendetta against him.

And now she was laughing and joking with Cian and Robert as they worked through their Chemistry homework. It wasn't to Matt's credit. Cian had made her happy again, and the realisation grated on Matt like nails on a chalkboard.

Heat rose in his chest until he was sure his heart would burn and turn to ash, but Matt managed to keep the anger in. Friends. Samantha and Cian were just that. Friends. And he couldn't take that away from her. He couldn't take her happiness away.

Which meant he'd have to deal with the gorgon himself. The less she knew about his family's most recent insanity, the better.

# Rachel

Somehow, Rachel found herself becoming Matt's confidante. Ever since they'd faced the drude together in his nightmares, he'd sought her advice on things. Or at least, on all things Samantha. Perhaps it was because she knew how to keep her mouth shut, or perhaps it was because she wouldn't get all overexcited over nothing, like Lucille. Whatever it was, it meant that Matt would randomly seek her out whenever he needed to and use her as a sounding board.

They shared Music class in the eighth period on Wednesday, a class which was nothing but a mindless point-gathering exercise for both of them, since neither was particularly interested in music. At least they were able to do Music without having to be actually talented, which the alternative—art class—didn't provide. Rachel even enjoyed the theory behind all of it. Much more than the often-asked-for singalongs around the piano at the end of the class.

Fortunately, they were spared that today, and Matt and Rachel made it out of there without second-hand embarrassment. As they walked down the hall, Matt launched into a rant about Cian.

"That snivelling bastard is worming his way into Samantha's heart, and I don't know why she lets him. He made her cry."

Rachel gave him a long stare. "One time. In terms of tears shed because of a boy, you've filled buckets."

"I know, but this isn't about me. This is about this double standard of hers. Disregarding that stupid spell of Lucille's, he's been hanging out with Cheryl since, what, eighth grade?" Rachel nodded vaguely. "That means he stood by, watching Cheryl bully Samantha for five years. How can she forgive that?"

Rachel didn't truly care for Cian. She'd lumped him in with Cheryl's posse and never given him much thought. "He's never bullied her." If anything, Cian had assisted Alan in harassing Fabian. But that had been ages ago. She liked to think people grew out of their childhood shortcomings.

"Doesn't matter. He's still with Cheryl."

"Is that why you don't like him?" Rachel asked in a flat voice.

As usual, Matt completely ignored her hint and barrelled on. "I just told you. He's not a good guy for her."

"And you are?"

He stopped short. "What? I didn't say anything about me. I just…"

Rachel clicked her tongue in slight annoyance. Matt was so emotionally stunted he sometimes needed things spelled out for him. "Let me be honest with you." Contrary to most people, Matt actually valued her insight. "You don't like Cian because he's shown an interest in Samantha. Who also likes him enough to get you all worked up."

"I'm not all worked up. I—"

"You're still in love with Sam."

Matt stared at her as if she'd told him he'd have to swim home. "What?"

*Plain words*, Rachel told herself. Matt needed super-plain, direct words to make sense of the human experience. "The one obsessed with Samantha is you. You want her approval and you want her to forgive you, because you're completely in love with her."

"Rachel, I can't be in love. I'm a half-demon."

She shook her head. "And demons are absolutely incapable of love?"

"Positive," Matt said without hesitation.

"And the same goes for half-demons?"

Matt shrugged, just a little less confident. "Chay never talked about a partner. And he's been around for almost three hundred years. It's not likely."

"One reference point is not a complete data set." When Matt only stared at her blankly, Rachel sighed. "What I'm saying is that I don't believe you. Because everything you say or do points to you having a massive crush on Samantha. One you can't move on from, despite it being nine months since she broke things off with you."

Slowly, he started shaking his head. "No. No, no. That's not it. I've moved on. I know that she has no interest in me. And never will. I made things right with her and that's all that's ever going to happen there."

Rachel's eyebrows rose with each passing word. "Is that so?" She didn't know anyone who was as good at deluding themselves as Matt, but maybe there was one thing he'd understand. "When was the last time you had sex?"

"What?" He shrugged quickly. "I don't know. I think at the student exchange."

"That's like three months ago!" Rachel exclaimed, surprised. She had expected the frequency to have gone down a bit, because he seemed solely focused on Samantha right now, but she hadn't expected it to be that long ago.

"What about it?"

"What about it? Matt, don't you get what that means? You're from the House of Lust, or whatever you call it. Your mother is *literally* seduction personified. And you are too."

Irritated, he glanced at her. "Are you trying to have sex with me?"

Horrified, Rachel took a step back. "Absolutely not. I'm just pointing out that you've started to abstain because—"

Before she could finish the sentence, a loud voice called. "Yoohoo, Matt! Over here!" A woman with garish green hair waved at him.

At first, Rachel thought it was his newest conquest, but then she remembered what they'd just been talking about. "Who's she?"

Matt had gone still. "A gorgon, sent by my mother to escort me back to Hescaryn. But she must've petrified parts of her brain, because first off, she thinks I need to be tutored in what it means to be demon, and second, she absolutely doesn't get the hint that I don't want to go back to Hell."

His answer spawned a multitude of questions in Rachel's brain, such as why his mother wanted him back in Hell. Or what could make this creature possibly think he needed tutoring in that regard. If anything, Matt needed a humanity tutor.

"Do you need help?"

She wasn't prepared for the gratefulness that washed over Matt's face. "Yes, please. Mostly to hold me back or I swear I'm going to rip her head off."

It was Euryale's idea to get a new haircut. When asked by Matt where one would go in Greenvalley, only her mother's hair salon had come to Rachel's mind. Partially, because she didn't truly trust anyone else to handle her hair. Her mum might have been negligent in any other aspect of her life, but she'd taken her profession seriously and learned about Black hair the moment she was expecting children with a Black man.

She also didn't balk at gorgon hair, instead keeping up her usual salon chatter and complimenting Euryale on the vivid green that didn't show any sign of growth or leeching out. "And it's so thick. Colour me envious, dear." Annette gave the hair a good wash before wrapping it up and guiding Euryale to a chair. "Let me just grab my tools. Do you want a drink or anything?"

Meanwhile, Rachel was sitting on an empty swivel chair, sipping on a clear glass of water, with Matt standing next to her. Both their eyes were glued on the gorgon, who seemed to truly be enjoying the attention. Unfortunately, Matt hadn't lied when he'd said she was trying to tutor him on demons.

"You need to concentrate more. Imagine the place you want to go to. If you don't do that, you could end up in a wall or under the surface, which is painful and sometimes deadly."

Annette probably heard all kinds of crazy stories all day long because she never even batted an eye. "How do you want them cut, darling?"

Rachel took the chance while Euryale was discussing her new style to check with Matt. "Have you ever landed yourself in a wall?"

"Not since I was four."

"There is a little trick to it," Euryale prattled on. "You send your spirit through first and pull the body in afterwards, but we can practise that later. For now, let's start with something simple. Move one step to the side."

Rachel concentrated hard on sipping the water to keep herself from laughing as Matt took a simple step to the side.

"Don't walk, jump."

He jumped. But not through space.

Euryale narrowed her eyes, which seemed to glow golden, and suddenly Matt's skin started to grey and his movements stopped. It only lasted two seconds, but it was enough for Rachel to realise how much danger they were truly in.

"Huh," Annette said. "I could've sworn your hair just moved." She laughed. "Silly me. And I haven't even had a drink yet."

Her casual mention of alcohol made Rachel wince. Sobriety hadn't lasted very long for her mother.

"I'm sorry," Euryale said. "I know I need to be more patient with you since this is all new. So, let's start again."

"Listen, lady." Matt took a step forward and lowered his voice to a hiss. "I know how to jump through space. You saw me do it at least twice. I also know how to shoot energy from my hands and that my body heals itself, but that doesn't mean I'll demonstrate it in front of all these people."

Feeling the tension in the room, Rachel got up slowly from her chair. "Matt..."

But Matt barrelled on as usual. "This has nothing to do with having become 'too human' or whatever you think of me. I don't want to go back to my mother, and I sure as hell won't go anywhere with some random gorgon. So, stop it."

He turned away abruptly, nodding at Rachel. "Come on, let's go."

Annette shrieked as the hair underneath her fingers turned into a lively bunch of snakes. To Rachel's horror, Euryale turned in her chair and shot Annette one of her golden looks. Instantly, Rachel's mother turned to stone.

When the gorgon turned back to them, Rachel quickly covered her eyes with her hands. "Matt, do something."

Matt swung around. "Turn her back." There was a sickening crunch and Matt gasped.

Through her fingers, Rachel glanced at the ground, finding his feet encased in solid stone. But the petrification wasn't complete. From the thighs upwards, Matt was still very much alive, fighting to retain his balance.

Euryale got up from her chair, and Rachel quickly squeezed her eyes shut again. She could hear her come closer, her snakes hissing. "I think I've had enough, young Matt. As refreshing as it is to see your streak of dominance well-developed for a human hybrid, your mother did me a favour, and I intend to keep it. Whether you want this or not. Come."

Matt's feet must've returned to normal, because Rachel could hear him stumble away. Slowly, the sounds of them receded, until Rachel heard the doorbell ring and the door shut. It was only then she dared open her eyes, half-expecting to find that the gorgon had remained behind.

The store was empty, save for her, and the garish statue of her mother. Rachel whimpered at the sight, but before she could do anything, the door opened again and an old woman came in.

"Oh, hi there," she said friendly. "You're Mrs Hadden's daughter, aren't you? Is she in the back?"

"Uh. No... I mean." What was she about to say? Or do? "She got sick. The flu. Yeah, I told her to go home."

The customer looked dismayed. "How unfortunate. But we had an appointment. Can you cut hair? Just the sides. They've gotten terribly long." As with most old women, she kept her hair quite short. The sides she referred to were sticking out about a centimetre above the ear.

"I can try." It wouldn't be Rachel's first foray into hair dressing, and this didn't seem too hard.

Relieved the woman took place next to where Euryale had sat, only then noticing the statue. "That's an interesting piece of art, you've got there. Is that supposed to be Mrs Hadden?"

Rachel laughed nervously. "Oh, you know her—my mother has always been a bit eccentric."

As she gathered some scissors and combs, Rachel tried her best not to panic. Hopefully, Matt wasn't going to find himself encased in stone by the time the day came to an end.

# Fabian

The moment Fabian had arrived at the Villa de Cerque in his father's suit, Lucille had been in a frenzy. The suit didn't cut it. He had no idea what she'd expected when his mother had suggested it, but naturally, it was a bit too short and too wide. After all, Fabian was the tallest in the family and had never really bulked up.

The hair was wrong too, and it had come as a surprise to Lucille, as if she hadn't seen him with the same haircut for a year. She immediately had him sit in her dressing room and started fussing with his hair. At the rate this was going, Fabian doubted they'd ever make it to the dinner table.

"Luckily, I've already tasked Albert with finding you a proper suit. Now, let me fix your hair." Lucille was so stressed she didn't even notice how her snobbish treatment affected him.

Fabian took a deep breath and reminded himself why she was so nervous. "Have you seen your brother yet?" he asked.

"We were introduced this afternoon," Lucille said, while she started putting product into his hair and slicking it back until Fabian hardly recognised himself anymore. "He's perfect. And by perfect, I mean a perfect fit to the Family de Cerque. Very polite, great manners, well-articulated."

Everything that Fabian was not. Suddenly, he understood her frenzy. He was supposed to be her support person, but instead, he'd become a liability. Her less-than-perfect boyfriend. "Do you still want me there?"

"Of course!" For a moment, Lucille looked panicked. "Don't you dare bow out now."

"I just don't want to embarrass you," Fabian muttered.

Lucille tilted his chin upward. "The only way you could embarrass me is by failing to show up. They know you're coming." She must've realised how that had come out and clapped her hand over her mouth. "Gosh, Fabian, I'm so sorry. I didn't mean it that way. I—"

He put his hands on her face. "Relax, Lucille. It's all going to be okay."

"You don't understand. I've never introduced a boyfriend to my family. Maybe this isn't such a good idea after all."

"You said it yourself. They're expecting me, so let's just get it over with." Fabian forced himself to smile the nerves away. "Look, it's going to be all about Pascal today."

Slowly, she relaxed into him. "You're right. My parents probably won't even notice you're there." Pain flashed in her eyes.

"Well, they'd be blind not to notice you, because you're going to be the most beautiful sight in that room." When Lucille smiled, he kissed her gently.

A knock on the door interrupted them before they got any further. With a sigh, Lucille extracted herself from him and called, "Come in."

It was her butler, Albert, carrying a much fancier suit in his arm. Or rather three. "I brought a selection. It won't replace a tailor-made suit, but I can make some adjustments."

True to his word, the butler was talented enough with a needle to get a passing grade from Lucille when Fabian was clad in a suit that didn't end above his ankles. He saw himself in her long, standing mirror and barely recognised himself. This was definitely not his comfort zone.

Lucille. All he had to focus on today was Lucille.

"What do you think, Albert?" Lucille asked the butler nervously, clearly looking for pre-approval.

The butler smiled benevolently. "I think that he makes you very happy, which is the most important thing here." Then he looked at Fabian. "If I can give you one piece of advice, Mr Bendtfeld, try to speak as little as possible."

Fabian knew the advice was well-meant, but his nerves instantly flared up. It wasn't just his looks that were on probation tonight. It was all of him, from his hair to the way he articulated himself. Tongue-tied before they even left Lucille's room, he hoped Pascal was indeed the main person of interest tonight.

Just as Lucille had said, Pascal was perfection personified. He was small for a ten-year-old but held his back admirably straight, his chin slightly raised so he could look down at people even when he was smaller than them. His blond hair was trimmed perfectly, and he wore the miniature suit as if he'd been born in it, which Fabian deemed entirely possible after ten minutes in his presence.

Pascal was sitting opposite him, and Lucille next to Linda, while the head of the table was reserved for Bastien de Cerque, who'd been a few minutes late to the dinner but immediately noticed Fabian's presence. "Who's this?" he asked Linda. "I thought this was a family dinner?"

Linda chuckled in an affected manner. "It is. Lucille insisted on bringing her friend, though. Apparently, she's eaten at his place a couple of times, so now we have to return the favour."

Bastien frowned. "Today?"

Subtly, Fabian nudged Lucille's knee with his, forcing her to say something.

"Fabian isn't just a friend, Dad. He's my boyfriend." Her delivery was uncharacteristically stiff. If Fabian didn't know better, he'd think she was embarrassed of him.

A searing gaze hit Fabian immediately. Despite the suit, he suddenly felt as if he'd shown up naked to the fancy dinner. Pascal seemed forgotten. "How do you know my daughter."

Somehow the first thing that popped into Fabian's head was how they fought monsters together. Instead, he opted for the much easier-digestible explanation. "We go to the same school."

The disapproving frown deepened even further. "I was under the impression that school was for learning, not..." Once more, Bastien looked Fabian up and down. "Whatever this is."

Yep, he was definitely naked.

"Oh, let's not pretend this is anything serious," Linda said with a smile. She hadn't looked once at Fabian. "This is quite an obvious attempt of Lucille's to show us her displeasure. Point taken, darling."

Aghast, Fabian stared at Lucille. He was nothing but a tool for rebellion to her?

Lucille seemed too stunned to come to his defence.

Instead, her father asked, "Is that so? Fabian, was it?" Fabian nodded slightly. "What kind of man are you, Fabian?"

"What kind of man am I?" What kind of question was this?

"I get the impression that he's not the quickest of mind," Pascal piped up. He glanced at Linda for quick approval, that he received promptly. "If this relationship is rooted in teenage defiance, then he must be sloppy, lazy, and underperforming. Or perhaps a troublemaker."

"What the hell?" Lucille had finally found her voice.

"Language, Lucille," Linda warned her.

Lucille huffed at her. "Excuse me, but where do these baseless accusations come from?" She fixed Pascal with a stare. "You don't even know him. And neither does anyone else at this table."

Pascal ignored her upset smoothly and looked at Fabian. "Was I right?"

Fabian could only stare at the pipsqueak. How on Earth had Pascal formed such a biting impression already?

"Well?" Bastien prompted. "Is he right?"

"About what?" Fabian squeaked. He suddenly felt too hot in his suit. The dress shirt was suffocating him slowly.

"How important is your education to you? Are you a slacker? Underperforming?"

Was this a job interview? Fabian felt the heat creep up his neck and knew he'd be bright red in a few seconds. "Of course, school's important to me, and I put effort into it. But there's more to life than—"

Bastien didn't let him finish. "Your education is the base upon which you'll build your future life. With good grades, nearly all doors will open to you. The worse they are, the more will close. In a worst-case scenario, you'll never amount to anything. So, please tell me, Mr... Fabian, what could possibly be more important right now than a solid education?"

Again, Fabian's mind had gone completely blank.

Fortunately, Lucille was finding her voice, though she was fiddling with the tablecloth. "I think what Fabian is trying to say is that there are other aspects outside of school that you shouldn't neglect either."

"Can't the boy speak for himself?" Bastien snapped, immediately shutting Lucille up. "I'm perfectly capable of imagining what you think is more important. Friends, entertainment, and my daughter. But I've got standards for Lucille. I'm not letting just anyone spend time with her."

Perhaps it was the avalanche of disdain that was burying Fabian under its brute force. Or it was the way Lucille swallowed while staring blankly at the table's edge. Whatever it was that made Fabian forget his place, he found himself snapping back, "As if you'd even notice who Lucille spends her time with."

Linda's spoon clattered onto the plate, Pascal's eyes widened, and Lucille gasped sharply. Bastien, however, kept remarkably calm. His voice turned to ice, though. "If you don't have anything else to say, I'll have to ask you to leave."

"Dad! He didn't mean it," Lucille begged, desperation thick in her voice. She was absolutely horrified how the conversation had turned out.

For her benefit, Fabian probably should've held back and meekly submitted to her father's general contempt. But the words had already been spoken, and there was so much more he had to say suddenly. "Oh, I meant it. And I've got more to say."

"Do I need to call the police?" Bastien's voice started to sound pressed.

"And tell them what? You want to control your daughter's friends, while at the same time not taking any significant part in her life? That's highly hypocritical, isn't it?" Ha! He even got a fancy word in. Eighteen years of friendship with Samantha were paying off big-time.

Next to him, Lucille shrunk into herself, her face full of pain. On the other side of the table, Pascal's eyes were growing bigger and bigger, while Linda had paled.

"The thing is," Fabian continued, returning Bastien's glare without wavering this time, "you don't give a sh... care at all about what Lucille wants or needs. You constantly close your door in her face and don't want to be disturbed. Your work is more important to you. And that's okay, I suppose, but if that's your choice, you don't get to demand a say in Lucille's life. In fact, she's an adult who makes her own decisions. And she has been for a way longer time than she should've had to."

Bastien massaged the point between his eyes, grappling for patience. "I never suggested I was intending to exert control over what she does or who she meets. I trust my daughter to make intelligent decisions about her life." Fabian highly doubted it. "That doesn't mean I will allow you to speak to me in this way."

Fabian couldn't hold in a derisive snort. "You started it." Bastien's eyebrows crawled up, probably wondering how he'd invited such childishness. "Yes, I don't think school is more important than anything else in my life. And I can tell you right now that work won't be like that either, whatever it's going to be. If I'm lucky, I'll follow my passions, but the people in my life will always be my top priority. If they need me, I'll *always* find time for them. That's so much more important to me than good grades or a lot of money. If anything, this conversation has just proved that to me." He got up. "And now I'll see myself out."

With a stiff nod at Linda and Pascal, Fabian strode from the room. He'd barely made it to the hallway when he heard quick steps running after him. He only managed half a turn before Lucille threw herself at him, slipped her hand to his neck, and dragged his head down to kiss him passionately.

His entire face was bright-red when she finally let go of him. "You're not mad at me?" He'd thought for sure that he'd absolutely blown it. Instead of keeping quiet as Albert had cautioned him, he'd exposed Lucille's feelings to her entire family and severely antagonised her father.

Lucille laughed and shook her head. "After you stood up to my dad for me?" Her hand slipped under his jacket and around the small of his back. "No, that was amazing. Amazing and incredibly hot."

Before Fabian had fully grasped the words, Lucille kissed him again. The look in her eyes made his pants too tight. He couldn't wait to get out of his suit.

# Jan

Jan had just finished mopping the floors at the youth hostel when a tornado of first-graders came past him, screaming as if dragons were after them. They were returning from a hike up the Witch's Hump and were dragging the mud of the mountain all over the floor. His hands tightened around the mop, nearly breaking the cleaning utensil, when he suddenly felt a pair of arms around his body.

"Hey, cutie. Are they trampling all over your nerves?" Meg's voice vibrated in his back.

"Kids are the devil's spawn. Remind me to never have any."

Meg laughed and let go of him. "But we can still practise making them, right?"

He answered with a teasing smile. "As soon as I've cleaned this up again."

She giggled, before walking beside him. "Hey, do you know a guy named Robert? He must've been in your year."

One of the best things about quitting school was that Jan's exposure to Robert had considerably lessened. He didn't feel like he was missing a lot. "What about him?"

"Well, Anne and he are going to the movies today."

Jan groaned. "You serious? He'd better keep his hands off my little sister."

Meg was less than impressed. "Is he that bad or is this some big brother shit?"

"Please." Jan almost spit on the ground but thought better of it at the last moment. "I couldn't care less about whose throat Anne chooses to stick her tongue down. But that guy's annoying. I was happy I didn't have to see him every day, and now he might be lurking in my own home." He shuddered just thinking about it.

Meg seemed amused and giggled. "Possibly. Anne has a major crush on him. She thinks he's really sweet."

Jan pretended to retch. Nothing about Robert seemed sweet to him. Dumb, maybe, completely obnoxious and incompetent, but not sweet. "Well, I never claimed she had a great deal of taste."

Again, Meg burst into giggles. "Oh, well, it's just her luck that the best guy out there is her brother."

That was more to Jan's liking. He leaned the mop against the wall, slipped his arm around Meg, and pulled her into him for a kiss. At first, she squealed, but then she slung her arms around his neck and kissed him.

Instantly, there were fake kissy-kissy noises behind them. A group of fourth-graders walked past and pointed at them. Annoyed, Jan let go of Meg and snatched up his mop.

"I hate this job."

A few hours later, Jan was getting everything ready for the night. He'd mopped the common room, emptied and cleaned the tea dispenser, and stored all information material in the office. It wasn't the most exciting job and the kids were getting on his nerves, but Jan felt a strange sense of accomplishment. Instead of learning useless stuff, he was completing tasks that struck just the right balance between diverse and achievable. They even trusted him with locking up at night. And as a plus, he was earning money.

Everything was going smoothly. Meg had gone home, the kids were in bed, and the hostel was as peaceful as a church.

Until he heard someone talking in front of the window.

"Stop dragging your feet. You cannot deny your demon heritage forever," a sharp female voice said, instantly putting Jan on high alert.

He almost breathed with relief when he recognised the answering male voice. "I'm not denying it. I just don't want to return to Hescaryn."

Jan peaked through the blinders of the office, but all he could see was the back of a tall woman and Matt in front of her. Annoyed, Jan clicked his tongue. Why did Matt have to bring his demon dates here of all places?

"I'll wipe out your humanity, don't you worry," the woman promised. "Tonight, you'll taste blood."

Jan gasped, then quickly bit his tongue. What was he witnessing here? A repeat of the Blood Night? Or Matt's true colours? Was he going to *kill* again?

"I definitely *won't* kill anyone," Matt said with a good portion of disgust. "Especially not here. This place is full of children."

"Exactly. Easy prey."

Jan felt the blood drain from his face. "No, no, no," he whispered. "What are you doing here, Matt?"

Matt crossed his arms defiantly. "I'm not going to kill anyone."

The woman huffed, exasperated. "Humans and their queer morals. Melchior, in our world, only power rules. It's natural to rise above the weak."

"Oh, stop with those hollow phrases. I've heard enough of that from Caspar. But this isn't Hescaryn. Here, terrible deeds have consequences."

Jan enjoyed a proud daddy moment. Matt was accepting consequences. They hadn't failed him completely.

"Human nonsense," the woman snapped, bringing back Jan's anxiety. "The only consequences you need to fear are those you'll experience if you don't follow me inside this instant."

Had he locked the front door yet? Jan glanced at the clock. No, it was still half an hour until ten. Not that a locked door would stop a demon.

"Oh yeah?" Matt's voice was still full of bravado.

"How about an eternity as a nice statue along the path?" the woman said sweetly, making Jan wonder what the hell she was. Even Matt seemed unsettled. "Children are easy prey. They don't run as fast, and they—"

"You want me to kill? Sure!"

A sudden bright light made Jan drop the blinds and duck. Matt's trustworthy energy hit something and crackled angrily. When the sounds ebbed away, Jan carefully peered through the blinds again.

The woman was plucking off an imaginary dust grain. "How rude. But at least you acted like a demon just now. Unlike your kind, however, I'm immortal. So, let's cut to the chase and get this over with. You'll see, once you've had a taste, the rest will come easily."

Horrified, Jan watched her grab a mortified Matt by the arm and drag him towards the entrance. He considered dashing over and locking it, but that would've betrayed his presence, and he wasn't quite sure he was ready for that yet.

In the end, his indecision led to him being trapped in the little office. The door opened and two sets of steps entered, the heavy footfall of the woman and the much lighter predator-like ones of Matt. Only he wasn't the predator tonight.

Jan crept over to the door and opened it as quietly as he possibly could. The woman was striding ahead, prattling on about demons and their killer instinct, with Matt dragging his feet behind her. Slowly, the distance between them increased. Jan seized his chance.

"Matt!" he hissed.

Instantly, his friend turned and spotted him. The woman continued on, just as Jan had hoped.

"Jan! What are you doing here?" Matt whispered as well, frequently glancing over his shoulder.

"I work here, remember? What is this?"

Matt sighed. "Ask me an easier question. This gorgon is adamant on repaying her debt to Melaney. I can only assume my mother didn't appreciate me returning to the human world. Euryale is supposed to show me the way back to Hell."

"And the way back to Hell leads through *my* hostel?" Jan stretched his neck to look for the woman Matt had called Euryale, but she'd vanished in the stairwell. "Shit."

Matt cursed too. "Jan, I don't know how to stop this. If I don't kill someone, she will. She's probably at it already."

He started to follow her, but Jan grabbed his arm. "Wait. Did you say she was a gorgon? Are those the…"

"…sisters who petrify you with their evil glares." Matt nodded.

"Like Medusa?" Slowly, an idea was forming in Jan's mind. "So, that means she's ancient. She probably doesn't know what a fire alarm is, then."

Matt was a total loss. "So what?"

Normally it was Jan who was the slow one. "That gives us time to get everyone out of the hostel. So, listen," he grabbed a key from the board next to the door, "you take her down to the laundry over there. Nobody will try to go in. Meanwhile, I activate the alarm and get everybody out of here. Then the two of us kill her."

"She's immortal. My energy blast did nothing but burn her dress."

"Then take her to Hell! Anywhere, just away from here. And now go, before she starts without you."

Matt found his confidence again and nodded. He plucked the keys from Jan's hand and jumped after Euryale.

Meanwhile, Jan took a deep breath, solidifying the plan in his brain. Then he stepped into the hallway towards the red button he'd always been tempted by. Only this time, he would actually press it. "If someone finds out about this, I'm so getting fired."

# Matt

Matt managed to catch up with Euryale moments before the alarm blared through the hostel. Within seconds, doors were thrown open and children cried out. Teachers burst into the corridors, trying to gain control of the situation.

Euryale had stopped walking and covered her ears with her hands. "What is this noise?"

"Come with me," Matt said. "I'll get you out of here."

Instead of using Jan's key, he visualised the location of the laundry then transported himself and Euryale there. The alarm wasn't much quieter, but if he didn't manage to kill her, then she'd be locked in, at least, giving the kids more time to escape. Now all he had to do was distract her long enough for Jan to come through and bring in the team.

Energy wasn't going to help, so instead, he drew his sword. According to the book Chay had written, the sword had the power to cut through anything. Perhaps even the immortal skin of a gorgon.

"What's the meaning of this?" Displeasure oozed from Euryale, and he knew she was running out of patience.

"I'm done with this farce. I'm not going to kill anyone, and I won't let you either. As for my mother, she brought this on herself." It still made him angry just thinking of her.

Euryale took a deep breath. "She mentioned you would be a hard-headed one."

"I'm not hard-headed. I just don't like to be told what to do." Especially not what his mother wanted him to do.

"What's a human life?"

"Damn much!"

Euryale started laughing. "Oh, boy. You might be half-demon, but you have no idea what eternity means. Wait until you get to my age and you'll see how insignificant a human life is. It's nothing really. A flame too easily extinguished."

"You want me to extinguish a flame?" Matt asked, his patience running low. "It'll be my pleasure!"

And with that, he threw himself at Euryale, intent to run her through. But instead of sinking into flesh, the tip of the sword was blocked, and Matt felt as if he'd run headfirst into a wall of stone. His shoulders hurt and so did the rest of his arms, but that wasn't enough to stop him.

He tried attacking Euryale from all angles, making use of every one of his demonic powers as he searched for her one weakness. It wasn't her heart, nor her neck. He couldn't even get the sword through her eyes. Even the snake hair was impervious to the cuts from his sword.

Through all of this, Euryale didn't move an inch. Only when he came to a stop in front of her with burning arms and lungs did she twitch slightly. "Have you tired yourself out, boy?"

Where was Jan? Where were the others?

*Take her to Hell!* It seemed like he had no choice. He'd have to go with her and stay there to make sure she wasn't going to continue what she'd started, something he wasn't willing to do. Not now, maybe not ever.

"Go to Hell, gorgon!"

He lunged again, but before he got a single step further, Euryale's hair rose, the snake heads hissed at him, and the golden gaze hit him. Matt tried to avert his eyes, but it was too late. He was unable to move an eyelid, much less his head. The sword vanished from his hands as his world turned grey.

The last thing he heard was, "Your mother never said you had to be brought back *alive.*"

# Rachel

It was already dark by the time Rachel heard someone knocking on the door of the hairdressing salon. She quickly got up, unlocked the door, and let Samantha in.

"Hey, sorry to keep you waiting." She pushed a stray strand of hair behind her ear. "What happened? You wrote you needed magical help? Is there another monster?"

Rachel locked the door behind her. "There is, but Matt is taking care of her... it."

"Okay." Samantha looked around, confused. "Why are we meeting in your mum's salon?"

"That's a long story." One she didn't quite know how to begin. For some reason, the first thing that came to her mind was: "Matt's in love with you."

Samantha's face fell and she closed her eyes, looking incredibly tired. Probably not the reaction Matt would have wanted. "What?"

Rachel shook herself. "Sorry, forget what I said. I mean, we all know he is."

"I don't think Matt has any idea what love is."

"Oh, he definitely doesn't. But that doesn't stop him from experiencing it and dreaming about it." For some reason, Rachel continued to dig her hole. "And so do you. From time to time."

"I do what?" Samantha's voice was overly sharp.

With a sigh, Rachel lowered herself into one of the hairdressers' chairs. "You dream about him, but don't worry, I didn't tell him. Besides, your dreams about him aren't all positive. Some far from it.

I'm just saying that he's on your mind a lot." In the dreamworld, the connection between the two was undeniable. Maybe it wasn't love, but their destinies were inextricably linked.

Samantha still stared at her, dumbfounded. Finally, she blinked. "Didn't you have a magical problem?"

Rachel was as happy as Samantha about the change of subject. "The monster is a woman who's supposed to lead Matt back to Hell. And she turned my mum to stone." There, she'd said it.

"Petrified? Like Lucille did to the ghouls?"

"No, not a spell. She did it with a look." Rachel almost slapped herself. "Sorry, she's a gorgon, a sister of Medusa, I think."

"How did he get tangled up with one of those?" Samantha complained, then quickly snapped out of it. "Scratch that. I don't really want to know. He'll screw anything, human or monster."

"Actually, he..." But this time Rachel kept her mouth shut. This was neither the time nor the place to discuss Matt's dried-up sex life. "Anyway, I need you to do that anti-petrification spell you did on Jan. Or at least I think I need you to do it."

Samantha raised an eyebrow. "You think? This is your mother we're talking about here."

"Exactly! She'd be much more bearable in stone."

Rolling her eyes, Samantha walked over to the statue she'd noticed now that Rachel had told her about the petrification. "Wow, that's quite something."

"You tell me. I had to answer so many questions about it." Nervously, Rachel watched as Samantha walked around the statue, examining it in detail. When she couldn't hold it in any longer, she asked, "And can you?"

"I think so." Samantha nodded at her. "It doesn't look too different from Lu's spell. So, yes, you'll have your mother back in no time."

Rachel sighed. "Too bad. I was kind of hoping you'd say it was impossible."

"Rachel!" Samantha looked at her in horror. "I know she's a walking red flag and has made your life a living hell, but we can't leave her like this. And she's still your mum."

The latter wasn't really an argument Rachel could get behind. "It would be easier this way."

"Only until the creditors come knocking because she's stopped paying her bills."

Now there was a valid reason. "Good point. Fine, let's get her back."

Samantha gave her one last look before turning back to Annette's statue. She ran her fingers over the stone, looking for a place to start. Meanwhile, Rachel was trying to think of an excuse for why they were standing in the dark in her hairdressing salon.

An idea struck her. Although Rachel secretly hated herself for doing it, she went to the back office to look for alcohol. The fact that she found a half-empty bottle almost instantly assuaged her guilty conscience. She grabbed it and marched back to the front room, placing the bottle in front of the statue as Samantha pulled the invisible threads.

The stone unravelled and Annette stumbled free.

Rachel caught her, simultaneously shouting in horror, "Mum! You're drinking at work?"

Next to her, Samantha frowned, but she remained silent when Rachel pointed to the bottle.

Annette looked confused, her brain struggling to compute. Then she snapped right back. "It's called pregame, Rachel. You'd probably benefit from it."

"Mum!" The indignation was almost real. Why did her mum always have to be so callous about it? As if it didn't matter

"Well, since you're here, you might as well close up," Annette said before taking her bottle and stumbling out of the salon.

Rachel immediately dropped the pretence, only to find Samantha staring at her.

"You want to tell me what that was?" Samantha asked, her voice less than impressed.

Rachel shrugged. "Blackouts aren't unusual for her. That way she won't ask questions I don't really want to answer." It had been the easiest and most logical way to deal with the situation.

Samantha made a face. "Sometimes, you scare me."

Sometimes, Rachel scared herself. But not by the way she dealt with her mother. "Let's go to my place and wait for news over pizza."

# Jan

With the hostel guests out of the way, Jan grabbed a mirror from one of the rooms and made his way over to the laundry. He told himself he wouldn't need the mirror, that Matt already dealt with the situation, but he wasn't going to go in unarmed, and while he might not have retained much Latin from school, he had remembered Medusa's story. A mirror was the only way to deal with a gorgon permanently.

His heart was thumping. As a precaution, he took a quick puff from his inhaler followed by a couple of deep breaths. Satisfied, Jan quietly opened the door with the spare key before pushing it open with his back, his eyes fixed on the mirror. Inside it, he saw the strange woman for the first time, nearly peeing his pants as he did so. She was quite tall, not as big as Fabian, but a few centimetres taller than Jan.

Right now, she had her back turned to him, but that didn't make her any less scary. In fact, it was the opposite. From his unique perspective, he saw a bunch of green snakes wriggling on the back of her head. There seemed to be no rhyme nor reason to it, until suddenly, they all raised their heads and hissed.

The gorgon started turning.

Jan watched it happen with bated breath, waiting to see what the eyes that could turn a man to stone looked like. He felt as if time was slowing down. Something hissed past his shoulder. A second later, the glass burst in his hands.

"Shit!" Instantly, Jan's heart jumped to his throat, and he squeezed his eyes shut. He hadn't even seen her throw something.

The door in his back was opened wider, and he could feel something slithering through his hair and across his cheeks.

*Please don't bite. Please don't bite.*

"Aren't you a clever one?" The voice had something seductive that it hadn't had outside. "Open them, my dear."

He squeezed his eyes shut even harder. "What did you do to Matt?" Matt should've been here with her. The fact that he *wasn't* concerned Jan a lot.

"What's he to you?"

"He's my friend." At least, he hoped that was true. Matt had abandoned them mid-battle before. Had he lured Euryale in here, locked her in, and thought he'd get a head start, leaving Jan to deal with the mess he left behind?

The gorgon laughed, a sound that could've shattered glass by itself. "He's a half-demon. He doesn't have any friends. Something he'll learn once I bring him back where he belongs."

Why was this woman so determined to deliver Matt to Hell? She almost made it sound as if Matt had run away from home, which surely couldn't be true.

Jan felt her squeeze past him and dared to open his left eye by the slightest of gaps, prepared to close it immediately if he caught a glimpse of her face. The gorgon had her back turned to him and bent down to search for something in the mirror shards. By the way she blindly tapped her fingers, Jan assumed she'd closed her eyes.

Which was good news. It meant she was vulnerable to mirrors, just like he'd thought. Too bad he didn't have access to another one. He needed to find a place with more mirrors.

As Jan thought about it, he noticed how Euryale's—that's what Matt had called her—fingers were closing in on a small orange object, a figurine of sorts. He made a split-second decision, grabbed the object, and ran for it.

"Give that back, you thief!"

He had no idea what he was holding, but he sure as hell wasn't going to give it back. Instead, he raced for the stairwell and took two or three steps with one stride. On the first floor, he took a moment to orient himself. In front of him were the double doors that led to the sleeping quarters. Behind him, he could hear Euryale's heavy steps coming up the stairs.

Without further hesitating, Jan ducked behind the doors and crouched down, ready to move. He held his breath as soon as Euryale stepped into the hallway.

"You can't hide from me, little mouse. I'll find you."

Fingers of ice trawled down Jan's back. The terror had him firmly in its grip. Slowly, the steps came closer. Jan wished she'd hurry up as he fought the urge to breathe.

"My snakes can smell you."

Could snakes smell? Jan ignored the stupid question that popped into his head and checked that the right wing of the double door was secured to the ground. Like him, Euryale would have to go through the left one and that would be his chance.

If the snakes didn't smell him.

The door opened and Jan squeezed his eyes shut. The pointy bits of the little figurine he'd stolen cut into his hand as he clutched it tighter. Any moment, she would grab him.

But Euryale went past. "Where are you, little mouse?"

Jan seized his chance. Before the door swung shut behind Euryale, he squeezed back through, then almost fumbled his keys as he locked it.

The snakes hissed and Euryale slammed her hand on the glass, nearly cracking it. "Do you think this will stop me?"

"Long enough for me to have a better idea," Jan called, hiding behind the door. Now if only he was someone who frequently had brilliant ideas.

He turned away to bring as much distance between himself and the gorgon as possible, when he heard a meek little voice on the other side of the door. "Excuse me? Do you know where the boys' toilet is?"

Why? Why was there a child left behind? What teacher had failed at their job?

Jan knew he had to act lightning-fast. He couldn't let Euryale turn. "Hey, silly woman, what's this thing anyway?" He took his first glance at the object in his hand. It was the figurine of a snake, similar to the ones on her head, but in a different colour. "Is it fragile?"

It couldn't be if she threw it before, but apparently the gorgon wasn't much smarter than him. "Don't you dare," she hissed.

A fire extinguisher caught Jan's gaze. "Run and hide, kid!" he called as he pushed the figurine into his pocket and grabbed the extinguisher.

Euryale turned away from him, likely trying to catch the boy first, but before she could grab him and force him to look at her, Jan brought the extinguisher down on her head, smashing the glass of the door in the process.

With a scream, Euryale turned back around. She barrelled through the door like a battering ram. Jan whirled around before he accidentally looked her in the eye and ran. Immediately, Euryale took pursuit.

At first, Jan only tried to lead her away from the boy, who seemed to be listening to him and running the other way. Had he slept through the blaring of the alarm? Just to wake up for a pee. *The boys' toilet,* really. No. Jan stopped for a moment. *The boys' toilet!* A room with mirrors on the wall. That's where he needed to lead Euryale.

The community restroom and showers were just ahead. Jan stumbled inside and held the door closed with his back, quickly casting his gaze around. He almost sighed with relief when he noticed the line of wall mirrors hanging above the sinks. To make sure Euryale would see them properly, he turned on the lights.

"You're pretty ugly, you know?" he called out when the door shook in his back. "You should take a look at yourself."

With a deep breath, Jan stepped away from the door and planted himself in front of the mirrors. Instead of opening the door, the gorgon kicked it open hard enough that it was lifted out of its hinges and went sailing through the room, nearly taking Jan out on the way.

Jan ducked down and closed his eyes. He wasn't even facing her, but you couldn't be too sure. The heavy footsteps entered the toilet. Any moment they would stop forever.

But the moment never came. Euryale kept walking. Instead of facing the mirrors, she must've been looking at him. "At some point you'll open them."

"Surely not. As if I wanted to see *that.* Did you check the mirror lately?"

"As if I'd fall for that. Now give me back my sister's lock."

From the scraping sound, Jan assumed she was picking the door back up. But before he was able to figure out what she was planning to do with it, the teeth-chattering sound of a dozen glasses breaking at once and a loud smash was heard. Shards of mirror glass rained down on him, then something heavy threw him to the ground.

Jan went down with an "uff". Splinters cut into his hands and for a few moments, he struggled to breathe. Groaning, he tried to turn his head.

Glass crunched under Euryale's feet as she slowly came closer. All Jan could see were the shards and her shoes. Carefully, he stretched out his hand towards one of the larger mirror pieces. As he closed his hand around it, the sharp edges cut into his fingers.

The crunching noise stopped, and Jan swallowed. The tip of Euryale's shoes were right in front of him. He took a deep breath, getting himself ready, when suddenly, her face appeared in the gap. Before he could fully see it, he pressed his forehead on the floor and squeezed his eyes shut.

Euryale lifted the door and dropped it to his side, sending a spray of fine shards into his hair and exposed skin.

"Look at me!"

The command tore through Jan's brain, demanding him to follow. He'd always hated authority, though, and remained just as he was.

Nothing could've prepared him for what happened next. Euryale grabbed the shirt around his neck, bunched it up, and lifted him up by it. The front of his shirt tightened around his throat and he gasped. By sheer luck, he managed not to open his eyes.

She slammed him into the mirrorless wall and pinned him there with her body. Snakes slithered over his face, across his lips, and close to his eyes.

"At some point, you'll open your eyes," Euryale said in no kind of rush. "They all do."

Jan shuddered, both because of the words and because of the snakes across his skin. How many people had she petrified in her long life already? Then something bit him just below the left eye. "Ouch." The pain only served to make him squeeze his eyes shut tighter.

Instead, his martial arts instincts kicked in and he pulled up a knee. Though it made contact with the soft parts of the gorgon, she merely huffed. He threw her sister's lock at her face in desperation, but it must've missed her, because he heard it hit the wall much further away. Then Euryale threw him across the floor.

Pain erupted from a hundred glass splinters ripping open his skin. Jan knew they'd be nothing but scratches, but it burned like fire.

"You want to fight me?" Euryale asked aghast. "Blind as you are?"

Jan scrambled up to a crouch and used his hands to find his way. He stumbled over the door at his feet, then knocked his hip against the sink. But then, his fingers found a toilet booth. He pulled himself inside and slammed the door shut, quickly barring it. Shaking, he sat down on the toilet and opened his eyes, staring at the bloodied mirror shard in his hand.

"When will you learn that you can't escape me, little mouse?"

Euryale punched the door open. Jan pulled up his legs in a quick motion and hid his face behind his knees, awkwardly holding the shard in front of him. He knew he was out of options. This was it. He was going to die on the damn toilet.

But the blow never came. The door slammed against the toilet, then back against another obstacle. Apart from his heavy breathing, the bathroom was quiet.

It took Jan nearly two minutes to work up the courage to open his eyes, keeping them trained on the floor just in case. He half-expected it to be a trick, that Euryale's gaze would wait for him right there, but all he saw were grey marble shoes. Slowly, Jan raised his gaze, trailing the stone until he landed on her impassive face.

Jan sagged backwards and let go of the shard that had saved his life after all. After a few minutes, in which he just breathed, he was suddenly grabbed by a moment of anger and kicked the statue with both of his feet. Euryale fell back and shattered into half a dozen pieces.

His gaze fell on the rest of the bathroom. The door she'd kicked open was broken in the middle, there was glass everywhere, and the empty wall seemed to glare at him. "Shit."

# Lucille

After Fabian had stood up for Lucille to her father, they'd stumbled into her bedroom, where they'd continued to kiss passionately. She pushed off his jacket, then pulled his shirt out of his pants to run her hands over the skin beneath.

"So, you thought that was hot?" Fabian asked between two sharp gasps.

Lucille laughed at him in pure delight. She put her hand around his neck and pulled him closer. "Incredibly hot." She hadn't had a champion in a very long time. As mortifying as the stand off had been initially, she'd loved every minute of it. Somehow, Fabian had said all the things she usually thought but had been too afraid to say out loud.

She feared losing her father so much she just let him walk all over her. But no longer. From now on she would demand her attention, and if he wasn't willing to give it to her, then, well, *screw him!* She was done vying for it. Let her new little brother have a go at it and see if his compliant adaptation of Linda's attitude served him any better.

She grabbed Fabian harder and pressed her lips onto his neck, just under his ear. "Everything you said was a revelation to me. You're so right. With everything." Starting to nibble on his ear, she said, "Especially about making my own choices. I know what I want."

"Oh yeah?" he sounded a bit hoarse.

It only turned Lucille on more. "I want you! All of it."

To her dismay, a knock on the door interrupted any more lovemaking. "Miss Lucille?" Albert's voice rang through the door.

Fabian stumbled backwards and quickly straightened his pants with some effort. Lucille sat up and took a deep breath. Then she exchanged a glance with her boyfriend. His eyes were wide. For all his bravery in the dining room, he was probably afraid of her father calling the police on him after all.

Lucille got up and opened the door just enough to peer through it. "I'm not letting him go," she declared icily.

Outside, Albert chuckled. "You won't have to. I'm here to let you know your father expects the both of you back at the table for dessert."

"Both of us?" Fabian asked in disbelief.

She couldn't blame him. There was absolutely no reason why her father would simply ignore how Fabian had called him out in front of the entire family. She opened the door slightly more, frowning. "Is it safe?"

Albert smiled at her. "Absolutely. I don't want to overreach, but it seems as if your words moved him." He glanced at Fabian and hid another chuckle. "Let me help you avoid other uncomfortable questions."

Lucille giggled then opened the door enough for Albert to come in, and turned to fix her dress and hair.

When they returned to the dinner room, their appearances were back in order. Only this time, they were openly holding hands, and Lucille had her chin raised in defiance. The main course had been taken away, but apart from that, everything looked as before. Pascal was shyly nipping from his glass, while Linda stared at her empty dessert plate with an unmatched ferocity.

Her father was the only one who looked at them directly, still regarding Fabian with a critical eye. "Sit, please. It's a show of poor manners to leave the table prematurely."

Fabian opened his mouth, but Lucille was faster. "If I remember correctly, you threw him out."

He raised a disapproving eyebrow. "Not quite. I threatened to do so." As if that made it any better. At last, his stance relaxed a bit. When he spoke again, his voice sounded pressed. "And that was probably equally premature. Now, please sit, so we can finish this dinner in peace."

Lucille and Fabian exchanged another glance before following the plea. The server brought out plates of tiramisu, as if he'd just been waiting in the wings for his cue. Which was likely the truth.

Despite the invitation, the tension around the table could have been cut with a knife. At last, Pascal couldn't keep it in anymore. "He likes your boyfriend," he announced.

"Me?" Fabian asked.

Meanwhile, her father seemed a bit annoyed. "That's not what I said."

"Not directly, but in a very convoluted way, you did," Pascal protested.

He truly seemed to have an advanced vocabulary for a ten-year-old. And Lucille recognised something else. Pascal was playing off what he saw, trying his best to grasp the family dynamics and find a safe space in it. And for some reason, he must've decided that aligning himself with his new sister was a viable option.

Bastien put down his fork and dabbed his mouth with a provided cloth. "I'm not agreeing with everything Fabian said, but I heard the critique and I'm willing to accept that not everyone shares my work ethics." Lucille doubted there were many people who did. "But most importantly, I realised that we want the same thing after all. The best for my daughter."

He flashed Lucille a quick smile that made her stomach all warm and fuzzy. "We might have differing views about what exactly that entails, but as long as my daughter is happy, I won't stand in the way."

Lucille couldn't help herself. With a squeal, she jumped up and hugged her father, kissing his smooth-shaved cheek. "You're the best, Daddy!"

She caught Fabian looking at her with blatant doubt in his eyes. Maybe her father wasn't exactly the best, but he loved her, in his weird workaholic ways.

"Let's eat now," her father said with a sigh as Lucille took her seat again.

Squeezing Fabian's hand, she couldn't help but grin widely. Linda shook her head slightly, then shrugged. Meanwhile, Pascal studied her with big eyes.

Her heart softened towards him. "I'm sorry our first meeting has been so dramatic. I promise we're not always that way." Usually, they all ignored each other. "Welcome to the family, Pascal."

The happy smile on his face was a balm to the soul. Together, they would work it out. And maybe, by the end of it, they'd be a real family.

# Samantha

Samantha and Rachel had just finished discussing Matt's weird behaviour at school and the last pieces of a family-size pepperoni pizza when the doorbell rang.

"Do you think it's your mother?" Samantha asked.

Annette hadn't been home when they arrived. According to Rachel, she'd found a party to go to. It wouldn't be the first time she'd been too drunk to work her keys.

Rachel frowned. "Can I leave her outside if it is?"

"Go!" This time, Samantha didn't believe for a second that Rachel meant what she said.

With a groan, Rachel got up and opened the door. To their surprise, it wasn't Annette but Jan. He looked pretty beat up, as if he'd suffered a severe case of road rash. A sloppy bandage was wrapped around his hand.

"Hey." He noticed Samantha. "Sam, perfect. Can you lend me a hand? He's a bit heavy."

Rachel and Samantha exchanged a confused look. Jan sounded drunk, though he didn't look it.

Samantha got up from the couch and followed the two of them out of the house, curiosity building in her stomach. "What happened? You look like you had a car accident."

"More like a monster accident," Jan quipped.

She raised her eyebrow. "You came across the gorgon? I thought Matt—"

They'd arrived at the open boot of the van Jan had borrowed from his workplace. Inside was the most handsome statue she'd ever come across, and one she recognised well-enough. "This isn't really his day, is it?"

"What happened to the gorgon?" Rachel asked, not surprised in the slightest.

Jan gasped. "You guys know all about her?"

"She petrified my mother."

"Oh. Well, she dragged Matt to the hostel," Jan started to explain. "We got everyone out with a false fire alarm. Matt was supposed to take her to Hell, but he obviously didn't manage to, so I stepped up to the task. I used a mirror, just like Perseus. She turned to stone and I broke her into pieces."

Samantha couldn't help but be impressed. "You know the story of Perseus and Medusa?"

"Only Latin class I paid attention to," Jan said with a grin.

Rachel burst his bubble. "Not quite. Perseus only used the mirror shield so he wouldn't have to look into her eyes when he cut off her head. It's a common misconception that she petrified herself."

Instantly, Jan paled. "Oh... Well, doesn't matter, right? It worked on her sister." Then he faced Samantha. "Is there a way we can help Matt crash-diet?"

She sighed in response. "I'm afraid so."

"My mother is alive and well and ready to party," Rachel said in a flat voice.

"Can't we leave him like that?"

Jan stared at her in disbelief. "Are you serious?"

Meanwhile, Rachel grinned. "But, Sam! I know he's acted like an idiot today, but well, we can't leave a half-human like this, and besides, he's our friend."

Samantha rolled her eyes and huffed. "You can be quite cold."

Rachel just smiled happily, while Jan was still trying to figure out what was going on between them.

With a heavy sigh, Samantha climbed into the back of the van to kneel over Matt's statue. Seeing his petrified expression, she felt like she understood Rachel's hesitation earlier. He would be so much more bearable if he'd just look pretty instead of opening his mouth and putting both of his feet in every so often.

She sighed and put her hands on his hard chest to loosen the spell around him. She was getting a lot better at it and found the relevant knot almost instantly. The stone unravelled quickly and Matt opened his eyes.

He hadn't been lying flat as a statue and was losing his balance now. Panicked, he wheeled his arms around until one of his hands landed on Samantha's hip and dragged her down with him.

Not expecting the movement, Samantha's arms gave way and she landed on his chest. Their eyes locked, causing her to catch her breath.

Confusion washed over Matt as he recognised her. "What...?"

Slightly embarrassed, Samantha pushed herself up again. Matt tried to follow her example but was still uncoordinated, and so the two of them bumped into each other a couple of times before she managed to extract herself from the boot. Heavily breathing, Samantha stumbled away, while Jan gave Matt a hand.

"Where is Euryale?" she heard Matt ask while she still caught her breath.

"In pieces. I beat her with her own powers," Jan boasted. "You can thank me later, because I need to get back to the hostel and clean up the chaos." He closed the door of the boot and climbed into the van.

Samantha still faced the other way as Jan drove away, leaving it to Rachel to further explain the situation. "You were turned to stone. Sam brought you back."

"Oh..." She could practically feel his gaze burning in her neck. "Thank you."

"No problem." The words came out rushed and in a high voice.

Behind her, Rachel giggled softly. "Oh well, I'll see you both in school. Goodnight, Sam."

"What—?" Samantha whirled around, but it was too late. Rachel had already hurried back into her house and closed the door behind her. Gaping, she tried to understand what was happening. Then she slowly turned to Matt. "Uhm..."

She found him smiling at her fondly. "It's late. Shall I bring you home?"

Nervously, she pivoted towards Rachel's house, then back again. "In case more supernatural babysitters turn up?"

He grimaced. "I hope not. But... yeah, basically." Tentatively, he took a step towards her. "So, can I?"

It took Samantha a couple of seconds to sort through her confusion for a simple, "Okay."

Slowly, the two of them turned their feet down the street, keeping a healthy distance between them. When her heart had recovered slightly, she asked, "So, you're supposed to go back to Hell?"

He sighed. "Yes. My mother doesn't like how human I've become."

His eyes were fixed on the street and his mouth had turned into a bitter line. Something big was going on, but Samantha hesitated to ask him about it. If she wasn't careful, she would be dragged back into the demonic mess that was his life, and that had already cost her so much.

"Walking around with Euryale made me realise something, though," Matt said suddenly, frowning slightly.

"What is it?"

"That a lot of what makes demons demons has become unfamiliar to me. Or maybe not unfamiliar but... it doesn't feel right anymore. Or normal." At last, he looked at her, then quickly averted his gaze when he found her staring. "A year ago, I would've done what she told me. I would've probably killed someone just to get her off my back."

Samantha swallowed heavily. "Charming." And that was exactly why she couldn't allow herself to open herself up to him.

"I know!" Matt said passionately. "That's what's so crazy about it."

She couldn't help herself. "What do you mean?"

"I'm also aghast that I ever thought that would be okay. Or rather, didn't think about it at all." He grimaced as if in pain. "It's like I don't know myself anymore."

Against her will, Samantha found herself smiling slightly. "Sounds..."

"Melodramatic?"

"Human," she suggested softly. It was just like when he'd hesitated to kill his uncle.

He stopped walking and stared at her. "Human? I hope you know that would be your fault."

She smiled again. "A fault I accept gladly."

Instead of returning her smile, the crease between his eyes deepened, his eyes looking uncharacteristically tortured. "I don't know what to do."

She felt the heavy load behind the simple statement. Once again, she got the impression that he was carrying something big around with him. Something that he wanted no help with, yet probably needed.

"Or who I am," he continued with a bitter twitch of his mouth. "What I want. What I want us to be."

Samantha sighed heavily when she heard the last one, reminded of what Rachel had told her. "Right now, nothing. I mean, we're friends, or well, we're working on it."

"Only right now?"

"Please." She couldn't stand the hurt in his eyes and averted her gaze. "Your other questions are so much more important."

"What do you mean?"

He sounded so terribly lost that Samantha gave herself a push and tried to elaborate on it. "Look, I'm sure it's hard to straddle two worlds. You've grown up in Hell—Hescaryn—with completely different values. Then you came here and experienced our world. It's normal to feel a bit confused. Or a lot. Humans and demons are fundamentally different, but you're both. And either you need to decide which one you want to be or you need to find a way to marry the two. But first off, you need to find out what you want. What you really want."

His eyes met hers as he said within the beat of a heart, "I want you."

Pain tugged at Samantha's heart. "And for how long?" She shook her head. As Rachel had said, he was obsessed with her. That was all there was to it. Despite what else he claimed, Matt was far from ready for a committed relationship. And she was just as far from entering one with him.

Before he could answer her ill-placed question, she hurried to speak. "Like I said, you need to work on yourself first before you... before you drag someone else in with you."

He lowered his gaze, visibly shutting himself off again, then nodded. "You're right. Thanks. That's great advice, really."

Relief filled her that they dropped the subject. She continued walking. "Tell me about Euryale. Rachel said she was extremely weird."

Matt chuckled as he fell into step beside her. "Weird doesn't even come close to it. She tried to reveal my demon side to me!"

Samantha laughed along as he detailed his surreal apprenticeship with the gorgon, as they both managed to push the heavier thoughts aside for the moment. It almost felt like before everything.

# Part 3

## Hunter & Prey

# Jan

Jan had been staring at the door of his parent's flat for the last ten minutes. Anger was churning through his body. Anger at the unfairness of it all, at the whole situation, and inexplicably at himself.

They'd fired him. After two months of exemplary work, the youth hostel people had fired him. He'd saved everybody's life, but the police investigation had found his fingerprints on the fire alarm and all over the bathroom. That stupid father of Alan's hadn't believed him when he'd tried to explain how he was protecting everybody.

Although he might have complained about the kids and everything, Jan had actually enjoyed working at the hostel. The routine and list of achievable tasks had agreed with him. As had holding a bit of responsibility. No one there had thought he was a total loser. Well, not until Euryale.

He'd lost his job and now he'd have to tell his parents. Jan would've much rather ripped his nails out, then swallow them, than do so, but that wasn't going to help, and with his healing power, the threat wasn't quite as severe. Healing himself was no joy. It worked but only to an extent, like a much-diluted can of soda.

"Let's get this shit over with." Jan set himself into motion and opened the door, instantly running into his little sister in the corridor. "Oh, hey."

"Hi!" As usual, she greeted him with a big smile.

One he answered with a frown. "Is Meg here?" When she shook her head, he was kind of relieved. He wouldn't have been able to do this in front of his girlfriend. Then again, Meg would've been the perfect excuse to not do it at all. "Are the old ones here?"

"Yes, they're watching TV." She gave him another glance. "Is everything okay?"

"Take care of your own shit."

Anne's face and shoulders fell and she quickly ducked into her room. Jan felt bad about it, but it was a kind of dynamic he found hard to break out of. Right now, he didn't need the golden child in his vicinity.

With a heavy heart, he made his way to the living room. His parents were sitting on the couch, eyes glued on the TV where one of those stupid daily soaps ran, and snuggled up. Jan rapped his knuckles against the door to get his parents' attention.

"Anyone home?" he asked, his voice naturally taking on an aggressive tone.

As predicted, his father looked up annoyed, while his mother bent forward to throw him a worried glance. It was she who said, "Food is in the kitchen, if you want."

"Cool, but I need to talk to you."

Instantly, the worry and annoyance grew, already turning Jan off. "About what?" his mother asked.

"I'm out of a job," he said, shrugging for added effect. "Just letting you know. So, yeah."

"What happened?" his mother asked, while his father was massaging the top of his nose, teetering on the familiar edge of exploding.

Jan didn't feel like elaborating. If he told them the truth, his father would have a stroke, and he wasn't in the mood to make up a big lie, so he kept it to the few facts that were indisputable. "I pressed the fire alarm and destroyed half a bathroom."

"What?" And there it was, the expected explosion. "Were you high or something?"

"Nope. I'm clean."

His father snorted. "And we're supposed to believe you?"

"Do whatever you want. I don't care." Jan turned away, but his father bolted from the couch.

"Not with that tone, my friend."

Jan's eyes rolled back so hard he got a headache from it. "I'm not your friend. Friends don't judge each other."

"Excuse me?" his father hollered. "You don't want to be judged? Well, then maybe stop doing stupid shit!"

"Stefan, please." His mother got up as well, putting a hand on his father's arm while throwing Jan a pleading glance.

But Jan couldn't appreciate it. His eyes were fixed on his father's reddened face and the contempt rose in his chest. "I wasn't doing shit." He'd saved a bunch of lives. But, of course, that remained between him and his friends.

"You *destroyed* a bathroom!" Spittle was flying from his father's lips. "Explain to me how that isn't doing stupid shit."

"Nah, you're right," Jan agreed with a shrug. "That was stupid of me. Oh well, better luck next time."

His response left his father speechless. His mouth opened several times, and the muscles in his face twitched uncontrollably, but he was too angry to speak. Jan used the opportunity to slip away.

As soon as the door closed on his back, he could hear his parents argue loudly. According to his father, Jan was never going to amount to anything. As if he didn't know that. He didn't even know what he wanted. Then the conversation turned and his father was threatening to throw him out. "He'll learn how to keep a job then."

Angry, Jan pushed himself off the door, grabbed a nearly empty water glass from his nightstand, and threw it against the wall, before kicking his nightstand for good measure. He'd saved lives! It wasn't his fault that they'd destroyed the bathroom in the process. As if he had the strength to kick doors out of their hinges. Well, that probably wasn't that hard, but flinging them through the room to take out every single mirror certainly was.

He stared at the shards and groaned. Way to prove his father's point about doing stupid shit. With a moan, he walked over to pick them up, when he stepped onto one.

"Damn it!" Biting his teeth, Jan hopped over to his bed and sat down on the mattress. A shard as big as his thumbnail was stuck in his heel. He groaned in pain when the door to his room opened and Anne peeked inside.

"Get out!"

Like all little sisters, she didn't listen. "Did you cut yourself?"

"No." He breathed through his teeth and hyped himself up to get the shard out, his fingers hovering over it.

"I can help you."

Damn, Anne was still in the room. Even worse, she'd come in and was reaching for the shard. Jan tried to be faster but failed and accidentally knocked her finger against the shard. Anne gasped. "Ow."

He grabbed her finger. "I told you to stay—" Pain jolted through his hand and a traitorous golden shimmer enveloped Anne's finger.

Her eyes bulged. "What is that?"

Jan feigned innocence. "What is what?" He took his hand off and plucked the shard from his foot, then lopped it into his bin.

Anne stared at her finger in wonder. "I cut myself, but now it's gone. You did something. You—"

"What a load of rubbish." Jan took off his sock and wiped the blood from his heel with his thumb, applying pressure. His stupid healing powers had healed Anne but they wouldn't come for him. "There never was a cut."

"There's blood."

"Yeah, my blood"

Anne narrowed her eyes. "I felt pain." She crossed her arms. "You healed the cut."

Amused, he looked up at her. "Did you smoke something or why are you talking so much nonsense?" The last thing he needed was his book-smart sister starting to ask questions.

She grimaced in disgust. "I don't smoke."

Jan groaned. "You're just as stuck-up as the old ones. You need to loosen up."

"You're mean." And with that, she finally left the room.

Jan dropped backwards onto his bed. Now, hadn't that worked perfectly? Everyone at home hated him, and it was all his fault. Maybe leaving home wasn't such a bad idea. He laughed mirthlessly. And live on what money? His parents would never support him, not until he'd shown he was able to hold down a job. He probably could demand their support legally, but that was usually reserved for people in tertiary education or doing an apprenticeship.

He ran his hands over his face, trying not to despair. What kind of apprenticeship would he even do? And wouldn't he just fail it, anyway? What was the point of signing up for three years if he did *stupid shit* again? Not that he planned to fight another gorgon.

Failing to find an answer, Jan just groaned.

To avoid more parental stress, Jan went over to his girlfriend's house. Meg managed to sneak him upstairs while her parents fought about who was responsible for cleaning up or something equally boring.

As soon as the door closed behind them, Meg threw her arms around his neck. "I'm so glad you're here." She kissed him and they tumbled onto her bed together.

Breathless, Jan laughed. "I can see that."

Instead of kissing him again, Meg pulled a face. "It's terrible. Day in, day out, non-stop fighting."

"At least they don't fight with you." Jan thought he'd rather have his parents fight than be the recipient of their anger any day.

"Why should they fight with me?" Meg asked. "I haven't done anything wrong."

"And I have?"

She gave him a long stare. Then her face softened and a cheeky smile played on her lips. "That's what I love about you."

Jan frowned. "That I do the wrong things?"

"You don't give a damn what anyone else thinks. If I quit school, my parents would have a fit. Not that I want to, but..." She leaned in and kissed him. "Your life is exciting."

"Oh, yeah, really exciting. I just got fired from the easiest job in town for vandalism, and narrowly escaped criminal charges." It was still so unfair. "And now I'm out of work and stuck at home with no money of my own."

Meg pouted. "Can we not talk about jobs and money? That's all my parents ever speak about."

If only Jan could just shrug it off like her. But he was well aware that, contrary to Meg, he was a twenty-year-old with no qualifications and no job prospects. How long would his parents put up with him if he didn't get a job? How long would he be able to put up with them?

"You're right. Let's not talk about it. Let's not talk about anything."

He swept her back into his arms and kept his promise, showering Meg with kisses until she was out of breath.

# Matt

After a year of living with his father, Matt was slowly getting into a routine. René had gotten used to having him around, and he'd gotten used to all the little things that made up their family life. Such as eating dinner. They never had the TV running through it, instead talking about whatever had occurred to either of them during their day.

René was the only person besides Chay he could truly be honest with regarding his conflicting feelings, not just for his demon and human sides, but also for Samantha. And contrary to Chay, he was always around.

Matt was clearing the table when he said, "We're talking again, yes, but I feel like I'm still walking on very thin ice. One wrong step, and we're back to where we started."

"That's only natural," René said, in his endless wisdom. "She has to relearn to trust in you, and you need to prove she's not putting her trust in the wrong person."

Carrying their plates to the dishwasher, Matt asked, "Why are humans so complicated?" There wasn't a single day he didn't ask himself that question. There were so many unspoken rules. Even after a year in the human world, he felt as if he'd only discovered a handful of them.

René appeared in the doorway and grinned at him. "It's what's makes us interesting." When Matt snorted, he chuckled and returned to the living room.

Matt checked if anything else needed to go into the dishwasher, when he heard a scream followed by a loud bang. Instantly, he dropped the plate he'd just picked up and ran to the living room where the bookshelf had tumbled down.

But not by accident. An ugly black scar marred the wall where it had been. Black magic. Courtesy of his brother.

Contrary to Balthasar, Caspar didn't bother with chitchat. He stretched a hand out towards René, who was kneeling on the ground and holding his arm in pain. Matt couldn't see if there was blood, but he knew he had to do something.

"Hey—"

Caspar turned and shot his energy directly at him. Matt barely managed to duck back into the kitchen. The distraction had worked, but not quite as he'd planned.

He pressed his back against the wall next to the door and listened for Caspar while he readied his own energy. All he could hear from the living room was René's heavy breathing. Had Caspar left?

From the corner of his eye, Matt caught a glance at Caspar as he materialised right in front of him, hand outstretched.

Only a space jump saved him this time, and he reappeared in the living room. In the kitchen, he heard another crash. The spice rack most likely.

"What are you doing, Matt? Leave!" his father said through gritted teeth. He was still cradling his left arm. With his right he was reaching for his jacket, which was hanging over a chair.

"And leave you alone with—"

Matt evaded another energy shot, but this time he used the attack to hide his path as he jumped through the abstract space, only to reappear behind Caspar and grab him by the shoulders. In front of him, René had picked up his demon hunter gun, but Matt wasn't ready to risk it. Caspar was a notoriously quick shot. Together, they tumbled out of the flat and into the empty zoo next to Matt's apartment block.

Appearing not quite on the ground, the two went down in a heap, rolling across the picnic meadow. Matt managed to get his legs between them and kicked Caspar away.

His brother stumbled backwards, but then he jumped and landed right back on Matt, pushing his face into the ground.

The pressure on the back of his head quickly became unbearable, and Matt struggled to breathe. He tried to wriggle free, but Caspar had managed to pin his arms to his body, his weight bearing down on Matt's lungs. "Die, bastard!" he hissed.

Matt decided to turn to his demon form. His wings practically exploded from his back, sending Caspar staggering back. Instantly, Matt jumped to his feet, ready for whatever was going to come next.

Caspar gave him a ghastly grin. Then he unfolded his own leathery wings. Their wingspan beating Matt's by two hands width. "What now?" he teased.

There was no way Matt could beat him. Especially not here. Instead, he jumped into Hell.

# Rachel

Some days, Rachel wished she'd never asked Samantha to undo her mother's petrifaction.

"Rachel!" her mother called, a bottle of champagne in her hand. It was only five in the afternoon.

"Really, Mum?"

"It's not just for me." Rachel guessed from her giggling that her mother was already half drunk. "It's for a date."

Rachel sighed. "Are you gonna bring your date here?"

Her mother wriggled her eyebrows. "Maybe. He's delicious." She said it conspiratorially, as if Rachel were her accomplice. "Tall, dark, sexy as sin. His body is to die for. You should see..."

"I don't want to see him. Like ever. Have fun."

Her mother winked at her. "Oh, I will."

Rachel shuddered as her mother sauntered past, grabbed her handbag, and left with the bottle of champagne. But then she was alone. As annoying as her mother was, at least she was another human being. Although Rachel preferred solitude, the absolute silence of her house was oppressive.

She tried to shake it off and went into the kitchen to check the fridge. As usual, she found it lacking. Dinner would once again be a tin of ravioli. Not that Rachel minded. There would be no one to tease her about it or appreciate her cooking. She half considered just eating it cold, but then decided she didn't need to stoop that low.

Fifteen minutes later she was sitting in Nico's old room with the plate of ravioli and a glass of Coke. The room had been converted into a guest room. Most of her brother's things had been given away or packed into boxes. There was hardly a trace of him left.

Still, Rachel decided to talk to him. "Don't laugh. You're not here to cook dinner." More often than not, it had been him who'd cooked and her who'd washed the dishes. "They're filling and the tomato sauce is full of vitamins." Well, maybe not full of them, but some must have survived. "I'll have an apple later, if it makes you happy."

Only nothing would ever make Nico happy, because the dead were neither happy nor sad. They were just dead.

"This is stupid." Rachel dropped her fork and took a deep breath. It'd been almost a year since Nico's death. One would think she'd be over it by now. She should be used to being home alone. Her mother had always gone out on dates or to parties, while Nico had fled home to spend time with his girlfriend.

Rachel knew she was kidding herself if she thought it would be any different with her dad. Much as she loved him, she was aware that he was a busy man, working long hours at the office to take care of his students. Besides, going to LA was out of the question when all the excitement was right here in Greenvalley.

The prophecy hadn't been fulfilled, which meant their adventure was far from over. It wasn't just monsters and threats, it was magic too. Her very own magic.

Determined, Rachel wolfed down her food. If she couldn't talk to Nico here, she'd do it somewhere else. The one place where she'd never be lonely.

The dreamworld felt like home to Rachel. Her meadow of dream flowers was as constant as the sunrise and sunset, swaying gently in the breeze. Sometimes, she had to venture out to the little house in the Orenjan desert to meet Nico. But this time, he was already there.

Hands tucked into the pockets of his oversized hoodie, he grinned at her, just like in the photos she cherished. It didn't matter that the figure in her dream wasn't really her brother. To her, he would be, for as long as she needed him.

"You're early," he greeted her.

Rachel had been in bed before six. She'd been so eager to escape the loneliness of her reality and join the sleepers. Her friends would be far from asleep, but their dreams didn't interest her much. Fabian would dream about water or Lucille, something Rachel really didn't need to see. Lucille would probably do the same. If not, her dreams would be full of family angst, the very last thing Rachel wanted to deal with. Jan's dreams were an acid-filled mess, while Samantha and Matt spent far too much time in each other's dreams, with varying imaginations.

No, she wasn't here to wander through dreams. "Show me more of this world."

Nico laughed. "This world is at your fingertips. Pick a dream and venture as far as your heart desires."

"Show me your dreams, then."

The smile slipped from his face. "You're not ready for those."

"Nico…"

"They're not Nico's dreams."

Rachel swallowed hard at the subtle warning. Nico's face seemed to waver, almost changing. She couldn't let that happen. With a huff, she forced the mask back into place. "Fine. No dreams, then."

As if her words had the power of Lucille's spells, the dream flowers blinked out one by one. Startled, Rachel spun around. "What's happening?"

The dreamworld was plunged into darkness. It took several minutes for her eyes to adjust. Her breathing was unnaturally loud, as if the walls around her were reflecting her own sounds. Some sort of cave.

Bright energy lit up the room like a flash of lightning, almost burning Rachel's eyes. The darkness returned.

"Light up!" Rachel ordered.

As soon as the light from electric bulbs flooded her surroundings, she wished she hadn't done it. She was in the Dûr Lôrac, the dark tunnels of Hell she'd traversed with Matt in his dreams. Instead of bare rock, blood-stained walls awaited her.

Shrieking, Rachel stumbled back. Another blast of energy bore into the rock, causing stones to fall and blood to spurt, as if the tunnel itself were a living being.

"What is this?" It didn't feel like a dream. More like...

"A vision," Nico said. "Something big is coming your way."

"My way?"

Rachel turned around, her eyes drawn to the row of lights above her. They looked familiar. As it hit her, the tunnels began to morph. Within seconds, the blood no longer covered the Dûr Lôrac but the corridors of the school.

Somehow, the sight was even more horrifying. Blood in Hell, Rachel could handle. Blood in her school was too real.

"How? When? Why?" she asked, breathlessly.

But as usual, the vision wasn't providing any answers. It only showed her endless corridors, some at school, some in the Dûr Lôrac.

Just then, energy flashed again. And this time, she heard a cry of pain.

"Matt?" she whirled around to find her friend dragging himself through the dark tunnels, smearing blood on the walls as he barely held himself upright.

"Is he being attacked?" Rachel asked.

A second later, his brother Caspar appeared and sent another blast of black magic straight into Matt's chest. Matt fell to the ground, bleeding profusely.

"Something's holding him back," Nico said.

Rachel was about to argue that if that was Caspar holding back, she didn't want to know what he was like when he didn't. But then she saw the ties around his body. Like bungy ropes, they pulled him back from the edge whenever he went too far.

Matt was on the ground, sputtering and coughing up blood. He tried to crawl away from Caspar, but his brother followed him mercilessly, moving forward regardless of the bonds around him.

In a split second, Rachel decided to leave the two of them and follow the ropes around Caspar into the darkness. She breathed a sigh of relief as she left the school corridors behind.

"Are you not going to help him?" Nico asked, striding beside her without a care in his voice.

"It's a vision, right? Not a dream, not reality."

"Yet."

She shuddered. She knew Caspar hated Matt with a passion, though the reasons made little sense. Not that demons needed a reason to kill. It just felt so personal. First Balthasar, then the gorgon, and now Caspar? What was going on in Matt's life? Maybe she should visit his dreams after all, once he was asleep.

The strings led her through red glowing tunnels, past silver streams of water until she came to a clearing with a single, ground-hugging, blood-red flower. A demon's dream.

"Should I?"

Matt's scream ripped through the tunnel behind her. The lines were slack. Nothing would stop Caspar. Unless...

She stepped into the dream and immediately tripped over the clutter on the floor. Something that looked suspiciously like a miniature guillotine crashed to the ground. Horrified, Rachel took a step back and smacked her arm against a cold box.

Breathing heavily, she took a moment to look around. She was in a sort of cave, filled from top to bottom with useless junk. Some of it Rachel recognised: simple household items, medieval weapons, and art. Others were more wondrous: small dioramas that moved on their own, carved wooden frames covered in cloth, and metal trinkets she couldn't even begin to understand.

It dawned on her that they were all part of a collection. A collection of human things, she thought as she noticed a TV from the eighties running in one corner.

Human objects in a demon dream.

"Menuha?"

"Oh, hi, Rachel."

Rachel jumped when her voice came from above. There, hanging from the ceiling in a purple silk hammock, was Menuha, as if she was part of a Cirque de Soleil show. Just now, she tumbled down at a sickening pace, stopping mere inches from Rachel's face.

"What are you doing here?" Menuha reached out and ran her fingers over Rachel's cheeks. "Pretty."

A strange jolt of electricity ran through Rachel's body and she jerked back. "Don't!"

"Humans." Menuha dropped to the floor, the clutter around her feet melting away. "You're always so tense. This is a dream, Rachel. Enjoy!"

She waved her hands, and Rachel's clothes came off.

Shrieking, she covered herself. "You can't do that!" In an instant, Rachel had put herself back into a dress. Then she whirled around to face Nico. "You didn't see that."

Nico's lips quirked upwards. "I'm your brother. Remember?"

"Twins," Menuha said, clapping her hands. "Let me get Caspar."

Horrified, Rachel lost control of her clothes again. "No!"

"Yes," Nico said. "You should get your brother."

"What? No!" Rachel looked at him fearfully. "I want nothing to do with Caspar. I certainly don't want to sleep with him. Or you. Or you!" She pointed at Menuha, who smiled lazily. Once again, electricity ran through her body.

Menuha took a leisurely step forward. Her dream responded in kind. Instead of human clutter, swathes of silk wrapped around a wide, comfortable bed. "Twins are special, Rachel. We're connected to each other. Caspar and me. You and your brother. You feel it, don't you?"

The silks wrapped around Rachel, binding her to Nico. She gasped as her body met his. "Stop it!" she shouted, but the silks were unyielding.

"It's an unbreakable bond," Menuha cooed.

Rachel felt a shower of ice run down her spine. "No, it's not."

The silk ripped with a heartbreaking sound, cutting her loose from Nico. He flickered, his face once more morphing. "Matt," he whispered, and then he was gone.

Lost to her.

A sob tore through her throat. "Don't..." She whirled around to face Menuha. "This is your fault!"

But it wasn't. She hadn't even known Menuha when Nico had died. And the dream figure wasn't her brother anyway. She remembered his last message and took a deep breath.

"Matt," she said, just to concentrate.

When she looked at Menuha, the demon had cocked her head, as if waiting for her command.

"You have to get your brother. For real!" With her words, Rachel sent a blast of black energy that put Caspar's attacks to shame.

The dream collapsed as Menuha was torn from the dreamworld. When it focused again, Rachel was back in the bloody corridors of the school. Alone.

"Hurry, Menuha," she whispered.

# Matt

Caspar had hunted him through the Dûr Lôrac all night long. Exhausted, Matt had managed to find a little cave that had no entry nor exit. The Dûr Lôrac were full of these kinds of things. They were the only places that offered some reprieve from what was otherwise an incredibly dangerous cave system. Not only was it a giant maze, it was also filled with lesser demons that were by no means any less *dangerous.*

None of them were as dangerous as the General of the Black Guard though, who happened to be his human-hating brother. By courtesy of René's blood in his veins, Matt had been the victim of his attacks since early childhood.

It was an irrational hate that he'd often lamented. After all, he'd been such a good demon boy. Did it really matter that his father was a human?

Apparently, to Caspar it did. Matt could hear his steps slinking around the outside of his refuge. "You can't escape me."

"What do you even want?" Matt found himself calling back. Internally, he cursed himself for giving away his position. For some reason, he never truly managed to ignore Caspar's taunts, often tempted to measure himself against the older one.

"I want to kill you." The answer came promptly. "So come out and face me like a demon, human bastard."

Matt laughed drily. "Sure, I'll come and let you slaughter me. Do you think I'm stupid?"

"I think you're a coward."

That drew a snort from Matt. If keeping your distance from Caspar made you a coward, then most of the demons in Hescaryn were cowards. They all knew better than to cross a wrath demon. Especially this one.

"Come on, bastard, you don't stand a chance against me. So accept your fate and die."

His brother was dangerous, like a wild animal on steroids, but he was also dumb. Especially when he raged. "I get why you don't have a place on the Council."

"And I know that you will never have one."

Suddenly, the wall behind Matt exploded. Jagged pieces of stone ripped through his wings, causing immense pain. But not as much as the heavy piece that smashed through his left shoulder, breaking every bone in it.

Time to leave.

Matt caught his breath and vanished again. He needed to get away from Caspar as quick as possible. After an entire night on the run, he was at the end of his strength. Any hope that Caspar would be, too, had been dashed hours ago. The general seemed to have endless energy when he had the opportunity to kill someone.

Matt reappeared in another part of the tunnels closer to Lucin, Hescaryn's bright capital, and the city where his mother lived. If he could get there, he might find true reprieve. His mother had always stopped Caspar before he could've gone too far.

His shoulder hurt so much Matt gritted his teeth. He leaned against the wall and took a couple of deep breaths. Sickness spread in his stomach when he felt the bones in his shoulder move towards each other, fixing themselves. Just a few more minutes and the joint would be good as new.

A sinister crackling was all the warning he got. Matt dropped to the ground a split-second before black energy shot through where his body would've been otherwise. Before he could get back on his feet, Caspar was on top of him and slammed his shoulders into the stone.

Matt cried out in pain, unable to contain the yelp. Lights danced in front of his eyes as blackness threatened to engulf him. But he couldn't allow that. If he lost his consciousness now, he'd never wake up again.

"Got you!" Caspar was positively mad, his eyes glistening in the darkness. Then he closed his hands around Matt's neck and pressed down on his windpipe.

With a good shoulder, Matt might have stood a chance. The way it was, his mindless flailing was laughable. The darkness crept in at the edge of his vision field as he gasped for air.

"And you thought you could escape me, bastard!"

"Caspar!" The voice of Matt's favourite sibling, Menuha, rang through the Dûr Lôrac. Matt had no idea how she'd found them, but he welcomed the shock in her voice.

His brother didn't seem to have heard his twin sister, his eyes fixed on Matt. "Almost. Almost."

The lack of air made Matt heady. He gasped and clawed at his neck, but to no avail. The darkness almost had him.

Menuha's voice started to sound muffled. "Caspar, let him go!"

"Most definitely not!"

A slap followed by a much more commanding. "Let. Him. Go!"

Matt didn't think he would. Not in time. But then the pressure on his chest and around his neck vanished and he tasted air. Wonderful, clean air.

"I don't know what you see in this weakling," Caspar complained.

"You wouldn't understand."

Something wet hit Matt's cheek. Spit. Then Menuha's face appeared in front of him, friendly as ever. It was the last thing Matt saw before he fell into darkness.

# Lucille

Ever since their fated dinner, Lucille and Fabian had been spending a lot of time in bed. She loved nothing more than to feel his firm body pressed against her and kiss him for hours. Just like now.

She was getting all hot and bothered when the door to her room opened and Pascal came in. Instantly, Lucille pushed Fabian away, causing him to tumble out of the bed.

"Ouch!"

Lucille sat up, pulling the blanket up to her chin to cover her underwear. "Pascal!"

Her little brother stood there impassively, staring down at Fabian, his eyebrows raised in a perfect imitation of Linda.

"Didn't I tell you to knock before you come into my room?" If this continued, Lucille might have to start locking her room. Actually, that wasn't such a bad idea. Maybe even magically lock it, just to be sure.

Pascal finally raised his gaze. "I didn't know he was here. Mum doesn't like him, you know?"

Lucille almost rolled her eyes at that. Linda had not been pleased by Fabian's performance at the dinner table. She had been even less amused when her father had accepted him.

"His name is Fabian," she hissed.

Meanwhile, Fabian pulled himself up and sat on the bed. "What's *her* problem?"

Pascal gave him another disapproving glance. "You. You are her problem. She thinks you're not proper conduct for Lucille. And you aren't."

"Proper conduct?" Fabian asked in disbelief.

"It means you're not good enough for my sister," Pascal explained in his smart-alec way. Then he changed his voice to imitate Linda. "Lucille could have any guy she wants and who does she choose? The son of a mechanic and a madwoman."

"Not any guy," Lucille muttered.

At the same time, Fabian bellowed, "My mother is not a madwoman." Then he turned to her. "What?"

Lucille waved him off in annoyance. "I just meant that I didn't get every boy I wanted in the past." And it definitely hadn't worked out with the ones that she had. But this was different.

She snaked her arm around Fabian and kissed his neck. "Ignore me."

He let out a soft whimper, causing her to grin and place another kiss.

"Your mother has a magic shop," Pascal pointed out in the meantime. "If that isn't crazy, I don't know what is."

Annoyed, Lucille stopped her fondling. "How does Linda even know that?"

"Naturally, Dad ran a background check on your boyfriend after the other night. Both parents have their own business. The father is running his into the ground, and the mother's isn't far behind. They own the house but it doesn't have a lot of value."

"What the—"

Lucille rammed her elbow into Fabian's back before he cursed in front of the child. Not that Pascal particularly acted like a child.

"My parents' businesses have been going strong. In fact, it's the Magic Circle's tenth anniversary next month. We're planning a huge party." It sounded as if Fabian was making it up on the spot.

"And it's a pretty cool shop," Lucille added. "I like it."

Pascal raised an eyebrow, seemingly questioning her reputability.

"I don't care what Linda or Dad think about Fabian. I like him, and that's that." As if she picked her boyfriends by their credit score.

Pascal nodded. "Because of your rebellious streak and because you need to prove that you hold the power in this house."

"Stop parroting everything Linda says!" Was that what her stepmum thought of her? That Lucille still hated her and had pulled her Dad card? The fact that there was a crumb of truth in it annoyed Lucille further.

She told herself that it wasn't really Pascal's fault, though. He was just a kid from the orphanage who'd dealt with a lifetime of rejection. "She's not going to return you if you don't share her opinions in every little thing," she said gently.

"And if I share those opinions truthfully?"

Or maybe those rejections were perfectly justified. "Then you can leave my room. Now."

Pascal huffed in indignation, but he squared his little shoulders and walked out of the room. As soon as the door closed, Lucille put a spell on it.

"So, I'm not good enough for you?" Fabian muttered, arms crossed in front of his shirtless chest. "Or rather, now my *parents* aren't good enough."

Lucille sighed. "Ignore them, please. Linda's beliefs are a tad antiquated." She wasn't some kind of noble lady who could only marry other noble gentlemen.

"Your father ran a background check on me."

"It's his way of showing he cares... about me." Lucille sighed. There was no good explanation for this violation of trust towards Fabian. She'd hoped everything would be okay after they'd had it out, but apparently, he was only tolerated, not accepted. If Lucille chose to marry Fabian—not that she was even entertaining the idea at this point—all hell would break loose.

She ran her fingers across Fabian's neck and started kissing the trail. "The only opinion," she said between kisses, "you should care about in this house is mine." Her hand cradled his chin and turned him to her, so she could look deep into his blue eyes. "And you're the best thing that's ever happened to me."

Instantly, the corners of Fabian's mouth moved up. He turned into her and slipped his hands around her back to pull her to him. "Let's continue from where we were so rudely interrupted."

Lucille laughed, enjoying his suggestion as much as he did. "Yes, please."

The next day, Lucille met Fabian, Samantha, and Rachel for third period in front of the Politics room. Samantha was carrying a thin pile of papers that Fabian seemed to be very interested in.

"Stop that!" Samantha said when he started flicking through them, upsetting her balance.

"Just let me look. One perk of being friends with you is getting first choice."

Samantha clicked her tongue. "The committees aren't limited."

Her curiosity piqued, Lucille stepped a bit closer so she could throw a glance at the sheets of paper. "What is this?"

With a sigh, Samantha explained, "It's the lists for the different Abitur committees. You know, who's doing the yearbook, Abi party, ball, shirt, trip... those kind of things."

Instantly, Lucille was hooked. It was the exciting part of graduating in June next year. They got to have all these special events and goodies. "I want to be on the ball committee! Please."

Samantha laughed. "As I said, the spaces aren't limited. You can be on as many committees as you want. I'm going to put them all up in the cafeteria after Politics. Then you can enter your name."

"There's no harm in entering it now, though, right?" Fabian managed to find the sheet he wanted and plucked it from her hand. "Abi prank, that's mine."

"Of course, it is," Samantha said with an eye roll. Then she handed Lucille the sheet for the Abi ball. "Knock yourself out."

Satisfied, Lucille put down her name, ideas already filling her mind. That Fabian was choosing prank really wasn't a surprise. Most boys would. Either that or the party at a club without the parents and teachers. Samantha would probably work on the yearbook with all their profiles and experiences, and join at least half of the rest because she couldn't *not* organise something. Rachel was a bit of a conundrum. The shirt maybe, or just help Samantha with the yearbook. And Matt...

"Hey, was Matt in Music this morning?" she asked Rachel.

"Haven't seen him."

"Huh. He wasn't in French either, though we had a test today." Lucille got her phone out and sent him a quick text. It wasn't like him to miss school.

By the end of the fifth period, Matt still hadn't replied. The friends left German class with Mr Zobel and decided to make their way over to the adjacent primary school to check with his father whether everything was okay. When they arrived, Pascal was waiting at the gate. His eyes lit up when he saw Lucille.

"Are you picking me up?"

Surprised by the question, Lucille frowned. "Hasn't Tobias come yet?" Her brother shook his head. "I'm sure he'll be here any minute. I still have classes." The break was just long enough to make their way over here and back again.

"At my school?"

"We're just checking in with a friend," Lucille said with a vague smile. She hadn't forgotten how he'd bothered her last night.

Pascal dropped the smile and shrugged. "Well then."

"See you later."

"Was that your brother?" Rachel asked after they'd put some distance between them.

Lucille rolled her eyes. "Yes, I'm afraid so.

"What happened to welcoming him with open arms?" Samantha asked.

"I'm trying, but currently he's like a little Linda, who tells me everything the big Linda only thinks most of the time."

"Especially about me," Fabian added.

Rachel frowned at him. "What does Linda think about you?"

"That I'm a poor wretch who only sullies her precious carpets, impregnates Lucille, and then leaves her."

Lucille couldn't help the bout of amusement and laughed. "Which is total rubbish."

They found René still in his classroom, tidying up and preparing for the next day. As soon as he saw them, his brow creased with worry. "Don't tell me he still hasn't come back."

"Still?" Samantha asked.

René sighed. He stepped forward to close the door behind them and gestured towards the tables. Since the chairs were much too small, Lucille and the others remained standing or leaned against a table edge.

"Caspar came to visit last night."

Fabian coughed instantly, his eyes bulging. "Isn't that the brother who's Hell's general?"

"Exactly. I had hoped to get a bullet into him, but he and Matt vanished before I could get the gun ready." René leaned against his desk and rubbed his forehead. "The fact Matt hasn't turned up again means that either they're still fighting, or he's dead."

Samantha shook her head. "He also could've decided to stay in Hell."

Next to her, Fabian nodded eagerly. "Yeah, that's his signature move. He comes and goes as he pleases."

Instead of joining the chorus, Rachel was chewing her lip.

"Not this time." René shut their hopes down. "At the moment, he's trying very hard to keep his distance from Hescaryn. And especially from Caspar."

"Why?" Samantha asked, sounding wary.

But René shook his head. "I can't tell you that. I promised Matt to keep it secret. For now."

His evasion only served to stoke the worry Lucille had felt before. "I'm sure he's fine."

"Menuha will see to it," Rachel added.

"Menuha?" Lucille asked.

"She's on Matt's side, right?" It sounded just a tad evasive. "She'll stop Caspar if Matt can't. And everything will be fine."

René smiled, but Lucille saw through it. He didn't think his son was well, and there was nothing he or they could do about it. Rachel's assurances didn't do much to calm her nerves either. What kind of trouble had Matt gotten himself into now?

# Matt

Matt woke to a bad headache among colourful soft pillows, on a bed shielded by a total of five sheer curtains that swayed softly in a breeze. Moaning, he tried to rise but only managed to sink deeper into the pillows.

Slowly, the memories returned. Caspar attacking his home and René. The two of them rolling across the zoo meadow. The endless cat-and-mouse game in the Dûr Lôrac. Caspar finally catching him and almost strangling him, if it hadn't been for...

"Awake at last?" The curtains were pushed aside, revealing a peek of the room behind it, which was filled with all kinds of contraptions, art, and weird figurines. Human collectables, amassed by the only sibling Matt could stand. Menuha.

"Was I out for long?" he asked lazily, waiting for his head to stop hurting.

Menuha offered him a goblet. "Just a few hours. Seems to me like you *really* needed to sleep. Are your wounds healed?"

Matt pulled himself up into a sitting position and rolled his shoulders. Apart from his head, everything seemed to be fine. "Of course. I just feel like I've been run over by a truck." When Menuha frowned slightly, he said, "One of the big boxy cars."

"Ah, yes. Ashuan's human goods transporters."

He took the goblet and drank from the watery nectar inside. Slowly, his head was settling down.

She sat down on the bed and put a hand on his thigh. "I'm sorry."

There was no way Matt could ever be angry with Menuha. On top of that, she had nothing to be sorry about. "Menu, do me one favour: don't apologise for Caspar's violent outbursts. You know he always hated me and now he hates me a little more. It doesn't matter." There really wasn't a huge difference between him trying to kill Matt, and trying to obliterate him.

"Did you talk to Melaney?"

Matt snorted. The days when he could rat out his brother to his mother were long gone. "What's the point in that? She wants this."

Menuha frowned unhappily. "Something doesn't make sense."

"Only something? Nothing makes sense." Matt had to catch himself when helpless laughter bubbled over his lips. He was *not* going to fall apart in Menuha's bedroom.

Nonetheless, she leaned over and gave him a hug. "I've seen humans do this when they're upset."

"I know what a hug is," he muttered into her shoulder.

"I promise to protect you," Menuha said as she let go of him again. "You're my favourite brother."

"After Caspar," he pointed out icily.

Menuha shrugged apologetically. "Favourite half-brother then."

"I don't know how you can like him even a little bit," Matt admitted. It wasn't the first time he'd wondered what the sweet, curious, and kind Menuha saw in his irritable, brutal, and vengeful half-brother. They were twins, but that couldn't be it.

"He's different in private."

Matt raised an eyebrow. "In private?" One would think being Caspar's little brother meant he'd met him in private before.

"With me," Menuha amended. "When we were children, he always protected me. Admittedly, most of the time his hot-headedness was what got us in trouble, but still. He always pretends to be so gruff and unapproachable, but beneath all that..."

She stopped when she noticed Matt looking more and more doubtful. There was *nothing* approachable about Caspar. "He's hated me since I was a baby."

Menuha sighed. "Yes, that's about right. But it's only because you're half human. It's nothing personal."

"Great!" As if that made the constant threat better. Besides, it felt pretty personal to Matt. He didn't know anyone else in Hescaryn who had to endure the ire of the General of Terror on a near-daily basis. Then again, everyone else who had to endure that fabled ire didn't have the protection of Melaney, and was probably already dead.

He'd been so close yesterday. Melaney's protection no longer held. Instead, she'd painted a target on Matt's back. A target on all their backs, but Matt had no illusions about who was going to be the first who'd get eliminated from the board.

"You're going to be fine," Menuha said while nudging his shoulder. "Let's get you home. I'll protect you until he's calmed down again... or found someone else to go hard on. Perhaps a new recruit."

Even if Caspar found a new recruit, he'd always come back to Matt.

With a sigh, he drained the goblet and swung his legs out of the bed. "Let's go."

# Samantha

After inquiring after Matt, Samantha returned to school and checked on the lists she'd hung on the big window near the stage. Satisfied, she noticed that quite a few people had already put their names down. Predictably, prank got the most interest, while the T-Shirt list was still bare.

Someone grabbed her hand and pulled her behind the big curtains. She gasped in surprise, ready to defend herself, when she recognised her "attacker" and let him have his way with her. Cian pressed her against the wall behind the curtain to kiss her passionately.

"Cian," Samantha said as she caught her breath.

He grinned at her. "Haven't seen you all day." Since Chemistry was their only class together, it came as no surprise. He leaned forward to kiss her neck.

Samantha moaned softly, then clapped her hand to her mouth. "What are you doing here? What if someone find us?" Someone could've seen her vanish behind the curtain. Or worse, someone could pull it back.

His laughter ran over her neck, sending delicious ripples of warmth over her skin. "So, now I'm your dirty little secret?"

The words did something to her, but they also brought a touch of guilt with them. "I don't want anyone to know," she admitted, only to realise, annoyed, that it was exactly the definition of a dirty little secret. "It's all so... unfamiliar."

Cian pulled back his head. "Do you mean someone specific or no one?"

Samantha hated how hurt he sounded. Cian had been nothing but honest with her. She loved hanging out with him. She also really enjoyed having sex with him, but that all made her feel like she was using him. Even though he'd said he was okay with it, Samantha wasn't.

"No one," she admitted. When he opened his mouth to protest, she put a finger on his lips. "Listen, please."

He shut his mouth again, but then he started to open his lips and suck on her finger with a cheeky look in his eyes.

Samantha laughed nervously. "This is all *very* exciting." His cheeky grin only turned her on more. "*But.* I can't deal with any more stress. If Cheryl, Ani, and—"

"Don't worry about Cheryl. I hardly hang out with her anymore, and if she's got a problem with who I'm dating, let her come. I'm not ashamed of you."

He said it with such conviction, Samantha melted into the wall behind her. "And that's great, but... it's not just Cheryl. I also don't want Matt to find out." Even though, they got along better these days, she still worried about what he was going to do to Cian if he found out they slept with each other. Matt had already acted weird when he'd assumed Cian was only flirting. He'd even tried to beat Cian up.

Cian paled as he heard that. "Oh, okay. Yeah, that poses a bit of a problem."

"I don't believe he'd kill you," Samantha hurried to say but then admitted, "I mean, I don't think so." She shook her head as if that got rid of the images that still haunted her. "Look, he and I are talking again, but it's all so very..."

"New?" Cian suggested.

"Fragile," Samantha said, and nodded when the word felt right. "I'm afraid what will happen if he learns of this."

Cian sighed heavily. "Alright. Matt can't know."

"And that means no one else can," Samantha hurried to say. "I didn't even tell Fabian, because he'd just blab about it by accident." The same was true for Lucille who definitely couldn't keep her mouth shut. Rachel might keep it a secret, but she had suddenly become a Matt supporter, only subtly, but Samantha knew they talked. "It's just too dangerous."

"Alan knows about it," Cian admitted, blushing slightly. "He's my best friend and he lives next door. He saw you come over yesterday."

When Samantha thought of yesterday, she just remembered the two of them having sex. If Alan had seen that through the window...

Cian's eyes widened. "He didn't see anything. I closed the curtains, remember?" She nodded breathlessly. "So, I told him about you, but if you want, I'll tell him to keep it to himself."

"Yes, please."

"No worries." He grinned cheekily at her. "I like being your dirty little secret." Then he leaned forward and they kissed again.

Samantha put her arms around his neck and pulled him closer, relieved that they'd talked about it. Just as his hands slowly started roaming her body, the bell rang.

She opened her eyes. "We're gonna be late."

Cian laughed, but he let her go and stepped aside. "You're such a goody-two-shoes."

With a mock gasp, she raised an eyebrow. "I beg your pardon? Goody-two-shoes don't kiss naughty boys behind school curtains."

"True." Cian grinned languidly, enjoying himself way too much.

She was about to hurry to Spanish when he called after her. "Speaking of Alan..."

Irritated, Samantha turned around. "What about him?"

"His mum's got a job opening. I can introduce you if you want."

From Samantha's memory, Alan's mother had a little flower business not too far from school. "Thanks."

"No worries," Cian said, before adding much more quietly, "anything for you."

When Cian picked her up after her last period to take her straight to the flower shop, Samantha wondered how much he'd already told Alan's mother.

"I don't have my CV with me," she protested. She was also supposed to meet the others in the Magic Circle to discuss Matt's worrying absence.

Cian snorted at her protest. "What's your CV supposed to say? You've never held a job."

"Not a job, but I've been on the student council for four years. And I'm the Student President now. Plus, I've got experience with paperwork due to my father's garage and..." she stopped when she saw him trying to keep his grin from growing too big. "What?"

"You don't need a CV for Pia. She's really nice and you're such a professional. She's going to fall in love with you based on the interview alone."

"Well, I'm not professional without a CV," Samantha grumbled. Then her eyes widened. "An interview. I'm not prepared. I'm not wearing—"

"Relax!" Cian laughed. He took her arm and patted it, but also used it to drag her along. "I've already told her about you."

Samantha looked at him in surprise. "You did?"

He shrugged and nodded. "Yes, of course. I asked her what she thought about hiring someone for the afternoon shifts. It's always busy around then, you know."

"You asked her for a job? For me?" Samantha didn't know what to say.

"In a way, yes." When Samantha wanted to protest, he raised a hand. "Look, I know you don't need my help. As you said, you're already so qualified you'll easily get a part-time job." That wasn't exactly what she'd said. "But when you told me you were looking for one, I had to think of Pia. Because of your flowers, you know?"

He knew her well. Not only were the flowers her magical emblem, Samantha also loved flowers and herbs and everything that grew. A flower shop was perfect. Even though she had little time to prepare, she really wanted it. It would help her family so much.

"Don't worry," Cian continued. "She really is a sweetheart."

"Who will give me a job, because I'm your... friend?"

Cian pulled a face at the reminder that she refused to be his official girlfriend. "No, I got you the interview. You need to convince her that she should hire you." His face relaxed again as he braided his fingers through hers. "Which I know you'll do in a heartbeat."

It felt nice to have someone believe in her. "Thank you." She leaned over and kissed him.

When she looked around again, she noticed that they'd arrived. The flowershop was on the corner, a selection of in-season flowers and larger plant pots standing outside. A hand-painted sign carried the name: *Aster Garden*. A few painted asters completed it. The only thing out of place was a parked police car.

Samantha was about to turn away, but Cian pulled her inside, and a tiny bell announced their entry. Immediately, the smell of dozens of different flowers hit Samantha's nose and she took a deep breath. The inside allowed for two different pathways, one past bigger plants, the other past layered shelves of buckets with cut flowers and ready-made bouquets. Bushels of decorative greenery stood in large pots on the counter.

A policeman leaned casually against the same counter, holding a cup of coffee. Samantha had only seen him once or twice, but she recognised the man as Alan's father, the local police captain. Of course, he'd be visiting his wife on a break.

"...and then they just vanished. Poof, gone." Captain Aster snorted. "Sometimes, I worry more about the people calling in than our actual criminals."

People vanishing sounded dangerously close to demons. Questions burned on the tip of Samantha's tongue, but asking them was strictly forbidden.

Captain Aster's wife was a pretty dark-haired woman, who wore her hair in a long ponytail, though several strands had escaped the confines. As she laughed with her husband, she bound a bouquet. She looked up with sparkling eyes, her smile only widening when she saw Cian and Samantha. "Hello, darling."

"Cian," Captain Aster said, then nodded at Samantha.

"Hello, Mr Aster. Mrs Aster."

The captain drank the rest of his coffee and put it down on the counter. "I'd better get back to work. Can't leave those idiots alone for too long. I'll see you later."

"Don't work overtime tonight, please. We've got guests coming," Mrs Aster called after him.

He knocked on the door. "I'll try." Then he was gone.

Mrs Aster finished her bouquet and placed it in a waiting bucket of water. Then she picked up the coffee cup and smiled at them. "You must be Samantha. Cian's told me of your love of flowers."

Nervously, Samantha brushed a strand from her hair. "That's right. I mean... Nice to meet you, Mrs Aster."

"It's not very busy right now, so why don't you come to the back with me and we'll have a quick chat. Cian can watch the shop in the meantime."

"You've got this," Cian whispered and rubbed Samantha's back as she walked past him.

Samantha thought she was going to pass out. When they'd done the student internship in tenth grade, she'd simply worked for Caroline for two weeks. This was her first proper interview, and without much warning.

But Pia Aster was truly as nice as Cian said, and within a few minutes, they were happily chatting about all things flowers and work experience. Pia loved that Samantha had already so much small business experience and a passion for gardening. After merely fifteen minutes, she'd offered her afternoon hours twice a week, as it fit her schedule, and Samantha left the flower shop beaming from ear to ear.

"I told you you'd get it," Cian said smugly.

She was so happy she threw her arms around his neck and surprised him with a kiss. "All thanks to you!" she whispered, then kissed him again.

Samantha managed to make it to the Magic Circle only a few minutes late. She greeted Caroline, then hurried into the back room. From the looks of it, Fabian, Rachel, and Lucille hadn't started yet. Instead, they were eating jam-filled donuts.

"There's one for you," Lucille offered with a big smile, clearly the sponsor of the afternoon snack.

She took one, feeling ravenous. "Where's Jan?" He wasn't working, so there shouldn't have been any reason for him to miss the meeting.

"On a date," Fabian said, grimacing. "Where did you go after school?" As usual lately, he had his arm around Lucille and leaned against her.

"Uh, I had a job interview." That shouldn't come as too much of a surprise. "And I got it."

Lucille clapped with delight. "Where?"

Even though, Samantha wasn't going to tell them about Cian, she knew the nature of her job would cause problems. Well, Fabian would just have to get over it. "I'm going to work at the Aster Garden near school. You know, the florist?"

"Doesn't Alan's mum run that?" Fabian piped up, predictably.

Samantha took a seat. "Yes, *she* is. I doubt he's going to be at the shop very often." How often did a teenage boy feel the need to buy flowers after all? She pulled a book on demonology to her and started flicking through it. "Anything from Matt yet?"

"No, I still can't reach him." Despite her words, Lucille tried again. With a sigh, she lowered the phone soon after. "I'm really worried."

Fabian rubbed her back. "I still think he's just gone for some time and he'll be back when he pleases. Nothing's going on."

That wasn't the impression Samantha had got. "He's got some family trouble, hasn't he?" Posing it as a question made it seem less likely the others would grill her about how she knew.

Despite her efforts, Rachel's eyes drilled into her. Samantha evaded the gaze by flicking through the book.

Fabian snorted. "Doesn't he always have family problems? He said he's going to take care of it."

"What if he needs help?" Lucille asked, calling Matt yet again.

This time, Fabian took his arm away. "Last time, Malcolm nearly killed us. Matt's always attracting blood-thirsty demons. It's not safe for us."

"That's why I'm trying to find a way to protect Ma—Greenvalley." While Malcolm had come to Greenvalley independently, Fabian wasn't completely wrong. Matt's mere presence here attracted his siblings, and maybe even his mother. And since Samantha was no longer trying to get Matt to leave, she needed to find a way to keep the others out.

"Like a ban?" Rachel asked.

Samantha looked at the complicated drawings in the book in front of her. Some of them were summoning circles, but circles of banishment existed. "I was hoping to rebuild the barrier our grandmothers erected, the one Malcolm tore down, but it's such a complex spell that I can't do that. Even Granny said it's no use right now."

Lucille nodded and added, "She said that there was a much higher frequency of monster attacks since... well, since we all came together."

"What?" Fabian looked at them aghast. "I thought the Spring of Magic was what drew them near. What do *we* have to do with it?"

"Less us and more our emblems, I suppose," Rachel said softly.

Samantha agreed. "Probably, yes. I mean, it's a miracle no one's tried to take them from us." Even Malcolm hadn't understood what they were until it was too late. "Anyway, there's no barrier. But I've found—" she pointed at the book "—that there are various ritual circles to ban specific demons from Ashuan. Not forever, but for a very long time."

"That sounds great. I'll start a list," Fabian offered, more enthusiastic than she'd ever seen him around monsters. "Caspar gets the top spot."

She really didn't want to curb his enthusiasm. "It's a bit complicated. We'll have to draw a circle of banishment and then get Caspar to step inside."

"He might not be very smart, but even he wouldn't do such a stupid thing."

"Matt!" Lucille jumped up and threw herself around his neck. "You're back."

At the table, Fabian coughed into his hand, probably not too keen to see his girlfriend hugging Matt. Samantha let out a sigh of relief at the sight of Matt and quickly stifled it behind her hand. Fortunately, even Rachel was too distracted to notice her, looking as if a giant weight had fallen off her.

Matt wasn't the only one who'd returned. Behind him, Menuha entered and immediately threw a curious glance at Samantha's open book.

"You're alive." Lucille had let go of Matt, her voice full of emotion. "Your dad was really worried."

"I know. I've already talked to him. He told me you wanted to meet here. So, what's up?"

Apparently, he was trying to do his usual evasion tactic, as if he hadn't just missed a whole day of school because he was being hunted by his demon brother. "We're looking for a way to banish your brothers from Greenvalley. Before they manage to kill you."

"They won't," Matt declared, though his voice wasn't quite as certain as he thought it would be.

"Can't we summon Caspar into the circle?" Rachel suggested.

Menuha shook her head. "That doesn't work. The spells are opposed to each other. The circle of banishment would forbid a summoning. Also, as the General of Terror, he has a slight resistance to summoning."

"Meaning?" Fabian asked, as if he wasn't quite sure he wanted to hear the answer.

"You can summon him, but that doesn't mean, he has to come," Menuha explained. "If one of the Archdemons calls, though, he has to jump."

Matt nodded in accordance. "It's a bit like Chay. Only, he worked very hard on building up a resistance." It sounded bitter, as if he'd tried to call Chay and had failed to do so.

"Too many people requested his help after he saved the first few worlds," Menuha explained.

Samantha supposed saving worlds was a lot more important than holding Matt's hand. "Well, in that case, we need to find another way to lure Caspar into the circle of banishment. Perhaps, by creating an illusion of Matt, and then Fabian pushes him with his water."

"Or you could just leave it."

She frowned at Matt. "Why would we just leave it?"

"Because it's dangerous, and I told you guys that I'd take care of it."

"Matt." Lucille took another step towards him. "We are a team. If one of us is in trouble, we all help out."

He wouldn't have it. Shaking his head, he turned toward the door. "These are my problems alone, and they won't go away by you banning Caspar. I want you to stay out of it."

While sensible, it wasn't the right thing to do, Samantha thought. "Matt."

"I mean it!" Matt's voice grew louder. "This is none of your business. He only wants me. If you get involved, you'll just get hurt."

Fabian raised his hands. "I'm not protesting."

But Lucille groaned with desperation. "Why are you being so stubborn? You can't keep going like this. If Caspar's hunting you..." She was losing Matt's attention fast. "Let us help."

Matt crossed his arms and glared at them. "I don't want you to get hurt. Happy?" Everyone stared at the table. In a demon against demon fight, they were all useless. "What happened to Samantha is not going to happen again," he promised, reminding everyone of Balthasar's birds. Or maybe how Malcolm had made her bleed. "I alone will keep him... them at bay."

"Matt..." Even Menuha felt sorry for him.

Samantha met his glare with one of her own. If Caspar hunted him only half as relentlessly as the birds had hunted Samantha, he needed help. Just as she'd needed help. But there was more to this than he saw. Matt might be able to fight his own battle, but Greenvalley could not. And frequent visits from Caspar were not conducive for the town's safety.

"Very well," she said and closed the book, but not before slipping a bookmark between the pages. "Have it your way."

# Matt

Judging by how Samantha had looked at him, Matt was convinced she hated him again. That or she was planning something incredibly stupid. If there was even the slightest chance it was the latter, he had to do something about the situation. Something permanent.

"You're planning to kill him, right?" Menuha was still with him, accompanying him like the good bodyguard she intended to be.

Matt closed his eyes for a moment before he answered. "I don't have a choice. He'll come after me again and again, until one day..."

"I'll stop him."

Matt didn't fault her for believing it. Menuha had always been the only one able to reason with Caspar. Even yesterday—or had that been this morning?—she'd stopped Caspar from killing him. But he couldn't hide behind his sister's apron strings forever.

"Forever? Menuha, this is Caspar we're talking about. He wanted to kill me when I was still in the cradle."

"And you're still alive."

Which was the biggest miracle of all, though Matt knew the reason why. Even Caspar wasn't stupid enough to cross Melaney. Not until she'd made Matt and everybody else fair game.

"Matt." Menuha's voice lost some of its softness. "I don't want you to kill him. Just as I don't want him to kill you."

Matt had only a long glance for her as they reached his apartment block. He felt sorry for Menuha. Her love for her twin might be undeserved, but he couldn't deny her that. In a world where blood meant nothing and sin was everything, twins were an oddity. They either killed each other early on to survive, or they stuck together like glue.

Despite all their differences, Menuha and Caspar were the latter. Stuck as she was between Caspar and him, Matt knew she'd choose the former if it came to it. And that was another reason he couldn't allow himself to rely on her. As much as he needed an ally, it was too risky.

"I can't allow him to hurt the ones who are important to me," he said as they stepped into the corridor in front of his flat. The words had never felt more honest, but Menuha started to grin. "What?"

"You almost sound like a human. It's cute." She chuckled when he pulled a face, but then she suddenly stopped cold, the blood draining from her skin. A hand flew to her mouth and she moaned softly.

"What's...?" Then he felt it too. Something sinister lurked behind his apartment door. Something that made him want to turn away and run as far as possible.

Matt shook his head. If there was something sinister, it was Caspar. And if Caspar had hurt René, then his brother had another thing coming.

Determined, he opened the door and gaped at the sight in front of him. On every single wall, protective arcane symbols glowed in bright blue, so repulsive Matt wanted to throw up. Just the sight of them made his skin crawl.

He was just about to turn away when René came around the corner, gun in his hand. "It's you." Instantly, he lowered the weapon.

"What is this?" Matt asked in disgust.

Next to him, Menuha retched. "Banning symbols."

René nodded with a severe expression. "I'm sorry, but that's how it has to be. Come on in, Matt."

It sounded like a threat. Matt took a step back, shaking his head wildly. "I'm not doing that."

"You're a half-demon. It won't be pleasant, but it's safe," René stressed. He held his hand out to him, inviting Matt into the most horrifying place he'd ever seen.

Just then, Menuha put a gentle hand in his back and gave him a slight push. "Go. Your father obviously knows how to protect you." There was no question about whether it'd be possible for her to follow. Even being this close had drained her completely.

*Safe.* Matt had never felt more disgusted by the word. He wanted to fight, to search out Caspar and face him in a life-or-death duel. But he wasn't ready. In his current state, without a proper plan, he'd be the one who'd lose his life.

With heavy shoulders and an even heavier heart, Matt stepped into the protective realm of the arcane symbols. Immediately, he stumbled, an indescribable weakness coming over him. René caught him and guided him into the living room, closing the door in Menuha's disappointed face.

By the time Matt had made it to the dinner table, he wanted to die. It was like he was back in the burning storage unit after Malcolm had tied his hands, banning his demon blood. Worse, because this was supposed to be his home, his safe haven. Now that safety came with a hefty price.

"I don't think I can do this," he confessed to René.

"It's the only way, Matt. You need a place where you can sleep and recover without being assaulted by that dastardly demon brother of yours."

Crumbs came and greeted him excitedly, running circles around Matt's legs. When Matt sat down, the dog put his paws on his knees and licked his face. He slung his arms around him and soaked in the warmth and unconditional love Crumbs showed him. It was the only anchor left in his demon-hostile home.

Matt couldn't get out of the flat fast enough in the morning. He'd lain in bed with Crumbs all night long, whimpering into his golden fur when the discomfort got too much. René had called it a place to rest, but there was no rest to be found when half of him was so fundamentally rejected. If this was what it meant to be fully human, then he pitied his friends.

After an extended round with Crumbs, he made his way into school early enough for the gates to be closed. Naturally, he ignored them and jumped into the cafeteria where he caught up on the sleep he hadn't truly found last night.

An hour later, he felt almost refreshed when he came across Lucille and was treated to her to-go coffee. "Thanks."

"You look like you need it more," she said with a laugh. But the laugh vanished quickly enough, replaced by worry. "Did he attack you again last night?"

Matt told her about the runes René had painted on the wall and shuddered. "I'm grateful for his protection, really! But my body can't take it for such a long amount of time. I hardly slept at all."

"Well, I wouldn't sleep well, either, if I knew my brother was trying to murder me."

He waved the concern off. "I can deal with Caspar." As soon as he'd come up with a plan.

"Well, if it's any consolation, I've got an annoying brother, too, now."

"Does he want to kill you?"

Lucille opened her mouth, grimaced, and shut it again. She sighed and then admitted, "No, he might be a little demon—not literally—but he's not *that* bad. He came into my room last night, though, and crawled under my blankets."

Matt stopped short. "I thought he was, like, eight."

Annoyed, she smacked his arm. "Not like that!" She shuddered. "Little kids do that when they have a nightmare. They crawl into their parents' bed to seek comfort. But apparently, Dad made it very clear to him that it would not happen. And I mean, he's *ten*. So, I told him he could sleep on my couch if he had to."

Matt wondered what René would say if Matt crawled into his bed to find comfort there. He scrunched up his nose. If it was a father thing, he'd probably lap it up. It beat crawling into his mother's bed by a mile, though.

Just then, Robert was passing them on the way to class. "Oh, hey, Matt. I heard you were sick yesterday. Don't forget to put your name on the lists."

Checking with Lucille, Matt asked, "What lists?"

"For one of the Abitur committees. Samantha put up the lists yesterday, and of course, she's signed up for almost everything. I chose the ball and the yearbook."

"You should join us for the prank. It'll be amazing!" Robert grinned.

"I'll think about it," Matt said, only to get rid of the other boy. He still had no idea what they were talking about. "What kind of committees?"

Amused, Lucille explained. "Graduation committees. They're various ways for how we want to celebrate graduation next year. That is, if we pass. It's tradition. Don't you remember the Abi prank last year? You know, when they filled all the rooms with balloons?"

Vaguely, a memory came to Matt. He'd been just as confused then as he was now. "Wasn't that followed by this really strange show on—"

The rest of his sentence was wiped from his mind when Caspar appeared in the middle of the school corridor. Instantly, he shot black magic at them.

Matt grabbed Lucille by the shoulders and threw himself on the ground, escaping the shot by a hair's width. The magic hit the wall behind them and plaster rained from the ceiling. The few students in the corridor started running and screaming.

Lucille had gone pale. "Matt," she breathed.

"Leave him to me." Matt got up on his feet, moving languidly like a cat. "You've become slow, Caspar." Then he ran.

As hoped, Caspar shot again, then took up pursuit. Matt ducked and jumped into the stairwell. Several students were coming up that way to his dismay.

"Go! Go!"

Another shot of energy hit the window next to him. Glass showered down on the stairs. The students screamed. Some scrambled up, some down, but a few just ducked as low as possible, as if the demon couldn't see them if they became small, and one girl just stood there staring, frozen to the spot.

Caspar appeared at the bottom of the stairs, just as Matt was running down the last few steps.

Cursing, Matt stumbled backwards, then thought twice about it and threw himself at Caspar. Caspar had anticipated his move, stepped aside, and used Matt's momentum against him.

Matt slammed into the floor. He gasped, but he knew he couldn't allow himself even a moment of reprieve. Instantly, he scrambled up and ran outside. If he could only get Caspar out of school, everything would be alright.

It had to be.

# Fabian

As usual, Physics was the low point of Fabian's day. He kind of wished he hadn't gained control over his water powers, so he could be saved by an unfortunate explosion of water pipes, but that avenue was closed to him now. Instead, he had to listen to Mr Herbert tearing his experiment report apart.

"You call this a sketch?" he asked, pointing to the perfect depiction of the experiment they'd done last class.

Fabian shrugged carefully. "Yes?"

"This isn't art class!" Mr Herbert snapped. "What I'm looking for is a schematic sketch, not a still life. Though, I have to admit, you've got a better chance at making it as an artist than you'll have at getting through the Physics exam."

At the moment, Fabian was willing to give his art career an honest shot if that saved him from having to sit through one more Physics class.

Mr Herbert harrumphed and put the report down, finally turning his attention to today's lecture.

Instantly, Samantha leaned over. "If he's only mocking your drawings for being too good, you must be getting better."

Fabian winced, not believing a word she said. Though he'd been crafting his experiment reports extremely carefully. He didn't always get it right, but they came close to Samantha's on details. At least he was learning something from this ordeal.

He sank as low as he could in his seat, trying to make himself small enough for Mr Herbert to overlook him for the rest of the period.

Fabian doubted it would work, but he couldn't keep himself from trying.

Just then, the carefully constructed experiment, consisting of several expensive electronic units, exploded.

It took Fabian a moment to realise that the window to their side had also broken, which meant… He looked outside and saw Matt vanishing. But he wasn't alone, a familiar white-haired demon followed him, shooting with energy as if there was no tomorrow.

"Fabian!" Samantha pulled on his arm.

He only noticed then that the entire class had taken cover. Quickly, he followed suit. "What's happening?" he asked Rachel and Samantha breathlessly.

"Caspar's happening," Rachel said.

In the front, Mr Herbert was hiding behind the counter, trying to figure out what he was expected to do. "Uhm… You… Stay low…"

"I need to get to my locker," Samantha hissed.

Fabian's eyes widened. "You need to *what?*"

"I've got the book on demonology in there. It was too heavy to cart around all day." She winced when another stray shot broke more windows. With desperation in her eyes, she looked up. "I've studied the circles of banishment. But I need the book. And everything else I brought for it."

Fabian didn't even question why she'd brought all that stuff to school. Of course she had. Samantha was always prepared and he loved that about her. Especially now.

"Mr Herbert," he called out loudly. "This isn't exactly a safe spot!" The students were all lying down, but the physics tables were nothing more than tiny folding trays, lined up on a sort of staircase so that everyone could see well. Which also meant that another stray shot could easily hit any one of them from the side.

His teacher's face darkened. "Bendtfeld, if—" He frowned and nodded suddenly. "You're right, of course. Everyone, keep low, but get into the corridor. Someone secure the entrance."

Instantly, Fabian, Rachel, and Samantha crawled over to the door. Before anyone could see or stop them, they ran outside and hid behind the Physics building.

Caspar was still alone. He stared up at the sky and laughed. "I'm tired of running after you," he shouted at the clouds, "so..." His gaze fell on Fabian, and a cruel smile appeared on his lips. "How about it?"

Just one look in his grey eyes and Fabian knew he was dead.

Caspar's smile turned into an insane grin as he raised his hand. Just then, Matt reappeared behind him, grabbed him by the shoulders and dragged him away. Hopefully, back to Hell.

"Come on." Once again, Samantha was tugging on Fabian's arm, her face devoid of any sign of blood. She was breathing as heavily as if she'd just run the 800 metres.

Fabian found himself nodding, and then he gasped, only now realising that he'd held his breath the entire time he'd been staring at Caspar. "Let's hope he's gone for good."

"Let's make sure of it," Rachel said with an admirable calm. If Fabian didn't know any better he would've thought she wasn't even the slightest bit afraid.

"Yes, let's go. Get your circle of banishment ready. Just in case."

With a nod, Samantha took the lead.

They ran into Lucille at the lockers. With a grave face, she was helping a younger girl calm down and breathe. Other students were gathered, looking confused, no teacher in sight.

As soon as Lucille saw them, she came over. "Did you see him?"

"He's gone," Samantha said. "Matt got him." Then she opened her locker and heaved out a bag.

"You see," Lucille said to the girl. "The shooter left the school. You're safe now."

The girl sniffled, but she drew courage from Lucille's words and managed to walk away, finding a friend among the crowd.

Samantha dragged the heavy bag into her arms and lowered her voice. "Everyone's talking about a rampage."

"Of course they are," Lucille whispered back. Her eyes filled with tears. "It was horrible. I hope Pascal is alright."

Fabian immediately wrapped his arms around Lucille. "I'm sure he is. His school is next doors. Caspar never got that far. And he's gone now."

Just then, Mr Zobel strode towards them. "Everyone please go into a classroom and take cover. Close the doors."

"But why?" Rachel asked.

The teacher scoffed. "Don't you see the plaster on the floor? There was a shooter."

"Yes, but..."

"Caspar!" Samantha called.

True to her word, the demon reappeared in their midst and started shooting energy without rhyme or reason. People screamed and ran into all different reaction, scrambling over each other, while Mr Zobel called for everyone to go into the classrooms.

Fabian knew he had to do something. There was water nearby. He could feel it. His eyes fixed the wall, and a second later the gypsum burst under the pressure, flinging first pieces of plaster and then water at Caspar.

"You again," the demon hissed.

And this time, no Matt appeared to save Fabian from the black magic coming at him. Instead, Mr Zobel nearly ripped his arm out of its socket as he hauled Fabian into a classroom and pushed him around the corner, before slamming the door shut.

About fifteen students had found cover here, most of them crying quietly. Lucille, Rachel, and Samantha had withdrawn into a corner, already deep in discussion. Fabian was about to join them when he stumbled.

Again, Mr Zobel held him. But then he paled. "Your leg."

"My leg?"

Fabian stared at his thigh. Inexplicably, the fabric of his jeans had started to turn red. Something wet and warm was spreading underneath. Blood.

The pain came after.

# Jan

After another useless visit to the job centre, Jan returned home an hour before lunch. From the shoes in the corridors and the sounds of the radio running in the kitchen, he gathered his mother was at home. He hadn't slept well last night, and the boring interview with the job centre employee had left him even more tired.

He went into his room to catch a nap when he froze.

Someone had searched his room. And they hadn't even bothered to cover their tracks. His clothes were lying in a heap in front of his cupboard and his drawers all stood open. Even the bed looked as if the mattress had been lifted. In the process, one of his largest berg crystals was lying in pieces on the ground.

"What the hell?" Then he roared, "Mother!"

He grabbed the broken crystal and stormed into the kitchen. His mother was sitting there with a coffee and the newspaper, though she looked at him in confusion. "What—?"

"Are you nuts?" Jan shouted at her.

She sighed, putting her newspaper aside. "Jan, please calm down. Your father—"

"—is a narrow-minded asshole, who doesn't respect my stuff!"

"Jan," she started sharply. "You've got to understand that with your past—"

"Past? Who the heck cares about my frigging past? I don't take drugs anymore!" He was not calming down in the least, still full-on screaming at his mother.

Her mouth had turned into a thin line. "That's great to hear. Really, but with your latest... well, with what happened at your job, he... we thought you might be taking some again."

Jan gasped. In pure disbelief, he started pacing the kitchen. That blasted gorgon. "You think I took drugs on the job?" His mother gave him a noncommittal shrug. "Woah, you guys really have no trust in me at all. Well, newsflash, I wasn't on drugs. I also didn't do it for shits and giggles. I was saving people's lives."

He didn't care that his mother wouldn't believe him if he told her the truth. She wasn't going to believe in him anyway, so he might as well hold his head high.

Tired, she rubbed her forehead and sighed. "From what? There was no fire."

"No, but there was something else." Not that he was going to dive into it. Instead, he waved it off. "Doesn't matter. What matters is that you're sniffing through my stuff, and that's not okay. I'm a grown-up!"

From the look on his mother face, she very much doubted that claim. But instead, she went for the gentle route. "You're still our son." She got up and tried to take his hand, but Jan backed away with a hiss, and she sighed again. "I'm worried about you. Your father is too. First you quit school, and now you've lost your job for vandalism. You're lucky they didn't press charges and—"

"Oh, stop selling me your shit as worry," Jan interrupted her rudely. The hostel had planned to press charges, but Lu and her law support had stepped in, and all he'd had to pay was the fee for ringing the fire alarm without a fire. The destruction was never proven to be his. "I'm not twelve anymore. I don't care for your gaslighting shit."

"It's not gaslighting!" his mother cried.

"If you want to force me out, just say so. I can pack my stuff right now." Though where he would go, Jan had no idea.

His mother was clearly overwhelmed. She shook her head, tears forming in her eyes, but then she suddenly paused, as if listening to something else.

Jan frowned and listened as well. The radio had changed to the news report.

"...active shooting," the radio reporter was saying. "The students are advised to hide in the classroom and wait for the police. Just now a special ops team has gathered at Greenvalley High School. The shooter..."

Jan stared at his mother in shock. Her face was pale, her eyes big. *Greenvalley High School. Active shooter.*

"Anne," she whispered.

"Meg," he answered.

Instantly, Jan ran into the corridor. His mother called after him, but he didn't stop. All he knew was that he had to reach his little sister and girlfriend and get them out of there.

# Rachel

The atmosphere in the classroom was overwhelming. Everyone was advised to keep quiet, but then and now, a soft whimper broke the smothering silence. Students huddled under the tables, while Mr Zobel was listening at the door. The classroom they were hiding in was on the second floor of the upper-class building, though the students hiding in here were from all levels.

Rachel, Samantha, Lucille, and Fabian were sitting in the back corner, where they could whisper softly with each other. Using a pair of Lucille's spare pantyhose and a PE shirt, Samantha carefully wound a pressure bandage against Fabian's bleeding wound. Caspar's energy had missed the femoral artery, but he'd still lost a lot of blood.

Blood-covered school corridors. Rachel shuddered. Waking Menuha to come to Matt's rescue hadn't stopped the vision from coming true.

"We need to do something," Lucille said softly. "Doors won't keep Caspar out."

"What's with that circle you were planning?" Fabian asked through gritted teeth, the pain evident on his face.

Rachel glanced at the other students. Two of them had devised a plan and were approaching a window. Apparently, they intended to climb out while Caspar was in the corridor and run for the fence. Not the worst idea... if they got out before he appeared in here.

"I can hardly do it here, right?" Samantha whispered.

Rachel stared at her, as if she'd gone mad. "Does it matter if anyone sees you?"

"Yes?" Samantha seemed unsure.

"Just a few months ago, you did a full-on magic display in front of everyone at Lucille's," Rachel reminded her. She hadn't seen it, but she'd heard the whispers at school.

Lucille nodded. "If we can save lives that way, we need to give it a shot."

A soft creak alerted them to the window being opened. Mr Zobel glanced over, looking horrified, but after a short, silent, mimed conversation, he gave his approval. The first student started climbing out.

"How do we get him in the circle?" Samantha hissed.

That was one part of the plan they hadn't figured out yet.

Fabian shrugged. "I could show my face. He doesn't seem to like me very much. He's probably still mad about the New Years' thing."

Rachel nodded. "Yes, we lure him in. If he's anything like Balthasar, he'll be happy to go after Matt's friends in an instant."

Speaking of Matt, they suddenly heard his voice ring loudly on the corridor. "Hey, Casp! Let them go!"

Rachel shuddered, thinking about whichever poor students had got into Caspar's reach. Meanwhile Mr Zobel looked absolutely horrified. "Is that Matt?" he hissed.

"I'm here," Matt continued.

Lucille breathed out in relief. "Matt's here."

"Where is my sister?" Caspar called back, taunting Matt.

"She's not coming. It's just you and me, just like you want it."

Mr Zobel frowned heavily. "Please tell me this isn't some relationship drama."

"It's not his fault," Samantha hissed back with surprising vehemence.

Rachel thought it was relationship drama, just not the usual kind.

Outside, Matt tried to convince Caspar to move their fight, but the older one wouldn't have it. "Oh, yes, we're doing it here. If you don't want anybody else to get hurt, then I would keep still."

Mr Zobel looked as if he was going to rip the door open. "He needs to leave this to the police. We don't need him to play the hero." Agitated, he massaged his temples, then he glanced at the group. "Get out. I'll take care of this idiot."

Samantha glanced at the others, then she nodded. "Let's find a better place. one where we don't have to move any furniture around."

Together with Lucille, Rachel helped Fabian stand and hobble over to the window, following the other students to questionable safety. Once down, they didn't go to the nearest exit but went the other way to the now-deserted table tennis area behind the building.

When they got there, they found Menuha watching the building with intense concentration.

"Menuha!" Lucille called. "You need to stop Caspar."

The demon turned to them with a conflicted expression. "He won't let me. And Matt insisted on facing him."

The bonds were loose.

"He wants to get himself killed?" Samantha asked, looking shocked. Apparently, she cared a whole lot about whether Matt lived or died. None of which surprised Rachel.

"Or kill Caspar." Menuha sighed heavily. "Melaney wanted this."

That was news to Rachel. When she'd last met Matt's mother, she'd turned into an outright fury when her precious little son got hurt. And she hadn't exactly hated Caspar either.

"We won't let that happen," Samantha said with admirable confidence.

It infected Lucille, who nodded wildly. "We follow our plan."

Fabian leaned against the table tennis table. "But how are we going to get Caspar from up there to down here? And preferably in the circle?"

"I'll help you," Menuha said without a moment's hesitation. "It seems like that's the only way to permanently separate them and keep them both safe."

Rachel didn't particularly care for Caspar's safety, but she'd be happy to send him to Hell. "Let's do it."

Samantha nodded. "I've got everything I need in this bag."

The plan had been to have Fabian do the chalk symbols, but with his injury, they couldn't ask him to get on the ground and draw. Samantha opened the book and handed the chalk to Rachel. "We need an exact circle of... let's do a two-metre one on the outside and then thirty centimetres smaller on the inside."

"Are we talking diameter or radius?" Rachel asked. It always paid to be exact.

"Radius."

Rachel nodded. "I can do that. You do the symbols."

Leaving the symbols to Samantha, Rachel started by measuring out as many points for her circles as she could in a short time. Meanwhile Menuha had jumped away and gathered proper first aid material for Fabian's wound, while Lucille fretted.

"What should I do?" Lucille asked.

"Once Rachel has finished the circles, we need a third one in salt. It's in my bag." Samantha knelt down with her book to copy the symbols as best as she could. Her hand was shaking, but fortunately, they were pretty geometric and easy to draw.

She wasn't the only one who was nervous. Lucille was pacing as well. She only paused to ask Menuha when she came back, "What did Matt do to make Caspar so determined to kill him all of a sudden?"

Surprised, Menuha glanced over her shoulder. "Didn't he tell you?"

"He doesn't tell us anything anymore," Samantha said with a heavy sigh.

"He's of the opinion that his family has harmed us enough and he doesn't want to drag us into his mess," Lucille elaborated.

Guiltily, Fabian added, "Perhaps because Jan and I said something like that. Because of that thing with Malcolm, you know?"

"Is it common for humans to keep important information to yourself and withdraw quietly from everyone that cares about you?" Menuha asked, sounding confused.

"That sounds pretty spot on," Rachel admitted, finishing the inner circle.

Menuha sighed. "In that case, he probably wouldn't appreciate it if I explained it to you."

Naturally, Lucille protested, "But we want to help!"

"And we're doing it," Samantha declared, "whether he wants us to or not." She got up from the last symbol and oversaw her circle. It looked like a pretty good representation of the one in the book. "I'm going to fill the symbols with magic now."

Rachel watched her close her eyes and concentrate on the river of magic that ran through the town. As she fed them into the salt, the symbols in the circle started to glow softly.

Next to her, Menuha made a retching sound. It was working.

Now all they needed was Caspar.

# Matt

Matt ducked under an energy shot and rolled across the floor before turning and checking no one was in his line of sight before aiming at Caspar. Taking care of innocent bystanders meant that he was much slower than his brother, who was going on a true rampage. Caspar's magic struck walls, doors, windows, and cupboards.

At last, Matt managed to lure Caspar into an empty corridor. If there was anyone on this floor, they were all hiding in the classrooms. He knew he couldn't defeat Caspar with magic alone and drew his sword.

Now that no one was watching, he used his space-jumping ability to launch at Caspar. Unfortunately, his brother had anticipated the move, jumped away, and shot from another angle at Matt.

Matt jumped a second time, evading the shot, and reappeared right next to Caspar, his sword already in full swing.

Caspar caught the sword with his bare hand and hissed. While the weapon cut deep down to the bone and he lost two fingertips, Caspar held the sword tight and managed to rip it out of Matt's hand. At the same time, he grabbed Matt's throat and slammed him into the wall behind them.

The plaster broke under the impact, and he gasped sharply as pain radiated through his backbone. Instead of squeezing his throat, Caspar threw him down on the ground and shot at him.

This time, Matt couldn't jump away quickly enough. The black magic hit him and catapulted him further down the corridor. When he came to a rest, his entire body felt as if it was on fire. His blood had left behind a red trail.

Moaning, Matt tried to get back on his feet. His sword wasn't too far away. If he just stretched his fingers enough, he could reach it.

But Caspar got there first. Instead of picking it up, he kicked the sword further away, then turned to Matt. "What now?"

Matt glared at him, resenting him for his taunt when he was already on the ground. He couldn't let Caspar win. It wasn't just that he didn't want to die, but that he couldn't be a hundred per cent sure Caspar would stop with him. He was surrounded by the humans he hated, helpless, defenceless humans, among them Matt's friends. And Samantha.

He had to keep fighting. With a sharp gasp, Matt pulled himself together. He jumped yet again, pinpointing his reappearance right next to his sword. Just as his fingers closed around the handle, energy hit him in the back and threw him against one of the doors to the stairwell. Matt's head hit the glass pane, and he suddenly saw double, darkness quickly encroaching on his vision. Something wet dripped down his neck.

"Die, Bastard."

Somehow, Caspar was suddenly right in front of him. He had his hand raised, his eyes shining with glee. Black magic crackled around his hand.

Matt knew he had to move. Instead, his knees gave way.

And Caspar vanished.

Gasping, Matt's knees hit the floor. For a few precious seconds, he fought for his consciousness. When he regained control of it again, he was still alive. No sign of Caspar.

Confused, he looked around. When he was sure that his brother had truly vanished, summoned from his death blow by Melaney—or maybe Volac, the Archdemon of Wrath, who wondered why his general was wasting time in Ashuan—Matt sent the sword away again.

He was just about to relax when the doors behind him were thrown open and a bunch of heavily armoured people stormed the corridor. From their guns, Matt surmised they were human police. A second later, those guns were all trained on him.

Not strong enough to jump away, he raised his hands shakily. It proved to be a wise decision. Instead of putting bullets through his body, two of them stepped forward and roughly tore his arms down behind him. A moment later, something metallic closed around his wrists.

Then they searched him for weapons. Finding none, one of them asked, "Can you stand?"

Matt nodded tiredly. He hadn't been so sure a minute ago, but his healing powers had kicked in just enough to stay on his feet when the two hauled him back up.

"Search the rest of the corridor," the commander of the group said. "According to reports, there were two of them."

Slowly, Matt realised what was happening. He was being arrested. Arrested for defending himself against his mad brother. How was he supposed to protect his friends and everyone else if he was stuck behind bars?

# Jan

When Jan arrived at the school, a crowd had gathered. He recognised Captain Aster near the entrance, handing the situation over to better qualified personnel, who immediately started establishing a cordon around the school.

Using his flawless knowledge of the school fence, Jan snuck around the school and entered campus from the other side before the barrier was fully erected. He dropped into a thicket, then waited, listening for anyone shouting. When he was sure no one had seen him, he hurried to the back entrance of the main block.

Inside, the school was eerily quiet. It reminded Jan of exam time, only it was far too early in the year for exams, and he knew for a fact none were going on right now. Where would Anne and Meg be this morning? If he remembered his girlfriend's schedule correctly, they had Art on the first floor of the main block.

He walked past the lockers when someone suddenly jumped on his back and bore down on Jan. His instincts kicked in instantly. By the time, he hit the ground, he had already half turned, and caught his attacker's next blow. He twisted the black-haired guy's arm and pressed him into the floor instead, before rotating his arm on his back and holding his head down with the other.

"Jan?"

The one who'd spoken wasn't the one beneath his knees but was standing behind him. Jan turned to see Cian, a heavy Chemistry book in his hands. Apparently, he'd been planning to drop that on Jan's head.

He now recognised the other guy groaning beneath him, as well. One Elite Idiot was rarely alone. "It's you guys." He let go of Alan. "Have you lost your mind?"

"Have *we* lost our mind?" Alan protested. "You're the one sneaking through school."

Jan got back up to his feet. "And the two of you want to be heroes, or what?"

"We were hiding behind the lockers," Cian pointed out. "We thought you were the shooter."

"Who is that, by the way?" It had to be someone from school, hadn't it? A former graduate? Or an active student?

Alan shrugged. "No idea. We just heard him."

Cian added helpfully, "The shots came from above."

"Where above?" Jan asked, annoyed. He was wasting his time with these idiots.

"First floor."

Jan started running towards the stairwell, not caring for Cian's irritated, "Hey!" or Alan's grumbled, "Who wants to be a hero now?"

This wasn't about being a hero. He needed to find his little sister and Meg before the shooter did, and the art rooms were on the first floor.

Jan took two steps at a time as he raced up the staircase. He reached out for the door in front of him, when instead, it opened from the other side. And there his sister was, her face wet with tears, her hands bloody.

Blinking, Anne stared at him. "Jan?"

Within a second, Jan had pulled her into a tight embrace. Again and again, he ran his hand over her hair as he pressed her against his chest and whispered, "You're okay."

Anne started sobbing and clawed his back with as much ferocity as he showed her.

"Where's Meg?"

Instantly, Anne pulled away from him. "You need to come." She grabbed his hand.

"Anne, you can't go back in! I'll bring you to safety and then I'll get Meg." There was no way he would let her go back inside.

"She needs you *now!*"

Instantly, Jan felt cold. Anne's voice was breaking. Something was wrong, very, very wrong. "What happened to Meg?" Whose blood was on Anne's hands?

Anne tugged at him again. "She's bleeding. You need to come, quick."

He followed without hesitation. Together they ran up to the first floor, which seemed to be free of shooters. Instead of the art rooms, Anne led him to the girls' toilets.

Whatever had hit the door looked much more like a gorgon attack than a bullet from some crazy shooter. Jan's heart leapt to his throat as he stepped past the broken pieces and saw the splintered mirrors and burst porcelain from one of the sinks on the ground. Blood was sprayed everywhere in the room, a trail clearly leading to the booth furthest from the entrance.

That was where Anne dragged him to. She knocked softly on the door. "Meg? It's me. Jan's here."

Behind the door, Meg let out the breath she must've been holding. "Jan?" Her voice was so full of fear, Jan's heart grew heavy.

He heard her unlock the door and open it. Anne nodded at him, so he pushed past her and squeezed into the tight booth. Inside, Meg was sitting on the closed toilet seat, her feet off the ground, as if that would obscure the fact the trail of blood led here. She had one hand on her stomach, where bright red blood flowed through the fingers.

"Shit! Sorry." For a moment, Jan's head was swimming. What was he supposed to do?

Get her out of here, of course. No, he had to deal with her injury first. Stomach wounds were no joke, and it was still bleeding.

"She was just behind the door when it happened," Anne explained. "It wasn't a bullet."

"Not a bullet?"

School shootings were incredibly rare in Germany, contrary to Greenvalley's monster attacks.

Jan put one arm under Meg's knees and the other behind her back. Then he lifted her up and managed to extract them both from the narrow booth. Gently, he placed Meg down on the cold tiles. To Anne, he said, "Grab me paper towels, will you?"

Meg's face was bathed in sweat. Her skin was pale, her breathing flat. The wound in her stomach was bigger than Jan had expected, but more superficial. Not the narrow hole of a bullet, but something equally deadly.

"Bright light," Meg said between pained grunts. "So hot."

Indeed, the rims of the wound looked burned. Unfortunately, the same couldn't be said of the rest, with fresh blood still bubbling from severed veins.

"Is she going to die?" Anne asked, her voice fearful.

Jan very nearly threw a piece of porcelain at her. Meg's eyes grew wide instantly, and her breath quickened. Her hand searched for Jan's and she started to cry. With a calming voice, he said, "Of course not. Meg, we're going to get you out of here. Paper towels now, please."

Anne brought a big wad of paper towels she'd ripped out of the dispenser and brought it to him. While Jan tried to identify the biggest bleed, she asked, "Can't you...?"

"Can't I what?" He pressed the paper towels onto Meg's stomach.

"Heal her?"

*Heal her.* Jan stared at the wound. So far, his healing powers hadn't switched into auto-pilot as usual. He had no idea if that meant he was getting better at controlling them or whether they'd noped out of this. Hadn't Matt said to never try healing a fatal wound? But when was it a fatal wound?

"Jan, please. If you have healing powers, use them," Anne pleaded. "You've got to try."

Outside the bathroom, shots were fired, though he didn't actually hear the shots themselves, only when they crashed into the walls. Anne whimpered, tears running down her face.

"Alright. Let's hope this works." He'd never done it intentionally before, and he would be lying if he'd said he wasn't scared of the pain.

*Pull yourself together.* If Meg could handle the pain, he could as well.

Carefully, he removed the paper towels and hovered both his hands over the wound, waiting for the golden shimmer to appear.

"What are you doing?" Meg whined, breaking Jan's concentration.

"Trust Jan. He knows what he's doing."

He had absolutely no idea what he was doing, but the trust his little sister had in him pushed him to try anyway. For a few precious seconds nothing happened—Meg's blood just kept seeping out of her—but then Jan felt something tickle in his fingertips, as if they were frozen and he'd put them too close to a flame. He kept pushing and the feeling intensified, like a thousand little needles. His vision shifted and he saw Meg's injury in all its gory detail. Then the pain hit full on.

Gasping, Jan withdrew his hands. The pain had been so intense his entire body was shaking. How did Meg stand it? He vaguely remembered Matt telling him that the patients themselves had their own hormones concealing the true extent of the injuries. A luxury, Jan didn't have.

"Keep going. I saw something happening." Anne was so engrossed with what she'd seen she didn't notice how hesitant he'd become.

How could he disappoint her now? *Easy, aren't you used to disappointing everyone? Especially her?*

Jan shook his head. *No more of that.* His parents may have given up on him, but Anne never had. Despite how much he pushed her away and how much better she was, she still looked up to him. He couldn't disappoint her. Not today.

Determined, he set his hands to work again. Although Jan expected the pain this time, it still hit him like a truck in full speed. He almost let go again. It was simply too much. Even Matt had said so. But Matt was a half-demon, and his only experience was Caspar, a full demon. Of course, no self-respecting demon would go beyond the most superficial injuries.

Well, Jan was no demon. He was human, and as such, he was going to face the pain, come what may.

With gritted teeth, he doubled down on his healing. The most important thing was to stop the bleeding. Somehow, he knew exactly how to identify the torn veins and how to fix them. Not that it made it easy that way.

If anything, the pain was intensifying. Jan heard himself groan and curse. Soon, his lips were bleeding from biting too hard on them. Cold sweat was running down his face, dabbed away by Anne. He might've even cried.

But he pressed on, refusing to give in until the girl he loved was no longer bleeding out under his care.

# Fabian

Lucille had covered the circle of banishment with an illusion to hide it from Caspar when Menuha called him. The demon must have been in mid-attack, because as soon as he arrived, energy tore through the bushes on the side, fortunately missing them.

Seething, Caspar turned towards Menuha. "You're kidding, right?" He sounded tense, as if he was only a second away from throttling his twin.

That was Fabian's cue. He had no idea how he'd got himself in this position. No, he knew. Caspar still had a score to settle with him. Fabian had humiliated him at New Years, something the demon hadn't forgotten. Plus, the circle was right between them. Caspar only had to step into it.

His voice was shaking worse than a leaf, but he got the words out. "Hey, asshole!" It was much easier to follow the challenge with a blast of water.

Caspar turned instantly. With a growl, he took one step towards the circle of banishment. To Fabian's dismay, he wasn't completely fooled by the illusion, picking up on something in the air. Instead of barging ahead, he jumped through space to land right in front of Fabian.

Fortunately, they'd been prepared for such a turn of events. While Fabian couldn't see it, Samantha had woven one of her anti-magic webs, the strings pulling tight around Caspar now.

With a grunt, he went down, and for a moment Fabian had hope. Demons couldn't survive in the complete absence of magic. But Caspar pulled something from the inside of his jacket and pressed it to the ground just as Lucille's black magic arrow soared over his head.

"Damn it," Lucille complained about her bad timing, drawing Caspar's attention to her.

In a second, the demon was on top of her, slamming her body into the ground. Fabian's insides went cold. Samantha screamed, running towards them.

Fear and anger concentrated in Fabian's hands, and a rock-hard jet stream of water shot out of his hands, pushing Caspar away from Lucille.

With enviable alacrity, Caspar got back on his feet, this time zoning in on Samantha. Her eyes widened and she began to weave, but Lucille was faster. "Scutum protecto!"

Energy hit the magic shield. Instead of ducking behind it, Samantha lunged forward, as if she planned to grab the magic with her bare hands, and suddenly, the shield backfired, the energy hitting Caspar instead.

Hissing, he bared his teeth. Blood was running down his face, but that only made him look more menacing. Just as he was about to try again, a book hit him in the head.

Even without her trusty crossbow, Rachel was an admirable shot. She'd positioned herself directly opposite Caspar, the hidden circle between them, taunting him.

Fabian knew it wasn't going to work. Despite moving around, Caspar had avoided the circle like a cat avoided water. He might not have guessed what was waiting there for him, but he knew to stay away from the spot. What they needed was a perfect hit that would send Caspar into the circle against his will. A strong push, just like before.

Sensing his chance, Fabian hobbled over to where Rachel was placed, hoping to get right in front of Caspar, but the demon was faster. He reached Rachel before Fabian was even halfway there. The angle was all wrong. All he could do was push him away from Rachel and hope for another chance.

When the water hit Caspar, he was pushed straight into Menuha's arms. His sister had timed her appearance perfectly. She grabbed hold of Caspar's arms and his chest, and threw herself into the circle.

The illusion fell apart as the symbols lit up with blue fire. Menuha screamed in shock, while Caspar roared. His rage knowing no boundaries, he fired wildly.

Fabian threw himself at Rachel and dragged her to the ground, hoping to escape the wild energy bolts. One tore through the sand in front of him and he squeezed his eyes shut. When he opened them, blue flames shot high into the sky before dying out with a hiss, leaving no trace of the demons and symbols.

Before Fabian could register what had happened, three special ops police officers stormed the area. They regarded the kids on the ground and asked, "Did you see him?"

Rachel had the presence of mind to point towards the main building.

The three police officers nodded to each other. Two started sprinting, while the third pointed the way they'd come. "Make your way to the exit. The path is clear."

Of course it was, Fabian thought. The demon siblings were gone. Gone forever.

# Lucille

The plan had worked! For a moment, it hadn't looked as if it would, but then Menuha had done what none of them had managed to do, and both demons had vanished in blue flames.

Lucille got to her feet and tried to brush the dust off her clothes. Throwing herself to the ground had left her with a few scrapes and scratches, but they didn't matter in the face of her success. Or rather, Menuha's success.

The realisation hit her like a ton of bricks. Menuha had stepped into the circle of banishment, and had been banished alongside her brother. They wouldn't see each other again in Ashuan. Not in her lifetime. The thought saddened Lucille. She'd liked the demon woman and her enchanting love for humans.

Next to her, Samantha moaned as she got to her feet. "That was close."

"You tell me." Lucille laughed, but the sound got stuck in her throat quickly.

On the other side of the no-longer-existant circle, Fabian helped up Rachel. Despite his injury, her boyfriend had fought admirably. Without him, Lucille might not even be alive now.

Overwhelmed by her feelings, she ran and threw herself at him with a gleeful shriek. "You were awesome!"

Fabian stumbled under her weight, and instead of catching her, he cried out in pain. Within seconds, the brave elemental mage vanished from his features, replaced by his usual whiny expression.

"Oh, I'm so sorry!" Lucille said, fussing over his leg. Together with Rachel, she helped him back to the table tennis table. "But you were fantastic. So were you, by the way," she said to Rachel, commenting on her impressive book-lopping skills.

"First time I was glad for Herbert's monster textbook."

"Can we get out of here? Please?" Apparently, all of Fabian's bravado had seeped into the ground along with his water.

"Of course." There would be time for a proper celebration later.

The four of them slowly made their way to the exit. It wasn't until Lucille saw the crowds gathered outside the school campus that she realised just how big the whole thing had been. There were so many parents, police officers, ambulance cars, and even news reporters.

"Samantha!" a voice cried out to their left; her mother. Juliane was pushing past other onlookers to make her way to the police-controlled exit at the same time as they did. As soon as the police had checked them, she fell into Samantha's arms, grasping her head with both hands and kissing Samantha's face. "You're fine. You're... Did you see your sister?"

Samantha shook her head, slightly overwhelmed by her mother's public show of affection. "I'm sure she's fine."

Fabian's mother made her way to the front as he arrived at the triage centre. Lucille knew without a doubt that her parents wouldn't be here. They probably hadn't even heard about it yet. Which meant...

"Pascal!" she told Rachel, the only one left over. "I need to check on him."

And with that, she took off, pushing through concerned parents and horrified onlookers until she got to the primary school, only to find it locked off.

"Lucille!" the familiar voice belonged to René.

She turned and saw him standing with his class of second-graders behind the police lines. Apparently, they had evacuated the entire school.

"How's Matt?" René asked when she ran to him.

"I don't know," Lucille admitted. For all she knew they could've been too late, Matt was already dead, and they'd banned Menuha for nothing. "But we banned Caspar. Menuha, too, though that was an accident. They can no longer come back to Ashuan and..."

She stopped rambling when René pulled her into his arms. "You did well," he whispered. "Really well."

"Lucille?"

At the sound of the young voice, Lucille whirled around. "Pascal!"

Her little brother looked pale but otherwise unharmed. His lip was quivering as he stared at her, unsure of what to do next.

Tentatively, Lucille opened her arms. A moment later, he was in her embrace, clinging to her with pure desperation.

"We played games and... They were distracting us, but they wouldn't tell us what happened. I knew it was bad when they started evacuating. What happened?" Pascal cried.

Lucille stroked his hair and planted a kiss on his head. "I'll tell you later, okay?" Once she'd had time to come up with a child-appropriate explanation. "Let's call Albert and see if he can pick us up, okay?"

She turned around to say goodbye to René and caught him on the phone. When he paled, her heart beat a hundred miles per hour. "Is it Matt?" she whispered.

René's conversation was still ongoing. "I understand. I'll be there as soon as I can. Thank you." As soon as he hung up, he stared at Lucille. "They arrested Matt. They think he's the shooter."

# Matt

It was Matt's first trip to the police station. A paramedic hat patched him up first but quickly claimed the wounds were only superficial. The pain itself had receded, replaced by a weird numbness as they drove him to the station.

There, they brought him into a tiny room with a black window and a microphone on the table. Then Captain Aster, who Matt surmised was the daddy Alan liked to brandish around, took over the questioning.

"What were you doing at Greenvalley High?"

"Going to school." The truth.

"Did you bring any weapons?"

"No." A lie. He always had his weapons with him.

"Why weren't you in class?"

"I tried to stop the shooter."

"Alone?"

Matt just shrugged.

"Did you know the shooter?"

What was he supposed to say to that? The truth? He couldn't possibly tell them about demons. They weren't going to do anything about him anyway. If they tried, Caspar would just kill them.

"It was my older half-brother."

Captain Aster raised an eyebrow, but caught himself surprisingly fast. "Name?"

"Caspar."

"Last name?"

Matt nearly told him of the Houses of Lust and Wrath, but realised at the last second that those weren't usual human surnames. He didn't want to leave René's name, so he came up with another one. "Volac." It almost made him smile using the Archdemon of Wrath's name like that.

"What was your brother doing at school?"

"Trying to kill me."

"Are you joking?" Captain Aster asked flatly.

Matt shook his head. "Dead-serious. He hates me."

"Why?"

It took Matt a moment to find the proper words since being half human wouldn't cut it. "Because I'm my father's son. He's not."

Captain Aster's eyebrows crawled up again. He was probably wondering what kind of giant chip Caspar carried on his shoulder to blame their parents' relationship woes on a younger brother. But then again, the real reason didn't make any more sense.

Before the captain could ask more questions, the door opened and he was called outside. Matt stayed behind, still handcuffed to the table. He could probably vanish, but then they'd find him guilty in absence, and he would never be able to return to Greenvalley. No, he couldn't flee from his responsibilities. If he wanted to stay in Ashuan, he needed to face the consequences for what he was.

It took Captain Aster ten minutes to return. When he did, he went straight to Matt's handcuffs and released him. "We've just received word from a credible witness that you were, indeed, just defending yourself. Also, your father is here to pick you up. Come on."

He led him down the corridor. René was waiting at the end. "Matt."

"Hey, Dad," Matt said sheepishly.

A second later, René had enclosed him in his embrace. "I'm glad you're alive."

"Me too."

"He said his half-brother attacked him?" Captain Aster asked, still a bit doubtful.

Fortunately, René was always good in a pinch. "That tracks. We received a threatening call, and two days ago, he turned up at our home.

When he left, I thought that was it, but... obviously he only waited until he could get Matt alone."

"Do you mind giving a report later? We still haven't found this... Caspar, was it?"

"Yes. And absolutely," René promised.

Captain Aster gave Matt a stern look. "Next time, don't play the hero. If your brother tries to contact you in any way at all, let us know immediately."

"Will do." Then Matt remembered something else. "Who gave the witness report?" The moment he asked he thought he already knew the answer. His friends had come through for him yet again.

"Your teacher, Mr Zobel."

"Mr Zobel?" Until now, Matt's experiences with the Politics and German teacher had been less than positive. In Marseille, he'd ruined all of Matt's dating prospects. In class, he was known as a fair teacher with an air of exasperation from dealing with smart-mouthed teenagers all day. Matt had always assumed Mr Zobel didn't particularly like him, but apparently, he was fairly decent.

René patted his shoulder. "Come on, let's go home."

"Are those... decorations still up?" Matt asked hesitantly, remembering the awful night he had prior.

His father laughed softly. "Yes, but I'll take them down. We won't need them any longer."

"What's that supposed to mean?"

"I'll tell you later."

Intrigued, Matt followed his father out of the police station.

Once René had removed the arcane symbols from the walls, they sat down in the living room with a bottle of wine. First, Matt told him all about the attack and the fight he'd had with Caspar. How he'd tried in vain to get him out of the school, but Caspar had refused, demanding their duel would be fought this day at this place.

When his story ended at Caspar's timely summoning, René took over. "Lucille told me they drew a circle of banishment and successfully banished Caspar from Ashuan. He won't be able to return in a very long time."

Matt huffed, amused. "I knew it. She had that look."

"That look?" René asked confused. "Lucille?"

"Samantha. She came up with this banishment plan. And of course, she succeeded where I couldn't." He was impressed, but that was nothing new. Samantha impressed him usually at least once per day.

René smiled wanly. Wringing his hands, he said, "They had help from Menuha."

"Of course. This way, neither of us has to die. I can stay in Ashuan, and Caspar gets Hescaryn." Matt hadn't wanted that to come out bitterly, but the thought of his home world being practically off-limits for him tasted like defeat. As if he'd gone in hiding, conceding the fight. "So, where is Menuha? Taking care of his hurt ego?"

"No," René said softly. "She was banned as well." Matt's eyes widened in shock. "She was the one who forced him into the circle."

Matt swallowed heavily. He knew what being in Ashuan meant to Menuha. She'd greatly enjoyed it here, forming friendships with the others, and soaking up all the new information. Now she was banned for an indeterminable time. Because of him.

"I'm sure she was aware of the consequences," he muttered.

René agreed, "I'm sure she was." He put the wine aside and took a deep breath. Matt waited with bated breath for what was going to come next. "You need to tell your friends."

"What? No!" Matt shook his head wildly. "It's okay now. Caspar is gone, the situation is handled."

"What about Balthasar? What about your mother?"

Matt glanced to the floor. If he just ignored Melaney's summons, she might force him one way or the other. "I don't want them to get hurt. They've already been through enough because of me."

René's proud smile was nearly unbearable. "Matt, the six of you are in this together. Haven't you learnt anything from today? Your friends will fight for you, even when you don't want them to. You're bound by fate. The least you can do is explain all of this to them."

With a heavy heart, Matt let himself entertain the idea. René was right. He usually was, it just took Matt a little longer to see it. His friends were there for him, even if he pushed them away. And despite all his failings, Samantha couldn't stop herself from helping him. Keeping them in the dark wasn't going to keep them safe.

"I'll tell them, but not today."

His body was battered, his mind even more so, and it was going to be a tough discussion. Jan and Fabian would complain again. Lucille would do something stupid, Rachel might invade his dreams, and Samantha would look for solutions again. Solutions that would attract the attention of his brothers. It was no coincidence that Balthasar had gone straight for her. Somehow, Matt would have to find a way to keep her safe, and to do that, he needed to rest

René nodded at him with a warm smile. "Let's get you some sleep."

It wasn't nearly late enough for bedtime, but Matt didn't complain. Even if he didn't fall sleep right away, he needed the time alone to fall apart.

# Jan

Bone-tired and aching, but stoically, Jan carried Meg in his arms. First down the stairs, then out of the building, and at last across the campus. A huge crowd had gathered outside, complete with police and press. As soon as Jan stepped past the barrier, he was swarmed by paramedics. They quickly relieved him of his burden.

"I tried to stop the bleeding, but she lost a lot of blood," he explained as they laid Meg down on a stretcher.

The paramedic was checking the wound under the soaked paper towels and gave instructions to his colleague. Jan saw that it had started bleeding again.

In the end, his healing hadn't been enough to close the wound completely. He'd stopped the bleeding for a while and repaired as much damage as he could. If there was a way to heal the blood loss itself, he hadn't found it. He'd decided to carry her out when she'd started to lose consciousness.

"Meg?" her mother's voice rang through the crowd. A second later, she, Samantha, and Jan's parents burst through the crowd. "Oh, gosh. Is she...? That's my daughter."

The paramedic updated Juliane, while Samantha came to Jan. "What happened?" she asked, her face pale.

"She got hit by a stray... whatever it was. She was bleeding out on the toilet floor, but I patched her up as best as I could. I mean, I hope I did." Hopefully, Meg would make it. He didn't know how to handle anything else.

Samantha hugged him fiercely. "Thanks for taking care of her." She paused and frowned. "What were you doing at school?"

"I came as soon as I heard it on the news. They said it's a shooter, but this wound—"

"Caspar," Samantha said in a flat voice. "Meg must've got hit when he tried to kill Matt. We managed to ban him, but… thank you," she whispered, before letting go of him.

Jan's insides had gone cold. "Caspar was here?" Slowly, heat was building, starting from his stomach. "Why was Caspar at school?"

"To kill Matt."

"Why? Why now? Why here?" He understood it wasn't Matt's fault his brother wanted him dead, but something must've happened to provoke this.

Samantha watched him warily. "I don't know."

"Is he dead?" Jan asked, surprising himself with how snappy his voice sounded. "Matt, I mean."

"Lucille said he was arrested."

Jan snorted. "Oh yeah, that's gonna help. He'll jump right out of that cell. Which suits me just fine, because I'm going to murder him."

"Jan." Samantha sounded exasperated. "This isn't his fault, so stop victim-blaming him."

"Victim? Matt?" Jan shook his head. "The only victims here are our little sisters and whoever else got in their firing line. This isn't normal. Demon battles at school aren't normal. I want to know what's going on. For real."

Samantha sighed. "Me too."

Before Jan could say anything else, Juliane came back and threw her arms around his neck. "Thank you, thank you, thank you. For bringing her out. They say you got to her in the nick of time." She let go of him and turned to Samantha. "Are you coming with us?"

"Yes, of course." Samantha formed another silent thank you with her lips, then followed her mother into a waiting ambulance.

Once they were gone, Jan felt as if he could drop dead on the spot. But his reprieve was only short-lived when Anne reappeared with his parents in tow.

"That was incredibly stupid of you," his father began. Before Jan could protest, he pulled him into an awkward one-armed hug and continued muttering. "You're such an idiot."

"Thanks?" The tone of his father's voice was in complete opposition to his words, making Jan decide that this was one of the rare moments his father was actually proud of him.

Somewhere in the back of his mind, he remembered the state of his room. His father would have to answer for that. But maybe not now. Maybe now they could pretend that none of this had happened and that they were just a father and a son, relieved to see each other after a frightening interruption of their day.

For now, everything was well.

Tomorrow, Jan was going to kick Matt's ass.

# Rachel

As expected, Annette hadn't come to school. Rachel had witnessed enough tearful family reunions to last a lifetime. Meanwhile, no one had come for her. If the school had called her, Annette hadn't answered the phone. And why should she, when she clearly had more important things to do?

Rachel lay in bed, trying to drown out the unmistakable sounds of sex coming from next door. Judging by Annette's moans, her mother was having the time of her life. Whereas Rachel could have been killed at school today.

If she'd been younger, Rachel would have been crying. Instead, she felt the anger boiling in her stomach. Would she ever be worthy of her mother's attention? Sure, it'd be the talk of the town tomorrow. Then Annette would come home and tearfully beg for forgiveness. And when Rachel refused, she'd drown her feelings in alcohol.

Or maybe in sex, if the enthusiasm next door was anything to go by.

Rachel turned up the volume on her headphones. For her birthday, she was going to ask for noise-cancelling headphones. Then she tried to breathe out her anger and get some sleep.

As soon as she appeared in the meadow, she sought out Matt's dream. Not surprisingly, he was already asleep. The flower gave off a deeply sensual yet threatening scent that both attracted and repelled Rachel. Whatever Matt was dreaming was not going to be pretty.

And yet, she had no choice. Last year Malcolm had targeted Jan, Lucille, and Nico because they'd annoyed him. It had cost her brother his life. Now Matt—and by extension the six of them—was being targeted by the rest of his crazy family. Rachel wanted to know why, hoping to stop it before someone had to die. They'd come too close today.

She scanned the meadow, but Nico was nowhere to be seen. Had she severed their bond permanently? Was the last she'd ever see of him his presence in Menuha's awkward dream? Rachel had to hope he was just busy elsewhere.

Taking a deep breath, she entered Matt's dream.

The heavy smell of arousal hit her like a wall. Praying to all the gods, Rachel prepared herself to find Samantha in the dream. What she found instead took her breath away.

"Matt?"

He was standing in the middle of a large room, his hands chained to the ceiling but pulling in different directions, almost tearing him in half. His hair was blonde from one angle, black from the other, his demon wings outstretched. Both Balthasar and Caspar prowled the room, frequently attacking Matt, who only escaped death by the irrational power of dreams. Still, the attacks struck, and he cried out in pain.

Undisturbed by the two demons tormenting Matt, his mother, the Archdemon of Lust, approached him. The one time Rachel had seen Melaney, she'd been scantily clad. In Matt's dream, she wore nothing but a sheer silk robe that revealed more than it concealed. She raised her right arm and drew it gently across his face, her curled fingers following the trail until they landed on his neck.

The long fingernails pierced Matt's skin as she grabbed the hair at the back of his neck and pulled his head back, ignoring the approaching brothers. Then, to Rachel's horror, she ran her lips down his exposed neck.

Matt struggled to escape the unwanted attention, but his mother's grip was unyielding. Just as he turned his face to the side, Caspar seized his chance and leapt onto his back. "Human," he hissed, ripping out his wings.

"Mum!" Matt screamed as hot blood rushed down his back.

"Kiss me," she cooed. instead of helping.

Then Balthasar was there, holding a narrow dagger to Matt's throat. "It's nothing personal."

"Mum!" Matt begged again as his older brother slit his throat.

Melaney wrapped both arms around his neck. "Kiss me or kill me. Your choice, darling."

Rachel had no idea how he could do either, immobilised as he was. The smell of blood and lust intensified until the room swam around her. Matt alternated between begging and screaming, but he couldn't escape the attention of either.

Unable to tear her eyes from the display of demonic deprivation, Rachel stumbled back. She had to leave. Had to forget what she'd seen. Had to—

Rachel woke with a start. She sat up straight in bed, one hand on her heart, breathing heavily as she struggled to clear her mind of the dream she had just experienced.

"What the hell, Matt?" she whispered into the room, annoyed at how flushed her cheeks were.

What was wrong with him? Why were his siblings so determined to kill him? And what had his mother done?

This couldn't be real. It had to be a metaphor. The power she had over her son. Was it pressure to continue his philandering ways? What would happen if he didn't heed his mother's call?

Rachel's head spun. She'd hoped to find answers in his dreams, not a bunch of questions. Not torment and depravity.

Still gasping for breath, she decided then and there that she'd ask him. No more wandering in demon dreams. They clearly weren't safe.

# Part 4

## Order & Chaos

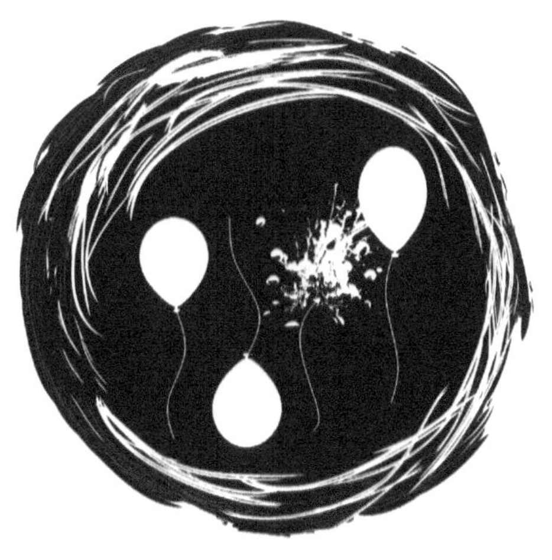

# Matt

Matt paced the backroom of the Magic Circle. Rachel was already there, watching him with unspoken terror in her eyes. As usual, though, she kept her thoughts to herself. A couple of times, he was tempted to start speaking, but every time he opened his mouth, the words stuck in his throat.

At last, he heard the chime in the door followed by friendly chatter with Caroline. Matt could easily pick out Samantha's voice among the four in the front room, and his heart grew heavy. What was he doing here, calling a meeting? Letting them know he had to tell them something when all he wanted was to keep it secret from them.

"I need to..." he started to say to Rachel, but then the door opened and Lucille walked in, shortly followed by Fabian and Samantha, "...pee."

Rachel groaned, but then she relaxed. "You're nervous," she said, so softly the newcomers couldn't quite hear her over the noise they were making.

Matt winced. He *was* nervous. More nervous than he'd been many times before. Where was his blasé attitude now? Why couldn't he summon some demon indifference and get this whole thing over with?

The others took seats around the table, then looked up expectantly, making Matt painfully aware of the fact that he was standing in the room as if he was planning some grand speech. Quickly, he sat down and tapped his feet instead. "Where's—?"

"I'm here!" Jan announced as he strode in and instantly planted himself in a chair. "Did we start already?"

"No," Rachel said, her gaze firmly set on Matt. As was everyone else's.

Jan harrumphed. "Good, because before you start serving us some wonky half-truths or demon make-believe stories... cut the crap, okay? Just give it to us straight."

Slightly overwhelmed by Jan's bluntness, Matt found himself nodding. "O-okay."

On the other side, he found Lucille smiling at him. "We're here for you."

Matt felt his throat grow tighter. For a moment, he wondered if it was a curse, some new surprise left behind by his brothers, but then he looked into Samantha's eyes and realised he was simply overcome by emotions. Human emotions.

The thought made him grimace, and in the bitterness he found the words he needed to say. Cold, hard facts. "My mother is being forced to abdicate."

"Abdicate?" Fabian asked with big eyes.

"They found someone hotter?" Jan said at the same time, earning a kick from Lucille.

"It's not that," Matt said annoyed. Annoyance was good. It helped him keep those other emotions in check. "The Council of the Seven claims she's become infertile, because she hasn't birthed a child in nineteen years. Intolerable for the Archdemon of Lust. So, Melaney gets one year to choose a successor or the Council will find one for her." There, that was half of it, at least. The easy half.

Samantha frowned at his explanation. "Is it just me, or does that sound sexist to everybody else? Would they follow-up on a male archdemon the same?"

Next to her, Lucille nodded emphatically. "Yes. Why does it even matter whether she has children or not. She's the Archdemon of Lust not Fertility, right?"

Those were surprisingly good points. When Melaney had told Matt about it, he'd found it odd, but not odd enough to question it. After all, his life experience was far too limited. Plus... "Look, I don't claim to know what goes on in the Seven's heads. It might just be a ploy to get rid of her." That fit.

"Wait," Jan interrupted. "Who are they? This Seven Council?"

True, his friends knew woefully little about Hescaryn. Partly because they were extremely reluctant to learn about it. "It is the ruling council of the seven most powerful demons in Hescaryn. Each of them represents one of the deadly sins. My mother is one of them. As was Malcolm."

"But Malcolm is dead," Lucille pointed out, sounding confused. "He is, right?"

"Oh, please tell me he's dead," Fabian whispered in dismay.

At least this one Matt was sure about. "Oh, yes, he's dead. That caused quite a ruckus in Hescaryn. The rumour mill was spinning, but as always, his powers simply moved to someone else."

"What's that supposed to mean?" Jan asked, sounding quite aggressive.

Matt sighed. "When a demon dies... their demonic powers transfer to the one... to the demon who killed them." It was one of the many reasons demons were so trigger-happy. "If Rachel had demon blood, Malcolm's powers would've gone to her, and Rachel would've been the new Archdemon of Greed."

Rachel looked amused for a moment, but then she seemed to think of something else. "I see. Was that another reason why you refused to kill him?"

It reminded Matt of what Menuha had said when they'd gone to fight Malcolm. *Melaney wants you to kill him.* His mother had wanted him be the one to take Malcolm's powers, and now... "Honestly, I forgot about it... but I'm glad I wasn't around. Sometimes, the proximity can be enough. Especially this far from Hescaryn."

"So..." Samantha started slowly, then carefully placed her words as if she was still building the thought. "If you'd killed Malcolm, you would've become the Archdemon of Greed, but that didn't happen. And now your mother is supposed to choose her successor... which in demon terms means, she's choosing the one who's going to kill her. And she wants you to do it."

Sometimes, Samantha's sharp mind frightened Matt. He'd only given them fragments, told them things that were completely new to them, and yet she'd managed to identify the core of his problem as undeviating as a Xerxes set on its prey.

His hands shook slightly, but despite how much it upset him, he managed to call back some casualness. "Well, me, Caspar, or Balthasar. She said it should be one of us." He shrugged dejectedly. "So, now they're trying to kill me."

"Aaaaalright," Jan said slowly. He clicked his tongue. "Well, I mean, look at it this way. You have a job waiting for you right after school, and hey, I don't know anyone who'd be more qualified." He grinned, undeterred by Matt's instant scowl. "You'll manage that kid issue, no problem."

Samantha massaged her forehead and muttered, "If you put it that way, there's probably already a few around."

Matt frowned. While the rational part of his brain completely understood why she'd come to such an assumption, that other stupidly human part was annoyed. Annoyed enough to set her right. "There aren't."

No one heard him, because Fabian was whining again. "But Matt doesn't want to become archdemon." His frightful eyes met Matt's. "You don't, right?"

There should've been a clear answer, but Matt only shrugged. "I'm trying to figure that out.

Fabian's jaw fell open. "You'd go for it, even with your brothers ready to kill you?"

"Oh please, just the mention of the possibility has painted a target on my back. They're going to come for me, again and again until this whole thing is resolved. That's why sometimes I find myself thinking, why not? Why not go all in and give it a try. I might just be the one who survives."

"But?" Samantha asked forcefully. There was a desperate need in her eyes that Matt couldn't meet.

He looked away and sighed. A year ago, he would've taken on the challenge without a second thought. He'd have welcomed it. Now...

"It would mean giving up my human side."

When he looked up again, Samantha had crossed her arms in front of her chest and was the one avoiding his gaze. He must've said something wrong again, but what?

"Do you have to?" Rachel asked, looking horrified.

Matt snorted. "Have you ever heard of an arch-*half*-demon?"

"A year ago, I didn't even know Hell truly existed." She shrugged, completely unaffected. "Why shouldn't there be arch-half-demons?"

"You don't understand!" Matt rubbed his face, quickly growing weary of all the explanations. And the emotions. There were so many conflicting feelings in his head. He wanted to accept the challenge. At the same time, he wanted to hide behind a rock. He couldn't bear the idea of Balthasar or *Caspar* becoming the next Archdemon of Lust. Even if he somehow survived the election period, he wouldn't survive *that.* The thought of Caspar taking his mother's spot was particularly galling. He couldn't let that happen, but would *Matt* be able to fill it, as his friends said? Did he want to do it?

"If I become the Archdemon of Lust," he started slowly, "then I'll have to leave Ashuan behind. That means, my father, school, you guys..." His eyes landed on Samantha. He quickly averted his gaze before she could catch him staring. "I would have to give up everything that makes up my life at the moment. I don't know if I'm ready for that." Later down the line, the idea had more appeal, but who knew when such an opportunity would present itself again.

He wished more than ever he could talk these things through with Chay. Even if the other would keep mum about what his future held, he'd leave him with some guidance. And Matt bitterly needed some guidance right about now.

"Plus, you'd have to kill your mother," Samantha added, her voice caught between a familiar tension and kind worry.

"What?" Fabian exclaimed, his eyes wide. "That's *crazy!* Matt would never do such a thing."

"You sure about that?" Jan asked, sounding unimpressed.

Rachel shuddered. "He'd have to if he wants those powers transferred to him."

For once quiet, Lucille was only looking at him, the worry in her eyes threatening to drown both of them.

Matt turned down his eyes. "Yes. It's what she wants."

"See?" Jan claimed loudly. "He'd totally do it."

"No, he wouldn't." The surprising voice of support came from Samantha. When Matt looked up, he found her staring at him. "You couldn't kill Malcolm when you found out he was family, and you actually love your mother."

He shook his head automatically, because who did? Certainly, no demon. Balthasar wouldn't have any qualms about killing her. She was a business partner to him, someone he would shed to get ahead. And Caspar... For Caspar, she was nothing but an obstacle, someone who'd stopped him one-too-many times from killing his half-human brother. Even sweet Menuha would do it if she thought she stood a chance.

And Matt? Matt pressed the balls of his hands against his brow, while his fingers dug into his hair until it hurt as he fought down a wave of emotion he was unequipped to handle. If she just died, killed by another, he believed he'd be fine. But now Samantha had planted this doubt in him. Would he really be fine? More fine than she'd been after Daniel, or Rachel after losing Nico, for sure, but not completely. His traitorous human heart would stop beating, just for a little bit.

A loud thump followed by the crash of something breakable from the room next door shook them all from their thoughts.

"Mum!" Fabian shot out of his seat and sprinted out the door. The rest of them looked at each other, before following him one by one.

Caroline was on the floor in the store room, surrounded by a dented box and what looked like broken dishes and potion bottles, the content of which was seeping into the floor boards. Worse, she was crying.

"Mum? Are you okay?" Fabian seemed a bit out of it, as if his mother's tears freaked him out more than the carnage of potions. Instead of answering, she only cried harder.

The tears certainly freaked out Matt. Adult humans didn't cry. Not in public. Not at work.

Meanwhile, Samantha and Lucille sprang into action. Samantha got out cleaning tools and was swiftly picking up the glass pieces, while Lucille carefully took Caroline's hands in hers and exposed a shallow cut, nothing worth so many tears.

"Did you hurt yourself?" Lucille asked.

Fabian was still on the retreat, unable to tear his eyes away from his mother.

"It's not a big thing, Caro," Samantha said with a gentle smile as she cleaned around her. "It's just dishes. We can replace them, and if you tell me what you had in the bottles, I can make new potions." Samantha, the reliable problem solver.

Lucille who only wanted to help and Rachel who stepped forward to do what she could. Even Jan found something to do by gently healing the cut on her hand. They all helped Caroline, while Fabian stared and Matt felt useless.

And still Caroline wouldn't stop crying.

And that was when Matt knew something was wrong, actually wrong. Once again, he was not equipped to handle it. He wasn't human like the others. But not really demon either. A bit of both and nothing genuinely.

He didn't belong here. But if he didn't belong here, where did he belong?

# Fabian

"This isn't normal." Fabian was pacing the kitchen back at home, while Samantha cooked dinner for his family. Lucille had offered to stay but he'd magnanimously told her she could go home. Meanwhile, his father had come and taken his mum to the doctor. Hopefully, they would fix her there.

Samantha put a hand on his shoulder as she passed him to raid their pantry. "She's human just like us, Fabi."

He winced at the reminder. Of course, his mother was human. She wasn't some scary archdemon who casually set her sons on each other to fight for the honour to kill her like Matt's mother apparently did. The whole thing was so messed up, and Fabian had already vowed that he'd stay out of it. There were more important things to care about, after all.

"It's not normal for her to cry over some broken cups," he maintained. "You know my mum. She'd never lose it because of that."

Samantha sighed heavily as she cooked up a tomato-based sauce to go with the pasta she'd already made. "Perhaps she's stressed. She's not only running the Magic Circle but does all the admin stuff for our dads' workshop too. Then all our current money woes. My parents fight. Your mother bursts into tears."

She made an awful amount of sense. His family was struggling. It was so apparent, even Lucille's father had found out about it in his awful investigations. They didn't have much savings, either. The Magic Circle had always been a bit weak on the financial side, but it was his mother's passion. She would wilt in an office job.

If she couldn't keep the shop open... Fabian bit his lip in frustration. "What am I supposed to do? I can't exactly quit school to help out with the shop."

Samantha poured both pasta and sauce into a casserole dish before sprinkling grated cheese on top. "There's a lot you can do. You could help out in the afternoons if you wanted to take care of the shop. Or you can help around here, small things that add up." She pushed the casserole into the oven and started cleaning up. "Take off some of the load."

It was true, his mother had carried most of the weight of the household on top of her business. Now that Samantha pointed it out, Fabian felt guilty for barely remembering to dump his clothes in the washing basket every other week. It wasn't that he didn't help out at all at home. Compared to his mother, though, he was doing awfully little. And contrary to her, he had spare time. If he didn't have to fight monsters.

"They're coming," Samantha warned him after a glance outside.

Fabian heard the crunch of gravel as his father parked the car, even if he couldn't see them from his position. At once, the nervous energy surged back and he picked up pacing again.

In the corridor, the door opened, and his mother softly complained that she didn't need help. Worried to see her in a cast or something similar, Fabian followed Samantha with great trepidation.

"Oh, it's all fine," his mother just told Samantha. "The doctor said, nothing's broken. I just sprained an ankle."

She looked fine, all tears dried and replaced by her usual warm smile.

Samantha gave her a hug nonetheless. "I'm glad to hear that. There's dinner in the oven. I'll leave you alone in a minute."

"What?" Fabian blurted. That was news to him. He needed his best friend. She was the one that held it together for him. She'd even made dinner while he'd been busy fretting. And now she was leaving?

"If you need anything, just call." Samantha gave Fabian a sharp look and he understood. She wanted him to look after his mother, not hide in his room and feel sorry for himself.

His dad smiled warmly at Samantha. "You're an angel, Sam. Will you update your parents for me? Ben was pretty worried."

"Of course. Goodnight." She slipped her shoes on, grabbed her backpack, and left the house.

When the door fell shut, silence spread between the remaining people. Fabian stared at his mum, and his mum stared at him, both devoid of words. At last, his dad took the initiative by clearing his throat.

"Let's all sit down in the living room, shall we?" he suggested.

One by one, they shuffled out of the corridor and took a seat on the big couch as if they were going to watch TV. But the TV stayed off, and instead, his father quickly ran through a proper update.

"The doctor said your mother needs to rest. So, we're going to close the Magic Circle for a bit."

Closing the Magic Circle? Somehow the thought was incomprehensible to Fabian. "But we've got the party on Saturday. We can't exactly cancel now, can we?" His mother was celebrating ten years in the business. It was a huge benchmark. There was supposed to be a cute little garden party and the addition of a little café on site, of course complete with magical teas and coffee.

"We'll have to move it to a later date," his dad said, though later sounded a lot like never.

"There's still too much to do, anyway," his mum added in a flat voice that scared Fabian more than he cared to admit.

His father rubbed her back, agreeing with her, but Fabian remembered Samantha's advice. "I could take over."

"Fabian." The plea in his mother's voice twisted Fabian's heart.

"I'm serious," he said, despite it. "You can close the shop, sure, but we can still celebrate your achievement. Everyone's looking forward to it."

"Like who?"

What kind of question was that? Did his mother really think no one cared about her shop? Had business been that bad? "Well, *I* do! Ten years is a long time." It was more than half his life.

"That's true." His dad decided to strengthen his plea, but he sought Fabian's eyes. "And you feel like you can really take over? Because I can't help you with this. I've got my hands full this week at the garage."

"Of course!" Fabian said immediately, not even thinking twice. Doing the party felt a lot like a plan. Something he could actually do.

"Sam will help me, and on Saturday, we'll all go to the party together. As a family."

His father checked with his mum. "What do you think?"

She only sighed. "If Fabian wants to do it."

"Alright." His father nodded at him. "The party's your responsibility now."

Fabian felt an immense bout of relief at that. He no longer felt listless, and worse, useless, but energised and motivated. "You can count on me."

Now he just had to rope everyone else in.

# Rachel

The reveal of Matt's big secret had been every bit as horrifying as the dream had made it seem. If anything, he'd been holding back how bad it truly was. Killing his mother, perhaps kissing her too... Rachel shuddered just thinking about it.

And on top of that, Fabian's mother had broken down over nothing. As shocking as that had been, Rachel felt more equipped to handle it. Both Fabian's and Samantha's families were under a lot of stress right now. Poor Caroline always held up the ship, helping wherever she could, taking on way too much. It might scare Fabian that she wasn't invincible, but not Rachel. She just felt sorry for her.

Caroline Bendtfeld deserved the world, *not like certain other mothers.* When it came to lust, her own was trying to give Matt's a run for her money. Even now, Rachel heard unmistakable moaning coming from the living room. She hurried to kick off her shoes and run up the stairs.

"Rachel? Is that you?" Her mother's call was slightly breathless.

For a moment, Rachel contemplated ignoring her, but she'd already paused. "Who else would it be?"

"Wait a second."

Rachel drummed her fingers on the banister and slowly counted to ten. She turned around just as her mother came into the entrance way.

Annette's face was flushed, while her top was exposing a little too much skin. On top of that, she bore the biggest smile on her face. "I want to introduce you to someone."

"No, thanks. I don't need to get acquainted with your lovers."

"Acquainted with." Annette giggled. "Such an old word. But it suits you."

Absolutely mortified, Rachel took another step up. She didn't deserve being called old by her own mother.

The smile lost a bit of shine. "This is different. He's going to move in with us."

"What?" Rachel stared at her.

Coquettishly, Annette gave her a one-shoulder shrug and giggled. "I know, it's a bit sudden, but I feel like I'm in love for the first time in a very long time."

Slowly, Rachel walked down the stairs. "Mum, no. You can't just decide this on your own. I live here too and..." Was her mother going to give Nico's room to this stranger?

"Rachel, before you go all high and mighty on me, how about you say hi first. You might come to like him."

*That* Rachel sincerely doubted. With a forced smile, she turned towards the living room and stopped cold. The smile slipped off her face like butter from a hot pan, while her feet were rooted deep into the floor.

She knew this man, knew him by his sexy smirk as well as his elegant features and the danger in his eyes. Her mother's *lover* was no one else but Matt's older brother. Balthasar.

"Hello, Rachel," he said in a honeyed voice that promised so much more.

Rachel shuddered. For a few seconds longer, she stared at the demon, noticing his half-opened shirt and the hard muscles beneath. A demon from the House of Lust indeed. She gulped.

Then she whirled around, grabbed her mother by the arm, and forced her up the stairs. "We need to talk now!"

"Oh, please! What's got into you?" There were no more love-struck smiles.

Rachel entered her mother's bedroom, since it was the closest to the stairs and closed the door behind her. "No, absolutely not. You don't know him."

Annette sighed. "Balthasar and I have been going out for weeks."

What fresh nightmare was this? Rachel felt as if she'd been slapped in the face. Her mother had been dating Matt's demon brother for *weeks?* It seemed like Balthasar had never truly left Greenvalley. And just as they'd banned one brother.

"Is it because he's younger than me?"

Rachel blinked, unable to understand what her mother meant. "He's what?" According to Matt, Balthasar was close to a thousand years old, the very opposite of *younger* than her mother.

"Do you find it weird a younger man could find your old mum attractive?"

"Yes!" Rachel eagerly accepted the explanation. "He looks like he could be your son." No lie, although realistically he could have been Annette's great-great-many-times-great-grandfather.

Annette huffed. "I'm not *that* old. He's thirty." She shook her head. "And I like younger men. They're more fun." That was way more information than Rachel had ever asked for. "Your father was also eight years younger than me."

"Balthasar isn't my father." That much was certain.

Her mother rolled her eyes. "Does it matter? I'm allowed to date whoever I want."

"Oh, you can date whoever you want. You've done that from day one, but that doesn't mean he gets to move in."

"Are you jealous?" For some reason, her mother seemed to find the notion adorable.

Rachel had no idea what to even make of the suggestion. "Jealous of what?"

"You're afraid that he'd come between us."

"Between us?" Rachel had to laugh. It wasn't a pretty sound. "The space between us is so big a whole truckload of men could come between us, and I wouldn't care at all."

Every trace of amusement was once again wiped from Annette's face. "Now you're just being mean."

"I'm not. We *aren't* close. We haven't been in a long time. But—" Rachel added before her mother could get a word in "—I care for you, and I'm trying to keep you from making a mistake." How could she stop her mother from getting entangled with a demon? Balthasar was dangerous! He was trying to kill Matt. Though why he had to do that from her mother's house, she had no idea.

At last, she found an angle that would make more sense. "You don't honestly believe that he'll stay true to you. Guys like him have a girlfriend on each finger of their hand." Not that Balthasar did girlfriends...

"That's enough," Annette snapped. "You said your part, but enough is enough. Ever since Nico died, you've been a vindictive little control freak. I pay the bills, so I decide who moves in. If you've got a problem with me being happy, you're welcome to leave."

"You..." Rachel gasped, so overcome with anger that she couldn't even form an answer. The mention of Nico had come completely out of left field. Unable to deal with the low blow that opened up all her wounds, she stormed out of the room.

She couldn't believe her mother would be so callous as to use her dead brother as a weapon against her. Tears shimmered in her eyes, threatening to overflow as she ripped the door to her room open. For the second time this afternoon, she stopped cold.

While she'd been arguing with her mother, Balthasar had invaded her personal space. He stood next to her bed, examining the dreamweb in his hands. *Her* Emblem of Power.

"That's mine," she snapped, but her voice shook.

"Is it?" Balthasar asked, mildly surprised, as if he didn't quite believe her.

Rachel wanted to do nothing more than to cross the distance between them and snatch the dreamweb from his hands, but even posing as some thirty-year-old toyboy, Balthasar's stance couldn't hide the dangerous predator he was. She knew first-hand how dangerous Matt's family was.

Still, she forced herself to say, "Give it back." Fear he'd simply vanish with her dreamweb struck her, and it took all composure she had to keep from charging him.

To her surprise, Balthasar lopped the dreamweb to her. Drawn out of her frozen state, she caught it clumsily. His eyes fixed on her face, he sauntered towards her, his limbs rolling sinuously like a panther.

Rachel gulped, more afraid than aroused. "Wh-what are you doing here?"

He stopped way too close in front of her, and looked down on her, his gaze smouldering. Rachel thought that it was this look he used on her mother, but it wouldn't work on her.

"I'm making your mum very happy." He raised his hand and ran his thumb along her jaw line until it came to rest on her chin, just a millimetre from her bottom lip. "I could make you happy too."

The insinuation of what he planned to do to her twisted Rachel's insides, and not in an enticing way. "No."

In a surprising testament to his standards, Balthasar dropped the thumb and stopped his advances. Instead, he passed her, whispering softly in her ear, "Tell Melchior he picked a boring entourage."

Rachel blushed heavily. "We're not... We're..."

Balthasar left her room before she could get her words in order. He didn't take her and her friends seriously, only saw them as Matt's extension, something expendable that he amused himself with. And while he hadn't crossed a line today, Rachel still felt threatened by his presence. Balthasar had a plan, and for some reason, that plan included her and her mother.

When soon after the moans continued from her mother's bedroom, Rachel could no longer hold it in. She ran to her desk bin and threw up into it.

# Samantha

Caspar's and Matt's fight had left the school on edge. While they talked about a shooter in the first few days, people weren't quite so sure about that in the aftermath. First off, they'd never found the shooter—Caspar was banned to Hell and hadn't figured out a way back—but the damage and the injuries didn't fit normal gunshot descriptions. Someone had started a rumour about bombs instead, which didn't really make it any better.

In the aftermath, police hung around for a bit, checking them all upon entry, while certain areas were cordoned off. But people recovered and soon, wilder rumours were spread. As much as Samantha strained to hear, though, she never heard anything about demons.

Standing at the locker, she glanced at the toilets that were still in disrepair. She hadn't known her sister had been hit by Caspar and bleeding out while they'd fought to ban him. If Jan hadn't been there, Meg might've died.

"Hey beautiful," a voice whispered into her ear. The warmth of Cian's breath caressed her neck.

She moaned softly before turning into him—and away from the grisly sight. In the middle of her parents fighting, the battle at school, and Matt's horrible secret, Cian was the only spot of sunlight in her days. "Hi yourself."

He bit his bottom lip, his eyes revealing he thought of afternoons spent in his bed or the break they'd spent "cleaning up" the chem lab. "What do you have next?"

"I'm actually free." Samantha's gaze fell on his lips.

"How fortunate. Me too." He leaned in.

Just then, Samantha saw Rachel coming down the corridor from the corner of her eye. "No, you need to do it on 350 degrees. Otherwise, the reaction won't occur."

Cian stared at her flatly, the corner of his mouth twitching. "Okay, I'll try to turn up the heat and see if I can get more sensible results."

Amused, Samantha pulled a face, which she barely managed to smooth when he left abruptly, no longer blocking Rachel's view. Samantha turned to her. "Hey, how are... *you?*" Rachel looked absolutely livid.

She hooked her arm into Samantha and dragged her along. "You need to come with me and help me talk to Matt."

"Okay. What did he do now?"

"Balthasar moved in with Annette and me."

Samantha nearly stumbled over her feet. "Come again?"

"You understood me perfectly fine. He's posing as her boyfriend, and if you ask my mum, it's Mr Right." Rachel's voice was full of tension, her eyes glittering with a hint of insanity.

"Every word you say is more absurd than the one before it," Samantha said slowly, her usually fast brain struggling to keep pace with what Rachel was saying.

"I know!" Rachel exclaimed loudly.

It was unusual for her to raise her voice, much less draw attention to herself. So, when Samantha saw other students looking, she knew her friend was really upset. Unable to come up with an instant solution, she simply patted her friend's arm.

Together, they marched into the cafeteria, though it was more Rachel marching, while Samantha stumbled along. The other three were seated around the table, lost in an intense discussion. Rachel didn't care.

"Matt!"

Startled, Matt looked up. His surprise only grew when he noticed it was Rachel who'd called him out. The others appeared just as confused.

"Did you sleep with Rachel?" Samantha heard Fabian whisper.

"What? No!"

Meanwhile, Rachel planted her feet in front of the table, glaring down at Matt. "Tell your brother to leave."

"Leave?" Matt asked. "Which brother are we even talking about?"

"Caspar is banned," Samantha reminded him. "Balthasar is dating Rachel's mum."

"Your mum and Balthasar?" Fabian sputtered. "Does she know—"

Rachel nearly ripped his head off. "Of course she doesn't know. She thinks she's some kind of cougar who snatched up a toyboy."

"What's a toyboy and cougar?" Matt asked with his usual oblivion.

Helpfully, Lucille explained, "When an older woman dates a much younger man."

That only deepened Matt's confusion, something Samantha couldn't even blame him for. The whole thing was ludicrous. "Balthasar is definitely not younger than your mother."

"As I said!" Each word of Rachel's was as sharp as a knife.

"Rachel, calm down, please. Did he hurt her or anything?" With a little tug, Samantha convinced Rachel to sit down.

"Not yet." Rachel's shoulders rose then sunk as she breathed out deliberately. "But the two are screwing so much I feel nauseous."

Samantha felt nauseous just hearing of it. She could only imagine how Rachel felt, with her room right next to Annette's.

"Maybe she summoned him?" Matt suggested.

Rachel let out a short sharp laugh. "My mother does a lot of stupid things, but demon summoning would be a first."

Though it was perfectly possible that Annette had stumbled across a summoning book and played around with it while drunk, Samantha didn't really believe it. Plus, Rachel had asked for her help. "It would be too much of a coincidence. You said it yourself—he's trying to test us. So, he's here because of you."

"Yes! Tell him to test something else," Rachel commanded. "But he needs to keep his fingers and everything else off my mother and leave."

Matt grimaced, clearly uncomfortable with the idea of facing his brother. "I don't think he'll listen to me."

"Then make sure he does!" Rachel snapped. "If he's so desperate to be close to you, he should move in with you."

Overwhelmed, Matt raised his hands. "Is after school alright?"

As if the promise was all she wanted, Rachel calmed instantly. "Yes, of course."

"Can't we just ban Balthasar too?" Fabian asked, looking around hopefully. "Then Matt wouldn't have to worry about him here, and neither would we."

"True," Rachel agreed. "Because according to your lovely brother, we're part of your entourage."

Lucille snorted. The thought that she could be part of anyone's entourage was entirely laughable.

Matt winced. "Friendship is a rather abstract concept in Hell," he explained. "Since we're running for the Archdemon role, he probably thinks I'm already forming my... *entourage.*"

It struck Samantha once again how different Matt's life in Hell had been. A family that was willing to kill each other, no real friends, apart from maybe Chay, who was way too busy to be called on often. She wondered if Matt had ever been lonely or whether that, too, was an abstract concept in Hell.

"We'd have to lure him in," Samantha mused, trying to think what that would look like.

Matt shook his head. "He's too smart for that. Caspar throwing a rage fit, sure, but Balthasar? Never."

"Well, think of something," Rachel demanded, though with much less ferocity. "He can't stay with us."

"I will," Matt stressed.

Rachel nodded sharply, then turned her attention to the paperwork on the table. "What are you doing there?"

Having made a few notes, Lucille smiled happily. "We're helping Caroline prepare the party for the Magic Circle anniversary."

"And we really, really need your help!" Fabian begged.

With a sigh, Samantha pulled a couple of notes to her and started reading. Helping Caroline was no question. She just wished her timetable wasn't already as full as it was.

Samantha loved her new job at the florist. The smell alone when she entered the shop made her sigh with pleasure. She hadn't realised how much she'd missed her old garden until she was surrounded by blooming flowers again. The work itself was fun, too. Pia kept the actual arrangements to herself, but she taught Samantha how to cut the flowers, how to display them in the buckets, and how to care for them so that they'd last longer. To top it all off, she got to take home the ones that looked on the verge of wilting. They were good for another day or two, and by then, she had to go back to work.

The pay wasn't bad either. It wasn't a lot of money, but she wasn't legally allowed to earn too much anyway. The only problem was that it didn't leave her much time. Not that it came as a surprise, but now that Caroline had had her breakdown, Samantha wanted to do so much more than she could.

Which was something Fabian hadn't quite figured out yet as he followed her around at work, telling her all about the party he was planning in Caroline's stead. "I thought it was as good as done and we only needed to decorate a little, but the bratwurst guy called and wanted to know when his deposit is coming, the flyers are neither printed nor distributed, and there's some kind of issue with consents from the city. Honestly, I have no idea what they even want."

"Why don't you ask your mother?" Samantha asked as she cut some lilies the way Pia had shown her.

"Because I said I can do it alone. She's supposed to rest, and if I ask her, she'll just do it herself."

Knowing Caroline, he was absolutely right. "Okay."

"Okay, you're doing it or okay—?"

"Me?" Samantha asked perplexed. It shouldn't have surprised her. Fabian always came to her if he needed help. It was her own fault for indulging him.

Fabian seemed oblivious as to why she would object. "Yes, you're good at that. Talk to officials and stuff like that. I only have ideas. You know how to make them real." The old troubled artist excuse.

"I don't have the time."

"It won't take that long," Fabian whined.

She gasped. "Of course it will. I need to get my head around everything and then pick up the phone. And don't believe for one second it's done after one call." She felt exhausted just thinking of the amount of work. "Normally, I would, but I can't. I need to work here, organise the Abi committees, induct the new student council, and at some point do my homework and prepare for the Abitur exams. Oh, and have a smidgeon of free time."

Fabian groaned softly, and she would've kicked his shin in response if it weren't for the counter between them. "It's only this week. The committees can wait a few days longer to kick off. And you're going to ace the exams anyway, whether you start preparing this week or next."

As if she'd only start now with less than half a year to go. "I still need to work until six, same tomorrow and Friday."

"That leaves Wednesday and Thursday."

"Way too little time!" Samantha complained. "Why is there even so much left to do?" From what Fabian had said, it didn't sound possible to pull the party off by Sunday.

He shrugged. "How am I supposed to know? Please, please, please."

"I can't."

"It's the Magic Circle." A little more sombrely, he added, "And my mum."

Just the memory of Caroline crying on the floorboards changed Samantha's mind. Caroline was her second mum, and she loved the shop to bits. She couldn't allow all her hard work to go to waste because of a minor hiccup. If it was only minor.

"Fine. I'll do it."

Fabian skipped around the counter and gave her a big hug. "You're the best."

The doorbell announced customers, and Fabian let go of Samantha. Instead of actual customers, though, it was only Alan, Cian, Ani, and Shayna. Alan nodded at Samantha before making his way to the back room where his mother was pouring over the books, while Ani and Shayna whispered with each other. Assuming by the frequent looks they threw Samantha, they were talking about her.

"Don't let them get to you," Fabian said as he got ready to leave.

"Get your girlfriend to call the city council and the bratwurst guy. She's good on the phone," she called after him. Those things couldn't wait for her to have time.

He waved at the door, ignoring the Elite Clique. "Will do."

When he was gone, Cian stepped forward, a single rose in his hand. "I'd like to buy this one."

"That's two euros," Samantha told him and smiled. "Do you want me to wrap it?"

"If you want to." He put down a five-euro bill. "The rest is for your tip."

She giggled in response. "It's a flower shop, not a café." Then she lowered her eyes to wrap the rose as she'd been taught; tight enough that the plant didn't move around, but not so tight that leaves and blossoms would be damaged. "Speaking of cafés, though..." Part of Caroline's plans for the big ten-year-anniversary were to establish a mini-café in the store. "The Magic Circle is opening on the weekend and throwing a big party. You might want to come?"

Cian leaned against the counter, slightly amused. "Is this a date?"

"More like a clumsy marketing attempt and a peace offering for having to rain check on tonight," Samantha said with a smile she hoped would make it all better.

Cian straightened with a groan. "Monsters again?"

"Not so far. But I need to prepare said party." She had to at least find out what needed doing, what she could delegate, and which tasks she might just cut. Then she had to make a plan and hope nothing else—like monsters—popped up.

"Alright. If that's the only way to see you," Cian said with feigned theatricality. How about I help you with your marketing campaign, and leave you to do the other stuff." He took the rose from her, only to offer it back. "This one was supposed to be for tonight. Since it won't hold until the weekend..." He shrugged sheepishly.

Surprised, Samantha took it. No one had ever gifted her red roses before. It was a flower that carried a lot of meaning, and just like that, Cian had made her smile again. "Thank you."

"Don't overdo it," he whispered, "or you'll be the next one who burns out."

His sweetness was enchanting, but it also made Samantha feel guilty. As if he gave her all of him, and she only had a part of her on offer.

Before she could say something in response, Alan came back out and rejoined his friends. Immediately, Ani asked him something, her eyes glued to Samantha. Without the slightest sense of propriety, Alan shook his head and announced to the world, "Nah, they're just screwing."

Ani looked scandalised, and Samantha felt as if someone had emptied a bucket of ice on her head. If Ani knew, Cheryl would be next.

Cian sighed softly. "Don't worry. I'll take care of it."

It was a testament to how busy she was that she believed every word of it. She had no time left to worry about Ani. Let Cheryl have her little tantrum. As long as Matt didn't learn about it, Samantha couldn't care less.

# Matt

Rachel's house had never struck Matt as particularly sinister before. It was one of dozens of one-family homes, and like most older Harzer buildings, it had the prominent outdoor wood beams that made up the charm of the area. Today, those wood beams looked menacing, as if they were going to come crashing down on him if he dared to blink.

The windows were dark against the setting sun, and the red light reflecting in them made Matt think of his home world. Which was only appropriate since a piece of home was waiting inside of it. A terrifying piece of home, but then again, everything about home was terrifying.

"Do we have to go in?" He hated how whiny he sounded. Almost like Fabian.

Rachel gave him a long stare. Yeah, they would have to go in.

She pushed the door open until it banged softly against the wall on the other side. They both stared inside, expecting the worst, but there was no burst of energy. Instead, they found the terrifying subject lounging on the living room couch, leafing through a copy of the *Greenvalley View.*

"How predictable," Balthasar said in his honeyed voice that always carried something dark and depraved in its silkiness. "Hello, Melchior."

Matt set his jaw. "Matt. If you are going to pretend to be a human for the day, then use my human name."

"Is this your declaration of forfeit?" Balthasar asked with a hint of a smirk.

Forfeit his demon side? Matt huffed. As if that were possible.

Rachel used his moment of hesitation to assert herself. "It's not. He'd be stupid to throw in the towel as the reigning favourite."

Matt gasped at her. What was she talking about? He was absolutely *not* the favourite. "This isn't helping." If anything, it painted an even bigger target on his back, and that target was already spreading from one wingtip to the other as it was.

"What makes you assume that Me—tt is the favourite?" Balthasar asked, each word making Matt's hairs stand on edge.

"Isn't that obvious?" Rachel said without a sliver of doubt. "You and Caspar are many times more experienced. You run the Small Council, he's the General of Terror. You've proven yourself over and over again. There is only one reason for Melaney to pick a greenhorn like Matt. Because he's her secret favourite."

"That's not true," Matt cried, then gaped at her. Was that how she had interpreted his explanation?

Balthasar, however, put the magazine aside and got up in a fluid motion. "I came to the same conclusion."

Balthasar came to the same conclusion? He felt threatened by the little brother he'd barely paid attention to all his life? Matt's brain was short-circuiting. Before it gave up completely, he asked, "If I'm truly favourite, why rile all of us up?"

"You want my opinion?" Balthasar asked, surprisingly open with information today. "Because she's not entirely sure you're up to the challenge. You're awfully young, my dear Matt, and very... how shall I say? Fickle." He gave him the once-over, clearly not impressed by what he saw. "I'm going to prove to her that she's right about her doubts. You're not up to the task."

"And you're proving this by screwing Rachel's mother?" Matt asked doubtfully.

"When was the last time *you* had sex?" Balthasar asked instead.

Rachel seemed less than impressed by this turn of conversation. "Is this some sort of pissing contest?"

Balthasar ignored her. "Your answer?"

Was he truly expecting an answer? Matt tried to think back when he last had sex. Down in Marseille with Amelie. And then... and then Samantha had protected him with her life despite hating his guts, and other things had been so much more important. Menuha had already called him out on it, and so had Rachel, even though she didn't understand why any of it would be an issue.

"It's none of your business." Matt didn't even know why he'd lost all interest. Maybe he'd already gone through the limited pool in Greenvalley and there was no one left to pursue. No one but *her.*

Balthasar snorted derisively. "Melaney won't like that."

"Why?" Rachel demanded to know.

"Oh, darling." Balthasar turned to her at last. "You figured out Matt's position in this race but not why his current *celibacy* would be a problem?"

Rachel's mouth made a tiny little 'o' shape.

"Let's worry less about me and more about you," Matt hurried to say. "What do you want here? It can't be sex. You've got enough of that and then some in Hescaryn."

"As I already told you last time, I would like to get to know you and the people you surrounding yourself with. Rachel here is very interesting."

"I am?" She seemed surprised.

"Of course, you are—"

They never got to hear what made Rachel so interesting as the front door opened from the outside and Annette came in, a bag of groceries in her arm. Confused, she looked at the congregation in the living room, then sighed. "Rachel, are you trying to intimidate my boyfriend to get him to leave?"

Balthasar coughed softly, likely balking at the idea of anything or anyone intimidating him.

Rachel's voice was incredibly flat when she replied, "I wouldn't dream of it." She totally would.

In the meantime, Balthasar had caught himself again. "No, on the contrary. It turns out that Rachel is good friends with my little brother Matt here." And then he stepped forward and put his arm around Matt.

Matt went completely still, well aware of how easily that arm could wrap around his neck or shoot energy directly at his heart. "Half."

The fingers rose. Matt's muscles went tense, ready to react. And then Balthasar lovingly tousled his hair, causing Matt to spring away to safety.

What was *that*?

"Oh, the two of you are brothers?" Annette asked. "What a nice surprise. I was going to cook dinner tonight. Are you going to stay for that, Matt?"

For some reason, the thought of dinner with her mother seemed to terrify Rachel. It definitely terrified Matt to sit down with his half-brother and endure any more of his fake shows of affection. "Uhm, no. I... My father is awaiting me."

"Matt!" Rachel glared at him.

He'd promised her he'd take care of his brother, but he had no idea how to make that happen. Especially in front of Annette. Maybe if they could talk alone...

"Give old Dad my greetings!" Balthasar said, with a cheesy smile.

"Maybe another time," Annette said, with a hint of remorse.

Matt nodded sharply and hurried out of the house. As soon as he stepped outside, he took the short way home.

Embarrassment struck him as soon as he arrived in his room. Not only had he run away from Balthasar, he'd also left Rachel alone with him. Rachel was capable in her own right, but if Balthasar chose to attack her or her mother, she stood no chance.

Not that Matt believed he'd fare any better. Truthfully, he had no idea. He'd never measured himself up against this particular brother, had never even seen him fight before. All he knew was that Balthasar, a politician by heart, despised Caspar's hotblooded anger and had managed to control the Small Council for nine-hundred years, which told him one of two things: either the Small Council was as boring as it sounded, or Balthasar had proved himself in subtle yet infinitely more powerful ways many times over.

Balthasar was dangerous, but how exactly, Matt couldn't figure out.

With Caspar, he simply had to hit back harder. With Balthasar, Matt had to work smarter. And at over nine hundred years Balthasar's junior, there was no way an ingenious idea would simply strike him.

No, he had to take a page out of Balthasar's own book. *Get to know him better.* Find out what he really wanted, but also how his mind worked, what his bigger plan was. It was clear to Matt now Balthasar wouldn't just try to murder him in his sleep, and if he was correct, that meant Rachel was relatively safe. For now.

It was decided. He had to get Balthasar alone.

In the middle of the night, Matt appeared straight in Annette's bedroom. The whole house was asleep. Soft snores came from the lump under the blanket. Matt stalked closer on tiptoes. Maybe the way to defeat Balthasar was this. No pure power, no smarts, but the element of surprise.

"Are you trying to murder me in my sleep?"

Matt sprung around, his heart galloping like a horse.

Balthasar stood in the door behind him, not an inch of clothing on him. Slowly, Matt turned to look at the lump on the bed. It was only one person, not two. Rachel's mother.

"Or maybe you'd like a threesome," Balthasar continued to muse.

Pained, Matt returned his glance. His voice was annoyingly feeble when he spoke. "Can we talk?"

Balthasar's chin dipped on his chest, and it took Matt a moment to realise his brother was softly laughing. "Talking, huh?" Then he jerked his head towards the corridor. "Come along, then."

Like a child caught trespassing where it didn't belong, Matt followed Balthasar downstairs to the living room. Once there, Balthasar turned on a dim light and poured himself a glass of red wine. He didn't offer Matt one, but sat down on the couch and crossed his feet on the armrest, blocking the space completely.

While Balthasar lounged there in his birthday suit, Matt felt like a lowly supplicant who wasn't even close to the same level of power. To top it all off, Matt's gaze kept falling onto something he didn't really care to see.

"Could you not cover up at least?" he asked, proud that he managed to sound more annoyed than overwhelmed.

Balthasar raised an eyebrow. "Since when are you so chaste?"

Matt decided to stare at the coffee table instead.

"Melaney won't be happy to hear that," Balthasar warned him.

It grated on Matt that he was right. It shouldn't upset him to see his brother naked. In Melaney's residence, one constantly ran into naked people. It used to be natural to Matt. It still was... but then why did the sight of his brother bother him so much? Probably for the same reason Matt wasn't naked himself. Not now, and not anywhere outside of actual sexual activities.

"It's a shame, really," Balthasar continued. "I was going to congratulate you on your success against Caspar. Banning him from Ashuan was a masterpiece."

"It wasn't my idea. Samantha banned him." As he spoke the words, Matt knew that the smart thing would've been to claim the victory for himself. Truth was, however, he still felt ashamed of how the whole thing with Caspar had gone down. He hadn't been able to stop him. Instead, his non-demon friends had to step in and do it for him.

Balthasar made an appreciative sound. "Samantha again. You like the little one, don't you?"

Matt jerked his head back around, glowering at Balthasar. "Why are you asking? Are you planning to surprise her with murderous birds again?" Smarter or not, Matt would kill him if Balthasar tried that again.

Completely unfazed by Matt's sudden anger, Balthasar took a sip from his glass. "Oh no, I've already learnt all I needed to know about her." He held up a finger. "One, she seems fairly capable for a human, both in wits and witchcraft. Second—" another finger followed "—you want to get between her legs."

Before Matt could protest, Balthasar pressed on, "And in regards to your other friends..." He spread his hands, and for a moment, there was a flicker of confusion on his face. "Why, Matt? What is it about them that holds you here? Why are you so attached to these humans?"

Stoically, Matt kept his mouth shut and glared at him. He was *not* going to discuss the concept of friendship with a demon. Especially not this demon.

"Let me guess, Chay's work?"

"What?" Matt gaped at him. "This has nothing to do with Chay. They're... my friends." Great, now he'd said it.

Balthasar was staring at him as if waiting for him to continue. Perhaps to declare the whole thing a joke, since demons didn't have friends. Not really. Not like here. Balthasar was the best example of it. He was surrounded by powerful people, or rather, he'd surrounded himself with powerful people, but they were partners, useful for the moment, nothing more. And that's why he couldn't grasp Matt's relationship with the other.

If Matt had understood it better himself, he might have argued. As it was, he knew that each argument he'd come up with was pointless. He wouldn't believe it himself if someone told him. He only *felt* differently.

When he didn't say anything, Balthasar scoffed softly. "A bit disturbing but cute, I suppose."

Matt clenched his fists. "I'm not cute."

"Then stop acting so damn human! It's pitiful," Balthasar said with a lethal sharpness in his voice.

Somehow, he'd managed to hit Matt where it hurt. In his goddamn feelings. Why did he suddenly have so many, and why were they all in direct conflict with his demon senses? He didn't want to be seen as weak, or worse, to be weak. Weakness got you killed. That was the very first lesson a demon learned in Hescaryn.

"Nobody's forcing you to watch," Matt growled in an attempt to harness his anger to disguise this momentary weakness.

"Fortunately," Balthasar said, unfazed. "It'd make me lose all interest in sex, too."

"Go away!" Matt hissed, now truly angry about his brother's insistence on his pitiful state.

Slowly, Balthasar rose from the couch. He drained his glass at a leisurely pace before setting it down on the coffee table. Then he crossed the distance between them. Matt almost backed away, wanting to leave some space in case of an attack. Then it occurred to him that he would have to resist that instinct if he didn't want to sink any further in Balthasar's eyes.

"I won't go until I know why you *and* Chay are so obsessed with these hormone-fuelled teenagers." He bent forward, his lips grazing Matt's ears. "Rachel has the Old Orenjan Dreamweb in her room." The words weren't of discovery. They were a warning, soft-spoken, but nonetheless lethal.

Matt held his breath as Balthasar turned off the light and walked back up the stairs to Rachel's mother. Several times Matt clenched his fists as if he wanted to jump on his back and beat the shit out of him. But it wouldn't help. Balthasar knew. Or if he didn't know, he suspected. And in his case, that was almost as bad as knowing.

In the silence of the room, Matt allowed himself a grunt of frustration directed at his mother. With her stupid announcement, Melaney hadn't just painted a target on *his* back, but on all of his friends' backs, too.

# Lucille

As soon as Lucille had heard there was a party to plan, she'd been ready to go all out. Unfortunately, Fabian wasn't willing to capitalise on her potential. He flat-out refused her offer to pay for luxury catering, rebuffed all ideas of making the party bigger, and to add insult to injury, had sought help from Samantha before he'd come crawling back to her.

Still, Lucille couldn't resist a good party. Even without all the creative control she yearned for, she was more than willing to pitch in. And she was willing to forgive Fabian, because after what happened to his mum, he was quite upset.

Like many boys, he didn't think of talking about his feelings and simply owning the sadness, but Lucille saw it in the tense lines around his mouth and the faraway look in his blue eyes whenever she tried to drum up some excitement.

Just like now, as they walked over to the Magic Circle after helping out with dinner at the Bendtfeld House. Lucille had a fantastic idea that wouldn't require Fabian to spend money and she was about to explain it to him. "It's a spell, not a complex ship of light or anything, just something to enhance the mood when it gets dark."

Fabian stared blindly ahead, lost in thought. When he said, "Is it safe?" it was more a reflex than a proper reply.

Frustrated, Lucille clicked her tongue. Sure, she'd made a couple of grave mistakes when she'd first learned her words carried magic, but it annoyed her to no end that this was the default response to every spell she proposed.

"I'm talking about fairy lights. Similar to those I did for the gnomes at Christmas. People will assume they're just fancy store-bought, electric ones, but they will be prettier and a little bit more magic."

He sighed as if the idea of someone *else* doing something tired *him* out. "As long as we don't need to catch actual fairies, I'm fine with it."

"Great," Lucille said, not without a bit of bite. He was supposed to be charmed by the idea, not *fine* with it.

With a shake of her head, she pushed the negative feelings away. Fabian wasn't himself right now. Since talking about the party wasn't going to improve his mood, she tried a different topic. "Pascal and I are getting along better now." The unfortunate experience of Caspar's shooting had brought them a little closer. Pascal sought her out more frequently, and to Lucille's surprise, she didn't hate it.

"Does he still think I'm not good enough for you?"

Lucille pursed her lips instead of an answer. Her entire family's opinion of Fabian hadn't changed, though her father had simply devoted no more time to it. Pascal's most common complaints were about Fabian lacking intellect. It wasn't a problem Lucille had ever had with him before, but now she couldn't help but notice how unrefined he was. And it annoyed her—not that he was, but that she cared.

"Did we leave the lights on?" Fabian asked, suddenly waking from his stupor.

She directed her gaze to the front. Sure enough, there was a light flickering behind the closed doors of the Magic Circle. Frowning, they approached the shop. They'd been in shortly after school to finish stocking the new café and sticking party notices on the door, but it had been a sunny day. No need for light.

Apprehensively, Fabian unlocked the door and pushed down the handle. "Maybe we left one on last—"

He stopped and stared, inadvertently blocking Lucille's entry. When she managed to squeeze past him enough to throw a look into the store, she froze just like him.

In the middle of the Magic Circle, just above the table of tarot cards and new book arrivals, floated a giant glowing orb. Light dropped from it like liquid, splattering the wood and paper beneath it. Black sooty stains spoke of where they'd landed before, as if the light had burned right through everything.

The long shelf on the left was half covered in a thorny bush. Something moved behind the thick vines. A mouse or rat, or something worse.

A creek of clear water flowed across the counter and created a waterfall in front of it. A puddle was forming, already warping the floorboards.

Something exploded to their right. Lucille and Fabian startled, expecting an attack, but only found a giant mushroom emitting a huge cloud of purple smoke.

Fabian's voice hitched in his throat. "What the hell is going on here?"

It took the others half an hour to join them in the Magic Circle. Fabian had drawn himself thick garden gloves with his feather and was attacking the bush rooted to the bookshelf, while Lucille had found a bucket for the water from the counter and was starting to clean up the puddle. They'd also removed the tarot cards and books and put a bucket on the table to catch the orb's droplets, which were now forming bright red little pearls instead.

"What did Lu do now?" Jan joked.

Lucille considered throwing her wet and dirty rag at him. The only reason she didn't was that her throw would probably fall short and embarrass her. "It's not *my* fault." So far, they'd been unable to detect any source for the wild magic in the shop.

Fabian was at the end of his wits and in full whiny-mode. "The whole shop is ruined. My mum will kill me."

"We can fix this," Samantha promised, but when she took a step deeper into the store, her right foot sank into the wood.

Before she could stumble and fall, Matt caught her. "Oops." He helped her sit down, but even with him pulling, her foot wouldn't come free.

"Uhm. I suppose these are usually the non-floating variety?" Rachel asked, pointing to a row of very well-behaved candles that floated just under the ceiling.

Meanwhile, Jan regarded the group of mushrooms in the corner.

"Don't get too close," Lucille warned him, but it was too late. One of the mushrooms exploded and covered Jan in purple spores.

"Ouch!" Matt cried out. "Something bit me." He had his hand in the wood, now just as stuck as Samantha.

Samantha shuddered, suddenly breathing in short shallow bursts. "There's something alive in here." Despite her apprehension, she moved her fingers in a quick weave.

"With sharp teeth?" Matt grumbled.

"Try lifting your hand again."

The floor seemed to be soft enough again for Matt to retrieve his hand and Samantha to pull out her foot. On the tip of her shoe sat a hornet-sized grey creature with spiderweb-like wings. Without thinking twice, Matt slapped the thing and flattened it on Samantha's shoe. When he raised his hand, grey slime covered it.

Lucille retched, imagining her own hand stuck in it. The floor, however, seemed to be firm enough again to stand on it.

Before they could discuss the creature, Fabian managed to tear the vines from the shelf with such aplomb that he fell flat to the ground, half-buried under books. Three more creatures flew over his head and relocated to the shelf on the other side. Seconds later, colourful flowers bloomed there.

"What is this?" Lucille asked, suddenly feeling weak.

Samantha caught her eyes. "No idea, but there has to be a nest of them."

It took them several hours to hunt down all the creatures and clean up the magical mess they'd left behind. When the botanic additions had been composted, the water had been soaked up, and the stock had been returned to its proper location, all six of them plopped down on the ground, exhausted.

"There is no nest," Jan declared. He pointed at the bucket of grey creatures, half of them more slime than bodies. "They're all dead."

"There's definitely a nest," Samantha said. Despite her exhaustion, she had surrounded herself with books and was doing her research thing. Apparently, she'd found success quickly.

The page she'd opened showed sketches of similar creatures, and one of a pipe-like object made of spiderwebs.

"I'm pretty sure that we're dealing with chaos imps. And these only occur close to their nest. We can kill as many as we like, there will always be new ones," Samantha explained, "unless we find and destroy the nest."

Next to Lucille, Fabian moaned. "Why? Why now? Why the Magic Circle? My mum's already overwhelmed enough without monsters taking over her store."

Now that Lucille thought about it, Caroline had stumbled two days ago. What if her foot had caught in the floorboards just like Samantha's before.

"I can stay tonight and keep searching," Rachel offered. "It beats listening to my mother and Balthasar next door."

Everyone grimaced at the reminder.

"Rachel's right," Samantha said. "As long as we haven't found the nest, we need to stay vigilant. Leaving the Magic Circle alone for twenty-four hours will just set us back right where we started." Fabian whimpered. "We need to make a plan and take shifts."

"What about school?" Jan asked. "You guys—" He stopped when everyone stared at him. With a true martyr grimace, he asked, "Really?"

"You've just pointed it out yourself," Lucille said smugly. "Thanks for volunteering for all the day shifts."

Jan glowered at her. "I suppose I won't get paid for it."

"Actually," Lucille said in a voice that caused Fabian to look up with sudden apprehension. "Why don't we let Jan run the Magic Circle while he's out of a job?"

Fabian's startled expression only grew worse. "You want Jan to run my mum's business?"

"I'm right here, man." Jan sounded insulted, which in Lucille's opinion meant he was no longer opposed to the idea.

"We can't afford an employee," Fabian said categorically.

"Not if the Magic Circle stays closed," Lucille said pointedly. "It doesn't have to be much."

"Again, right here!" Jan complained.

Lucille waved him off. "It's not a real job." Before Fabian protested, she hushed him, increasingly aggravated. "Of course, it's a real job for your mum. I'm saying that Jan's not applying, and there's no proper contract. He's just helping out, just as you've helped out countless times before. I mean, if it's such a problem, we'll just go back to plain store sitting, but I think it'd be a waste of the Magic Circle's potential if we kept it closed while we're sitting inside."

"And squashing imps," Samantha said softly. "It's not exactly safe to open the store to the public while we struggle to locate the chaos imp nest."

"They're not dangerous," Lucille argued.

Matt raised his perfectly healed finger. "Their teeth beg to differ."

Frustrated, Lucille shot to her feet and stomped her foot. "I'm not the one being ridiculous here!" Agitated, she gesticulated each pause and full stop in her explanation. "We've got a store that's doing nothing but accruing costs. We've got a friend who's doing nothing but wasting his time, and who could really use both money and experience. And we've got a big party that's supposed to celebrate the magic of this place. The chaos imps are not a bug, they're a feature."

Everyone stared at her, as if she'd gone mad.

"Guys, this is *Greenvalley*. The whole town thrives on magic tourism. This store is part of it. So what if a couple of customers come across something truly wondrous? It'll just add to the entire atmosphere. There'll be rumours and there'll be excitement. People will come to see the magic in action. We can work this to our benefit. It's not that hard."

She glared at Fabian, but he was still unconvinced. "I don't know."

"I don't care," Matt said, sounding tired.

Samantha sighed. "We'll have to find a solution to keep the imps in check to guarantee it's safe. And of course, find the nest, but then, yes, I think it could work."

"Thank you," Lucille said pointedly. Since Rachel only shrugged, she turned to Jan. "Do you think you've got it in you to be a responsible adult for once?"

Next to her, Fabian winced, clearly uncomfortable with the idea of letting Jan loose on the Magic Circle.

Jan, however, returned her glare with one just as sharp. "If I don't get fired again for saving lives, I'll do just fine."

"Then it's decided."

"Well, no," Fabian muttered. "But I'll ask my mum if she'd be happy with an arrangement like that."

In her fervour, Lucille had almost forgotten that the store didn't actually belong to them but to Caroline. She sat down, properly chastised. "Of course. I hope it doesn't stress her out too much. I just want to help."

Fabian reached over to grab her hand and squeezed it gently. "I know."

# Rachel

In the end, the group decided on four shifts to work around their individual schedules. Lucille and Fabian were inseparable these days, and Jan and Matt were both confident they could handle the imps alone. Meanwhile, Rachel and Samantha were taking the first night shift, giving Samantha an excuse to brew a potion in the café. According to her books, it would take care of the little bursts of chaotic magic with one simple application.

In the meantime, Rachel wandered the dark shelves, on the lookout for more imps or hints where their nest could be. Neither task could fully occupy her brain. Instead, her thoughts always returned to the demon in her house.

The plan with Matt had completely backfired. Balthasar walked around the house as if he owned the place, while Matt had run away with his tail between his legs. Rachel should've been deeply afraid for her life. Instead, she was annoyed. Balthasar seemed to be more interested in what was between her mother's legs than he was in killing her.

While the memory of hearing her mother have sex with Matt's brother made Rachel shudder, it also turned her thoughts towards the current demon family issue. A year ago, she would've had no doubts that Matt was perfectly suited to replace his mother. Now, things had changed. And the one who'd changed them was currently stuck with her in this room.

"Were you aware that Matt hasn't had sex in over three months?"

As suspected, Samantha stared at her, outraged. "Do I look like I care?" She shook herself out of the shock and returned her focus on the potion. "Why is he telling you such things?"

"It came up…" Samantha was right. Rachel shouldn't even know such an intimate fact about their friend. But with Balthasar hanging around her house, she couldn't stop thinking about it. "I'm just so used to him flirting with everyone constantly that it's weird he stopped."

"Maybe, he's just through with Greenvalley," Samantha remarked offhandedly.

While that was a possible explanation, Rachel knew from her dreams that it wasn't the issue at hand. "I don't think so."

Samantha snorted coldly. "Do you think we need to worry about him?" It didn't sound half as biting as she probably intended.

"Only if we want him to be the next Archdemon of Lust."

"Oh, please no."

Curious, Rachel turned a corner to observe Samantha more keenly. Her friend was stirring her cauldron a little too agitated. "You don't want him to ascend?"

Samantha noticed her stare and answered it with a glare. "That would complicate things immensely, wouldn't it?"

"Oh, I see." Slowly, Rachel walked over. "This is just practical concern."

"What else would it be?" Samantha sounded tired.

Rachel wondered how she could breach the idea that Matt was abstaining from sex because it didn't offer the distraction it once had. That his yearning for a particular person had overtaken everything. Lucille would totally do it, but Rachel usually had better sense. She sighed.

"Balthasar thinks he's unsuited to the job if he keeps forgoing sex."

A little tense, Samantha muttered, "Probably a reasonable concern."

"I guess so." Rachel pursed her lips, slightly frustrated with the apparent lack of care in Samantha's voice. The others might not see it yet, because Samantha was doing such a fabulous job of lying to herself, but those lies didn't last in the dreamworld. Despite her better sense, Samantha cared for Matt.

And now she'd become the one who was distracting herself.

"I saw you with Cian."

Confronted with the statement, Samantha almost dropped her ladle in the cauldron. "You what?"

Rachel groaned at the little act. "You weren't exactly inconspicuous this morning at the lockers. Are you two a couple?"

"No," Samantha said instantly, but at last, she dropped the act. "Not really. We're more like friends with benefits."

Rachel scowled. "Was that his idea?" It wouldn't have ever crossed her mind that Samantha could date one of the Elite Clique guys. Too much danger was lurking in that direction, and by the sounds of it, Cian was using her.

"No, it's not him," Samantha rushed to say. "It was my idea. Cian is in love with me." She made love sound as if it was as foreign a concept to her as it was to demons. "If it were up to him, he'd shout it from the rooftops and into Cheryl's face. But I'm not ready to deal with the consequences. I don't want Matt to know about it."

"Because you don't care about him," Rachel couldn't help but say.

Samantha glared at her. "You know exactly why."

Now that she said it, Rachel was only annoyed with herself. There was a very real reason why Samantha wouldn't want the murderer of her last boyfriend to know about her new relationship. What Matt had done to Daniel might have been the result of a bigger power than himself, but jealousy had ruled his hand that night. And jealousy still ruled him whenever Samantha showed an inkling of interest in another—or in this case, Cian showed in interest in *her*.

"Well, if it's okay with you, and we don't have to hang out with Cheryl and her cronies, I'm happy for you. He seems to be a... nice guy." There was this German saying that nice was the little sister of shit, and in a way, Rachel felt that way. She found Cian incredibly boring. She thought about searching out his dreams and would've rather counted the dust grains on the Magic Circle shelves, but maybe he was great in bed or something else Rachel cared little about.

"Thanks," Samantha said with a small, slightly pained smile.

Rachel sighed, resolving herself to make more of an effort. "Just keep your distance at school if you don't want Matt to see you."

She hadn't intended it, but the pain in Samantha's smile etched deeper. "Thanks for the tip." Samantha shuddered and returned her attention to the potion. Clearly over the topic, she asked, "Is Balthasar truly living with you?"

"I have no idea what he's doing during the day, but apparently, he likes my mother." The thought that anyone could like Annette well enough to stick around for longer than a date or two, weirded Rachel out. She couldn't see her mother's appeal in the slightest.

"Strange."

"Oh yes. Very strange." Eager to move on herself, Rachel asked, "How's the potion?"

Samantha glanced at it, as if she was seeing it for the first time. With a hint of surprise she said, "Done." She shook herself out of the weird trance. "Now all we need is one of those little imps."

Rachel turned to check the room. A rainbow was spanning the distance between the books and the tarot cards. "How about that one?"

Satisfied, Samantha took her ladle and carefully snuck up on the rainbow. With her finger, she snipped some potion liquid at the rainbow. Within seconds, the rainbow unravelled. "Perfect. This should make the shifts a whole lot easier."

The potion worked splendidly. The outbursts of chaos became discretely manageable once Samantha had filled the potion into spray bottles. And one spray from it usually took care of the chaos. A more intense spray even subdued the imps themselves.

But all they were doing was fighting the symptoms. The cause—the imps' nest—remained hidden.

In the meantime, Lucille, Samantha, and Fabian prepped the Magic Circle for the big party. Flyers popped up all around town and school, the phone never stood still, and decorations went up. And all the while, Jan wasn't doing too bad of a job of keeping the actual shop running.

While her friends were busy with the Magic Circle, Rachel was coming to terms with the strange new situation at home. Balthasar wasn't going anywhere, but he was surprisingly civil about the whole thing. If one ignored the frequent sexual escapades.

At the beginning of the week, all of Rachel's nerves had been taut to the max whenever she found herself in a room with him. When he hadn't murdered or assaulted her by the end of the week, she'd begun to relax around him. Unlike Caspar, Balthasar wasn't a wild animal ruled by rage and blood thirst. Instead, he was refined, charming, and a surprisingly good conversationalist.

On top of that, he had the most interesting effect on Rachel's mother. Somehow, Annette had begun to come home earlier. She cooked, and while she didn't abstain from her beloved wine, it was now a glass at dinner and perhaps one after, and not half the bottle before she was even through the door. And while her attention was often captured by Balthasar, she also showed more interest in Rachel.

"So, what do you do with maths?" Balthasar asked after inquiring what Rachel enjoyed most at school. It wasn't the usual dumbfounded question people so often asked when told someone could possibly entertain the idea of studying maths, but rather genuine interest.

Rachel assumed there wasn't a lot of need for complex maths in Hell, though some people might argue that was where maths truly belonged. "It's the basis of a lot of applications nowadays," she said, traipsing around using the words *"human"* or *"magic"*. "Physicists use it to make projections and explain what they observed. There's a ton of maths involved in space exploration, and of course computing, though I'm not particularly interested in that part."

"Rachel's father is a maths professor. He makes a nice amount of money," Annette added, as if money was the only reason people should choose to pick up a profession.

With a little eye-roll, Rachel quickly glossed over it. "If I'm being completely honest, I don't exactly care about the practical application of it. Other people can worry about that. I'm more interested in doing maths. I like how logical it is. The patterns and rules. Everything in it makes sense."

"Huh." Balthasar sounded surprised. "I would've thought you were more of a dreamer?"

"What? Rachel?" her mother intercepted. "She's the most sensible person, I know." It didn't sound derisive as usual, but instead as if she was in awe of Rachel.

Slightly confused, Rachel struggled to think of a straight answer for Balthasar. It pleased her somehow that he'd picked up on her dreaming ability despite her staying far away from *his* dreams. She had absolutely no illusions that his words had been coincidence.

"Dreams aren't quite as chaotic as they seem. Like, for example, everything we dream about comes from deep within us. It might be a wild mix of different impressions and memories, but it's not something completely new. It's just a whole lot more complex than maths."

"A challenge then," Balthasar mused, toasting her with his wine glass.

Rachel felt chuffed he seemed to recognise her, if not as his equal than as someone worthy to waste his time on—even without sex. She could sense that Balthasar valued intellect, and somehow, she'd passed.

"I don't know how you do it," Annette said, shaking her head. She laughed softly, "But maybe it *is* the maths. I never had a head for that, and hence, I'm completely lost in my dreams."

For a moment, Rachel's heart went out to her. She'd seen Annette's fractured dreams. The shards of her life scattered around her. If only those shards didn't cut Rachel so badly.

"You dream too?" Balthasar asked, quickly glancing at Rachel for confirmation.

"I used to," Annette answered with a wistful smile. "But Rachel is much better at it. Her dreams aren't tainted by life yet." She reached over the table. "And here's to hoping they never will."

Rachel stared at her mother's hand as if it was a strange insect. She wasn't sure how much she could trust this new version of her mother. It was at the same time strange and yet familiar.

"Oh, I'm sure Rachel will surpass all our expectations." There was a glitter in Balthasar's eyes that reminded Rachel sharply of the lethal predator he was.

Annette laughed nervously, but then her features smoothed with an unfamiliar sense of confidence. She took back her ignored hand and smiled warmly at Rachel. "I already know she will. Rachel will go places. I'm sure of that."

A strange warmth spread within Rachel. A warmth she didn't truly know how to trust, but a warmth nonetheless.

# Fabian

"Mum?"

Fabian stood at the door to his parents' bedroom, leaning his head against the frame as he listened for the reply. Merle slunk around his legs, mewling for attention, but he couldn't allow himself to be distracted by the needy cat.

He had his backpack packed with the last things for the festival. It was all prepared and ready to go. All they needed was the woman of the hour, but there was nothing but silence from the room.

"Mum? We've got to go."

When he still didn't get a reply, Fabian closed his eyes against the wave of sadness that seemed to overwhelm him. This wasn't like his mum. Caroline Bendtfeld rarely missed a day of work and always gave a hundred per cent, or more often, one-hundred-and-fifty per cent.

Which was precisely what had landed her in this predicament, according to the doctor.

Fabian sighed, then he set down his backpack and gave Merle a quick stroke to reassure himself. "Mum?" he asked yet again, but this time, he opened the door and put his head in.

She was awake, and yet far, far away. The sight of his mother lying motionless in her bed, staring at the cupboard next to it, as if she was counting each grain in the wood, made him swallow heavily.

"Why aren't you dressed yet?" he asked, trying his best to sound upbeat. "We have to go."

His mum blinked and took a deep breath, as if she had to physically pull herself out of whatever trance had captured her. "I can't."

Fabian struggled to keep his smile, if it even resembled a smile. "What do you mean? It's your party."

"Didn't you take care of everything?"

"Sure, but this party is for you. We're celebrating *you*." His voice faltered around the words, and he had to swallow again. "It's your achievement."

A wan smile crossed his mother's face. "You go ahead. I'll might come a little later."

Instantly, Fabian shook his head and crossed his arms. "I'm not going without you." With a sigh, he let go of his stubborn stance and sat down on the edge of the bed instead. "I don't get it," he admitted. "This is the Magic Circle."

His mum sighed greatly. "You're right." But she still didn't move.

Fabian felt his throat swell. Swallowing hurt now. "Mum?"

"I just can't," she whispered.

"What?" It came out more forceful than he'd intended.

Her eyes shimmered slightly. "Get up. Get dressed. Walk over there... I just..."

"Mum, please," he begged. "Just tell me. Make me understand." He didn't care that he sounded like a little child. This was his mum. "I'm scared."

A tear rolled down her cheek, and he felt awful about it. "I don't know what to say."

"Just say something," Fabian whispered.

"Can you imagine that even that seems nearly impossible right now?" She tried to smile, but the expression didn't manage to stick.

Fabian closed his eyes for a moment, allowing the hovering fears to crawl a little closer. Until now, he'd managed to tell himself that all his mother needed was a little help and a little rest. But this didn't seem so little anymore.

"You won't be back at the shop for a while, right?" he said at last.

His mother winced slightly. "How's Jan doing?"

"Okay." Fabian shrugged. He hadn't paid too much attention to Jan's performance. So far, he'd neither stolen from the cash register nor burned down the store. It was good enough for Fabian. All he cared about right now was his mum. "This is more than a little rest, isn't it?"

She sighed heavily. "It looks like proper burnout."

Burnout. The word had little true meaning to Fabian. He'd used it before in a lighthearted warning or as a joke about Samantha, despite knowing it was a real affliction. A disease that somehow rendered his beautiful, supporting mother into this lethargic woman.

"It was probably too much stress in the last few months," she explained softly.

Fabian found himself nodding. "Because of Dad and the workshop."

"Yes."

Somehow saying it out loud had given his mother enough relief to sit up in bed. Gently, she patted the space next to her. Obligingly, Fabian crawled onto the bed and sat down next to her.

She took his hand and put her head on his shoulders. "I always forget how big you've become," she mused.

When he didn't answer, she took a deep breath. "I struggle with admitting it, but the last few months have been very hard for me. Helping your dad isn't a problem in itself—I enjoy the work—but all the other things need to be done as well. And the Magic Circle. You know how much I love my work, but lately it all feels so senseless," she admitted, to Fabian's horror. "I'm on my feet all day long, then do all the other stuff at night, and all of that for a margin that's not much better than a regular student job."

"I didn't know it was that bad." Fabian had never thought about how much the Magic Circle actually made. It had been a fixture in his life for as long as he could remember.

His mother shrugged. "I managed to stay afloat and pay all the costs over the years. It's never been about the profit, you know? The Magic Circle is my passion, and it's so vital for the Harzer witches. I rarely take more for the real ingredients than I paid for. If at all. I mean, Elda and Sam can take whatever they need." Quickly, she added, "And I don't want money from them, especially not Sam when she uses it to keep all the monsters away, like those chaos imps you've been trying to hide from me."

"Sorry." Fabian didn't even think of denying it.

"I know, darling." She patted his hand and continued, "And Elda supplies me from her own garden. So, I couldn't possibly charge her in return." She shook her head and blinked a couple of times, trying to keep the tears at bay. "I feel like I'm stuck. As if I'm little crazy Caro again, who'll never amount to anything real, just like my sisters always said."

"Mum!" Fabian protested. "The Magic Circle is amazing. *You* are amazing and..." He was completely lost for words. Samantha might have known how to fix this, but he felt completely helpless. "What should we do now?"

"I don't know." His mum shrugged again, equally helpless. "My thoughts are circling endlessly. There's no pause, no solution. Apart from throwing it all away and trying to get a fixed position. It might not be fulfilling, but even part-time would get us more money, and I could help your father."

The thought made Fabian's stomach turn. It didn't sound like a solution, it sounded like giving up. "But you love the Magic Circle."

"Do I?" she asked in such a tiny voice, his heart broke into a thousand pieces.

How many times had he wished his mother didn't have a such a weird and ridiculous job over the last five years? Truth be told, however, without it, she just wasn't his mum. Especially now that he knew she was a proper witch and played such a vital part in the community.

Overcome with sadness at the prospect of a future without the Magic Circle, Fabian put his head on hers. His phone vibrated, but he ignored it for his mother's benefit. If all he could do was be there for her, that's what he was going to do.

He would keep her dream alive until she was ready to dream again.

# Jan

The party was about to start and the man of the hour was nowhere to be seen. Jan and the others busied themselves getting the shop ready for a massive sale, while outside, the barbecue was fired up and soft music played. As throughout the entire week, their progress was constantly hampered by chaotic outbursts.

Such as the giant, yellow chicken walking into the store.

"Can you take care of it, Jan?" Lu begged. "Please."

Jan groaned. In his opinion he'd already taken care of more than enough things this week. Nonetheless, he grabbed the nearest spray bottle and began to attack the chicken with it.

Squeaking, it raised a wing. "Stop that."

"Robert?" Jan stared at the chicken in disbelief, his brain failing to compute what was happening.

Samantha was approaching them, carrying a box of flyers. "Oh, hey, Robert. You're here early."

"Sam!" Jan barked. "You can't just pretend you're not seeing the whole chicken thing." Had he worked so much this week that he was seeing things?

She gave him a flat stare. "I can see the chicken, and I know it's Robert in a costume. Cian talked him into walking around the neighbourhood to pass out flyers and get more people to come."

"As a chicken?" Someone had to explain to Jan what chickens had to do with magic.

"Look, I don't get it either," Samantha admitted. She sounded as if she'd given up caring a long time ago.

A muffled voice came from the chicken, babbling about some costume mix-up or whatever.

"Bro, open that beak when you speak," Jan snapped.

The chicken seemed to teeter on its balance as it raised both wings in an exhaustive effort to remove the headpiece. Underneath, sweaty, red-faced Robert appeared.

"It's from a summer job," he explained. "I was working for a birthday party company, but they went broke and so I was allowed to keep the costume in lieu of payment."

Jan was still convinced they were all messing with him. "Why would you want to keep a chicken costume?"

"Because it's cute?" Robert asked instead of answering. Then he mumbled something that sounded suspiciously like, "Anne likes it."

Before Jan could worry about his sister's mental state for liking both Robert *and* a chicken costume, Samantha stepped in and handed Robert the box of flyers. "Thanks for doing this. If you run out, call me, and I'll print some more."

"Will do." Robert put his head back on and took the box.

Once he'd left, Jan turned to her. "Are we not going to talk about how we're promoting the Magic Circle with a *chicken?*"

"I don't have time for that." Samantha already turned away and called out to Lu, who was polishing the café counter. "Where's Fabian?"

"Great question," Lu called over, sounding equally stressed. "Next?"

Jan stared at her. "Don't we need him?"

"I'm sure he'll be here at some point," Samantha said, already moving on. "I'll run the café and keep an eye on the reserve potion. Lucille is taking over the shop. Matt..." She stared at the aforementioned boy who was currently standing around. "You're gonna be at the entrance, charming people out of a donation."

Matt raised his eyebrow, looking rather pleased with himself. "Sure will."

"Rachel will be here later," Samantha continued, "She's keeping an eye on Balthasar. That leaves..." She turned around to face Jan.

"Me," he offered with a half-grin.

Samantha nodded hectically. "You're our floater. Start by helping Matt and then move around to help where needed."

"Sounds riveting." While he thought about something to say that wouldn't insult Samantha's efforts, she'd already moved on, rushing to address some other last-minute task.

Jan shrugged and strolled outside. The gate didn't need a warden yet, but some of the stalls might need some help, and he figured some networking couldn't hurt if one of them was looking for an assistant.

At around one in the afternoon, Jan joined Matt at the entrance and leaned against the outside wall of the Magic Circle, half-closing his eyes again the sun. Next to him, Matt looked as handsome as always in a cream-coloured shirt that formed a light contrast to his darker, bronze skin. His blond hair was fashionably tousled, and the sunglasses he wore were pushed up on his head so nothing would distract from his pretty eyes.

Jan watched as Matt welcomed the first couple of guests with a wide smile and smooth talk. Every single one of them left money in the box.

"It's not fair," he grumbled.

Matt half-turned to him. "What's not fair? That you're just standing there, doing nothing?"

"While you what? Dazzle everyone out of their money?"

"Isn't that what I'm supposed to do?"

Jan snorted at his obliviousness. "If I'd been standing there, we'd be done counting in a second. I need a job, and people just hand you their money."

"It's for a good cause."

Jan didn't bother to reply because he could see his sister and his girlfriend approaching. Matt did his spiel and both girls parted with some of their pocket money as well as a whole lot of giggles. It took Meg nearly a minute to notice Jan standing right there.

"Oh, hey," she said, then came over for a kiss. "How's it going?"

He glanced at the party. This early, not much was happening. The bratwurst guy wasn't ready yet and there were too few people to mingle or dance. The ones who'd arrived were mostly strolling through the Magic Circle. "Great. What are you doing here?" Jan could think of many things that were more exciting than this neighbourhood party. Besides, Meg was supposed to rest.

As a reply, Anne giggled, blushing slightly. "We were invited by a cute chicken," she squealed.

Jan withstood the urge to rub his forehead in annoyance. "Pretty ridiculous, isn't it?"

Meg slapped his arm, while Anne just swooned a little. "I think it's adorable."

"Sure, let's go with childishly adorable."

"Ugh." Meg groaned before putting her arm around Anne and leaning against her slightly. "Don't listen to him. He thinks anything that isn't strong and tough is somehow less manly. Robert *is* sweet."

Jan considered shouting after them but couldn't be bothered on Robert's behalf. If his little sister wanted to date a loser, that was her problem.

Instead, he turned back around, noting that, for once, Lu's mother and brother had made it. Perhaps having an actual child again made them feel like they needed to put in a bit more effort and do performative outings, and such shit. It came as no surprise to Jan that Linda de Cerque put a generous donation into Matt's box. He didn't see it properly, but it was more than one bill.

As soon as they were gone, Jan leaned over Matt's shoulder. "How much did you swindle out of her?"

"Do you want me to count now?" Matt asked, annoyed. Since new people had arrived, he didn't actually follow through.

His megawatt smile failed him, though, when the next guests were Rachel, Annette, and Balthasar.

"Welcome!" Jan said, since Matt seemed to have forgotten what his job was.

"Oh." Annette looked at the store with undue excitement. "I never knew this enchanting little shop existed. Do you go here all the time?" she asked her daughter.

Rachel gave her a non-committal, "Mmmh."

"I need to check this out." She pulled on Balthasar's hand. "Are you coming?"

"Sure…" But before he did, he put a coin into Matt's box. "For your piteous look."

Matt glowered at Balthasar's back when he followed Annette into the store. "It's high time he leaves," he growled.

"I don't know. I kind of like him," Rachel admitted.

Both Matt and Jan stared at her. "You like Matt's demon brother?" Jan asked in disbelief.

She shrugged dejectedly. "I'm not sure I like specifically *him*, but I like what he does to my mum."

Matt made the most hilarious face, and Jan both felt sorry for him and laughed his head off. At least his sister didn't date demons.

Rachel clicked her tongue. "Take your minds out of the gutter. Since she's been dating him, my mother is much more balanced. She's home more often and she takes an interest in what I do." With a big dose of irony, she added, "We're almost like a real family."

Jan spluttered. "Come again?"

Next to him, Matt frowned heavily. "I'm going to pretend you didn't just say that."

Rachel looked as if she'd woken from a dream. Horrified, she shuddered. "Oh, yes. He needs to go. As quick as possible."

Finally, something they agreed on. Jan had no idea what Balthasar was planning, but whatever it was, it couldn't be good. It was like an itch he couldn't scratch. Something was going to happen. And judging by how Matt's demon family usually operated, it was going to be something big.

# Samantha

As far as Samantha could see, the party was going well. Fabian and Caroline still hadn't showed, but everyone else had. Both the store and outside area was full of people, while she rarely had a chance to breathe in the café. Everyone wanted the magical brews she'd come up with: *Charming Coffee with a Splash of Optimism* or *Good Mood Tea*. The only worry was the frequent burst of chaos magic, which would make mushrooms grow in the window or objects float through the showroom. But Samantha had the feeling everyone just thought they were a bunch of very clever tricks, and she was happy to keep that belief alive, frequently joking about it.

She was just washing returned cups to reuse when Cian came by.

"Hey, little witch."

Laughing, she continued her work but asked, "How do you like it?"

"Pretty good for a neighbourhood party. I'm surprised so many came."

"Yes!" Surprised and pretty chuffed about it, Samantha put the cups away and beamed at him. "Thanks to you." And Robert.

Modest as always, Cian shrugged, "I just told a few people." He put his elbows on the counter and leaned forward with the big lazy grin she'd come to enjoy. "So, can I kidnap at you some point?"

Samantha mirrored his pose, putting herself into kiss-likely territory. "I'm afraid the answer is no." She laughed when he hit his chest with the flat of his hand and dramatically grimaced. "I know." Getting kidnapped by Cian sounded incredibly tempting. If it wasn't Caroline's shop, or if Caroline and Fabian were actually here, she would've gone with him. They could've gone for a little walk that would've ended at his place or hers, and then...

Her cheeks warmed, and Cian's grin deepened, his eyes growing darker with desire. "Next week will be better," Samantha promised, then quickly averted her gaze to glance at the shop. "You can see how full it is, and then all the chaotic magic." That was another reason why she couldn't abandon ship.

"You told me about that. So, you still haven't found the nest then?"

She shook her head. They'd searched the Magic Circle from top to bottom three times without any luck, and any location spells only told them one thing: the nest was here.

A customer came in and studied the list of drinks. Cian pulled away from the counter. "Alright. I'll leave you to your work, but call me as soon as you get off."

"I will," she promised before turning her attention to the customer. "What would you like?"

"The *Dream Well* tea sounds nice."

Samantha smiled. "Absolutely. That's two-fifty, please."

Once he'd paid, Samantha turned to the water boiler and froze. The water inside was bubbling, as if it was already hot. It was also poisonous green.

"Uhm, I'll have to put on a new pot of water. If you don't mind waiting, I'll bring it outside once it's ready."

The customer nodded and left. Samantha grabbed the spray bottle hidden under the counter, but before she could address the issue, the door opened again.

Ani walked in, a haughty look on her face, and Samantha's stomach turned. There was no good reason for Ani to be at a party for the Magic Circle much less approach her.

"This a silly little party you've got here, Sammy." Ani used her old childhood nickname with the usual dose of condescension. It was the reason Samantha had come to hate it. "I hope you don't think everyone's here because you've suddenly found popularity. We're only hanging around because there's nothing else to do in this backwater town."

Every single word was carefully placed to hurt, and all Samantha could do was bear the insults and turn the other cheek. "What would you like to drink?"

Ani pretended to look at the menu but really just took in the whole set-up. "Do you sell normal stuff or only this vomit-inducing green dishwater?" Her gaze stuck on the outburst of chaos magic behind Samantha.

She tried to block her view and offered to bring her a glass of water instead.

"Oh, yes, please," Ani said patronisingly. Then she smiled like a shark would smile at its prey. "Oh, and one *Stay Away from Cian*, please."

There it was, the true reason why Ani was here. Thanks to Alan's big mouth, the Elite Clique knew all about their little affair. And of course, they'd come to ruin it, just as Samantha knew they would. "We're out of that unfortunately," she managed to say as she filled a glass with water.

Ani wasn't used to her talking back, so she huffed in an affected manner. "Oh, you seem to be hard of hearing. The party, I assume." Enunciating every word, as if Samantha was deaf, she said, "We don't want you. Nobody wants you."

The words didn't sting as much as they used to. Mostly, because Samantha knew they were wrong. She had a big group of friends now and a relationship other than her childhood best friend. And someone who wanted her a little too much. In a way, two people did. "Did you explain that to Cian, too?"

"Oh, we will," Ani promised. "He's obviously lost his mind."

Annoyed, Samantha slammed down the glass on the counter. Some liquid sloshed over the top and pooled on the wood beneath. "Your water."

Ani ignored it. "Look. Cian seems to have a thing for nerds right now, but he'll quickly realise that there's a difference between a regular nerd and someone who's not quite right in the head like you. I mean look at you, selling silly *potions* like you did in kindergarten." She shook her head in fake amusement. "Cian deserves better, and he knows that."

"Like who? You?" Samantha asked, her voice annoyingly brittle. Though, she knew the words were poison, she hadn't built up enough immunity yet.

With a grimace, Ani faked a shudder. "Uh, no. Not everyone's desperate enough to climb into bed with her best friend."

Samantha tapped her fingers on the counter, looking for another customer coming to save her, but no one seemed interested in buying a coffee or tea right now.

"Face it. You're a nobody," Ani continued, enjoying herself immensely. "I bet once the news of the two of you breaks at school, people will be asking, who?" She laughed in an affected way, then said in a different pitch, "Oh, look, it's Cian and his weird girlfriend."

"You still owe me fifty cents," Samantha said in an attempt to make her go away.

Ani snorted. "I don't want your yucky tap water." Still, she threw a coin at Samantha. "You can keep the rest for your efforts."

"How gracious," Samantha muttered, her answer too quiet to be heard.

Fortunately, her torment appeared to be over, though. Ani turned and stepped right into a neon pink puddle. With a scream, she suddenly vanished.

Surprised, Samantha threw herself over the counter, knocking over the glass of water. It poured down onto a thumb-sized Ani, drenching her completely. The glass followed straight after.

"Ani!"

Instead of breaking on impact, it simply covered and locked her in.

Before Samantha could fully process what had happened, the door was pushed open, and Lucille stumbled in. Samantha held out a hand before she could step into the puddle herself. "Careful."

Lucille's gaze dropped to the neon pink, and she shuddered. Because of the milky bottom of the glass, she hadn't seen Ani yet. "We need more anti chaos potion. The imps are going absolutely crazy out there."

Wordlessly, Samantha handed her two more bottles. "I put on a new batch. Is everyone okay?"

"No." Lucille sighed. "I mean, no one's been hurt yet, but we need to send people home, or... There's a jungle behind the store. A grass *jungle*." Her voice got whiny. "And I haven't seen Pascal anywhere. Linda lost him."

"You go back outside, I'll take care of the potion." *And Ani,* she added silently.

Well, Ani could wait. Samantha slipped a piece of cardboard under the glass and put it behind the counter, ignoring the furious little person and how she banged on the glass. Then she removed the puddle and got rid of the green water.

A glance outside told her that Lucille hadn't lied. There were no screams, but a lot seemed to be going on at once. Bratwursts flew through the air, and something squawked.

With a sigh, she checked on her cauldron and started yet another batch.

# Matt

When Fabian finally showed at his own party, the chaos had completely taken over. Matt was so captivated by the sausages lining up on the counter and performing a weird line dance that he didn't even notice his arrival until Fabian cleared his throat.

"What's going on?"

Matt was about to explain when a series of explosions distracted him. Apparently, the soda bottles had all shaken themselves until the carbon burst the glass. At the same time, a chicken squawked. Lucille rushed over and sprayed Robert with potion. This time, it was well-appreciated.

"Well, uhm. The imps." Not his most eloquent explanation, but it would have to do.

Fabian looked typically pale. "Great."

Sudden loud music made them both flinch. Most of the guests startled, but then the high ratio of teenagers worked in their favour and dancing ensued.

"Where were you?" Matt asked.

But before Fabian could think of answering, Lucille had found them. "You're here. Finally."

"Sorry, I—"

"Pascal's gone! I can't find him anywhere." A cloud of glitter rose above the dancers. "Oh, damn it." And she rushed off again to attend to the chaos.

Fabian took a deep shuddering breath, clearly wishing he hadn't turned up when he did. "So, I take it we haven't found the nest yet?"

"Sorry."

But instead of whining as usual, Fabian just straightened his shoulders. "Very well, let's get those outbursts under control and find Pascal."

"I should probably find my brother before the chaos turns bloody," Matt mused.

The look Fabian threw him told Matt that he should've dealt with that much earlier.

Surprisingly, it wasn't hard to find Balthasar. He was leaning against the wall of the Magic Circle, looking highly amused by the obvious bursts of magic and chaos around him. When he saw Matt coming, his eyebrows rose, and his mouth twitched. "Tore yourself away from your post?"

Matt didn't deign him with an answer. Instead, he grabbed him by the elbow and dragged him behind the store where they would be out of sight from the party guests.

In the back, the grass had grown as high as the Magic Circle itself, creating a surreal landscape that made Matt think he was truly only ten centimetres tall. It only served to set him even more on edge. "When are you leaving?"

Balthasar feigned innocence. "Are you tired of me already?"

"I was tired of you on Monday."

"Ouch." With a mild smile, Balthasar put a hand on his heart, though he didn't look particularly wounded to Matt.

"If you hurt even a hair on Rachel's or her mother's head, I—" Matt broke off when Balthasar started laughing.

"Are you threatening me?"

It was the amusement that set Matt's nerves on edge. As if Balthasar thought he didn't have it in him to attack him. "Is that a surprise to you? Do you think Melaney only favours me because of my good looks?"

Balthasar gave him a long stare until Matt felt completely naked in the field. "That's pretty much the only argument I can get behind."

To Matt's great embarrassment, he blushed. And thus, he wasn't prepared for it when Balthasar grabbed him by the collar and slammed his back into the wall behind them.

Balthasar held his face so close to Matt's he could feel his hot breath on his skin. "Do you really think that you'd be a match for me and Caspar with your eighteen puny years of experience?"

Somehow, the switch to physical violence relaxed Matt. Despite Balthasar's words, he no longer felt outmatched. They were on his terrain now. "Maybe not alone," he mused, thinking back to how Caspar got himself banned. "But see, that's the good thing about hanging around humans. I'm not alone."

"Those children?" Balthasar smirked at him. "Look at them! They can't even handle a simple chaos imp nest. I have no idea why you even bother with such incompetent people."

Matt was about to defend his friends when it hit him. "Wait. Who told you about the chaos imps?"

Balthasar snorted. "Do you think they moved here on their own?"

"You!" Matt threw himself on his older brother and pulled him down with him.

They both flattened a bunch of thick grass blades underneath them. Matt was about to punch Balthasar when the other raised his hand for an energy attack. Reflexively, Matt jumped away. The energy tore through the grass instead, leaving behind a black swath of burned ground.

Suddenly, there was a little boy. *Pascal,* Matt thought as he noticed his huge eyes and pale skin. The energy had missed him by the width of a hair.

Balthasar smiled coldly and raised his hand. Black magic crackled around it. His eyes gleamed with intent, for once betraying the monster behind them.

Matt didn't hesitate and threw himself at Balthasar. He got a grip on his wrist and managed to turn it downward just moments before the energy was released. Soil splattered them and momentarily blinded Matt when it landed in his eyes. He had hardly registered the grainy impact when a knee landed in his stomach, and he was thrown to the ground.

His hands were grabbed and pushed into the ground over his head, Balthasar's weight on top of him. "The boy isn't even yours."

"Doesn't matter," Matt snapped. He blinked furiously, managing to dislodge enough soil to see his brother hovering on top of him.

Furious, he pulled up his legs and kicked Balthasar in the groin, before using the swing to roll himself to the side. He was barely up when Balthasar's fist connected with his chin and threw him down again.

This time, Matt didn't bother to try and get up. He just held onto Balthasar and peppered him with kicks, fists, and energy. His brother did the same as they rolled through the grass forest, somehow making it back onto the party grounds. There, Balthasar picked him up and threw him into the table with the sodas.

The table collapsed under Matt, and he could feel a couple of bottles break. Blindly, he grabbed one and threw it at his brother. In the corner of his eye, he noticed Pascal running into Lucille's arms, babbling about Balthasar and him.

Matt knew he had to get Balthasar away from here. Just like Caspar, his older brother didn't care who got hurt in the process. He might not hate humans, but their lives didn't matter to him, either.

Together, they crashed into the bratwurst stall. A pile of napkins dropped onto the grill, catching fire immediately.

Water followed almost instantly. It extinguished the flames before it slammed into the two of them. Fabian. Matt could only hope that Lucille was covering their tracks with illusions.

He escaped the onslaught of water and stumbled back towards the grass jungle. Balthasar had had the same idea, but Fabian's water became hard enough to bruise.

"Do you want to die?" Balthasar snarled.

The look in Fabian's eyes was murderous. "Do you?"

Horrified, Matt noticed the moment Balthasar's focus left him entirely and hit Fabian. The demon's hand was raised, but Fabian was quicker and directed the water straight at Balthasar's palm, forcing it down again.

Balthasar grunted. Then he jumped through space, grabbed Fabian's T-Shirt, and slammed him into the bratwurst stall.

Fabian gasped in pain, and the water vanished.

Matt knew he was going to be too late, but he ran anyway.

The air behind Balthasar flickered. Just as the demon was about to raise a hand, another's shot out and grabbed it. Matt skidded to a stop when he recognised Chay.

Balthasar turned his face agonisingly slowly and stared at Chay. Then his gaze wandered to where his skin met Chay's. "Enjoying the view?"

"Hardly." Only the tension in Chay's voice betrayed the agony he always felt when watching a person's life pass before him. Matt hoped, in Balthasar's case, there wasn't much left of it.

"Then let me finish this quickly, so we can talk."

Chay gave a sharp shake of his head. "I don't want you to kill him or any of the others."

"All of them?" Balthasar asked. A sly tone entered his voice when he repeated. "All *six* of them?"

Matt didn't dare to close his eyes as he felt the weight of Balthasar's revelation settle on his shoulders. If he hadn't known before, Chay's presence had confirmed it. They were doomed. Utterly doomed.

Chay nodded once, and to Matt's great surprise, Balthasar let Fabian go with a groan. Quickly, Matt moved to his side and steadied his friend, ready to protect him if Balthasar chose to kill them anyway.

But his brother only glanced at the two of them, then Lucille who still held Pascal, Jan who had his fists clenched, Rachel with her spray bottle, and Samantha who stood at the door to the café with a wild-eyed stare.

"I see." Balthasar snorted and turned back to Matt. "What do you want with Melaney, then?" When Matt only stared at him in confusion, Balthasar jerked his head upwards. "The nest is on the roof." And with that he turned and walked into the crowd, Chay on his heel.

Matt stared at their backs, still struggling to understand what had just come to pass. What did Balthasar know? And since when had Chay had such power over him? The habitual joy at seeing Chay again was severely marred by the fact that he and Balthasar seemed to have an understanding. One that eluded Matt.

"On the roof?" Fabian said, steel still in his voice. "Let's get a ladder."

# Rachel

With the location of the nest revealed to them, they quickly got the chaos under control. Samantha was brewing a new batch of potion in front of everyone, while Lucille sold spray bottles to the enthusiastic party goers who went around and sprayed everything they thought looked weird. They were all convinced that it was an amazing marketing gag.

Meanwhile, Matt and Fabian climbed the roof and seemingly extinguished the nest, which burst into a crackling and colourful display of fireworks, creating the perfect ending to the impromptu show. After that, Rachel and Jan had their hands full with moving stock as people stormed the shop and bought nearly everything.

"Got to hand it to Balthasar," Jan mused when the last customer had gone and they'd sat down to balance the till. "He made this party a huge success."

Leave it to Jan to appreciate a fight. Rachel rolled her eyes and left him at the counter to lock up.

She'd just reached the door when she noticed Samantha running up to Cian, Alan, and Shayna who were in the process of leaving.

"I need to kidnap Cian for a minute," Samantha announced, slightly out of breath, as she grabbed Cian's arm.

Cian immediately leaned into her direction. "Looks like I got no choice. Tell your dad to send a search party if I miss school on Monday," he joked with Alan.

His friend rolled his eyes so hard Rachel thought they'd get stuck in his head. Apparently, he knew everything about their secret relationship and didn't approve in the slightest.

Curious whether Samantha was really going to make out with Cian while they were all still around, Rachel followed her progress through the glass windows. Her luck was with her when the two of them entered the Magic Circle through the café door.

"And what's your plan now?" Cian asked, amused and curious at the same time.

Samantha pulled him behind the counter. "I've got someone for you."

Rachel crept closer until she'd reached the last shelf that separated the café space from the main show room. Samantha pulled a glass up and seemed to point at something. That something started talking in a high-pitched voice. It took Rachel a couple of moments to understand it.

"I promise you won't be able to put a single foot into school without being at our mercy," the tiny voice screamed. "We're going to end you. You'll be running home crying or throw yourself from the bridge."

"Ani?" Cian asked, his voice full of wonder.

Now Rachel recognised the voice as well, though the pitch was off. She still couldn't *see* Ani, only hear her.

"Cian?"

"What happened to her?" Cian asked Samantha.

Samantha looked down at the counter with a surprising amount of attitude. "Chaos magic. She stepped into an imp and was shrunk."

Rachel gasped. It was one thing for Samantha to keep up a secret relationship with Cian, quite another that he apparently knew all about magic now.

"Don't believe a word she said," the apparently tiny Ani screamed. "She bewitched me."

"Can you turn her back?" Cian asked, not hugely concerned.

"Sure," Samantha said and placed a big cake knife on the counter. Rachel couldn't help but snort when she heard Ani squeal. "You should know that Ani is concerned about you. You deserve someone better than me."

That sounded like Ani, but apparently it no longer applied to Cian, whose lips quirked upwards. "There's someone better than you?"

"Charmer," Samantha said with a delighted smile.

Meanwhile, Ani still screamed, "She'll ruin your reputation!"

Samantha casually dropped a couple of herbs around Ani. In the meantime, Cian took out his phone and took some pictures.

"What are you doing?" Ani asked, suddenly fearful.

"Making sure you keep your mouth shut and your nose out of my relationship. One word to Cheryl and these photos will be printed in the yearbook. I've got a direct line to the committee organiser, you know." Cian smiled at Samantha.

Ani was furious. "You've ruined him."

Rachel smiled to herself. Samantha had indeed totally ruined Cian for the Elite Clique as it seemed. She was starting to see the appeal.

"Me?" Samantha asked. She carefully picked up the knife. "When I'm such a nobody." She was clearly quoting some earlier words. "Shall we begin with the counter spell? Or should we leave things as they are, since I'm obviously just playing pretend as usual."

Ani's voice was like a mouse's. "Do you have to use a knife?"

Samantha laughed. "No. Not really." She put the knife down and grabbed Ani, who let out a high-pitched squeal. Then she placed her on the ground and flicked her fingers in a quick weave.

A moment later, Ani shot up to her proper size. Shaking, she wagged her finger at Samantha. "You'll pay for this."

"Great. I still have a couple of spells I always wanted to try on someone."

Ani paled. With a last squeal, she fled the shop, nearly running over Rachel. In her panic, she struggled with the key in the lock. When she finally managed to let herself out, Cian burst out laughing.

"That was quite impressive, little witch." He slung an arm around Samantha and pulled her close.

"I hope that'll keep her quiet for a bit," Samantha admitted, her voice devoid of previous confidence.

Cian tucked a lock of her hair behind her ear. Then he kissed her softly.

Rachel cleared her throat and stepped out from behind the shelf, as if she just appeared there. Instantly, the two of them separated. "If you really want to keep this secret, you need to be a lot more secretive about it." Then she allowed herself to smile. "That said, you dealt with Ani beautifully."

Too bad that method had little odds of success if Matt ever found out.

Rachel returned home, bone-tired. She'd attended a few neighbourhood parties in her lifetime but never organised one. Much less while fighting chaos imps. It wasn't an experience she was particularly keen to repeat.

After the fight at the party, she was a bit apprehensive about returning home. Over the last few days, she'd somehow managed to tune out that Balthasar was an actual demon. He'd acted too civilised, too refined. They'd had surprisingly good chats, and he'd treated her mother and her with kindness. But the mask had slipped tonight. Behind it all, he was just as dangerous as Caspar had been. Perhaps even more so.

Would he wait for her at home and continue his farce, or would he finally snap and kill her in her sleep? Would he threaten her mother? Only Chay's sudden appearance had stopped him from killing Fabian. Who would stop him from killing her?

Her teeth dug into her bottom lip as Rachel opened the front door. Only a single light was burning in the living room. She listened hard for the sounds, bracing herself against the inevitable sex noise. But there was nothing. No talking, no kissing, nothing but a soft snivelling.

"Mum?" Worried, Rachel stepped into the door frame.

As so often, she found her mother alone with a wine bottle. A few crumpled up tissues covered the coffee table. Instantly, Rachel was in high alert mode.

"Where's Balthasar?"

Annette turned to her and gave her a broken little smile. "I broke up with him."

Of course, he'd break her mother's heart. That slimy bastard had wormed his way into their home and then... "Wait. Did you say *you* broke up with him?"

Her mother patted the empty place on the couch next to her. "You were right."

Uncertain, Rachel followed the invitation and took a seat next to her. They were still getting used to being just the two of them. With Balthasar, they'd been three again. He'd acted like a buffer, or maybe a conductor, something that allowed them to bridge the chasm between them. Now that he was gone, the chasm lay wide open again.

"He was nothing but a toyboy. Way too immature for me," Annette confessed. Rachel had to bite her lip harder so she wouldn't burst out laughing. "I mean, really. He was so obsessed with you teenagers all the time. And that fight? So childish."

Annette put her head on Rachel's shoulder, ignoring how stiff her daughter grew under the unfamiliar sensation. "I miss having a real man. Like your father."

Rachel coughed. The confession hit her from left field. Was that true? After all these years, was her mother still in love with her father? Rachel thought she'd known the truth. They'd married too early, rushed into it because of the pregnancy, and then the reality of parenting had caught up with them, ending in a bitter fight and divorce that drove her father to cheat and her mother to alcohol. Rachel keenly remembered her mother talking about the terrible man her father was back when they'd still lived with him, though he'd never come home until long after she and Nico were in bed.

But there was the shattered dream. The sharp-edged pieces of Annette's life. Maybe the reason Annette was still caught in them was, even with all the alcohol in the world, she'd never been able to let go.

Her mother put her arm around Rachel and hugged her. "Who needs men when we've got each other?"

It wasn't a concept Rachel was familiar with. She'd always felt like her mother had never had her back. Annette hadn't even been able to take care of herself, much less the children she took along with her.

But things had changed. They'd both lost Rachel's father, and then they'd lost Nico. For the longest time, Rachel had tried to hold on to her grudge. In her opinion, her mother hadn't deserved her.

And maybe she didn't. But she was also right. They had no one else but each other.

Tentatively, Rachel put her head lightly against Annette's. This experience was something completely new. Strange and unfamiliar. And yet oddly comforting. Perhaps if Rachel could find it in herself to forgive a little, and if her mother could find it in herself to care a little, they could start again.

Rachel noticed she wasn't completely opposed to the idea anymore.

# Lucille

Lucille had wanted to take the party somewhere else. After all, the anniversary had been a huge success, despite the little hiccup of Matt's and Balthasar's fight. With a little help from her illusion magic, they'd managed to make it all seem like a grand show. One could only hope that the Magic Circle was going to be extremely popular now.

But none of their friends were ready to celebrate. Fabian had gone straight home after missing most of the action. Samantha had claimed exhaustion, Matt had gone with Chay, and Rachel had been too worried about Balthasar taking revenge on her mother. To top it all off, Jan announced that he was taking Meg out on a date, flaunting his relationship in her face.

Instead, she'd gone home and decided to celebrate alone with some rubbish TV that Linda would never approve of, pyjamas, and pecan ice cream. She was starting to feel a little sleepy when someone knocked on her door.

"What?" she asked, a bit annoyed.

The door opened, and Pascal slipped in, clearly having climbed out of bed again.

Lucille sighed. She was growing fond of him, but the frequent visits at night had to stop. "Another nightmare?"

Pascal shook his head. "Not yet. I'm sure I'll have one after today, though."

Instantly, Lucille was overcome with pity. Pascal had come running to her after nearly getting caught in the crossfire between Matt and Balthasar. "Come here."

He came closer, but instead of sitting down, he remained standing, his brow knitted in deep thought. "I need to ask you a few questions, and you need to tell me the truth."

Lucille raised an eyebrow. "The truth?"

"None of the lies you tell our parents. Or that show you put on for the other guests," Pascal demanded. "I'm not stupid. I know what I saw and what I heard."

Lucille swallowed. She wasn't sure she was ready for this kind of conversation. The truth suddenly seemed a little too big and scary for a child, no matter how smart. "What do you know?" she asked before she walked into a trap and accidentally told him more than he could handle.

Pascal nodded sharply. "Okay. But you're not allowed to laugh." He put up one finger for each truth he told. "Magic is real, and you are a witch."

Gasping, Lucille couldn't wait to hear what else he'd divined in the short amount time he'd been here.

"This town is full of magic. It's strong here, though I don't know why. And there are monsters." He switched to his other hand. "The shooter at school was a monster. That's why the police never caught him. Your stupid boyfriend can manipulate water or something. Your other friend has a brother who tried to kill him. Their fight wasn't a scuffle, it was life or death. His brother is a monster. Your friend is too." He'd run out of fingers before reaching the end.

Lucille gaped at him. "You got all this from...?"

"I'm a keen observer," Pascal claimed proudly. "People don't pay much attention to me, but I pay attention to everything." He looked at her and sighed. "You think I'm creepy." His bottom lip started quivering slightly.

She shook her head and laughed helplessly. It was only a short burst that died out quickly. "What's creepy is that we *do* have monsters, and yes, technically, Matt is one of them. Though he's half-human, so..." She took a deep breath. Matt's complicated family history truly wasn't the best example of Greenvalley's magic.

Tentatively, Lucille regarded Pascal. His small, wiry frame made him look so much younger than he was. But apparently, he was an old soul. And something else. A keen curiosity held in check by some soul-crushing fear. "Are you scared of the magic?"

Pascal shook his head. "It's real." Rather than a statement, it sounded like a plea. A desperate plea.

Should she really tell him? A memory came to Lucille of confronting her father just like Pascal had confronted her. Her father had grown angry, denied everything, and tried to gaslight her, stomping out all hopes of connecting with each other. Pascal yearned for connection as much as she did. She saw the hunger in his eyes, and so she decided to tell the truth. "Yes. It's very real."

Relief flooded his little face. "I knew it."

"How?" Lucille asked. "I know, you're smart and a *keen observer.* But most people deny magic exists, even if it jumps into their face. You saw the people today."

"You mean the adults?" Pascal asked dismissively. Then his face took on something eager. "Can I show you something?"

"Sure."

Lucille had no idea what it could possibly be and expected to have to come with him. But Pascal remained standing and looked at the remote next to her with an intense expression, as if he was severely constipated. She was just about to ask him whether he was okay when the remote started to float into the air.

"How?" Lucille whispered, gaping yet again.

Pascal still fixed the remote with his stare, clearly moving it around just with the power of his mind. "Telekinesis," he said, tense lines around his mouth. "It's a form of magic."

The remote control fell into her lap. Lucille stared at it in confusion. Then she laughed. A real pearly peal of laughter, born of pure joy. "This is amazing."

"Amazing?" Pascal asked surprised. "You don't find it creepy?"

Lucille shook her head, still grinning from ear to ear. "No, it's astounding. Magical. Oh, you're going to fit right into Greenvalley."

Inadvertently, she must have found exactly the right words, because Pascal cried out and threw himself into her arms. "Really? Do you really think so? They're not going to send me back because of it?"

Her heart hurt for him. She could only imagine how many times Pascal had been close to adoption, only to have his hopes dashed because his new parents found out about his telekinetic powers. Instinctively, she slung her arms around him and held him tight. "I won't let them. It's better we keep this between us, but you can tell Albert. He's one of us and really kind."

"You're really kind too," Pascal sniffled.

Lucille stroked his hair and planted a kiss on his head. "You're not too bad yourself when you want to be."

He laughed softly, fighting with sobs at the same time. "I'll try to be nice to your boyfriend. But for the record, I do think you deserve better than him." Pascal raised his head and smiled at her. "You deserve the world."

# Fabian

It was dark when Fabian came home from the anniversary party. According to the others, it had been a huge success. Fabian had seen the sales numbers and had to agree. Objectively, the party had exceeded every expectation. But in his heart, it had been a big failure.

The anniversary was supposed to celebrate his mother's work. He'd taken over because he truly believed in her and what she'd achieved. He'd wanted to prove that people felt the same. But no one had thought of his mother today. They hadn't even noticed that the woman of the hour had never attended her party. There had been no speech and no toast. Everyone had had a grand blast, everyone but the one who mattered.

The TV was running in the living room, but Fabian knew he wasn't going to find his mother there. She was exactly where he'd left her in the afternoon. Sitting in her bed, staring at the wall.

Without a word, Fabian climbed back into bed with his mother, put his arms around her and held her tight.

He contemplated telling her about the party or about Balthasar. Or that they'd dealt with the chaos imps at last. But all of that seemed so irrelevant when faced with the heavy sadness in this room.

Something was fundamentally broken, and there was no easy fix. All Fabian could do was let her know he was there for her.

# Part 5

## Cure & Disease

# Matt

Matt was used to not seeing Chay for months or even years, and he'd never minded before. But lately, he wished there was a way to contact his old friend more reliably. So much was happening that worried and confused him, and he needed someone to explain it to him.

Chay was the only other half-demon he knew, but he was incredibly busy. He'd even managed to find a way around the summoning curse. While it made sense to Matt—if he were a high-in-demand world saviour, he'd shut down the direct phone line too—as a friend, it sucked.

He'd tried to summon Chay several times in the last weeks. After Malcolm's death, Chay had dropped a giant truth bomb—the prophecy had nothing to do with the Archdemon of Greed—and then went off grid again. Now that Matt's own life seemed to be entangled in countless prophecies and fate, it seemed highly irresponsible of Chay to ignore his summons.

It was what he told him when they returned home—without Balthasar. "You need to get a cell phone or something."

Chay looked slightly amused. "Look at you, adopting human ways."

Matt rolled his eyes. "I mean it. I have no way to call you. It's always you who decides when to show up."

"And you don't think I show up exactly when I'm needed?" Chay asked gently.

"No. Because I—" Matt swallowed the rest of his words before he said something embarrassingly human. "Are you here because of Melaney? Is it important?"

"Everything you do is important."

Matt groaned. "To whom?"

Chay didn't miss a single beat. "To me."

*Then why weren't you here?* Matt stared at Chay, unable to get those needy words out. Annoyed, he walked into the kitchen and poured himself some soda. "You want one as well?"

"Yes, please."

He took out a second glass and filled it too. "I assume you know all about Melaney's challenge?" When Chay nodded, Matt took a contemplative sip from his soda. Even though Chay's ability only showed him the future, he was always excellently informed. "I couldn't kill Malcolm, despite him threatening my friends. And now my *mother* wants me to kill her."

Chay took the second glass from him, his fingertips merely brushing Matt's. It would be enough for him to catch a quick glance of the future. "It wasn't your destiny to become the Archdemon of Greed."

Matt knew as much. "But is it my destiny to become the Archdemon of Lust?" Things would be so much easier if he knew what was supposed to happen. If the future ordained his fate, at least he wouldn't have to make the decision.

Naturally, Chay didn't provide a straight answer. "Do you want to be the Archdemon of Lust?"

And just like that, Chay had put his finger into the wound. There was no use pretending, so Matt told him the truth. "I don't know. Actually, I don't know anything anymore. All of this is complicated enough without my mother wanting me to kill her or my brothers trying to *murder* me."

He knew he should sit down and think about how he truly felt about the issue, and what he was willing to do about it. Balthasar hadn't been completely wrong when he'd said Matt was hiding in Ashuan. It wasn't just to get away from Caspar; he was getting away from all of it. It was easy to forget Hescaryn and the Council of Seven existed when he was busy learning for exams and preparing for graduation. A graduation he might never need.

"What's 'all of it'?" Chay asked, slightly intrigued.

Matt leaned against the kitchen counter with a sigh. "I don't feel like myself anymore." When Chay raised an eyebrow, he elaborated, "My mother wants me to replace her, but how can I do that when I'm not even interested in sex?" The eyebrow crawled higher. "I mean, I *am* interested in sex. It's just that I only want it with Samantha. It doesn't make any sense. What's wrong with me?"

Chay's eyes glittered, and he let out a soft laugh. Not exactly the reaction Matt had hoped for. "What's wrong with you? Nothing." But then his laughter slipped off his face, leaving behind the melancholy that always surrounded Chay. With a sigh, he answered, "You're in love, Matt. That's what's wrong."

"I can't be." Matt shook his head. "I'm a demon. Love... Look, I know, you're going to say I'm also half human, but... love?"

"Honestly, I don't think it's a strictly human thing," Chay admitted. "It happens to demons too, as unlikely as it sounds. It definitely happens to half-demons."

Matt was about to protest before he realised Chay was speaking about himself. "You were in love?"

"A long time ago." Chay shrugged dejectedly. "I was young, too, once. But that's the thing. Just because I can't have any kind of meaningful physical contact doesn't mean the feelings don't develop. It just means that there's no future for them."

Matt caught his breath, suddenly feeling heady. "Is there a future for me...?" While he couldn't say the words *"and Samantha"*, they hung heavily between them.

The look in Chay's eyes wasn't promising. Before he could answer, Matt waved him off. "Don't bother. I know you won't tell me my future. It doesn't matter, anyway, because I'll get over it soon." It was nothing but a phase. A temporary infatuation that wasn't going to go anywhere, because Samantha wasn't interested and he needed to back off. "Tell me why you're here," he begged instead.

"Because even though I couldn't get away earlier, I heard your summons." Chay took his soda and returned to the living room. "So, let's talk."

Slightly unwilling, Matt pushed off the counter and followed him. "Talk about what?"

"All the things you keep stuffed inside of you," Chay said with a little smile. "Shouldn't you know by now that it never works?" He sat down on the couch. "So, what do you really think about Melaney's request?"

Matt groaned. "I told you. I don't know." He plunked himself down next to Chay and let his head fall back on the couch. "I keep going back and forth. For one, I'm only eighteen. That's very young to become an Archdemon. The youngest ever, considering most demons barely figure out how not to die in flight at that age."

"True."

"On the other hand, it's an enormous chance that definitely won't present again itself anytime soon." The power of an archdemon wasn't usually this easily attainable. Positions changed in brutal coups, long-winded intrigues, or stealthy attacks. In comparison, killing his willing mother required very little effort.

"I'm tempted," Matt admitted, tasting how that thought felt on his tongue. Prickly and slightly bitter. He would've spat the words out again if he could. Instead, he washed them down with a good dose of contempt. "I definitely couldn't bear Caspar becoming it."

Chay shuddered, and Matt hoped that meant Caspar had little hope of succeeding. "I suppose stranger things have happened."

"So, what do you think? Should I go for it?" Matt bit his lip and squinted at Chay, as if he somehow could gleam the future from his friend's reactions.

"All I know is that, either way, it'll be life-changing for you."

Matt snorted. "Very helpful. Really." He shook his head and leaned forward to take another sip.

"I support you," Chay said in all seriousness. "No matter what you choose, I'll be there for you. But whether you want to take on Melaney's challenge is up to you. No one can make this decision for you. Not even your brothers."

Darkly, Matt stared into his glass. In a way, his brothers were forcing his hand. Whether he was willing to follow through or not didn't seem to matter. They wouldn't stop even if he publicly announced his resignation. "What did you say to Balthasar?" His older brother had left after a single short conversation with Chay.

"I only confirmed his suspicions."

Matt's heart fluttered. "You told him about the prophecy?"

"He *knows* the prophecy. A lot of demons do. Some humans, too." Chay swirled the contents of his glass thoughtfully. "It's been around for a while. What Balthasar didn't know was that the prophecy is about you."

"Now he does."

Chay nodded. "Now he does."

"Is that bad?" Surely, Balthasar wouldn't just sit by and let them fulfil their destiny.

"If I play my cards right, it could be a good thing."

Matt glanced at Chay in surprise. His friend rarely admitted to his own hand in the grand scheme of fate, much less allow a glimpse of what his game was. "A good thing?" he asked doubtfully.

"He's gone, isn't he?" Chay answered his question with another one. "So... Samantha, huh? Have you made any progress in the matter?" He didn't sound particularly interested in the answer, but this was Chay. He wouldn't bring it up if he wasn't.

With a groan, Matt leaned back again. "Not at all. We're friends again, but nothing more." He supposed that was quite some progress. Unfortunately, it didn't feel like it, since his longing remained annoyingly unwavering.

"But you want... *more?*" Chay made it sound as if the idea disgusted him almost as much as it would Caspar.

Raising an eyebrow, Matt asked. "Is that wrong?"

"Depends on who you ask."

"I'm asking *you.*"

Chay's face distorted as if he was suffering from some great world-bending pain. "To be honest, I don't know. Samantha's Emblem carries the Power of Change. She'll definitely change you, but whether that's for the better or worse..." He shrugged helplessly. "I saw both." With a sad little smile, he added, "It would be far less complicated if you didn't have those feelings for her."

Matt sighed. It wasn't like he'd planned on them. They were simply there. And if he interpreted Chay's ambiguous advice correctly, it was not a *phase.*

Chay's words still swirled in Matt's mind when he sat with the others at school. Samantha was seated across from him, lost in concentration as she prepared flash cards for the next exam.

*She'll change you.*

Matt didn't want to admit it, but she already had. She'd turned him into this bloody mess of illogical feelings and doubts. Would facing his mother and brothers have been easier if he'd never met Samantha? Or was that too much credit for her subtle power?

"I wonder what's going on there," Lucille mused, her eyes fixed on the back of the student hall, where the Elite Clique had taken up seats.

Cheryl and Ani were pestering Cian, who had his arms crossed and looked so over it. When they kept harping on, he rubbed his face in annoyance, before grabbing his belongings and stuffing them into his backpack.

"He probably picked the wrong outfit or something superficial like that," Fabian suggested, not bothering to spare the drama more than a glance.

Lucille rolled her eyes. "You're such a boring gossip," she muttered. Her eyes lit up suddenly, though. "He's coming to us."

This time, Fabian looked up for real. "What? Why?"

Matt tensed as he watched Cian march down the rows of tables, his gaze clearly fixed on their table. Across from him, Samantha only dared to look through her eyelashes, clearly pretending she was still focused on her school work. It pained Matt to notice. She shouldn't feel guilty about showing an interest in someone else. But why did it have to be Cian of all people?

The other boy had finally arrived, and Matt felt a sliver of satisfaction when he realised how pale and sweaty he looked. The very opposite of attractive. "What do you want?"

Cian ignored him, staring at the table instead. "Can I sit?"

Without looking up, Samantha lifted her bag from the chair next to her.

"You want to sit with *us?*" Fabian asked, still dumbfounded.

Samantha paused in her action.

Glad that Fabian had given him an opening, Matt continued his line of thought, "With us losers?" It was a word Cheryl frequently threw at them, though rarely at him personally.

"What was going on over there?" Lucille asked, not willing to pass on a juicy piece of gossip. "Cheryl looked livid."

"Nothing," Cian claimed. "Cheryl's just going into full diva mode, and I'm so through... with..." He looked as if he was going to drop dead if they didn't let him sit soon.

Softly, Rachel remarked on it. "You look very pale."

"Nah. It's nothing. I'm just—"

Without a warning, Cian's eyes rolled back in his head. He swayed and crumpled on the spot.

"Cian!" Samantha jumped to her feet, in full alert mode. The worry on her face was like a bucket full of cold water emptied over Matt's head.

*She cares for Cian*, he thought and hated himself for it in the next minute. Right now, his self-proclaimed rival needed medical attention not his jealousy.

Nevertheless, Matt couldn't help but hope there'd be an easy way out of his moral dilemma, and the worst bit was he couldn't tell whether that thought made him undeniably demon or human.

# Samantha

Cian's collapse had been a great shock to everyone. Although the crowd of onlookers hadn't been particularly helpful, he'd recovered sufficiently to be taken to the infirmary. Samantha had to wait patiently until Alan and Shayna had left his side before slipping into the room when no one was looking.

Cian was lying on the bed, an arm over his eyes.

When Samantha approached him, she saw sweat on his forehead and in his hair. Cautiously, she put the back of her hand on his forehead and gasped. He was burning up.

With a groan, Cian lowered his arm to look at her. When he recognised her, his lips curled into a delirious smile. "It's you."

"You're pretty hot..."

"Thanks."

Samantha chuckled. "Let me rephrase that. You have a fever. Do you have an exam today, or why else did you drag yourself to school?"

"I was fine this morning," Cian claimed. Then he sighed. "I think it's the flu. I feel awful. My mum's going to pick me up soon."

"Good. Promise me to rest." Gently, she brushed his sweaty hair from his forehead when suddenly she noticed something on his arm. "What's this?"

Without waiting for him to answer, she grabbed his arm and twisted it to get a better look. Under the hem of his sleeve was an alarmingly red, swollen spot.

"What is it?" Cian asked, swallowing hard at the sight.

"I don't know, but you should definitely check in with a doctor as soon as possible." Samantha glanced at her phone, noticing that she had to leave for PE soon.

Cian sat up and gingerly felt around the swelling. When he touched the red skin, he winced and pulled a grimace. "What the fuck?"

Samantha gave him a pitiful look. "It's going to be fine. Probably a sting or something."

"So, I've got malaria?"

"I don't know…" She sighed, then leaned in to kiss his cheek. "I've got to go. Just rest, drink lots of water, and go to the doctor. Love you."

"I love you too."

Samantha winced, not having meant it in such a profound way. "I'll see you later."

She didn't like leaving him alone, but she didn't want to be late to class either. When she hurried down the stairs of the admin building, she promptly ran into Matt. "What are you doing here?" Even in their short interaction, he had been incredibly hostile yet again.

"I have to hand in an apology for the other day. And you?" He studied her thoughtfully, as if he could see a trace of Cian on her.

"Um… I was doing student council stuff." There was always something to do, and it usually involved admin.

Matt's eyes narrowed. "Should've thought about that." He ran his tongue over his lip. "Did you hear how Cian's doing?"

*Shit, shit, shit.* She couldn't have given herself away, could she?

"Cian?" Samantha asked, trying her best to sound confounded. "Oh, yes. The secretary said he had a fever. They're sending him home. I… I've got to go. PE's starting soon." She switched positions with Matt and walked backwards down the stairs to slowly get away from him before he asked any more questions.

"Are we going to meet up later at the Magic Circle?"

It must have worked. Samantha smiled. "Sure. See you later."

He returned the smile slightly. "See you later."

Samantha shook off the strange tension and walked away. Under no circumstances could Matt find out that she was sleeping with Cian. The consequences would be too much for her.

Disgusted by her thoughts, Samantha grimaced. When was she finally going to stop seeing each relationship as terribly doomed? Matt had apologised and learned.

Problem was, she didn't know if that changed anything.

After Caroline's breakdown, the six of them had sort of taken over the Magic Circle. Since Jan was currently unemployed, he ran the shop during the day, and in the afternoon, they all chipped in to keep the store afloat. Most of the time that meant the six of them hanging out in the store and newly opened café.

"There just aren't a lot of customers," Jan was updating Fabian on how the morning went. "I don't know how Caroline lured them in, or whether I just imagined there'd be more. It's a pretty relaxed job. Much better than the hostel. A little boring, though."

Fabian stared at him flatly. "So, what you're telling me is that the store isn't running."

"I'd say, it's not running, it's creeping."

Samantha felt sorry for Fabian. He desperately wanted to bring the store back from the brink, as if that would miraculously heal Caroline's burnout. But the Magic Circle had always been slow. It ran a little better on the weekend and in the holidays, but when the tourists stayed away, the store grew quiet. There were only so many ritual bowls and athames you could sell to Greenvalley's general population.

Even the little café hadn't attracted many customers yet. Maybe if they started a proper marketing campaign... Just thinking about it made Samantha groan. She was busy enough with her paying side job, all the exam prep, the graduation committees, and her general homework, which was currently spread across two tables.

Bored by the chat at the counter, Lucille slipped into the seat opposite her. "I asked around, and people are saying that Cian ended his friendship with Cheryl."

"Is that so?" If he did, it had been merely a formality rather than a new development. The only reason Cian still hung out with Cheryl was because Alan and Shayna did.

"Maybe people are staying away because the place is full of teenagers." Jan pointed at them.

Fabian looked over, irritated. "Wouldn't that entice people to check the place out?"

"Not really. Plus, Sam took home more ingredients last week than we sold the entire month."

Samantha felt her ears burn. Caroline had always told her she could take whatever she wanted, but now she realised there must have been a cost attached to that. On the other hand, it wasn't like they went to waste. "I'm taking them home to make potions. Potions that kind of save our ass from time to time." Since hunting monsters, her demand had definitely risen.

Fabian jumped to her defence. "Sam's got a deal with my mum, same as Elda."

"Almost no one buys those potions," Jan complained.

"Hey guys," Rachel interrupted. She had a newspaper in her hand and frowned heavily. "Did you read this article by Vendenberg?"

"Who's Vendenberg?" Lucille asked.

"One of the writers for the Greenvalley View," Samantha explained. "He's known for writing ridiculous articles about supernatural events in the city."

Lucille raised an eyebrow. "For real?"

"It's just fake. Entertainment at best. As I said, ridiculous articles."

"Well, this one isn't ridiculous," Rachel claimed. She walked over and took the seat next to Samantha to show her the newspaper. "Look at this. Apparently, a mystery disease is ripping through Greenvalley."

A mystery disease? Samantha's thoughts immediately brought up the swelling on Cian's arm.

Before she could read the newspaper, though, Matt had plucked it from Rachel's hands. "'The Black Death is back! Mystery sickness leaves Greenvalley doctors clueless'. What's the Black Death?"

"The Plague," Samantha answered automatically. It always threw her when Matt missed references almost every child knew. It reminded her he wasn't, in fact, fully human. "A disease that killed millions of people like six or seven hundred years ago. Hence the moniker."

"I see." He continued reading. "Well, here it says the disease's symptoms consist of high fever, loss of appetite, and apathy. In later stages, painful black boils form under the skin that darken over time. At this stage, the disease attacks the inner organs. Greenvalley's ICU currently reports six patients."

"Cian." His name slipped from Samantha's tongue before she could stop herself.

Matt looked at her questioningly. "Cian?"

"Um." How was she going to get out of that? "He had a fever, didn't he?"

"People have fevers all the time," Rachel said, throwing her a pointed look.

It was enough for Matt to keep reading. "Anyway, they tell you to go to the doctor if you exhibit any of the symptoms and not to panic. It'll all resolve itself."

Jan walked over to the kitchen to grab some coffee while he asked, "And how's that supernatural now?"

"The Black Death is back!" Lucille said with much gusto. "It's the title."

"Well, Jan has a point," Samantha had to concede. "The Plague didn't have any supernatural causes."

Fabian huffed. "You don't believe this idiot, do you? The Plague is a thing of the past. Long ago past. It's no longer around, is it?"

"Technically, it is—" Samantha started. She'd researched it a couple of years back when she'd gone through her medieval phase.

The door opened, and all six spun around to see who it was. Instead of a customer, Robert hurried in, seemingly out of breath. "Jan."

"What?" Jan barked back, mocking Robert's dramatic entrance.

"Your sister. She collapsed."

# Jan

Jan hadn't been thinking straight since Robert dropped his bomb in the Magic Circle. Instantly, he left everything behind and raced towards the hospital, which fortunately wasn't too far from the store.

Wheezing from an oncoming asthma attack, he barged towards registration. "Anne Kerscher!"

The woman behind the glass shield looked at him, unimpressed. "And you are?"

"Her brother, Jan Kerscher."

She sighed then pulled up the patient information. "She's in Internals, Room 17. Please report to the head nurse upon arrival to—"

Jan rushed away before he could pick up the rest. He barely made it into an elevator before the doors shut and hammered the button for the third floor. The elevator moved way too slow for his nerves, but it gave him some time to pull out his spray and take a couple of puffs.

When the door finally opened on Level 3, he hurried into the corridor. Usually, the doors opened instantly on request, but today it was all shut down. Jan pressed the doorbell again and again until he finally heard crackling on the intercom. "Yes?"

"I need to see my sister, Anne Kerscher, she's in Room 17. Please," Jan hastened to say.

"I'll be with you in a minute. Please be aware that we're operating on a strict quarantine plan."

Quarantine? How bad was this?

It took the head nurse more than a minute to arrive at the door. Through the window, he saw her clad in full protective gear, complete with mask and gloves. She opened the door. "Come with me. I'll take you to disinfection and give you some gear. I also need to see your ID."

Every passing minute grated on Jan. He just wanted to know how his sister was faring. Again and again, he heard Samantha's words. *The Plague. Millions dead.* It couldn't possibly be true.

The outfit was ridiculous, but it brought Jan to Anne's room. Just as he was about to knock, the door opened and his mother came out. She looked at him surprised. "What are you doing here?"

"I heard about Anne. Is she alright?"

"She needs rest." His mum glanced over her shoulder, betraying more than her answer did. "It would be better if you didn't go in. The quarantine rules aren't in place for fun."

After he'd got all dressed up and disinfected? Small chance. "I just want to see her."

"Ida?" Another nurse called his mother. "Could you help for a second?" She was accompanying an orderly pushing a patient's bed.

His mother threw Jan a stern look. "I'm serious. This disease is something else." Then she left him to his own devices to help the nurse.

Jan watched in horror as they pushed the bed past him. The patient inside it was pale and sweaty. Black boils covered most of his skin and a bloody cotton plug hung from his nose. He had his eyes closed, breathing heavily through the mouth. Disgusted, Jan turned away and opened the door to Anne's room.

His sister was awake, though she looked utterly exhausted. Like the other patient, she was paler than usual, but there was no black marks on her skin, just a bunch of red sores. "Hey," she whispered, the ghost of a smile on her face.

"Hey." Jan took another step towards her. "Do they know what it is yet?"

"Mum says, it's probably bacterial. They put me on antibiotics." She pointed at the IV.

Another step brought him right next to her bed. "How do you feel?"

"Shit." She coughed and grimaced. "Everything hurts when I swallow or when I move. I can't sit up on my own; that's how weak I feel. Did Robert tell you?"

Jan pulled the chair closer and sat. "Yeah, he was a mess. When did you get sick?" He tried to remember when he'd last seen her, but couldn't pull up a visual.

"I felt unwell for two or three days, but since I'm on my period, I didn't pay it much attention. Then I noticed the spots."

He glanced at the angry red spots. Some were only as big as the nail on his thumb, but at least one was as big as a table tennis ball. "Do they know what they are?"

"Mum says they're infected lymph glands. She mentioned the bubonic plague." Anne's face fell. "Jan, I'm scared. Are you going to stay?"

"Of course." There was no question about it. "Rest a little, okay? I'll stay here." *And do something about this.*

When Anne closed her eyes, he pulled off his glove and took her hand in his. Concentrating deeply on his magic, he hovered his other hand over the big swelling and dipped into Anne's body. He had no idea how to do this, but as usual, the magic had its own mind. It sank into the swelling and drew out the infection.

Jan winced when he felt a sharp pain in his own body in response. No wonder Anne had complained about pain. This was vile.

"Have you gone mad?"

Startled, Jan dropped Anne's hand and turned towards the door. His mother had come back, her eyes wide with shock. "I only—"

"Broke about seven quarantine rules at the same time?" Ida bellowed. "I already have one sick child. I don't need two."

Jan rose from his chair as he mumbled, "As if there'd be any question whose bed you'd be sitting at."

"What?" Judging by her expression, she hadn't heard what he said.

"Just forget it."

His mother took a deep breath. "I'm sorry. This is all very stressful. Please go and make sure you sanitise your hands properly. If you have any symptoms—"

"Yeah, yeah." He probably wouldn't be let out without lathering his hands anyway.

Without another look at Anne, Jan left the room. Outside though, he took a deep breath. Whatever this was, it was actually serious. His mother was a professional, but she couldn't hide how much this disease worried her, and Jan had seen a glimpse of what it had done to Anne's body. He doubted the doctors were going to find a cure soon.

# Lucille

"I need to tell you something," Lucille announced when she, Samantha, and Rachel were out in the forest, accompanying Elda to the Spring of Magic for some magic maintenance. "It's about Pascal."

"What did he do this time?" Samantha asked.

Lucille laughed. Her little brother had managed to gain quite the reputation in the short time he'd been in Greenvalley. "Nothing. But it turns out that he's magical too."

Both friends turned to her. "Proper magic? Or is this a euphemism?" Rachel asked.

"Proper magic. He's a telekinetic. I saw it with my own two eyes."

"Really? That's cool," Samantha said. "So, did the two of you bond over it?"

Lucille shrugged. "A little, yes. He's obviously not the easiest kid, though Linda can't stop bragging about him." She told them about Pascal's experiences before he was adopted into the de Cerque family and how his power proved to be a hindrance. "He honestly thought he was creepy." It still broke her heart.

"Well, ask Fabian, and he'd probably agree," Samantha joked.

It didn't sit right with Lucille. A nearly nineteen-year-old shouldn't have beef with a ten-year-old. Then again, it *had* been Pascal who'd attacked Fabian in a desperate attempt to score brownie points with Linda. "About that. He doesn't mean it. He's just taking his cues from Linda."

"That's a great choice," Rachel commented drily. "She'd win mother of the year if it weren't for mine."

"Uh-oh, what did yours do?" Where Linda was often out-of-touch, Rachel's mum had serious issues.

Rachel shrugged, looking slightly perplexed. "Honestly, it hasn't been too bad lately."

"Not too bad is as far as Annette goes, I suppose," Samantha muttered.

"No, it's... she's... better, I think." Rachel wrinkled her nose, her confusion seemingly growing. "When she was with Balthasar—which was weird, for the record—she became somewhat attentive. My guess is that because *he* took an interest in me, it sort of rubbed off. Anyway, we've been getting along lately."

Samantha didn't appear too impressed. "That's a lot better than my parents at the moment. They wouldn't get along if they were both drowning and could only survive by putting their differences aside."

"Do you think it's serious?" Lucille asked, concerned.

"Caroline said the two of them need squabbles like others need air to breathe. Supposedly, it's a sign of passion." Samantha shuddered at bringing her parents and passion into one sentence.

For Lucille, it reminded her of how there hadn't been a lot of passion in her relationship, lately. Fabian was always working at the shop or taking care of his mum. As sweet as it was, it wasn't terribly exciting. "Passion would be great," she mused.

"Not if you have to duck out of the way when they show their passion for each other."

"Girls?" Elda called from the front. She had already reached the clearing and sounded concerned.

The three of them hurried to join her, only to stop short when they arrived. The beautiful clearing had been defiled. Someone had dropped off a pile of metal barrels which were leaking a sticky, brown liquid. Underneath them, the always-verdant grass had died off.

Samantha gasped. "This is horrible." She looked around, her mouth wide open in horror. "The rivers are turning black."

Lucille had seen the rivers of magic in this place. They were as vibrantly green as their surroundings. When she closed her eyes now, she had trouble finding them at all. But then she saw what Samantha had.

Instead of green, black sludges of magic rolled down into the valley. "What is this?"

"Toxic waste," Elda said. "If we don't get rid of it quickly and clean the Spring, our magic will dry out. Or worse."

Lucille thought back to Vendenberg's article and the news of Anne's collapse. "I think it's already much worse."

# Rachel

After they'd contacted the authorities to have the barrels removed, they all gathered at Elda's house. Rachel sat in one of the comfy armchairs and hugged herself. She loved Greenvalley's beautiful nature. To see all that toxic waste piled up was doing something to her. Almost as if she'd been forced to drink it herself.

"Let me guess," Jan said to Matt as he walked around in agitated circles. "This is yet another test by Balthasar or maybe a gift from Caspar now that he can't come here personally."

"How would I know? Is it?" Matt checked with Chay, who was still around after the anniversary party. Probably for this exact reason, if Rachel knew him at all.

Chay shook his head.

"Because I swear if Anne dies because of your garbage brothers…"

Rachel cleared her throat. "I don't think demons produce a lot of toxic waste." Admittedly, she didn't know much about demons, but the barrels had looked distinctly human. Some sort of factory trying to cut corners or something.

Jan snorted and rolled his eyes. Meanwhile, Samantha gave Fabian a book to read and quickly gathered some more to work through.

"I'm sure Anne will feel better soon," Lucille said, though the smile on her face seemed a bit forced.

"I'm not sure about that. It sounds really bad," Fabian muttered.

Lucille boxed his arm, annoyed. "Don't you think we could use a little bit of optimism at the moment?"

"What? No!" Fabian rubbed his arm, then pointed to the book. "I meant what it says here. The poisoning of magical rivers is often accompanied by the Blood Plague."

"Blood Plague?" Jan repeated loudly. "Please tell me you only get a nose bleed from that."

Quickly, Fabian read some more of the book. "It says here that the incubation period is about one to three days. Early signs are loss of appetite and nausea. High temperature is possible. Within hours of the first outbreak, the lymph nodes begin to swell." He grimaced. "This is followed by fever and increasing muscle weakness. Purulent abscesses form, especially on the neck. They often burst and the pus flows into the nose or throat. A wet, often bloody, cough follows." Fabian dry-retched and pushed the book away. "This is disgusting."

Jan had stopped pacing. He stood rigid, his muscles tense. "Is. It. Deadly?"

Fabian picked up the book again and quickly scanned the page. "In extreme cases, it can result in organ bleeding. In its final stages, severe muscle cramps cause organ failure and... Yes, it's deadly."

"Fuck!" Jan grabbed his jacket and threw it on.

"Where are you going?" Lucille exclaimed.

"Anne. I'll heal her from this Blood Plague. I won't let my sister die."

Matt blocked his path. "Are you stupid? You can't heal diseases."

"I've got healing powers."

"Yeah, since like yesterday." Matt shook his head, calming himself. "Jan. Your powers can heal injuries, not diseases. You can only heal the symptoms, not the cause. Whether you heal her or not, it won't change the outcome."

As adamant as his reasoning was, Rachel noticed that his tone wasn't unkind. He pitied Jan, not like back when Nico had fought with an incurable disease. She shuddered. Thinking of Nico wasn't going to help.

"Well, if you say I *can* heal the symptoms, it could give her time. Time enough for the doctors to come up with a solution. Or you." Jan looked at Samantha, buried in books as she was.

"There's another reason," Chay explained calmly. "Attempting to heal a disease, is highly infectious." He regarded Jan with pity. "But you already know that, don't you?"

"What's that supposed to mean?" Fabian asked, his voice shaky.

Lucille looked concerned. "Jan?"

Rachel knew when someone looked guilty. And Jan looked especially guilty. He cracked soon. "It's just one spot. It's tiny."

"For now," Chay said.

No one doubted what he said, and an uneasy atmosphere took hold of the room. When Rachel felt as if she was about to throw up, she forced herself to say, "I have to admit, I feel a bit nauseous."

"I've been feeling nauseous since I read this," Fabian muttered.

Next to him, Lucille had gone pale. "Pascal stayed home today because he threw up."

"Please stay calm," Elda said, smiling kindly at each of them. "Since the disease is caused by magic, the easiest way to heal it is by—well, magic. All we have to do is clean the Spring. That's what you're looking for, isn't it, darling?" she asked Samantha.

When Samantha looked up from her reading material, Rachel felt sick again. Her friend's expression wasn't very optimistic. "Normally, it regulates itself, but that's only in case of a naturally occurring contamination. I could probably do some kind of weave, but that's as infectious as Jan's healing powers. Plus, worst-case scenario, I could be accelerating the spread."

"You're definitely not cleaning the Spring by yourself," Matt decided.

Samantha sighed. "I wasn't planning on it. Unless we get a full witch coven here, it probably wouldn't work anyway. But..." Her voice took a positive spin. "There apparently is a potion, which was designed specifically against the Blood Plague."

Rachel let out a sigh of relief. When Nico had contracted the werewolf virus, Samantha's potion had healed him. It hadn't saved his life, but this was different. She had full faith in her friend to pull this off, too.

Jan seemed to think the same as he nodded eagerly. "Perfect. How long will it take? You can have all the ingredients from the Magic Circle. Everything."

"A few days, but first we need to gather all the ingredients, and unfortunately, not all of them are available at the store." Despite her solution, Samantha didn't look too happy.

Her grandmother said, "I've got some contacts I could call."

"I know." Samantha's voice became more strained by the second. "But you can't get Lucifer's Shine."

"What's Lucifer's Shine?" Rachel asked.

It was Chay who answered. "A plant. It grows in only one spot: Hell."

After a long discussion, Rachel arrived home exhausted. It hadn't taken long for her friends to decide they'd go to Hell to grab the plant. Chay had explained it would be a trip of at least three or four days, since the stupid plant didn't just grow in the most dangerous place known to them, but in an area that was inaccessible to space jumps. Hell's Gardens. To reach them, they'd have to travel by foot through a dangerous cave system Rachel had already forgotten the name of. She hadn't forgotten how they'd felt when she'd seen them in Matt's dreams, though.

The mission was almost as risky as staying in Greenvalley. Jan had already declared he was staying here. The thought of leaving his sister without his supervision for a few days was unthinkable. Rachel was a bit torn. It was true that hearing of the Blood Plague had left her uneasy. Maybe it was only psychological, but right now she didn't feel like she could last four days of hiking in an area full of monsters.

If she was infected, the strain could kill her. In addition to that, she wasn't too keen on getting to know Hell intimately. Matt's dreams were bad enough.

She dragged herself to the living room and was about to drop onto the couch when she heard a retching noise from the bathroom. Her own nausea responded to the trigger, but she kept it in as she made her way over to the downstairs bathroom.

As expected, her mother was hanging over the toilet, throwing up the contents of her stomach. From her position, Rachel had an excellent view of the black spots on her neck.

Maybe visiting Hell wasn't such a bad thing, after all. Unfortunately, Rachel knew it wouldn't matter. The nausea she felt was real.

"Rachel?" her mother asked weakly as she noticed her standing there.

"Looks like we both have the Plague."

# Samantha

There wasn't much time before they'd leave for Hell. Samantha's heart was racing just at the thought of it. Hell. World of demons. Matt's home. The very home that made him the kind of person who'd just shrug off a death. How would it change them? Would they be able to pass through it unscathed?

Samantha shuddered. If it wasn't absolutely necessary, she wouldn't think about going there, but time was running out. The number of patients had already doubled. In a day or two, Greenvalley Hospital would reach its capacity. People might die.

Like Cian.

She swallowed heavily as she stood in front of his hospital room in full protective gear. Her head felt dizzy as the unbidden thoughts continued spiralling. She couldn't do this again. Couldn't lose someone else.

That's why she had to go. With a sharp exhale, Samantha straightened her shoulders and knocked, then opened the door.

Cian was lying in the bed at the front—they were already doubling up rooms. His hair was so sweaty it stuck to his forehead, but when he recognised her, he smiled. "You didn't have to come," he whispered, his voice scratchy from coughing. "The doctors said it could be dangerous."

"They have no idea."

"True." His voice faltered and he swallowed hard before wincing in pain. Then he realised what she'd said. "Wait a minute. This disease isn't supernatural, is it?"

Samantha came closer so she could lower her voice, but stayed a safe distance from his bed. "I'm afraid so. Someone poured toxic waste into the spring and now the magic is spoiled."

"But you can fix that, right? Right? That's why you're here. To tell me that I don't need to worry, because you've got it all sorted." When Samantha's eyes filled with tears, Cian winced. "I'm scared."

Another little step. Samantha wanted to reach out so badly it hurt. Instead, she forced herself to give him the cold facts. "There is a potion, but the vital ingredient only grows in Hell. So, that's where I'll be for the next few days."

Cian's eyes widened. "You're going to Hell?"

Samantha grimaced at the unfortunate turn of phrase. There was a lot of truth to that statement if Matt's stories could be believed. "Yes, apparently the plant we need grows exclusively in Hell's Gardens, which is a place outside of reach from space jumping. It's a two-hour hike. I have no idea what the witches who developed the potion promised the demons, but we're going to go and pick a couple of roots. And then, hopefully, we'll be back in time." Meanwhile, her grandmother would start with the potion.

"I trust you," Cian said, but his voice was shaky.

She couldn't blame him. Her own voice was merely a whimper. "Last time someone trusted me to do a complicated healing potion, he died."

"But this is different." Nonetheless, Cian swallowed. "It has to be different."

"I'll try my best." While the memories of Nico's death still haunted her, the alternative was unbearable. The potion was their only hope.

Cian nodded, trying to be brave. "Be careful down there."

If only the potion was the hard part. "We'll see."

Samantha blew him a kiss and left before she'd crumble completely. *It won't be the last time I see him,* she told herself over and over in her head as she returned the protective gear and sanitised her hands.

At the elevators, she ran into Jan. He wasn't going to come with them, opting to stay with his family instead.

When he saw her, his face fell. "Is it Meg?"

Confused, it took Samantha a moment to realise why he'd be asking after Meg when he knew she'd been released weeks ago. "Oh, no, don't worry. Meg's fine. I was visiting a friend." She gave him a thorough look. "You're not here to heal Anne, are you?"

Jan left the elevator and held it open for Samantha. "Does it matter? I'm already sick."

"Don't let the nurses hear that."

Jan grimaced. "Good luck and... be quick."

The doors of the elevator closed and Samantha leaned against the inner walls. The mission was absolutely vital. So many lives were on the line. Failure was not an option.

She pushed up her sweater sleeve and gingerly tested the red spot on her elbow. No, it really wasn't an option.

# Lucille

"You're home, great," Lucille was greeted by her father. If that wasn't unusual enough, he shooed her into the house. "Albert, we can shut the house down now."

"Excuse me?" Lucille looked around, noticing the copious amounts of sanitiser and masks in the entrance hall. "What's happening?"

Her father had a list in his hand, which he was ticking off. "We're isolating. No one will come or leave who isn't on this list of approved people. Interaction with personnel will be reduced to a minimum. Necessities will be delivered. Each of us is only allowed in their own room and bathroom."

Slowly, Lucille backed away. "But we're able to leave, aren't we?"

He looked up, perplexed. "This is a complete lockdown. So, no."

"Uhm..." Lucille thought better of it and smiled. "You seem to have it all under control."

"Hopefully. Now go to your room. Dinner will be delivered soon."

She turned and hurried up the stairs. There was absolutely no way she was staying in the house. Not when the only thing that could save her family was tied to her meeting her friends in an hour at Matt's.

As soon as she reached her room, she took a backpack from her cupboard. She didn't usually bother with them as she'd yet to find one that worked with her style. But this was Hell, not a fashion runway. The first thing that went in was her spell book. Then she gathered way too few clothes for her taste. Fabian would probably carry her bag for her if she asked, but it was better to assume she'd be stuck with it for the four days it would take them.

Just as she was stuffing a thin blanket on top of everything, the door opened. Lucille dropped the backpack and regarded her bookcase with great interest.

It wasn't her father, though, but Pascal. And by the looks of it, he was already sick. "Pascal! Shouldn't you be in bed?"

"I'm scared."

"Oh, Pascal." If only it was sensible to give him a hug, but she needed to stay healthy. Going into Hell was bad enough at full strength, it would be outright stupid to do so sick.

Pascal's keen eyes fell on her backpack. "Where are you going?"

Lucille had learnt her lesson. She wasn't going to lie to him. "We're going to find a cure. You'll feel better soon."

"Do you have to go?"

"There's safety in numbers." It was how she'd managed to convince Fabian to come along, despite his reservations. "But don't worry, I'll be back." For the most part, Lucille was excited to finally visit Matt's birthplace, but there was an instinctive fear that she couldn't quite shake.

Despite herself, she reached for Pascal, then remembered that she couldn't risk touching him. Pascal, too, was aware and took a step back. "Papa's locking everything down."

"I know." Hopefully by not arguing with her father, she'd shaken any suspicions. "I'm going to take the back door. Do you think you can act as a lookout for me?"

Pascal brightened up a little. "Of course." While pale, he didn't seem too sick.

That was good, Lucille thought. It gave her time to do what she had to. She grabbed her water bottle, intending to refill it at Matt's place, and shouldered her backpack.

Despite her best attempts to pack light, the straps cut into her shoulders. Gritting her teeth against the pain, she turned to the door. "Let's go."

Pascal took up position at one end of the hallway, while Lucille hurried down the other. She reached the back door without any problems, but found it locked.

"Oh, come on, Dad." Maybe she could climb through a window like some sort of criminal.

"I can open it." Pascal had followed her, keeping a two-metre distance. "Just a moment."

He frowned, and Lucille knew he was using his telekinetic powers. A few seconds later, she heard a click in the door.

"Not bad. Promise me you'll stay on the good side of the law."

Pascal grinned.

Lucille opened her arms, then closed them slowly, bringing her fingertips to her mouth, as if she were hugging him. She kissed her fingers and blew the kiss towards them.

"Come back quickly."

"I will."

And with that, she hurried out of the house.

When Lucille arrived with Samantha and Fabian at Matt's place, he, his father, and Chay had done an impressive job of preparing two huge hiking backpacks. A selection of daggers were lying on the table next to them.

"Have you got everything?" Matt asked, all business-like.

"I don't know," Lucille admitted. "It would've been helpful if you'd told us what weather to expect."

"No sky, no weather, remember?"

Next to her, Fabian sighed. "True. There wasn't even a wind."

It took Lucille a moment to remember that they'd already walked through Hell before. Admittedly, it had only been a short stretch, but the experience hadn't been particularly nice. She shuddered as she thought of the weird animal that had covered her in snot. Hopefully, those didn't exist in the cave system.

"If I remember correctly," Samantha said, "We need to worry more about things on the ground which could kill us."

Matt's badass mask fell and he whined, "Last time was a bad example. We won't be crossing the Black Guard training grounds this time."

"Awesome, I feel so much more confident about this trip now," Fabian said.

Lucille chuckled at his obvious sarcasm. "Pretend you're going on holiday."

"Adventure holiday?" Fabian asked doubtfully.

"Let's go before Fabian decides to stay behind," Matt said, handing each of them a dagger. "Where's Rachel?"

As usual, Samantha had the answer. "She told me she wants to stay to keep an eye on the situation. If there's a new development, she'll find our dreams and let us know."

"And how am I supposed to know the difference between those and my normal Plague nightmares?" Fabian whined, holding his dagger as if it was going to jump out of his hand and stab him.

Annoyed, Lucille clicked her tongue. "Rachel will find a way." She stowed the dagger in the side pocket of her backpack.

"Shall we go then?" Matt asked, extending a hand to Samantha.

To Lucille's surprise, Samantha shirked away from it. Were the two of them getting worse again?

"I'll take care of that," Chay announced and offered Samantha a hand. His were gloved. The two of them vanished almost instantly.

Matt let out a heavy breath. "What did I do wrong now?"

Lucille and Fabian exchanged a look, but neither knew any more than he did. "Let's just go."

One second they'd been stood in Matt's flat, the next they'd appeared in a cave. When they'd walked across the training grounds the time before, the ceiling had been so far above their heads it had almost given them the illusion of an open space. This place was undeniably underground, but it wasn't completely dark.

The stone around them was glowing a soft red, while a silver waterfall plunged into an abyss to their side. Several tunnels led away in different directions.

Lucille had barely taken a look when she was pulled into a hug.

Matt's sister Menuha grinned at her. "You're here." She moved on to give Fabian an equally exuberant hug. Then she turned to Matt. "A few soldiers were sneaking around here earlier. Death Army ones. I chased them off, so we shouldn't be bothered."

"What about Caspar?"

"You don't need to worry about him. Volac sent him with a special unit to the fire swamps. The neckars are revolting yet again. Apparently, they joined a group of rebels, who are already on the black list of the Seven. Anyway, he won't be back for days. You know how messy those swamps are."

Fabian was staring at the ground, swallowing repeatedly. He probably thought they'd have to navigate fire swamps.

As horrible as those sounded, the area they were currently in was beautiful. The silver water rushed down a ledge, providing an enchanting background mumble, while lush plants covered the edges of the tunnel system. The red light made it all look so comfy and warm.

"It's beautiful here," Lucille admitted.

Samantha joined her, still spinning around in awe. "Not at all how I imagined."

"The water is probably poisonous and the ground will open up and swallow us any minute, but yeah, it's nice to look at." As usual, Fabian's assessment was bursting with pessimism.

Contrary to him, Matt was grinning like a little child. "I told you last time was a bad example. The biggest part of Hell is gorgeous."

"And still, Fabian's right," Chay interrupted. "It's not known as one of the most dangerous environments for no reason. We should get on our way before the soldiers return." He led them towards one of the tunnels.

Matt threw a last glance at the waterfall. "I love this space."

Lucille chuckled softly. So far she'd found no reason to argue otherwise. She could only hope Hell would continue to show its best side.

# Fabian

They left the red-glowing bigger cave behind and followed the silver stream down a long dark tunnel. Since no one else bothered with a torch, Fabian held back as well. Better to keep their eyes sharp.

"Look at that." Matt pointed to the ceiling, which was covered with a large variety of colourful sparkles.

"So beautiful," Lucille whispered.

Even Fabian couldn't resist the beauty—or the curiosity. "Are those glow worms?"

Matt shuddered. "No worms." Fabian hadn't even thought of his phobia. "More like a kind of coral."

"Corals? On the ceiling?" Samantha asked.

"Yes, beautiful, aren't they? With their sparkling, they attract all sorts of animals, which then get stuck on the surface and will be slowly reabsorbed," Matt explained with pure delight.

Fabian swallowed. "Of course."

"Oh, come on," Matt complained. "It's not *that* sticky. Touching them isn't any worse than the sting of a burning jelly fish."

"Much better." The sarcasm dropped from Fabian's lips, almost as venomous as the creatures around them.

"Can't you show a little bit of enthusiasm?" Lucille asked him, sounding annoyed.

Confused, Fabian asked, "For burning jelly fish or for acid sparkle corals?"

Lucille turned up her nose. "Well, I think it's fascinating."

Fascinating it was, but Fabian still ducked his head to avoid getting too close to the deadly corals. He was about seventy per cent sure that they were going to die on this mission. Maybe not all of them, but if it had to be him, then not as food for these corals.

Behind them, he heard Samantha tease Matt, "I didn't know you loved your home this much." Whatever had caused her to shirk away earlier seemed forgotten again.

"Of course I love it. There are so many awe-striking locations. Someday, I'll show you my favourite places. Lucin or the Glowing Lakes."

"Will you, now?" Samantha's voice was fraught with tension.

"We should find a place to rest soon," Chay announced. "It's getting late."

They'd been walking for three hours at most, but it had already been late afternoon when they'd left.

"There should be a rune alcove ahead," Menuha said.

Curiously, Lucille asked, "What's a rune alcove?"

"Something deadly, I'm sure," Fabian mumbled.

"Not quite." Menuha sounded amused. "It's a place where you can rest. The runes protect you from the lower demons who hunt these corridors."

"It would still be good to keep a guard," Matt added.

So far, their passage had been uneventful, but the reminder of other demons made Fabian's stomach turn. How had he gotten himself into this? "I don't know if I can sleep here."

"Well, I'm sure I will be fast asleep," Lucille said, as if to spite him. "My legs are dying. And I'm hungry."

"My dad made sandwiches," Matt said.

"Plus, I'm sure we'll find some Gavashi Shrooms and Firali. I'll keep my eyes peeled," Menuha said, upbeat.

With their luck, demon food would burn their throat and put holes into their stomach. After all, demons healed quickly. It could all be part of the experience.

"Sandwich for me," Fabian muttered.

"Is the water drinkable?" Samantha asked. "We could refill our bottles."

Matt grimaced—of course, he did. "Only if you suffer from constipation. It's not water but sylver. Tastes horrible and gives you diarrhoea. But don't worry. There's a multitude of water veins in the stone around us."

That explained why the vegetation was hugging the walls rather than lining the river next to them.

"Well, I'll trust you," Samantha said, her voice just the tiniest bit strained.

Matt obviously didn't notice it, because he practically beamed at her.

At some point, Menuha disappeared to scout ahead. When they found her again, there was a bloody cadaver in front of an alcove, the inner walls of which were inscribed with numerous runes.

"What's this?" Fabian asked.

The cadaver was nearly unrecognisable. All he could see was a lot of fur, tusks, and claws. And blood, so much blood.

Menuha touched the cadaver with the tip of her shoe. "Just some lower demon. Come on in. I've already started a fire." She ran her fingers across one of the runes before stepping inside.

As they followed her, it felt as if they stepped through a waterfall, only it was hot, not cold. Before Fabian could feel uncomfortable, though, the feeling passed.

"A lower demon?" Lucille asked as they all sat around a fire with a pot hanging over it. "I thought demons were like us. Humanoid for the most part."

"That's only first and second-grade demons," Menuha explained. "That demon out there was fourth grade at most."

"You have a class system?" Samantha asked, surprised.

Matt cocked his head. "Yes and no. It's quite simple, actually. Everything endemic to Hescaryn is a demon."

"Including those corals?" Fabian asked.

"Yes, they're sixth grade. Small, no considerable brain activity, sedentary, and not really worth the trouble."

Despite himself, Fabian whistled. "Demonic biology. Who would've thought?"

Lucille leaned into him, grinning again. "And you said it wasn't fascinating."

"How did you come up with the grading?" Fabian couldn't help himself. This *was* interesting. "Did you evolve from those corals?"

"No, it has nothing to do with evolution. It's what's called a biosocial system." Everyone looked at Chay who grinned sheepishly. "Second year Interglobal Studies—biological systems and their development." As if that explained it all, he continued, "Demons are classified by power. Matt's siblings are typical first-grade demons. As Lucille noted rightfully, they're humanoid, very strong, have healing powers, retractable wings and all that. The second-grade demons are much the same, though they tend to be less powerful and are unable to pose as humans since their wings are fixed. They also can't jump through space."

From there, Matt took over. "From third grade on, you definitely can't mistake them for humans anymore, though those of third grade still walk on two legs and are technically humanoid. Think banshees, vampires, and all that kind."

"And then they get more animalistic," Chay continued. "Fourth grade is usually big and dangerous. Well, all of them are dangerous, but the lower you go, the less intelligent they get. A reanimated corpse falls in the same category as the corals, despite its size."

"I feel like it doesn't matter what grade they are," Fabian surmised. "They'll all be able to kill me."

Next to him, Lucille inhaled sharply. "Fortunately, you don't live here."

"But, if you'd grown up here, you wouldn't be such a coward," Matt chimed in.

Drily, Fabian replied, "True. I'd be dead."

Matt and Chay laughed good-naturedly, but Lucille took another deep breath, her shoulders tense. Something was up, and it made Fabian almost as nervous as he was about the demons of whatever grade sneaking through the corridors.

"Food's done!" Menuha announced, before handing each of them a neat little package. Wrapped in leaves, it felt warm in Fabian's hand.

"What is this?" Lucille asked, disproportionally excited.

"In Firali leaves roasted Gavashi-Shroom-Ragout," Menuha declared equally happy.

"Are those leaves?" Fabian asked.

Menuha nodded. "Yes, you can... no, you *must* eat those. Without them it only tastes half as good."

Matt, who was still chuckling to himself, added, "And you won't die from it."

If only Fabian could bring himself to trust Matt's assessment. He knew he was being overly cautious, so he squared his shoulders and bit off a tiny piece, barely big enough to get to the ragout. When he finally did, though, a rich earthy flavour exploded in his mouth, quickly followed by spice.

"It's hot," he said, "but yummy."

Lucille looked at him triumphantly. "See, Hell has some good sides." Then she turned to Chay before Fabian could protest. "Chay, I hope you don't mind me asking, but Matt once told us that you only found out you were a half-demon after you'd lived to a hundred or so. How is that possible?"

"I wasn't born in Hescaryn like Matt. My home world is Lukrya, the centre of the interglobal community. During my first life-span, demons were largely unknown to them. In comparison to other worlds, Hescaryn and Ashuan are much closer to each other."

"An interglobal centre?" Samantha asked. She was sitting a little further from the group, already huddled into a blanket, and hadn't touched the food yet.

"Yes, the Interglobal Parliament is located in the Eastlands of Lukrya. It's one of the first worlds that reached out to others... at least those in the East." Chay took a deep breath. "That's where I studied Interglobal Studies after realising how much time I had available to me. It's the biggest university in all known worlds, over a thousand faculties. When you visit the Eastlands, it's hard to believe how far behind the neighbouring states of the world are." He shrugged. "But they don't have dragons."

Fabian nearly dropped his food. "Dragons? As pets or...?"

"Oh no, I wouldn't dare call any dragon a pet. I'm talking about those giant flying lizards so common in your mythology, though I've yet to establish a link between Ashuan and Lukrya, in that regard. In either case, my people—the High North—ally with them. At least the Dragon

Lord does, our head of state." In the warm shine of the fire, Chay looked uncharacteristically wistful. "I grew up by the Dragon Lakes and saw several of those majestic creatures flying during my youth."

"Do you ever go home?" Lucille asked softly.

"Not really." Chay shook his food and grabbed another Firali package from the skillet. "Anyone want more food?"

For as long as Fabian had known him, he'd never really understood the enormity of Chay's life. Unlike Matt, he'd grown up in a human world and lived a human life, or as close as you could get to such a life without ageing and seeing other people's futures. And despite being one of the most revered and knowledgeable people in what seemed to be an interglobal community, Chay somehow managed to make immortality look like a curse.

There was a sadness in everything he did, whether it was the way he supported Matt or how he looked at Samantha as she got ready for bed. Fabian thought he knew exactly where it came from.

As a demon, death mattered little. As a half-human, Chay had seen far too much of it. And not just in his past, but his future, too.

Fabian could only hope he hadn't seen it on this excursion of theirs.

The thought, plus their environment wouldn't let him sleep. He was lying next to Lucille with closed eyes, trying not to freak out. The real hike was still ahead of them. They'd been fairly lucky today, but Fabian doubted their luck would hold. He hoped... but as usual he didn't feel very confident in his apparent power.

Lucille was sound asleep. They hadn't had a chance at all to talk about what had happened today. On her other side, Samantha tossed and turned on her bedroll, though judging by her whimper, she was having a nightmare rather than being awake, like he was. It was another reason Fabian didn't dare sleep.

Matt and Chay were keeping watch. For the most part, they kept their silence, two unshakeable sentries who'd already seen too much.

"I'll have to leave you," Chay said after a while.

"Leave?" Matt asked.

"I just had a vision... I'm sorry, Matt."

"You said you had some time." Matt's voice was uncharacteristically emotional.

Chay sighed. "I thought I did. Sorry, but another world needs my help."

"Another world." Definitely hurt.

And why wouldn't he be? Chay was going to leave them here in the middle of Hell without an easy escape.

Matt got up. "It's fine. You do you. I mean, you wouldn't leave if you didn't think we had it all covered, right?"

Fabian desperately hoped he was right. Surely Chay had already seen their success and survival.

"She's sick, Matt."

Or maybe not.

There was no doubt about whom they were talking nor what sickness *she* had.

"Sick?" Matt asked, his voice thin. He must have been standing right next to Samantha.

"She'll be coughing blood by tomorrow."

Fabian squeezed his eyes shut, trying his hardest not to give himself away as he fought the sudden urge to burst into tears. *Chay wouldn't leave... Chay wouldn't...* He inhaled sharply. *Tomorrow, we'll find the cure, and no one will have to die.* Especially not her. Not his best friend in the world.

# Jan

Jan stared at the TV, struggling to keep his eyes open and process any of the information. In the corridor, his mum scurried around, grabbing supplies, clearly not interested in checking in on him while she was home.

"Greenvalley Hospital reports its first death to the mystery sickness."

He felt numb. His friends had only been gone a day, and people were already dying. There was no way they'd make it back in time before the Black Death took any more lives. Jan thought he should be doing something about it, but as much as he racked his brain, he couldn't quite grasp *what* he could do.

Something wet tickled his lip. Jan raised a finger to wipe it off, then stared at the bloody pus on his finger. Between the joints, two black boils had formed.

"Jan?"

Quickly, he covered his mouth with a tissue before his mother could see it.

"Have you seen—" She stopped cold. "Is that blood?"

"Nonsense." He turned away, internally cursing that he forgot the blood on his finger while trying to hide the sores on his mouth.

"Jan..." His mother's voice was weak. "What are you keeping from me?"

"Don't you have to go to work?"

"Yes, of course. But maybe you should come with me?"

Jan snorted. "I thought the hospital is over capacity."

"You're my son."

He shook his head. "And you think that makes beds magically appear? I'm not interested in getting locked up."

His mother sighed. "Jan, please. Don't be ridiculous."

"I'm not being ridiculous," he barked, dropping the useless tissue. "There's no cure, so why would I go there? I can quarantine here just fine."

There were tears in his mother's eyes, but she took a deep breath. "Alright. If you prefer that. But if you need something or if it gets worse... I'll be back as soon as I can."

"Sure." He knew he wasn't going to see his mother anytime soon.

For half a minute more, his mother stood in the door, obviously torn. In the end, her work and Anne won, as always. She left, and Jan was alone again.

He bent to pick up the tissue and started coughing. Droplets of blood landed on his pants. In pain, Jan threw his head back and groaned. If his friends didn't hurry, it was going to be *him* who didn't make it out alive.

Despite what he'd said to his mother, Jan decided to go to the hospital, after all. Not for himself but for his sister. With great care and a stolen access card, he managed to make it to her room. He'd forgone the whole protection crap, not seeing the sense in it when he was already sick.

However bad he felt, Anne looked worse. The nose plug was soaked with blood. Her eyes were feverish, and when she coughed, fine drops of blood covered her lips.

Without hesitation, Jan stepped closer and exchanged the nose plug for a fresh one. Anne coughed again, spraying his arm with blood.

"I'm sorry," she whispered.

He plucked a tissue from the box next to her and wiped his arm. "Don't worry about it. What are you doing?" he asked, as if Anne ever had any choice in this.

"Jan, it hurts so badly. Make it stop."

He swallowed hard. "Anne..."

"Will I die?" Anne's voice broke. "I heard someone died."

Jan took her hand. "No, you won't. I won't let you. Do you hear me? Besides, Sam and the others will fix this. I promise."

Anne started coughing again. This time, her lungs cramped and she grimaced and moaned in pain. Gasping for air, she swallowed blood and pus instead.

"Anne." Jan sat on her bed and pulled her into his arms, rubbing her back until she calmed again.

"You're going to stay, aren't you?"

"Until the end."

Jan swallowed. What was he talking about? The end? There would be no end for Anne. Not like that. Not while he was still here.

He sank his healing magic into her and aggressively pulled the sickness from her body. *Ease the pain here, draw out the infection there, stop the bleeding, clean the lungs...* His head swam, and he groaned as a wave of pain washed over him.

"Jan, stop!"

Not until she was all better.

Anne cried, whispering, "Please stop. It's not worth it. You're just going to get sick."

Exhausted, he pulled back and laid her down gently. "I'm already sick, so don't worry. I can't see you suffer like this. You're my little sis." He glanced at the clock. "I need to go before Mum catches me, but I'll be back tomorrow."

"Promise?"

"Promise."

Jan pushed himself off the bed, biting down on the pain that had multiplied tenfold over the course of a minute. His head was still swimming, but he forced himself to put one foot in front of the other.

Another step, and the room was spinning. His heart started racing, and he struggled to see.

"Jan?"

Darkness closed in quickly. The last thing he heard was Anne's panicked scream.

# Matt

They were making remarkable progress, and yet Matt found it hard not to hurry them on. Especially as they traversed the Slum Chute, a section of the Dûr Lôrac filled with deformed demons, hungrily watching their every move. But it wasn't the lesser demons or the danger of a hunter on their tail that Matt feared. No, what worried him was the invisible threat in their midst.

Samantha hid it well. She never complained, never hung back. But she wasn't talking or asking a ton of questions like Lucille and Fabian did, which was unlike her.

Sometimes, Matt caught her grimacing in pain or moaning softly, but whenever he checked on her, she had a smile for him, telling him not to worry, without uttering a word. She was determined, he'd give her that. But then again, she'd always been stubborn.

He was so caught up in his thoughts that he didn't notice the demon who suddenly stumbled into his way. Instinctively, he unfolded his wings and hissed, his hand flying to his hip. Then he recognised it was a little girl and felt embarrassed.

She had two clumps on her back where her wings would've been. Matt couldn't tell if she'd been born like that or had her wings taken in a fight. If he had to guess, she was no older than him, which put her as the demon equivalent of a five-year-old. With big eyes, she stared at him, completely frozen in fear.

At the sides, other demons watched them. Not a single one moved, though one was covering her eyes. An older friend, perhaps even a relative.

They all expected him to blast the little girl from existence for daring to cross his path.

"I'm hu…" she whispered before the fear silenced her.

"Go!" Matt growled. He couldn't give her food. If he did, the rest of them would swarm them. And though alone they were no match, together, they could easily overwhelm them. All he could offer the girl was another day alive.

She scurried back instantly, hiding at the side of the demon woman who'd assumed she was as good as dead.

His jaw set, Matt lengthened his strides. The sooner they got through the Slum Chute, the better.

"Who are these people?" Samantha whispered.

If she'd been healthy, she probably would've argued with him. Or maybe not. Samantha was sensible enough to know why he couldn't show more mercy.

"They're lazars, born with little or no magical powers. Some of them are chronically ill. Elsewhere, they'd be killed instantly; here they have a fighting chance," he explained, as matter-of-factly as he could bear.

"Is no one taking care of them?" Lucille asked.

"Of course not," Fabian muttered. *He* would never understand why self-preservation was more important than pity.

"It's not our way," Menuha pitched in. "Most demons would murder them on sight."

Drily, Matt added, "Caspar."

"The rest don't care."

"Balthasar."

"That's horrible," Lucille exclaimed.

Before she could start a revolt, Matt shrugged. "It's survival. You either kill or you get killed."

"Disgusting," Samantha whispered behind him.

He squared his shoulders. Before coming here today, he'd never paid the lazars much thought. They were just a part of the Dûr Lôrac. Now, he felt something. It took Matt a moment to notice it was shame. Yes, the situation was horrible and he understood how reviling it would seem to his human friends, but that was just the way it was. There was no space in Hescaryn for the weak.

"That's Hell for you," he said, his voice somewhere between callous and resigned.

Instead of answering, Samantha coughed. Matt whirled around in concern, as if he expected her to drop dead right there and then. But before he could come to her help, a scream tore through the cave.

A demon lunged at Fabian. Instinctively, the elemental mage raised his hands and shot water at him, pushing the demon back against the wall. It could go one of two ways: either the other demons would be too scared to try again or they'd realise they had nothing to lose.

Naturally, it was the latter.

In a flash, the entire horde of demons attacked. Wings snapped, claws extended, horns came out. Rays of energy shot across the cave, hitting as many of their own people as were aimed at them.

"Run!"

Menuha showed no mercy. She tore off a demon's head and shot another in the face. Matt drew his sword and cut off a demon's wings. The woman crumpled screaming.

The red shimmer of Lucille's magic shield extended above their heads. It was just in time as a swarm of energy bolts slammed into it. A demon crash-landed on top and dug his claws into the shield. He was thrown off when a second demon attacked him.

The six of them managed to burst through the crowd into a larger cave. Unfortunately, more lazars awaited them, instantly joining the fight. Within seconds, they were surrounded.

"Damn it! There's too many of them," Matt shouted.

Next to him, Lucille was breathing heavily. "Why are they even attacking us? I thought they were so much weaker than us." She threw a fireball, burning a swath of destruction through the demons behind them.

"Because they're so many and there's not enough food," Menuha explained.

"I don't want to be eaten!" Fabian cried, and washed away the next wave of attackers.

More and more demons flocked to them. Matt doubted the ones in the back even knew what was going on. They just moved with the crowd, hoping for scraps, whatever they turned out to be.

The shield was starting to weaken. Matt knew Samantha was weaving something more permanent, but she kept coughing, clearly struggling to retain her hold on the magic. Subtly, he put himself in front of her, his sword ready to skewer the demons one by one when the shield fell, but then he had a different idea.

"Lucille, can you craft an illusion? Something big and dangerous? We just need to get to that tunnel over there," he pointed at the dark opening currently blocked by the horde of demons.

"I'll try my best!"

She closed her eyes and took a deep breath. Only seconds later, a dozen of very healthy and vicious-looking demons flew into the cave and started throwing energy at the deformed lower demons below. Their arrival broke the momentum, and soon the lazars were fleeing from the cave.

Fabian laughed with relief and slung his arms around Lucille. "You're fantastic!"

"Not really," Lucille said, frowning heavily. "I think those are real."

Matt gripped his sword tighter. If those demons attacked them, he doubted they'd emerge unscathed. Just as he was sizing them up to identify the strongest and largest of them, he recognised the one in the lead.

Jet-black hair and vivid green eyes. Adrianes was nearly fifty years his senior, which made them roughly the same human age. His eyes lit up when they met Matt's gaze. "Uncle Melchior!"

"Adrianes." Matt pushed past the others and pulled his favourite relative into an embrace.

Adrianes laughed, then studied him with curiosity. "Is that your human form? You're so blond."

Matt couldn't help but laugh along. It had taken him some time to get used to as well. During his time in Hell, he rarely switched, as if the demons could see the human in his features if he did.

He turned to the others, still grinning and said, "May I introduce you to Adrianes? He's Balthasar's son and my nephew. Adrianes, these are my friends: Samantha, Fabian, and Lucille."

The three seemed a little confused about the sudden change in atmosphere. Lucille gave a shy wave.

"Humans in Hescaryn?" Adrianes asked. Apparently, you could truly see the human in them. "What are you doing here?"

"We're on our way to Hescaryn's Gardens."

"Well, in that case, you found the right demon." Adrianes raised his chin with a wide grin. "I was made Chief Gardener last year."

"Balthasar's work?"

Adrianes shook his head. "As if he remembers I exist. No, my own success."

Matt clapped his shoulder proudly. "That's great." When they'd both studied at the City of Youth—Hescaryn's only remotely safe place for growing demons—Adrianes had spent most of his time researching and caring for the plants in the outer rings. He'd had a fabulous knowledge of the deadliest plants and how to harvest them safely, to aid in the fight for survival against bigger crews of adolescent demons.

"I didn't know Balthasar had a child," Lucille whispered behind them.

Menuha took it upon herself to cheerfully explain, "He's almost a thousand years old. Of course he has children. As do I and... Actually, I don't know if Caspar has any. He so rarely sleeps with anyone." She seemed a bit confused for a moment, as if it had only just occurred to her.

"What about Matt?" Samantha asked softly. "I mean we all know *he's* been sleeping with people."

Matt felt the heat creep into his cheeks. "I heard that. And no, I don't have any children." More gently, he admitted, "At least, I don't know of any." It wasn't entirely out of the realm of possibility. He'd never thought much about it. Would it be a deal breaker for Samantha?

What was he thinking? That deal had been broken long before any of this.

"Come on," Adrianes urged them. "If we stand here any longer, they'll come back. The gardens are just two-hundred wingbeats from here." As a second-grade demon, he flew almost everywhere.

Matt and the others followed Adrianes and his guards through the tunnel until they reached a huge brass gate. Hundreds of wondrous plants had been etched into the doors. The detail of it was astounding, but even that paled in front of the actual gardens when the gate opened.

After two days spent in the darkness, only surrounded by red-glowing stone, they were suddenly overwhelmed with green. Plants grew on the ground, on the walls, and even on the ceiling. There were bushy ferns, tall trees, and soft moss. Flowers in every shade and hue bloomed amidst the green, and the sound of several sylver streams and low-grade bird-like demons wove into a melodic tapestry. Although a golden path led into the thicket, Matt lost sight of it only ten metres in.

"I get what they mean when they say 'green hell' now," Fabian said, his voice awe-struck.

They all looked overwhelmed by its beauty. Even Samantha's eyes had lit up again. "I think this is my favourite location."

Matt struggled to keep the giant grin off his face for the rest of their walk.

# Samantha

Hescaryn's Gardens were certainly not made for walking. Sometimes, there was a path, but most of the time, they had to climb over roots and fallen trees, and push through the undergrowth. By the time they were halfway through, Samantha was sweating profusely.

Or perhaps that was the fever.

Lucille and Fabian walked with Adrianes. For once, Fabian had lost his shyness about the supernatural and asked a ton of questions about demon botany, his curiosity overcoming his fear. They didn't even notice how far behind Samantha was.

The same couldn't be said for Matt, who leisurely strolled behind her, as if she wasn't going at a snail's pace. Samantha didn't know whether that was because he wanted to make sure no lesser demon snatched her up on the way or whether he'd guessed she wasn't feeling well. Whatever his reason, he never pestered her.

At last, the beautiful but exhausting greenery gave way to an open space. A wooden bridge spanned a wider sylver stream and led to a settlement high up in the trees. At the foot of what looked like a rudimentary staircase, the others waited. Fabian was still deep in conversation, while Menuha was flying up to the tree tops.

Lucille waited for them right at the forest's edge. Her eyes lit up when she saw them. "There you are."

"Yes." There she was, ready to collapse right on the spot.

"Who would've thought that Hell could be so vibrant and beautiful?"

Samantha shrugged. It had surprised her too. She just wished she was well enough to enjoy it to its fullest.

"Even Fabian's stopped yammering," Lucille said with a laugh.

Samantha frowned. It didn't sound very nice coming from his girlfriend. "Everything okay with you guys?"

"Yes, I think."

"You think?"

Lucille rolled her eyes, laughing again. "It's nice..." Then she sighed. "I mean it was nice, and I really like him... in the beginning... but lately... I don't know, maybe I'm bored, but all I see are our differences. Like, I find this exciting, he wishes he could be anywhere else. I want to go out clubbing, he wants to stay in cuddling. He's getting more and more clingy, and I want to do things on my own."

"I see." When Fabian was in a relationship, he always went full in. It was nice, but apparently not for everyone.

"So, break up with him," Matt said, shrugging dejectedly.

Samantha groaned. "Matt." There were more nuances to a relationship than on or off.

"What's the point of being with someone when you don't want to be with the person?"

He did have a point there. From Lucille's admission, she didn't sound like she wanted to be with Fabian anymore.

"I like him," Lucille protested. "I just wish he was a bit more... spontaneous. Daring." She shrugged. "I'm probably overthinking it."

On one level, Samantha understood those thoughts, but aimed at Fabian, they didn't seem fair. "Whatever you decide, please be honest with him. He's my best friend."

Lucille immediately changed her tune. "And he's awesome. Don't think I don't know what I have in him. He can be very passionate. Like now." She looked at the two of them. "I'd better join them. Gotta take advantage of when he's not talking about dying all the time." True to her word, she hurried along and joined Fabian, hooking her arm into his.

"Someday, you'll have to explain this to me," Matt mumbled.

Amused, Samantha turned to him. "Am I your relationship counsellor now?" When it came to Lucille, there wasn't really much to explain. The girl was in love with love itself. She loved the flirting, the early stages of a relationship, but the longer it went on, the more dissatisfied she became. Samantha wasn't sure there was a man yet who could keep her interested long enough to be kept around.

"Would you do it?" Matt asked softly.

Explain human relationships to him? Half a year ago, it would've been unthinkable, but Matt had changed. He really wanted to learn, and that could only be a good thing for all of them.

"Maybe."

They reached the tree. Adrianes joined Menuha by flying up, while Fabian and Lucille had begun the long way by foot.

Samantha regarded the stairs with trepidation. Normally, it would be an adventure, and after the climbing park with Cian, she was a little more confident with heights—as long as there weren't any birds attacking them—but right now, the climb seemed daunting.

"You know you can just fly," she said when Matt stepped on the stairs behind her.

He raised an eyebrow. "I'm okay. Do you want me to fly you up?"

As tempting as it was, she couldn't risk it. If Matt knew how sick she was, he might decide to take her straight home. As botanically inclined as Fabian was, he wouldn't know what to look for. "I'm good."

The ascent was an ordeal. Every few steps, Samantha had to press herself against the tree to combat a spell of dizziness. Her legs were aching, and every time she looked up, the treetop seemed just as far away as before. Like before, Matt didn't complain, and she was secretly glad for his presence, knowing that if she fell, he'd catch her. Together, they made it to the top after one endless climb, but without an incident.

The others were already seated on a terrace surrounded by blooming flowers. As soon as Samantha and Matt sat down, Adrianes passed out cups filled with a thick, yellow liquid. "Our best nectar, you can't get it anywhere else. It's nutritious and refreshing."

Samantha was a bit doubtful, but the drink held what he'd promised. It was not too sweet with a faint citrus note, cool and yet as filling as a thick smoothie.

"So, tell me," Adrianes said when they'd all been tended to, "what brings you here?"

"We're looking for a plant," Matt started explaining.

"Well, you've come to the right place. Any in particular?"

Samantha stared into her nectar, waiting for the liquid to settle in her stomach. "Lucifer's Shine."

Adrianes' eyes widened in surprise. "You've got taste! I'll lead you there tomorrow morning. It's about half a day from here, so you'd better rest up."

Another day away from the cure. Samantha closed her eyes.

Despite her exhaustion, Samantha only managed about an hour or two of sleep before she woke up in pain. As soon as she was awake, the cough wouldn't let her go back to sleep. Unable to find a comfortable position, she decided to give up and make her way outside.

Despite there not being a sky, Hell had light and dark phases. Up here in the gardens, it wasn't a complete darkness. Some of the flowers that bloomed at night were glowing—probably to attract prey—and there were sparkling insect demons, though they all seemed to avoid the tree settlement. Below her feet, the sylver stream was emitting a metallic light.

It was beautiful, breathtaking really, and completely different from what she could've ever imagined. All she'd known about Hell was how deadly it was. She'd thought a world that housed demons would be as cruel and hard as them. And while there definitely was cruelty abound, there was also all this beauty.

Samantha coughed yet again. If only she was well enough to appreciate it all. At this rate, she wasn't sure she'd even make it back alive. Not because she felt like dying right now—it was bad, but not that bad—but because she knew how the sickness would progress. Her time was running out, and no matter how she tossed and turned the plans in her head, there was no other way than forging ahead and hoping it all miraculously worked out in the end.

She was startled by sudden steps on the wooden floor. Instinctively, she pulled on the magic around her, weaving half a shield before she recognised Matt. "It's you."

"What are you doing here?"

"Keeping guard." She might as well watch over everyone if she couldn't sleep.

"We're safe here."

"You may be. But we're humans surrounded by demons." The end of the sentence was spoiled by a coughing fit that felt like needles in her lungs. Matt came close, reaching for her. "Don't!"

A look of dismay went over his face. "You're sick."

"It's just the flu." Samantha didn't know why she kept lying about it. It wasn't like they could go anywhere else, as deep inside Hell as they were. Perhaps to protect herself from the implication.

Matt pouted. "That's not what Chay said."

Blasted Chay. Of course, he'd known from the start. That's why he'd offered to take her. With his gloves, she'd felt safer with him than potentially infecting Matt.

"It's Cian, right?"

Samantha's eyes flew open. "What?"

"That's where you got it from. The Plague." When Samantha shook her head, Matt's mouth turned into an angry line. "Sam, I'm not stupid. You and him, there's something."

"Matt..." A useless whimper escaped her mouth as bloodied snow appeared in front of her eyes. She sighed. It was no use. At least down here Matt couldn't act impulsively and kill him. If Cian was still alive, that was. "It's not what you think."

"It's not?"

"We're just friends." What kind of stupid answer was that? They obviously weren't *just* friends. But the truth was a bit embarrassing. As much as she enjoyed it, it wasn't like her. "Friends who occasionally have sex with each other."

Matt snorted. "Just occasionally?"

"Perhaps I got it from you." He was, after all, the poster boy for casual sex.

"But you won't have sex with me."

The directness of the statement blew Samantha away. Who asked a question like that? As if sex was the most important thing. "Is that what you want from me? Sex? That's why you're so obsessed with me, because you told me you want me, but I refuse to spread my legs for you?" This right there was exactly why a relationship with Matt of any sort was out of the question.

Matt's eyes widened with horror. "What? No!" He sighed heavily and finally took a seat, keeping the same distance between them. "I'm sorry. That wasn't what I meant to say."

"What do you want then?" Samantha felt exhausted. Matt's confusion around his emotions was hard to untangle on a good day. It was impossible when her body already hurt so much.

"I want you," Matt admitted, looking at her like a lost puppy. "I want to be with you, make you laugh, kiss you and... yes, yes, of course I want to have sex with you, but I want all of it. The being close to you, the talking with you, the staying in and spending every second with you." He swallowed hard. "Look, I don't know what this means. Chay said I'm in love, but what even is love? I know what it is in theory, but it makes no sense. None of those definitions explain why it's so overwhelming, why I can't do what you want and just..." He searched her face, swallowing again. "Stop."

Samantha stared at him, her heart beating a mile an hour. Her face was flushing with heat as she struggled to find her senses. Just as she thought she might have words for him, she started coughing yet again.

This time it was worse than ever before. The cough bit into her lung tissue and throat, tearing them to shreds. She covered her mouth with her hand and felt the wetness on her fingers. Matt's hand closed around her wrist.

"Don't," Samantha warned.

But he pulled her hand away regardless, turning it so he could see. "Shit!"

# Rachel

Two days after her friends had left for Hell, Rachel and her mum were well and truly sick. Neither had gone to the hospital since they'd heard it was over capacity already. And knowing what she knew about the cause of the sickness, Rachel wasn't willing to deal with all those other people when none of them could help them.

What she needed was for her friends to return, and for Elda and Samantha to brew the potion that would clean the magical rivers. In the meantime, she took care of her mother—and vice versa.

For the first time in a very long time, her mother had made her soup and hot cocoa. The liquid was as much as they both could stomach, and even that was painful. Together, they sat on the couch, both huddled in blankets, unable to find the energy for anything other than coughing their lungs out.

"Do you need something?" her mother asked. The sicker she got, the more caring she seemed to become.

"A cure?" Rachel joked. It was the only thing she truly needed right now.

Her mother's lips quirked up. "That would be amazing."

She coughed for the better part of a minute, triggering Rachel's own coughing reflex. When she was well enough to speak again, she gave Rachel a sad smile. "I'm so sorry for everything."

"Everything?" There was so much she blamed her mother for.

"Everything," her mother confirmed. "I made your life pretty horrible, didn't I?"

"Mum..."

"No," she said, then coughed again and held up a finger to show she was going to continue. "I failed you and your brother. When I brought you here, away from your dad, I thought it would be a new start. I was motivated. I really wanted to make this work for the three of us."

Rachel kept quiet, knowing she'd be unable to hold back the truth, and that the truth would only hurt her mother.

"And then I got here, and it was all so stressful. I had to find a place to stay, move all our belongings, run to a million ministries to set up everything, arrange school, launch my business... and you weren't talking to me. Both of you were so angry. You blamed me."

"Was that wrong? You broke our family." There, the hurtful truth had come out anyway.

Annette looked away in pain. Tears shimmered in her eyes, betraying the hurt she could never get away from in her dreams. "That's not what happened."

"Is it not?"

"Your father cheated on me."

Rachel's eyes widened. "What?"

"I'm sorry. Maybe I shouldn't say this. See, I never wanted to... You love your dad so much, and you always resented me from taking you away from him." Her mother shuddered, clearly still harbouring some resentment of her own. "I didn't want to destroy that. But I guess... you deserve the truth."

"The truth?" It turned out Rachel's truths weren't the only ones that could hurt.

"Look, your father and I married for the wrong reason. We were both young, he even younger than I was, and it wasn't that serious. I got pregnant four months into our relationship, and your father being your father, well... he wanted to do the right thing. So he proposed and I said yes."

"And that was wrong?"

Annette nodded with a bitter little smile. "Oh, yes. Because sure, we got married. And thanks to his wealthy parents, he was able to provide for us, but that was the end of it. He'd done his duty and he still wanted more. From his own life, I mean. While I stayed home with you, he continued his studies, stayed late at the office, and went out with his friends. I hated him so much by the time you were five."

She took a deep breath. "Sorry, I know this isn't what you want to hear."

"No," Rachel said a little forcefully. "Keep talking, please." As hurtful as it was, it explained some of the inconsistencies in her early memories.

"He always loved you two," her mother said softly. "But he never loved me. Not for long, anyway. And agreed, I didn't make it easy for him. I didn't speak up, giving him the silent treatment, instead. In my darkest hours I believe that I drove him away, that I made his home so hostile he stayed as far away as he could possibly could. I mean, we always fought when he was home."

Rachel remembered that, though she didn't remember what they'd been fighting about. She and Nico had always hid in their room, playing games instead.

"And I turned to drink, which... well, we both know what a great decision that was. A glass of wine for mum quickly turned into a bottle for mum."

*Or two or three,* Rachel thought.

"Anyway, one day, he left his phone on the counter, and when I made you guys breakfast, a million messages from his girlfriend or whatever she was came in. I was so angry, I threw the phone at him and broke a window. And you know what he did?"

"No," Rachel whispered.

"He admitted to all of it. And when I said I wanted a divorce, he was glad I asked. He never once fought me for custody. Not because he didn't want you or anything—I don't want you to believe he didn't love you. He did and he does!—but because he thought it was the least he could do for me." She laughed softly. "That bastard took the blame in his stride, no emotions whatsoever, just accepted it and moved on."

The tears were streaming down her face now. "I was screaming and fighting, and he stayed calm the entire time. As if we were nothing but a business decision."

Rachel stared at her. The thought of her own stoic reaction came unbidden. Nico had always been the emotional one, while she seemed to have inherited her father's dissociation. Or so she thought. The father she knew was always kind, always willing to talk, and had been a rock to her throughout the divorce, but he'd never actually fought *for* her.

As much as it hurt, Rachel understood where her mother was coming from. How frustrating it must've been. How lonely and abandoned she must've felt all the time. On a superficial level, Rachel understood, but on a personal level, she wanted to scream that it hadn't been *her* fault.

"I messed up," Annette confessed, without being prompted. "I made a big mess out of all of it. And now you hate me, and your brother is dead."

And soon they'd both be dead as well. Rachel wanted to slap herself for the cold and callous thought. This was exactly what her mother had just talked about. The lack of emotion. The dissociation. Had she always been like that?

"I don't hate you." Rachel tested the words and was surprised to find they were true— with a small caveat. "Not anymore."

A bright smile bloomed on her mother's face. "That... that's good to hear." For a moment it looked like she wanted to invite her over to her side of the couch, but they both knew Rachel would never allow that. "You should call your dad."

"Why?" What good was that going to do?

"Because you're sick and... You should talk to him."

When Rachel finally understood what her mother meant, it nearly broke her. Annette wanted her to seek comfort from her father, because she wouldn't take it from her mother. And to say goodbye to him. Just in case.

But Rachel wasn't going to die, and neither would her mother. Her friends would come through. Samantha always did. And then when she was better, she would have a proper chat with both of them.

"I'd rather spend my time with the one who didn't give up on me."

"Oh, darling."

Tentatively, Annette opened her arms. And though it didn't come naturally to Rachel, she forced herself to shift over and accept the embrace for what it was. In a way, she needed it as much as her mum did.

# Samantha

Samantha found a little bit more sleep, but when she woke up, she felt as if a bus had rolled over her. The pain from the boils and internally were nearly unbearable with a straight face. And no matter how much she tried to hide it, the coughing always broke her cover.

Matt wasn't the only one who'd found out how sick she was. When she finally managed to get up, she noticed Fabian watching her with a haunted look.

"It's going to be alright," she whispered, knowing where his thoughts would go.

He set his jaw. "I won't accept anything else." His confidence—whether fake or not—gave her the strength to smile.

After a small breakfast that seemed to revitalise her even more, Adrianes led the group through the gardens. Not all sections were as massively overgrown as the first. There were ceiling-high rows of fruits and vegetables, which were delivered to Lucin and the other big cities on a regular basis. Herbs grew along pathways, emitting strong and heavy smells. And from a bridge, they looked down into an elaborate underwater garden.

As urgently as they needed to get to the plant, Samantha was grateful for the many breaks she suspected Matt of initiating. He allowed her some grace, and that was more than she'd expected of him. That and last night's chat made it hard for her to hold on to the healthy distance she'd achieved.

It scared Samantha. They were in a good place at the moment, one where they wouldn't hurt each other. A balance of sorts, but a precarious one, because she still felt as if one wrong move would send them both tumbling off the cliff.

She'd always known that he was obsessed with her—it was the reason he'd gone after Daniel after all—but she'd never believed he'd ever learn what real love was. Did it change anything? Did it matter to her if he loved her or not? How did *she* feel about him?

Samantha honestly didn't know. Her head told her to run the other way, that nothing good would come of his affection, that it would be a betrayal to Daniel to even think about it. No, returning Matt's affection was out of the question. Now matter how irresistible the pull was.

As exhausting as contemplating his confession was, it distracted her from the creeping death claiming her body. Despite that, she was glad when they reached their destination after three hours of walking.

They arrived at a circular plaza. Between the cracks of pavement, sylver flew towards a plant in the centre of the circle. Even from a distance, its golden blossoms dipped the cave into glorious sunlight. At least that was what it reminded Samantha of.

"Lucifer's Shine," Adrianes announced proudly. "Hescaryn's most beautiful plant and the only surviving one of its kind. It takes a thousand years to grow from its seed, a thousand more to bloom. There's no plant like it in any world."

Lucille cleared her throat. "Wait, are you saying this is the only specimen there is?"

"Yes, there were more, but most demons have no concept of conservation. This was the only one we could save and protect."

"Damn," Fabian whispered.

Samantha swallowed hard. She had expected a field of them or at least more than one. "Are you—" she licked her lips and tasted something metallic and bitter "—growing more?"

"We've been trying, but it takes time, and we won't know whether we've succeeded for another five or six hundred years."

Oh, sweet mercy. She suddenly felt very weak on her legs.

Matt walked over to Adrianes and put an arm around his shoulders. "We need to talk." He led him away, leaving the other three and Menuha alone.

Samantha turned to Fabian and Lucille. "We can't take it. Not if it goes extinct."

Fabian shook his head, a grim look on his face. "Usually, I'd agree, but as noble as the thought is, *people*—" he said the word very pointedly "—will die if we don't take it. I'd rather have a plant die than *anybody* else." Again with the emphasis.

Samantha knew it was aimed at her. And the thought of having to give up after all the pain to get here was nearly unbearable. However... "What if the Blood Plague breaks out somewhere else? It's happened before, it's likely to happen again, and then what? There'd be no cure."

"As horrible as that scenario is," Lucille started, her voice determined, "it's purely hypothetical. Meanwhile, *we* need a cure now. So much time has already passed."

Matt and Adrianes returned, the latter looking distraught and angry. Matt, however, pointed his finger at her. "There's no discussion. I won't let you die for a plant."

Next to Matt, Adrianes ground his teeth. He clearly would be happy for anyone to die if it kept his precious plant safe.

"Sam's going to die?" Lucille asked, instantly frowning.

"She's sick," Fabian said, more forcefully than he probably meant.

Samantha couldn't bear it. "I'll find another way."

"When?" Matt asked, outraged. "There is no time. We need the plant now. Adrianes has already agreed."

She looked at the lesser demon. "Have you?"

Adrianes' shoulders rose. "If you don't brew that potion, the Blood Plague will sweep over Ashuan. Millions will die. And apparently, that's a problem." He snapped his wings. "Melchior is my friend. If he says he needs it, then I'll have to hope the seedlings we have will bloom."

In several hundred years.

Samantha swallowed. "Once I feel better, I'm happy to see what I can do with my magic."

That made him relax his scowl slightly. "I'll hold you to it." He clapped his hands and turned towards the plant. "Let's get it out of the ground."

Half an hour later, Adrianes handed Samantha Lucifer's Shine in a pot with a secure cover to protect the plant from being jostled too much and her from being blinded. Then he took a can and filled it with sylver.

"It needs to be soaked with sylver every twelve hours to maintain its potency," he explained.

Samantha nodded, but before she could shift the pot to take the can of sylver, Matt grabbed it and poured it into his drink bottle, instead. Then he took off his shirt and tucked both, shirt and bottle, into his belt. A second later, his wings extended with a powerful whoosh.

"What are you doing?" Samantha asked, slightly flustered by his muscular upper body.

"You and the flower have to be back in Greenvalley as fast as possible. I'll fly you there. It'll be faster."

"Fly?" Samantha took a step back. "I'd infect you." With that much skin exposed, there was no doubt she would.

Matt shrugged his shoulders, the muscles rolling deliciously. "If I get you back in time, it won't matter." When she gave him an exasperated look, he smirked. "If it makes you feel better, there's a high probability I'd heal easily." His eyes hardened again. "I won't watch you collapse on the way back. So, better say your goodbyes. We're leaving."

His determined response took her breath away. Exasperated, she turned to the others. "I can't abandon you."

"Sure, you can." Fabian nodded nearly as grim as Matt. "Look, we'll be fine. Menuha can take us back alone."

"I will protect them," Menuha promised.

Lucille implored her, "Go, save my brother and everybody else. Please."

That settled it. It was one thing to risk her own life, quite another to risk everyone else's. Samantha nodded at Matt, who immediately stepped closer. Shyly, she put her arm around his neck, jostling the pot into the crook of her other elbow.

Matt slung one arm around her back and bent slightly to put the other under her knees. With ease, he lifted her. The movement caused her to inhale sharply as his touch put pressure on some of the boils under her skin.

"Sorry," Matt whispered, then he pushed off the ground and they were in the air. "We'll meet again at home," he told the other two before setting off towards the exit.

Soon, Fabian, Lucille, Menuha, and Adrianes were lost behind a curtain of greenery.

# Matt

Matt flew above the crowds of deformed demons, easily avoiding their badly-aimed energy attacks, then dove into the darker tunnels under the light of the glowing corals. In his arms, Samantha flinched and moaned. He didn't know whether it was due to the fast flight, pain, or because of their forced proximity. Judging by his previous track record, it was all three of them, and neither changed anything.

"I'll bring you home, if it's the last thing I do."

"Thanks," she whispered. Her arm around his neck tightened as she tried to change position. Pain it was, then.

He tried to help her, adjusting his grip until she could breathe a little easier. Exhausted, Samantha leaned her head against his chest. Where her skin touched his, heat spread, but it was nothing against her hot breath.

"This thing with Cian." Her voice was so quiet he almost didn't hear it over the headwind. "I'm sorry."

The apology twisted his stomach. It didn't feel right. "Are you two in love?" he asked, steeling himself against the answer.

"Cian is."

Matt's throat was suddenly dry. "And you?"

"I... I like him. What we have is... nice. It's a good thing." Samantha looked up at him, her eyes hardening slightly. "You know I don't owe you anything just because you happen to..."

She was as unable to define what he happened to be. "Of course, you don't owe me anything. And this thing with Cian..." What he should say was that if Cian made her happy, that would be enough for him.

But it wasn't, and Matt was unable to lie. "It makes me mad, but for you, I'll pretend it doesn't." Surely, without the pressure of the Blood Night, it shouldn't prove too much of a challenge to ignore the intense pain he felt just thinking of her and Cian together.

To his surprise, Samantha didn't get mad at him. Instead, she sighed softly, her head dropping again. "Oh, Matt. This is really hard for you, isn't it?"

She shouldn't be so understanding. Matt knew he didn't deserve it. He didn't deserve anything. He lost the right to be upset last winter.

"I wish it wasn't," he admitted. "These feelings I bear for you... they seem so bothersome. They don't serve you or me." What good was his love if it hurt them both? "I wish I didn't have to pretend. That I really didn't care." He gritted his teeth, struggling with the frustration building in him. "I used to be better at this."

"Better?"

"Of letting go. Letting all of it go. All those doubts and fears, the irrational anger, the jealousy. I never used to be jealous before. It wasn't a sin I identified with. I'm from the House of Lust. Pleasure was all I ever cared about, and no, I wasn't ever picky about it."

"Oh, I noticed."

Matt chuckled softly. "I know you did. But everything's changed. I haven't slept with anyone in five months. When I was younger, it never mattered to me who it was with. If they weren't interested, I'd move on to the next. And now I'm... stuck?" It wasn't a pretty word, but since there was no hope of Samantha suddenly falling into his arms—well, unless she was as sick as she was right now—it was the right one. "Like, I want to move on. I really do."

"Sorry?"

"No, no, it's not you. It's me." He closed his eyes and took a deep breath, nearly knocking himself out on a rock nose protruding from the ceiling. "I wish I could move on so I could stop making you feel so damn uncomfortable."

Samantha sighed and shifted yet again. "I don't think anything can make me comfortable right now." When she noticed him watching her with concern, she ordered, "Keep talking. We might as well hash this out, once and for all."

He raised an eyebrow, doubtful.

Exasperated, she snapped, "It distracts me from the fact I'm dying."

"You're *not* dying. I'm bringing you home."

"Sure." If it wasn't for all the other symptoms, Samantha giving in was all he needed to know about how bad she was.

Distraction it was, then. "Being human is hard," Matt admitted. "Much harder than being demon. Like, two years ago, if the opportunity to become an archdemon had opened up, I would've seized it, no questions asked. I would've killed Melaney without a second thought. And now I can't bring myself to even imagine it. And we're talking about my mother, the one who left me in Caspar's care to entertain a lover, or who didn't notice I was gone three years, stuck in the City of Youth. That's like a hard-ass boarding school for demons. She doesn't care for me, so why do I?"

"Because she's your mum." Samantha coughed again.

"What does *that* matter?" It was a rhetoric question. By now, Matt knew that against all reason, it did.

Samantha shifted slightly. "It just does. You could have the worst parents in the world and you'd still find it hard to shut your feelings off. It's complicated. Ask Rachel."

He didn't think Rachel particularly cared about her mother, but maybe he wasn't looking deep enough. "Complicated is exactly what being human is. All of this would be so much easier as a demon. I could kill my mum, become the Archdemon of Lust, leave you alone and live happily ever after."

"Is that so?"

"What?"

"Would that make you happy?"

Matt glanced down at her, nestled against his chest. "Not anymore."

She sighed heavily, her muscles cramping for what looked like a painful moment.

"I'm sorry," he whispered, slowly coming to realise how much pressure he was putting on her to reciprocate his feelings. He didn't want to force her into anything. Once he'd saved her life, Matt decided he'd walk away. Somehow, he would make it work. Even if it meant returning to Hescaryn. "I'm happy for you and Cian."

"No, you're not." She glared at him for good measure.

Samantha was right, of course. The words hadn't captured what he'd wanted to express. They didn't ring true. "What I meant is that I won't interfere. I won't destroy this for you. If Cian makes you happy, then I'll learn to be content with that. I'm not there yet, but it can't be harder than anything else I've had to learn in Ashuan. And I *am* glad you found someone who makes you happy again." For some reason, Samantha was still glaring at him. "What?"

She shook her head slightly, moaning softly. "I don't know."

"You don't know?" Samantha knew everything!

"I like you."

"What?" Surely, he'd misheard that.

"It makes no sense and I feel terrible about it, but despite everything you did, I somehow still like you."

She was breathing heavily. Whether from the enormity of her confession or because of the plague, Matt couldn't tell. His head was suddenly filled with nothing but air. He struggled to hold on to any thought but the constantly repeated, *"She likes me."*

"This thing with Cian is not that deep. He's madly in love with me, but we're just friends. I like hanging out with him, and I also like the sex."

Matt's momentary euphoria ended sharply.

Samantha looked up at him, tears in her eyes. "I don't understand it. How can I still have feelings for you? How can I even *stand* you? Daniel must be turning in his grave. He deserves better. And I know all this. So why..." She took a shuddering breath. "I should be happy with Cian. He's literally perfect. We get along both inside and outside the bed, so why... why can't I love him?"

Matt struggled to hold her haunting gaze. He wanted to say something clever, something meaningful. Something that would bridge this chasm between them and tear away all obstacles. But that was impossible, and so all he said was, "Because he's still an Elite Idiot."

"You're the idiot," Samantha said, laughing softly. Exhausted, she leaned her head against his chest. "You broke me."

It didn't take long after that for her to fall asleep.

Matt flew on, pressing Samantha and the vital plant to his chest. He didn't know what to make of her confession yet, whether to have hope or stick to his earlier decision. The only thing he knew was this: "You broke me, too."

# Fabian

Fabian had to accept that a quick return home was impossible. Whether Samantha lived—or Jan or anyone else infected—was out of his control now. There was not a single thing he could do. He wouldn't even be home to see fate unfold. Instead, they were stuck deep in the underbelly of Hell, surrounded by demons.

Chay had already abandoned them, Matt and Samantha were gone, and all he and Lucille had left was Menuha. He tried to not let his fears get away from him, but as lovely and exuberant as she was, she was also Caspar's twin sister and had expressed her support for the evil twin. Then again, she'd helped ban him to Hescaryn.

"Wait a minute," he said, stopping short. "How are you going to get us back to Ashuan? The ban hasn't passed yet, has it?" That would be a catastrophe.

"Nice," Lucille hissed.

Menuha stopped to think for a moment. "We'll find a way. I'll just summon Matt as soon as we've left the no-jump zone. Or Chay, if he's available. If all else fails, there are gates you can use. I just have to check where they are, because I never bothered with them."

"That sounds like a lot of maybes."

"No, it doesn't!" Lucille barked. "It sounds like a lot of options. We're going to get home safely. So stop worrying."

Irritated, Fabian looked at her. "Is everything okay?"

"Just walk."

Definitely not okay then.

Fabian mulled her words over in silence as they slowly made their way through the gardens. They would sleep at the tree house again before diving into the tunnels. Adrianes had promised to send a troupe with them to guard them in the sketchy section they'd been attacked in before they were left to their own devices.

He wasn't too worried after having managed it once, but you could never be too careful in Hell. Something that Lucille didn't seem to get. He didn't understand why she was so prickly lately, but every time he opened his mouth, she shut him down. Had he done something wrong?

"Lucille…"

"It's fine, Fabian," Lucille interrupted him. An exasperated smile made its way onto her face. "Everything's good. We'll be good."

*Will we?* Fabian clamped his mouth shut. The need to talk about this was overbearing, yet she obviously didn't want to. And that was the worst of all. Just like Rachel, who instead of communicating with him, worked it all out on her own, then sent a vengeance goddess after him. And before that Samantha had made the decision for him. Somehow, all his girlfriends had an expiration date, upon which they'd quietly withdraw, leaving him no chance to fix things.

What was he supposed to do? Respect Lucille's wish for silence or fight for their relationship? Fabian didn't even know whether it was worth it. He had the sinking feeling it was already too late anyway.

Just then, Lucille turned to him and sighed. "I can't deal with your negativity right now."

"My negativity?"

"Your constant worries and pessimism. All the problems you see." She closed her eyes and reset. "I'm not saying they're not valid concerns—they are—but I don't want to think about everything that can go wrong, because of Pascal."

Startled, he stopped. "Pascal?"

"He's sick, and you know children." Her voice broke a little in the end.

"Oh, Lucille." Fabian opened his arms, his own insecurities instantly unimportant.

But Lucille backed away. "No. I'm not going to dwell on this, because everything will be fine. Understood? Matt will return Samantha and the plant, and Samantha will save all of us, and nobody has to die. Okay?"

After such a plea, he had no arguments left. "That's exactly what's going to happen."

Her smile was much warmer now. "Thank you."

If a positive attitude was what she needed, he'd give her that. After all, the power of hope was his.

Fabian offered her his hand, and this time, she took it gladly. Everything was going to be fine.

# Samantha

## Samantha

The flight through the Dûr Lôrac was pure torture for Samantha. It wasn't so much the act of flying, which was much gentler than walking would've been, as it was that every bone in her body hurt. She was coughing near constantly and drifting in and out of a fitful sleep that left her worse every single time.

Matt's arms around her body hurt. No matter where he placed them, he always put unbearable pressure on a tender spot. She tried shifting, but that did nothing to alleviate the discomfort. All she could think about was that surely, they'd arrive soon.

However, demon flight wasn't that much faster. There was a reason they preferred to jump from place to place. Though Matt beat his beautiful wings continuously, they moved at the pace of a horse's trot. He could probably go a little faster, but it was a long trip and she knew he was already exhausting himself by keeping up the pace.

"We can have a break," she whispered.

"No, we can't."

"Matt..." He was so damn stubborn. "I need a break."

That worked like a treat. He stopped almost immediately near a grove of purple mushrooms. "What do you need? Toilet? Food? Drink?" Carefully, he set her down, eager to jump into action.

"I need to water the plant. Or sylver the plant."

"I can do that."

"Sit!"

The tension between them could've been cut with a butter knife. Matt held her gaze, the muscles in his face moving with unspoken words. Then he sat. Glowering, he asked her, "Happy?"

"Yes." She dropped down next to him and took a minute to breathe before she asked for the sylver, carefully opening the protective cover on the plant.

Matt winced. "That's bright."

"Very." The light hurt her eyes, but she forced herself to pour slowly until the soil around the plant was well-soaked. They were both relieved, yet equally blind, when she covered it again. "I've never seen anything like it."

A coughing fit prevented her from saying anything more. Matt moved instantly, his arm already halfway around her body when he tensed. "Quiet." The word was barely a whisper.

Samantha held her breath, hanging onto the next cough for dear life. It was impossible. Five seconds, almost ten, then she burst into an even worse fit. Blood splattered the cover and her lungs screamed in pain.

Matt's arm around her tightened. He lunged into a roll, taking her with him. A second later, a stream of fire charred the spot she'd been sitting at. "Stay low." He pressed her down to the ground, forcing her into a crevice near the cave wall.

Her body didn't respond well to the rough treatment. Sweat broke from her pores and she kept coughing, while her mind was racing. Where had the fire come from? What had he heard? Lucifer's Shine! "The plant!"

In an instant, Matt jumped back to grab the plant from where he'd left it. Before he could bring it to safety, though, a second stream of fire was blown at him. He used his wing to shield the plant, hissing in pain as it burnt through the sensitive membrane.

Meanwhile, Samantha got a look at the creature, which appeared to be a monstrous tardigrade, a thick worm-like creature with thick rings of fat, no eyes, and a circular mouth from which it shot its fire. A worm!

It wasn't thin and wriggly, and close to an arm long, but that hadn't mattered when they'd encountered the wyrm either. Sure enough, Matt's phobia kicked in. His eyes grew wide and his throat bopped.

"Just kill it," Samantha said. Knowing how heavily his phobia had stunned him before, she reached for her magic. Instead of vibrant green strands, everything she touched was sticky and flimsy, like tar-covered spiderwebs. She couldn't weave that.

Matt evaded another attack, but his movements were almost as sluggish as the tainted magic in her hands.

"So, the rumours were right."

A chill went through Samantha's spine. She knew that voice. And so did Matt. "Caspar?"

The demon appeared with another one of the creatures on his shoulder. Contrary to the last time she'd seen him, he was wearing a fearsome armour full of spikes with a blood-red coat, holding a grisly helmet under his arm. "I wouldn't have thought you'd be so stupid as to show your face in Hescaryn after the stunt your friends pulled."

He didn't seem to have noticed her yet. Or maybe he'd dismissed her instantly. It wasn't as if she'd be able to hold back the blasted cough anyway. It was already creeping up her throat as she thought of it. Which meant she'd have to weave fast. But what?

"You weren't supposed to be around." Matt sounded breathless.

"Did Menuha tell you that?" Caspar scoffed. "You're going to pay for that."

"For what?"

"Taking Menuha from me."

Matt gasped, helpless. "I did no such thing." Unable to move away in time, the fire hit his leg. Matt sagged to his knees and moaned.

"Do you like my new pets? Found them on my campaign." Caspar stroked the one on his shoulder. "They made me think of you, bastard."

The inevitable cough broke free from Samantha's lungs, betraying her presence and location. At the same time, she had an idea. The tainted magic was no good for anything. Nothing but what it was already doing to her.

She dipped her hands into it with all her heart and wove it around Caspar in a sloppy, sticky fashion. Since it wasn't visible, he didn't seem to notice, though his eyes burned in her direction.

"You brought your pet human to Hescaryn? What's this? A research trip? A romantic stroll?" He spat out viciously. "You're the one who banished me."

Samantha froze.

"Touch Samantha and I'll stuff your fire worms down your throat until you explode," Matt hissed.

Caspar started laughing. "Will you now? I'm tempted to watch you try. I'll even tell her to hold her fire."

"Her?" Matt pulled a disgusted face. He wasn't going anywhere near the creatures.

With luck, he wouldn't have to. Samantha's sticky web of pain and disease didn't seem to have an effect on Caspar, but the tardigrade on his shoulder was squirming. Quickly, Samantha tightened her web, then threw a second one over the female that had Matt in a chokehold.

The one on Caspar's shoulder coughed, belching fire close to Caspar's face. Startled, the demon jerked away, sweeping the creature off his shoulder in the same movement. It splatted on the ground, still sputtering fire like a dying motor. At first, it tried to creep forward, but then it convulsed.

Samantha felt terrible for causing it such horrible pain. It might have been a lesser demon, but it was much more animal than demon.

"What the human?" Caspar stared at his pet, just as the second one started malfunctioning.

Slowly, Matt crept towards Samantha, his eyes never leaving the fire-belching worm in front of him.

Then Caspar coughed. Motivated, Samantha stuffed more and more tainted magic into him, barely registering her own coughing. The tardigrades were dying. With luck, Caspar would too.

Suddenly, Matt jumped into action. He shot energy at Caspar while he was distracted, grabbed Samantha, and launched himself into the air. He gritted his teeth, hissing in pain.

"Your wing."

She was barely holding on to him, stuck under his arm like a lumpy package. The weight distribution and his injured wing made for a lopsided flight that saw her scrape against the cave walls more than once, but it also saved them from the black magic hurled after them.

"Don't you dare run away!" Caspar screamed, then coughed again. "What did you do to me, witch!"

Matt snapped his wings, flying as hard as he could. "The wing will heal. Hold this."

She reached out to receive the plant, breathing heavily from the exertion. When she had it safely in her arms, Matt swung her around to carry her as before. She felt a little more comfortable in that position.

Caspar was still following them, but he seemed to be getting worse, or else he would've caught up with them. His shots were as deadly as ever, though. One missed Samantha's feet by a mere millimetre.

Matt accelerated even more. "That was stupid."

"What?"

He didn't answer, evading yet another shot, nearly causing him to crash into the wall. Samantha figured she didn't need to know what he meant. She felt it in her body. She hadn't just given Caspar a speed treatment of the Plague, but herself, too.

Despite the adrenaline rushing through her veins, she felt the darkness closing in. Something was wrong with her. Really, really wrong.

"I don't think..." *I'm going to make it,* she wanted to say but couldn't find the strength to do so. At least, if Matt brought the plant home, her grandma could save everyone else.

# Rachel

When she wasn't tormented by her coughing, Rachel dreamt. There was little else to do and she needed to know how far away her friends were. Or whether they'd failed to find the only plant that could save them.

But her fever-filled dreams were hard to navigate. They pulled on her much more strongly than before, launching her into vivid nightmares and horror-filled visions. She fell into her mother's first, finding herself back in their Los Angeles kitchen, which was flooded with red wine.

"Oh no. No, you don't." The smell of alcohol was overbearing, much worse than Rachel ever experienced it before. And there were screams. Her parents fighting.

"I'm always alone!" Her mother hurled a glass at her father. "You're always gone."

He didn't duck. The glass burst on his forehead and cut into his skin. Dark drops of blood welled up, while he never even twitched. With a sneer, he answered, "And why would I want to come home to this?"

Annette just screamed, while Rachel's stomach did a flip. He hadn't said that. Her father couldn't possibly have said that.

But the wine rose, quickly filling the entire room. Against her will, Rachel swam towards the door. Away from her fighting parents.

"Nico!" she called, trying to remember which way the children's room was.

At first resisting, the wine suddenly swept her down the hallway and straight into Nico's bedroom. But it wasn't the dream presence she was searching for. Instead, Nico was lying on the ground, convulsing as blood streamed from his leg. They were outside of Elda's house.

Rachel turned and ran into the house. "Elda? Sam?"

A potion was bubbling in the witch room, but there was nobody there. It didn't look like it was done either. Samantha wasn't back yet.

"Samantha!"

Rachel held onto an image of her friend, forcing the dream world to bend to her will. When it finally gave way, she tumbled into a terrifying scenery.

Giant black, pus-filled boils covered the space she stepped in next. Accidentally, Rachel stepped into one. It burst, and pus soaked her leg. Disgusted, she shuddered. "Samantha?"

This couldn't be real. It wasn't allowed to be real.

Rachel stumbled on, suddenly coming across a hospital bed. Jan was lying in it, a multitude of machines stuck out of his body. His mind was so weak he barely even dreamt.

"You had to heal her, right?" Rachel felt tears on her cheeks as she regarded his deadly pale skin. "Hold on. You need to hold on. Please, Jan."

He was just one in a long row of hospital beds that seemed to lead into eternity. Rachel was too scared to see who else she might recognise and ran the other way, bursting through the boils of Samantha's dream.

If Samantha was sick, Matt would be bringing her home. Successful? Or in failure? She tried to reach his dream, but he must've been awake. Rachel decided to count that as a good thing. Though she didn't have much hope it'd be any different for Fabian and Lucille, she reached out to them.

Surprisingly, she found their dreams. Lucille was at home, sitting at Pascal's bed, who seemed to be sick. She held his hand, checked his temperature, and stroked his hair.

"Lucille? Did you find Lucifer's Shine?"

The sun was shining in Lucille's dream, but that did little to ease the worry on her face. "Pascal, please. You've only just arrived, you can't leave."

"Lucille, the cure. Did you find it?"

Doors slammed shut, startling Lucille. "It's a trap. If I don't leave soon, I'll be trapped." Despite her words, she sat still. The doors closed in, locking her in smaller and smaller rooms, suffocating the sunlight.

Annoyed, Rachel gave up and lunged into Fabian's dream instead. She'd avoided his dreams since they'd broken up, but the familiar sight of water brought her an instant ease. "Fabian?"

She found him in a foreign garden, studying unfamiliar plants with great interest. When he saw her, his eyes lit up. "Rachel? Look at this."

He cautiously held a stick to a bright, orange flower. As soon as the wood touched a blossom, it went up in flames. Instead of shirking away, Fabian grinned. "Pretty cool, right?"

"Yes." She could only assume that meant they'd made it to Hell's Gardens. "Did you find Lucifer's Shine?"

"Come along."

Rachel followed him, stumbling over monstrous roots and vines, while flowers snapped at her, hissing viciously. Fabian led her with a surety he seldom displayed in real life. Soon, they'd left the jungle behind and arrived at a circular plaza. In the middle of it, a bright shining flower stood.

So, Lucille's sun-filled scenery had shown her the plant after all—in typical dream fashion.

Relieved, she dropped down next to it. "You found it."

"It's an incredible plant. The only one of its kind. They take a thousand years to grow and another thousand to bloom," Fabian told her excitedly.

"But you took it, right?" Rachel asked, suddenly nervous. If it was the only plant, would they have had to steal it from the demons? Was that what Matt was currently doing? If so, how long would it take them to get back? Jan had maybe a day left, if that.

Fabian kept talking about the amazing properties of the plant. "It has to be handled with great care. If it gets touched too much, it'll dim, and its potency will reduce for a couple of years or decades. It's really sensitive."

With a sigh, Rachel watched the plant. Hopefully, Matt knew that.

# Matt

Energy tore through Matt's right wing. He tried to jump in reflex to balance himself, before remembering that space jumping wasn't an option at the moment. He lost his momentum to his indecision, careened to the left, and crashed into the wall, unable to hold onto Samantha and the plant.

Samantha had lost her consciousnesses shortly after they'd fled from Caspar. Now, she cried out in pain. Lucifer's Shine fell from her grasp, the pot splitting on the cave floor. The protective cover slipped and a sliver of sunlight peeked out.

Matt pushed off the wall, ignoring the pain, and lunged for the pot.

Meanwhile, Caspar had reached them, coughing blood as he dragged himself closer. "What did your witch do to me?"

"Killed you. Hopefully." Matt closed his eyes and tore the protective cover from the plant.

Caspar's painful scream was like music to him. Even with closed eyes, he noticed the brightness. He left it going for five seconds longer, then covered it again.

"You're dead. You're so dead. I'll kill your witch too!"

Matt glanced at Samantha. Blood on the floor. Curled up in a tight ball. Heart-wrenching moans.

She hadn't moved from where she'd landed. Couldn't move.

Panicked, he went to scoop her up. They were almost at the crossing. He tried jumping, hoping the border extended into the tunnels, but to no avail. Flying was out of the question. His left wing had healed but the other was in tatters. Useless.

Matt balanced the plant and Samantha. He was just about to start running when something slammed into his back. Caspar.

"You're not going anywhere, bastard." Hot blood hit Matt's neck as Caspar coughed. His grip's strength dwindled.

Caspar was sick, perhaps even dying. Unfortunately, Matt was nearly as exhausted. He broke the grip, but staggered backwards under the weight. The pot slipped from his arm and burst on the ground. Not good.

The protective cover slipped, but instead of bright sunlight, it was more like the light from a lightbulb. "No, no."

He shot black magic at Caspar, pushing him away from the plant, then bent to gingerly pick Lucifer's Shine up by the trunk. "Sam," he whispered, his mind reeling as he watched the light dimming in front of his eyes. "What do I do?"

She was barely conscious enough to look at it. "Sylver," she whispered. "Home."

"Go." Matt set her down. "I know it's hard, but go ahead. I'll follow you."

Samantha sighed heavily, wincing as soon as her feet touched the ground. With both hands and half her body on the tunnel wall, she dragged herself towards the crossing.

Matt threw a glance at Caspar, who was suffering from yet another violent coughing fit. He could probably kill him now, freeing himself from the constant threat, but that wouldn't help Samantha. Instead, he got out his sylver-filled water bottle and gingerly threaded the roots through the opening. The decay halted and for a moment, the plant seemed to perk up, but then it dimmed again, though much slower.

The sylver helped, but the only thing that would not make this a colossal failure was getting it home before it died. Before Samantha died.

And unfortunately, before Caspar died.

Energy missed him by a hair's breadth. Balancing his water bottle, now re-functioned as a flower vase, Matt hurried down the corridor. He could already hear the noise of the sylver waterfall. Halfway there, he found Samantha collapsed on the ground.

"Don't you dare." He set down the bottle and threw Samantha over his shoulder, then picked it up again. "Home. We're going home."

Behind him, Caspar was on his feet again. The bastard simply refused to lay down and die. "You can't get away from me," he slurred.

Matt tried to ignore him. With every step, he made another attempt to jump, groaning in frustration when he failed over and over again. The waterfall was so close now.

Just then, Caspar gained a spurt of energy. "Stop running away!" He launched himself at Matt and slammed them both into the wall.

Samantha screamed, bearing the brunt of the attack. Just what she needed when she was already suffering from the Blood Plague.

Matt couldn't defend himself, not while holding on to both the plant and Samantha. He trudged on, even though Caspar wrapped a hand around his wing stumps and nearly tore them off his back. Hot blood was trickling, then gushing, down his back, the pain nearly blinding him.

It was only due to Caspar's dwindling strength that Matt managed to make any leeway. Steeling himself against the pain, he continued on, dragging Caspar along.

His left wing tore from his back, searing pain shooting through his entire body. In response, his knees gave way and he dropped to the ground, nearly burying Samantha under him as he protected the water bottle. "Leave me..."

Caspar pounced on his back. "You're not getting rid of me that easily."

*Home.* He had to bring Samantha home. The plant. Elda. He pictured Elda's living room, or maybe the witch room, and dragged himself towards it.

"Matt? Oh my god."

He was even imagining her voice.

"Give her to me."

No, she was there. *He* was there. In Elda's witch room, collapsed next to a cauldron. Instead of handing her Samantha, he pushed the water bottle into Elda's hands. "Quick. It's dying. Everything's dying."

His eyes felt too hot, as if he'd finally caught Samantha's fever. He didn't realise he was crying until he wiped the sticky wetness from his cheeks. "You need to hurry."

Elda was already onto it. She didn't ask any questions, didn't fuss over Samantha, or the fact that he was bleeding profusely from his back. Within seconds, she'd harvested the roots and added them to the potion, then added a few other already-prepared ingredients to round it off.

"Did it work? Is it still good?" Matt closed his eyes, feeling faint. Suddenly he remembered Caspar. He looked around frantically until he remembered that Caspar couldn't go to Ashuan. He'd been forced to stay back when Matt had jumped from one world to the next. Lying in his arms, Samantha's eyelids fluttered. She looked so pale in the daylight. Ugly boils covered her neck and her arms, while bloody blisters marred her beautiful lips. "You can't die."

"Listen to him, Sam!" Elda said while steering the cauldron. She looked a bit concerned. Too concerned.

"Please... There is no other plant. It's the only one." Never mind how long it would take him to go back to the Gardens.

"Better pray to all your gods."

The bleeding had stopped by the time Elda announced the potion finished. Matt didn't waste any time and brought Elda, the potion, and Samantha to the spring. What was usually a verdant clearing was now dry and grey. If there were any fairies, they lay dead between the crumpling leaves and moss.

Matt held onto Samantha, refusing to let go of her. Her breaths were so shallow now he constantly feared they stopped.

Elda used a big ladle to spoon the shimmering-gold potion right into the centre of the spring. It was hardly the sun-filled cure it was supposed to be.

Numb, Matt watched her continue. He couldn't lose Samantha. The very thought was unbearable, which scared him. What kind of hold did this girl have on him that he couldn't imagine a life without her?

*It's the exhaustion,* he told himself. *You fought so hard to get her here. It can't have been in vain.*

But in his heart, he knew it was something different. Samantha had changed him. Broken him.

Just then, the moss next to Elda's feet turned to green. Green, soft, and full of life. Sunlight shone through the bare trees, just as their leaves grew again. When Matt looked down, the entire spring had come back to life. "It worked," he whispered. He pressed Samantha against him, laughing all of a sudden. "It worked."

"Of course, it worked," a soft voice said, still weak from the disease.

"You're awake."

Her eyes were open. The colour of the boils was fading fast, the swelling reducing a little more slowly. As he watched, she drew deeper and deeper breaths. "I always knew you'd make it."

"Did you?"

Samantha smiled at him. "You wouldn't let anything happen to me."

She had him there. As disturbing and confusing as his love for her was, it was the reason he was here now. The reason he'd persevered despite the pain and despair. For her, he would've dragged Caspar to the end of the world. It was both a frightening thought and an empowering one.

Maybe being human wasn't all that bad.

# Jan

"It's a miracle, you know?"

Jan blinked. Fluorescent hospital light was blinding him, and he struggled to place the sniffling voice.

"I thought we'd lost you."

Was that his mum? Was his mum crying over him?

Cautiously, he tried to open his eyes again. It was true. His mother was sitting at his bedside, holding his hand with tears in her eyes. "Lost me?" His voice was little more than a croak.

Her eyes brightened a little. "There you are." She stroked his forehead, smiling at him. "You're a fighter, huh? Always fighting us, the world, even death."

"Death?" What was that woman talking about? Slowly, the memories came back. He'd healed Anne and then... he couldn't quite remember.

His mum nodded. "Yes, darling. You kept how bad you really were from me. Good thing you came to the hospital, and good thing Anne called for help so quickly."

"What happened?" Jan still couldn't place himself in space and time.

His mother sighed, slowly returning to her professional nurse's ways. "Well, you collapsed in Anne's room. They took you to the ICU, gave you fluids and antibiotics, but you continued to deteriorate like everyone else on the ward. Yesterday, you went into a coma. Your organs started to fail. I thought that was it, but then this morning..."

She laughed, in disbelief of whatever had happened. "Everybody's improving. We've already discharged the first few patients. And you came back from the literal brink of death. Just suddenly improved. I've never seen anything like it."

"It's magic."

His mother laughed even harder. "Oh, Jan, you and your magic." Then she wiped her tears. "But maybe you're right. It definitely feels like magic."

If he could've, he would've rolled his eyes. It truly was magic. His friends must've come through, just as he thought they would. But he didn't argue. He was just glad his mum was there. At his bedside, for once.

As it turned out, the entire hospital was in disarray. For five days, doctors and nurses had fought against a mystery illness. Six people had died. And just as suddenly as it had come, it had gone again, leaving everyone who'd fallen ill to improve instantly. There were news reporters all over the hospital, but of course, none of them got the real story. Instead, the hospital's strict quarantine and exceptional care were credited.

It grated on Jan. The doctors and nurses might have done their best, but they hadn't known shit. His friends had saved Greenvalley and the only healing done at the hospital had been by his hands.

The door opened and Anne's head appeared. She smiled shyly at him. "Can I come in?"

"Knock yourself out."

"That's your thing," she answered cheekily and stepped inside.

Days ago, she'd looked like the living dead. Now her cheeks were rosy again, her eyes clear and alert. "So, you're better."

"Much better. I'm getting discharged."

"Well, that's not fair." The doctor had just told him they were keeping him in a few more days for observation. Apparently, people didn't just get up and walk away a day after organ failure.

She came to sit on his bed, then suddenly laid down and put her head on his chest. "Thanks for trying to help me. I'm sorry it had such a bad effect on you."

Tentatively, Jan put his hand on her hair. "You were sick and needed help. I just did what anyone would do."

Anne raised her head and looked at him. "Most people wouldn't."

"When it's their little sister, they would."

She smiled as if he'd called her pretty or something stupid like that. Then she sat up again, her face serious. "You can't do this ever again."

"I'm a healer, Anne, this is literally my..." Jan paused. What was this? His destiny? A quirk of fate? Some kind of cruel joke?

"Your job?" Anne said smugly.

His job? He wanted to laugh. He didn't have a job. At least not a real one. "Don't be ridiculous."

She laughed. "Admit it. You're like Mum. Working yourself to the bone to make other people better."

"Have you met me?" Working himself to the bone. As if!

"I think you're kidding yourself." She poked his chest. "You think you're nothing but a troublemaker, a loser, a failure."

"Gee, thanks, Anne."

She clicked her tongue. "My point is you're not. You just haven't found what you're good at. Well, actually, you *have* found it. Healing."

He bridled his protest and looked at his hands instead. Could he really use this power in his real life? Miracle Doctor Jan, bringing people back from the brink of death—and then dropping dead himself. He snorted. "Anne, magic won't get me a job. No one's going to pay for a miracle healer."

"Then become a real healer. Doctor, I mean."

"They gave you too much pain medicine. You're high. I don't even have my Abitur. Studying medicine is completely out of the question." Especially if he imagined all those years of studying and studying. No, even if he went back to school, he'd never make it that far.

Anne frowned, but then she lit up again. "You don't have to be a doctor. You could be a nurse like Mum."

"And change other people's bedpans. Woohoo."

"That's it!" Her eyes were sparkling dangerously. "You have to become a paramedic."

"A paramedic?"

"Yes, the first on the scene. You don't need an Abitur to do the training and you can secretly heal people, but also learn how to help them without making yourself sick. Ask Mum."

Jan glared at her. "I will *not* ask Mum." But the idea wasn't half as stupid as he thought it was. Annoyingly, Anne was right, he might just have what it took to work as a first responder. Plus, he could see himself driving an ambulance, sirens blaring, ignoring all the red lights. He smiled. Put that way, it sounded like something right up his alley. "I'll think about it."

Anne beamed at him. "You're gonna be great!"

# Lucille

It had taken Lucille, Menuha, and Fabian another two days to make it to the crossing. Few demons had dared to attack them, none of them even remotely human. Between the three of them, they'd got rid of them without too much trouble. The entire way, Fabian's behaviour had been exemplary. Always encouraging her, never once whining. She knew it was an act for her benefit, but she still appreciated it. He was sweet like that.

At last, they arrived at the crossroads, and Menuha summoned Matt. He appeared instantly in his demon form, hands raised ready to attack, causing Fabian and Lucille to duck preemptively.

"It's just us," Menuha announced cheerfully.

Matt relaxed his hands and nodded. "Good. Did you see Caspar?"

"We've just arrived."

"I was hoping you'd come across his corpse."

Menuha cocked her head. "Did he wait for you in the tunnels?" She sounded annoyed.

Matt's face darkened, despite him changing back to his human form. "He almost ruined it all."

"But only almost, right?" Fabian asked, tense as a bow string. "It wasn't ruined. Everyone is well. Samantha is..."

"Alive and well." Matt nodded. "Sorry. Yes, the mission was a success. Jan's still in hospital, but everyone else is recovering nicely. Samantha's already researching ways to help Adrianes grow his seedlings."

Lucille let out a huge sigh of relief and leaned against Fabian. He slung an arm around her and muttered, "There you go. All went well."

"Just as I told you," she joked.

"That you did." He kissed her head and squeezed her a little tighter. "Let's go home."

Matt offered both his hands to them. "Alright then."

"Wait," Menuha called as they grabbed his hand. "What happened to Caspar?"

"I don't know. He attacked us in the tunnels. I think Samantha infected him with the Plague but, like, turbo-charged it. He looked like death when we made it out of here. I guess it would be too much to hope he actually died." Matt shrugged. "If he's somehow still alive, tell him Samantha's off-limits."

Lucille inhaled sharply. It was damn hot when Matt said it like that. Samantha was one lucky girl. Or not, considering how far Matt had actually taken it before.

Before she could add anything to the conversation, Matt took them back to Ashuan. "Do you want me to bring you straight home or do you prefer to walk?"

"I think we've walked more than enough this week," Fabian said, making Lucille laugh.

She nodded. "I'd rather not waste another minute."

"Home it is, then." He dropped her off first before vanishing with Fabian.

Lucille regarded the big empty villa. A little less empty now, perhaps, with Pascal there. The thought of her little brother gave her the strength to return home after blatantly ignoring her father's security measures and fleeing like a thief in the night.

"Welcome home, Miss Lucille," Albert said as he held the door for her. "You've been sorely missed."

"By my father?"

"By the young master." He winked at her. "Your father was a bit perplexed when he found you gone, but I told him you'd decided to quarantine with your boyfriend, instead. I hope you had a nice trip."

Lucille chuckled. "An adventurous one."

"Good to have you back home. Master Pascal should be in the music room."

She heard the piano long before she reached the music room. Pascal had taken to the classes with delight, already playing better than she had in the same time frame. At the moment he was only playing for fun, though, no teacher in sight.

"Knock, knock."

"Lucille!" Pascal jumped from the bench and came running. "You did it! You fixed everything." His eyes were big with admiration.

She pulled him close and gave him a big hug. "I told you I would."

He slung his arms around her. "You're the best witch in the world."

She'd hardly done anything to ensure the mission's success, but there was enough time to explain later. For now, she just enjoyed mattering to one person in her family.

The next day, they all visited Jan at the hospital, uniting for the first time since their return. The doctors must have decided to keep Jan in, because to Lucille, he looked as healthy as ever and a little annoyed with all the attention, save from Meg, who doted on him.

"You guys were so lucky they didn't trap you at the hospital," he told Samantha and Rachel.

"Oh, yes, it was so much better to suffer at home without all the fancy pain medication and caring personnel," Rachel said, sarcastically.

Samantha laughed. "Or getting jostled around while coughing your lungs out." While she'd healed from the Plague, there was a nice collection of bruises and scrapes on her body.

Lucille checked with Matt, who, sure enough, looked at her dismayed. She was sure he'd done his best. Fighting with Caspar, while trying to get a deadly sick Samantha home, couldn't have been easy.

"I owe you," Jan said. Meg slung her arms around his body as if she was never going to let him go again.

Samantha shrugged. "We just had to eradicate the most beautiful plant in Hell."

Jan chuckled. "I'm glad I was more important to you than a plant."

"We had to convince her of that," Fabian joked.

They all laughed, while Meg slung her arms around Jan and held him tight. "Don't scare us like that ever again."

"Yes!" Anne joined in. "I thought you'd dropped dead."

"Sorry."

"So, when are they letting you out?" Lucille asked. "I thought the Plague was officially gone? Even Vendenberg wrote about the *Miracle of Greenvalley*." She rolled her eyes at the ridiculous news article.

Jan grimaced. "Tomorrow or the day after. After the coma and my stint in the ICU, the doctors are being cautious and want to keep an eye on me. They can't really explain why my organs decided not to fail after all. Funny, huh?"

"Well, they won't find out anytime soon," Matt said with a snort.

"It's a *miracle*," Fabian repeated, causing Lucille to giggle. Their relationship may have been a bit rocky, but in moments like this, she couldn't help but love him. He had a way of making her feel better.

When he wasn't whining.

# Samantha

At some point, Samantha managed to slip out of Jan's room and visit Cian. As one of the first patients, he'd almost died, though he didn't have a huge group of people crowding his room. At least, not at the moment. She found him playing on his Switch, a sure sign that he must have been a lot better.

Cian looked up and smiled. "Ah, my lifesaver."

"I didn't do it alone." If it weren't for Matt, Greenvalley would've experienced a huge tragedy. One she wouldn't even have been alive to see unfold.

"As if I care about the details." He stretched out his hand and pulled her onto his bed to kiss her.

Samantha returned the kiss, but she couldn't stop thinking of Matt and his stupid confession. Just as she'd started to move on from the whole thing. Annoyed with herself, she wrapped her arms around Cian and snuggled against his side.

"He knows," she whispered.

Cian moaned softly. "So, do I need to write my will, after all?"

"I don't think so." The Matt she'd talked to in Hell was not the same Matt who'd killed Daniel or refused to take responsibility for it. He'd been a deeply tormented boy, struggling with his identity, and feelings he'd never learned to cope with.

"He's okay with us?" Cian asked doubtfully.

Samantha sighed. "I wouldn't exactly hold hands around school or... you know, kiss, but... I trust him. He won't harm you." Not unless there was another secret demon ritual that turned his head.

"Wow." Cian exhaled audibly. "Okay. If you trust him, I do too." He put his arm around her and pulled her close. "You know you're the most remarkable person, giving him a second chance like that? It's why I love you."

She groaned. "Stop saying that. I don't think I'll ever... I'm not ready."

"I know." Cian grinned, despite her lacklustre response. "But that doesn't change the fact that I love you. I love you. I love you. I love you."

With a grunt, Samantha rolled on top of him and shut his mouth with a kiss. Cian laughed, then returned the affection with enough passion to make her forget all about Matt and her ridiculous feelings for him.

# Caspar

Two days! Two days, Caspar's healing powers had battled it out with the mystery sickness. He'd used runes and other magic to try and break the curse, but it had been to no avail. At one point, he'd even believed he was going to die like those fire swamp flareys had. He'd felt absolutely miserable. And all because of Melchior and his human witch friend.

Overcome with anger, he threw his bed through the sparsely decorated room, smashing it to smithereens. That was fine; he preferred sleeping on the floor anyway.

"You're alive. Good."

Caspar whirled around to find Menuha standing in his door, arms crossed and glowering at him. He spat out, "Why did you invite them here?"

"That's none of your business."

"Humans have no business in Hescaryn. They certainly don't get to experience our magical places." Just the thought of three humans walking through the Dûr Lôrac, as if they'd earned the privilege, made him seethe. They'd only survived because of Menuha and Melchior watching out for them.

Menuha snorted. "Since when do you care for the Gardens? There's nothing for you to kill there."

"You let them take a plant." Caspar was still trying to make sense of it. He had no idea what kind of plant it was, only that it had been powerful.

"And you came back from your mission just to fight Melchior," Menuha hissed.

"Of course I did. He banned me," Caspar roared back. "How else am I going to kill him if I can't go to him?"

Menuha groaned and rolled her eyes. "Maybe you could *not* kill him?"

"And let Melaney choose him? I don't think so." Melchior didn't deserve to be archdemon. He wasn't even a full-blooded demon. It was bad enough that their mother had favoured him his entire childhood, coddling him like a precious little pet.

"This is your fault." He poked a finger at Menuha. "If you hadn't collaborated with those humans, I wouldn't have been banned from Ashuan. He would already be dead."

Angrily, Menuha caught his finger and broke it cleanly.

Caspar hissed in pain.

"Because of you, *I* can't go to Ashuan anymore. You know how much I love it, but you don't care about anyone else but yourself. If you did, you'd be begging me for forgiveness."

His sister should've been glad he liked her or she'd be dead just for suggesting it. "Surely not." He freed his finger and stormed out of his room, promptly running into Balthasar.

His older brother smirked at him. "You've recovered. How unfortunate." His grin widened. "I heard Samantha got you good. Again."

"Again?"

"Well, she's chiefly responsible for your banishment. A fine thing, too. How will you kill Melchior now?" All of it seemed to amuse Balthasar greatly.

"I'll think of something. Until then, I'll kill you." Caspar shot a powerful blast of energy at Balthasar.

Tiredly, Balthasar waved his hand. The energy returned and threw Caspar against the cave wall. In his weakened state, he was no match for the older one. Not that it would stop Caspar from trying. Someone *had* to die. It was the only way he'd sleep tonight.

Meanwhile, Balthasar strolled over and grabbed him by the collar. "Careful, little brother, you don't want to exhaust yourself."

Caspar bared his teeth, growling.

"Now, listen: if you don't want Melaney to choose Melchior as her successor, you need to start using your brain. Assuming you have one."

"He's hiding in another world," Caspar snapped. Who was the one without a brain now? A banishment of the kind those kids had pulled off lasted half a human lifetime, if not longer. "A world I can't enter."

Balthasar smiled slyly. "Then you need to be creative." The smile deepened. "*We* need to be creative."

Stunned, Caspar stared at him. There had never been a "we" before. He'd always been beneath Balthasar, or at least that was what his older brother had made him feel. Caspar didn't trust him. Then again, at the moment, they had a common enemy, and Balthasar was clever. Together, they might just pull it off.

"Fine," he growled. "But I get to kill him."

# Dramatis Personae

## Family de Cerque

**Lucille** – 18, one of the Six, a witch and illusionist
    **Bastien** – Lucille's absentee father, a busy man
    **Linda** – Lucille's stepmother, a designer
    **Pascal** – 10, Lucille's adoptive brother, a telekinetic
    **Cecille** – dead, Lucille's witch grandmother, killed by the Archdemon of Wrath
    **Alena** – dead, Lucille's mother, died in a car crash

## Family Kollmer

**Samantha** – 18, one of the Six, a witch and potion maker
    **Meg** – 17, Samantha's little sister and Jan's girlfriend, best friend of Anne
    **Ben** – Samantha's father, runs a car workshop with Joachim Bendtfeld
    **Juliane** – Samantha's mother, an aspiring actor
    **Elda** – Samantha's grandmother, the Greenvalley Witch, lives in the forest
    **Erich** – dead, Samantha's grandfather, a demon hunter

## Family Bendtfeld

**Fabian** – 18, one of the Six, a water elemental mage
    **Joachim** – Fabian's father, runs a car workshop with Ben Kollmer
    **Caroline** – Fabian's mother, runs the Magic Circle, a magic shop
    **Merle** – the family cat

## Family Hadden

**Rachel** – 18, one of the Six, a dreamwalker
    **Nico** – dead, Rachel's twin brother, appears in her dreams
    **Annette** – Rachel's mother, a hair stylist with an alcohol problem
    **Mick** – Rachel's father, a Maths professor, lives in LA

## Family Kerscher

**Jan** – 20, one of the Six, a healer, works at the youth hostel
    **Anne** – 16, Jan's little sister
    **Stefan** – Jan's father, a coal miner
    **Ida** – Jan's mother, a nurse

## Family Trede and Matt's demon relatives

**Matt/Melchior** – 18, one of the Six, a half-demon of the House of Lust
    **René**– Matt's father, a former demon hunter and elementary school teacher
    **Crumbs** – the family dog
    **Melaney** – Matt's mother, a demon, the Archdemon of Lust

**Balthasar** – Matt's oldest brother, a demon of the Houses of Lust and Greed, leader of the Small Council

**Caspar** – Matt's older brother, a demon of the Houses of Wrath and Lust, Menuha's twin brother, the general of the Black Guard

**Menuha** – Matt's older sister, a demon of the Houses of Wrath and Lust, Caspar's twin sister

# School

**Alan** – 19, part of the Elite Clique, son of the local police chief

**Ani** – 18, part of the Elite Clique, Samantha's former friend

**Björn** – 18, part of the Elite Clique, Jennifer's boyfriend

**Cheryl** – 18, the Greenvalley High Queen Bee, leader of the Elite Clique

**Cian** – 18, part of the Elite Clique, in love with Samantha

**Mr Herbert** – teaches Physics, hates Fabian

**Jennifer** – 19, part of the Elite Clique, Björn's girlfriend

**Mrs Renner** – the Greenvalley High headmaster

**Robert** – 18, a friendly guy who follows the Six around

**Shayna** – 18, part of the Elite Clique, parents own an inn

**Mr Zobel** – The Six's tutor teacher, teaches Politics and German

# Demons

**Adrianes** – Matt's nephew, Balthasar's son, Chief Gardener of Hell's Gardens

**Chay** – "The Seer" a half-demon, Matt's best friend, can see the future

**Hel** – the Archdemon of Pride

**Iyaga** – the new Archdemon of Greed

**Malcolm** – dead, Melaney's brother, the former Archdemon of Greed

**Moloch** – the Archdemon of Gluttony

**Pyke** – the Archdemon of Envy

**Volac** – the Archdemon of Wrath
**Yash** – the Archdemon Sloth


## Others

**Albert** – the de Cerque butler, a mind reader
**Captain Aster** – Alan's father, the local police chief
**Pia Aster** – Alan's mother, runs the Aster Garden, a florist
**Tobias** – the de Cerque chauffeur

## Hell hath no ambition like a demon in politics

.

Jan had one hell of a year. First he lost his job, then he almost died, and now his parents are kicking him out. The last thing he needs on top of all that are Matt's demon brothers wreaking havoc in Greenvalley. It's already nearly impossible to find a place to rent when you have no money; it's absolutely hopeless when a magical storm blows through your town, you have to deal with snow-witch squatters, and possession by an ancient evil spirit. But Jan's done being the butt of every demon's joke. He's determined to make a life for himself, monsters be damned. If there's one thing he's learnt from demons, it's that if you want to get ahead, be prepared to fight for your dues. Or die trying.

.

*Hell Hath no Ambition* is the fifth book of the action-packed *Ashuan* series, continuing the *Ashuan Lust* trilogy. If you like *Buffy's* wit and snarky one-liners, the magic of *Charmed*, and the supernatural drama of the *Vampire Diaries*, you'll love this monster-hunter urban fantasy series.

.

**Buy *Hell Hath no Ambition* now to discover what adventures are in store for the Greenvalley Crew in their sophomore season.**

# JANNA RUTH

# HELL HATH NO AMBITION

## ASHUAN LUST BOOK 2

**To see the Erlking's face is to see your own death**

.

Nature spirits have ravaged the world with natural disasters for millennia. They're dangerous, unpredictable, and largely invisible. After eight years living on the streets, Rika is one of the few people in the world that can see them. Most of the time, she keeps a fragile peace with them, but when the Erlking, a powerful storm sprite, attacks Berlin, Rika is drawn into the war against nature.

She joins the spirit seekers, a group of elite soldiers trained to defend Berlin and other cities around the world from nature's wrath. Currently bereaved of their acting commander, the spirit seekers look to Rika to be their eyes, but when Rika befriends a young sylph, she isn't even sure she wants to fight spirits. Her hand is forced when she comes face to face with the Erlking though, an incident that can have only one possible outcome: her death.

.

**Join the Spirit Seekers in their first, stormy adventure and start your European journey today!**

JANNA RUTH

# A FORCE OF NATURE

SPIRIT SEEKER BOOK 1

I'm a ghost whisperer, not a catacomb crawler. But when you live in Paris, sometimes you end up being both.

·

Hi, I'm Alix. During the day, I'm a history student at the time-honoured Sorbonne University. After class, I hang out with the ghosts of the revolution, the many undead misunderstood Parisian artists, and adventurous scientists that glow in the dark. None of them are alive, but they come to me to solve their problems with the living. When a recently deceased catacomb tour guide asks me to retrieve a mysterious personal item from the underground, things take a turn for the weird. Suddenly, I find myself in a city of ghosts, hunted by murderous cave crawlers, and stumbling across haunting secrets. If I'm not careful now, I might end up a ghost myself.

·

Urban Fantasy with a French twist. If you like cave-crawling adventures, hopeless romantics, and ghosts, you'll enjoy Ghosts of the Catacombs, the first book of the Parisian Ghosts series. Travel to Paris today to embark on your catacomb adventure.

JANNA RUTH
GHOSTS OF THE CATACOMBS
PARISIAN GHOSTS 1

www.ingramcontent.com/pod-product-compliance
Lightning Source LLC
Chambersburg PA
CBHW031740180726
48283CB00005B/1594